OPINICUS

GRYPHON INSURRECTION BOOK 7

K. VALE NAGLE

Cover art and map by Jeff Brown.

Interior artwork by Brenda Lyons.

Oilbird gryphon artwork by Maria Puenchir.

Interior graphics by Crystal Gafford of Crafty as a Coyote.

Published by STET Publishing, Denver

WWW.STETPUBLISHING.COM

WWW.KVALENAGLE.COM

Last updated 2-13-2023.

Dust Jacket Hardcover
ISBN: 1-64392-047-2
ISBN-13: 978-1-64392-047-4

BELAMURIA

ALABASTER EYRIE
REEVESPORT
CRESTFALL PALACE
WHITEBEAK
DUCKBILL
ARGENT HEIGHTS
ABYSSAL NAZE
NIGHTSKY
NEW EYRIE
ALWREN
JADEBEAK MOUNTAINS
EMERALD JUNGLE
FLOWER OUTPOST
SUNKEN EYRIE
STORMTAIL
RAFTWORK
KING'S REACH
SUBMERGED FOREST

Blacktalon
Mothfeather Eyrie
Blackwing Eyrie
Pitohui Eyrie
Glassworks
Glacier Pride
Poisonmaw
Crackling Sea Eyrie
Redwood Valley Eyrie
Kjarr Nests
Taiga
Kjarr
Weald
Strix Plateau
Luminaire

For Chris Fox, whose encouragement and guidance have helped me since the start of my author career.

THE WHITE REEVE

Emin looked down at the dying seraph. Her blood soaked the sands of the remote city of Alwren. Across the beach, large rodents spilled out from the wreck and fled for the relative safety of the jungle. The ship's design was unlike anything the locals had ever seen. The metalwork alone required skills beyond the best craftsopinici of the Alabaster Eyrie.

With his bodyguards and escort ordered to round up the strange, furry beasts, Emin found himself alone with the stranger. When he attempted to approach her, she hissed, calling him *gryphon* and ordering him not to touch her.

It was a strange word, gryphon. Its root hinted at a kind of de-evolution. As an opinicus from the largest eyrie on the continent, it wasn't the sort of thing anyone had ever called Emin. Though, in fact, it had come to his mind, too, when he'd been called out to the beach to witness her dying moments. The messenger had been unable to figure out what she was and suggested she might be a new type of gryphon.

The stranger's plumage shimmered like pearl in the light. Her feathers were unlike anything he'd ever seen. She had wings in the traditional sense: long, broken things that spread out along the beach. Yet her forelegs were almost like a second pair, and even her back legs showed off flight feathers.

What would she look like in the air? Emin wondered.

He pushed a bowl of drinking water to her, but she just glared at him. There was a lot of fear and hatred in her eyes for a creature he hadn't even known existed before this afternoon. Despite her otherworldly appearance, if she knew the word gryphon, she probably knew others.

"My name is Emin." There was recognition in her eyes at his words. "I'm the heir of the Alabaster Eyrie. What eyrie do you hail from? Are you from the east?"

The blood coast and desert had turned the far side of the continent into a mystery, even with the few trade routes willing to make the trip. The eyries there, especially the ones in the south, had gone silent or turned feral, and there were rumors of gryphon prides the likes of which no opinicus had ever seen hiding out in the mountains and redwood forests.

She snatched away the bowl, drinking it and coughing. Her injuries were severe, and if she didn't let his medics near her, she would soon bleed out.

He changed his approach. "I'm an alabaster opinicus. Opinicus, you know that word, right? What are you?"

"Don't use that word." Her voice was beautiful, musical.

He couldn't place her accent. "Alabaster?"

"Opinicus." She looked up from her bowl. "You are all *gryphon*. You are no longer opinicus. You have been quarantined down here for so long you have forgotten what that word truly means."

Emin regarded her, weighing the information. The

problem with speaking to someone dying was there was no way to know how much of what she said was true.

He changed tack. "What news of the king?"

"Dead," she said.

"And the other eyries?" he pressed.

She shook her head. "Buried in ash, like the king. There are no eyries left on the mainland. Would I have fled if I had anywhere else to go?"

No more king.

The entirety of the eyrie and reeve system was built upon the idea they all served at the pleasure of the king. It was what kept one from attacking another. If the king found out, the offending eyrie would be burnt to the ground.

But what the stranger said rang of truth. He'd never met the king. His father or grandfather or great grandfather hadn't. There was no living opinicus who knew the king's name. All they really knew were the stories, stories from long ago.

Yet, if the king was really dead, that meant there was nothing stopping the eyries from tearing each other apart. They'd need a new king to guide them, and the Alabaster Eyrie had been the first in Belamuria. If there were no eyries left in the homeland, that meant they were next in line.

"An entire continent of eyries buried under ash?" The medic came up from behind. Her osprey features showed she was local to Alwren. "It's not possible."

And yet, it was. Ash covered most of Emin's continent now, bringing with it a blizzard that had supposedly ended eyries and gryphon prides on the east coast. That ash had come from somewhere.

Home.

Emin stood, and the stranger flinched. Even that small

movement was enough for him to see the box she guarded with her body. It had a seal with six wings, an image not too dissimilar from her own.

He offered her one last choice. "You won't survive much longer. Either allow my medic to save you or hurry up and die so I can board your ship."

When the medic stepped forwards, the stranger hissed. "I would rather die an opinicus than live long enough for this cursed land to transform me into a gryphon like you."

It made no difference to Emin. "As you wish."

His guards finished off the stranger, a clean, brief death. He ordered her body sent north to the Alabaster University, then had one of his guards smash the lock on the chest.

The medic looked disappointed there weren't jewels or precious metals inside. Perhaps she'd hoped to see the hidden treasure of the king inside this strange boat with only one survivor. *And a hundred strange beasts.*

Not Emin, though. The Alabaster Eyrie's heir wasn't disappointed at all. Inside the chest were books and maps. All the questions the stranger had been unable to answer for him, he'd be able to locate in their pages. He opened the top one and began reading. It was illustrated with animals and flora he'd never seen before.

He flipped through the pages, looking for the names of the strange furry creatures that had escaped the ship.

"Capybara," he said, pointing to the larger one. He flipped a few more pages, trying to locate the name of the small ones with furry tails that had disappeared into the Emerald Jungle earlier. "Squirrel."

He closed the book. He had a lifetime of learning ahead of him. For now, there were more pressing matters, like the

Alabaster Eyrie messenger waiting for him to acknowledge her presence.

Her hesitation told him all he needed to know. There was only one reason why she'd defer to him like he was a reeve.

"What news of my father?" he asked.

"The alabaster reeve passed away yesterday morning." The messenger bowed her head. "You must come north to accept his crown. You are now a reeve."

He looked back at where the medic moved the body of the stranger.

Not just a reeve. Tomorrow, I become a king.

EMIN STUMBLED through the doors to the university of medicine, clutching at his wing. Outside, an army of peafowl attacked his harbor, making one last-ditch attempt to free Reevesport from his grasp. Their merchant ships, full of apples, had hidden a small army beneath. An army that made their assault on the palace in the middle of a parade, hoping to catch the Seraph King unaware.

And they had nearly succeeded, were it not for the intervention of his youngest general, Hi-kun. Emin would see to it that the opinicus received the highest honors. Even now, he was retaking the palace.

The university hospital was empty.

"I need help," he called out. Most likely, the doctors and nurses would have continued hiding if it hadn't been his voice. As it was, opinici appeared from all directions.

"Your Majesty?" A duckbill opinicus approached, her head a green as vibrant as the blue markings on her wings. "How bad is the injury?"

It was a strange question for a doctor to ask her patient. What she was really asking was whether it was time to use the strange salts again. They'd been less effective last time, and he'd had to pick and choose when to use his limited supply.

The king looked back at his wing and the way it drooped. He'd hoped to get a few more years, but a king without flight was a sitting duck, no offense intended to his current physician.

"It's time." Emin allowed himself to be pulled back through the hospital to a hidden room where only reeves and their families were treated. Once, reeves had come to the Alabaster Eyrie from across the continent for medical care. Now, they hid in apple crates attempting to overthrow it, unsuccessfully, as the body of the ruler of Reevesport floating in the harbor attested.

The physician set his wing as best she could while her nurses prepared the bath. Part of the reason for his push east was necessitated by the limited supply of essential salts remaining. He needed to put pressure on Crestfall, which was why he'd ordered his armies to take Reevesport. If he could block off Crestfall's nearest trade partners, they'd be more willing to listen to his commands.

The mixture reached its optimal temperature, and Emin allowed himself to be lowered into the tank. The salts were a surprising, but timely, discovery. He'd nearly reached the end of his lifespan when he first started taking them. The way things were going, he'd soon pass a hundred years old.

His body warmed, and he closed his eyes. He always told himself the process was no worse than molting, but that wasn't remotely true. The more he did this, the greater the pain. But it was worth it to feel young again. To *be* young again.

More shouting came from the hospital. He recognized Hi-kun's voice squaring off against the sounds of more peafowl. Several screams, the scrape of metal, and then the sounds of some of his nurses dying.

The king opened his eyes. Staring back at him was an albino peafowl opinicus. Dark, cobra-like circles were painted on her tailfeathers. She wore a single set of long metal talons —*cobra fangs* the farmers called them—and she reached back to stab him.

Featherless and without armor, the naked king twisted as the talons entered the vat. They still caught his side, spilling his blood, but he trusted the salts to fix that. She pecked at his eye, and he caught her head and held it away.

A moment later, Hi-kun slid into the chamber. With one slice, he severed the head of the opinicus. Her blood spilled into the vat, but her body fell limp.

"I'm sorry, your Majesty," Hi-kun said. "They'd already hidden a team of assassins near the hospitals before the main assault came. We didn't find out until it was too late. It's over now."

The king's body burned, but something was wrong with this infusion. His skin felt wrong. The salts had always restored him, but now something was off, twisted. He shouted for the doctors, and they pulled him out early.

"It must be the peahen's blood," the duckbill physician said. "It spilled into the mixture."

Emin tried to stand, but his legs were still weak. His feathers grew in, a process much faster and more painful than a normal molt, and he resisted the urge to cry out in pain in front of his subjects. Instead, he gritted his beak and waited.

When he finally caught his reflection in Hi-kun's polished armor, he didn't recognize himself at first. The long, black markings of a white-tailed kite were gone from his face. In fact, all of his markings were gone. He was as white as the peafowl who had tried to assassinate him.

"What happened?" he asked at last, beckoning a servant over to bring him food and water. "How is this possible?"

The physician signalled her assistants, who ran off to fetch the royal scholars. "It's too soon to know. It could just be an effect of the salts. We haven't been able to experiment with them while they remain so rare."

Several of Emin's scholars had been targeted by the assassins, and two were being treated outside his room. One of them stepped forwards, an osprey who had been fisherfolk before the king had forced Alwren to bow before him lest another ship wash up on its shores.

"I've heard stories of this." Despite having grown up isolated in the southwest corner of the world, she always managed to know what was going on. "It's said a Redwood Valley scholar has performed a similar trick with eggs, influencing how they hatch."

Two maps decorated this chamber. On the west wall hung the map of Belamuria from the stranger's ship. It didn't have a Redwood Valley Eyrie, being far too old, but it included three eyries not any other maps—the Emerald Arkhaiopolis, the Plagued City, and an eyrie whose fate was uncertain, but whose inhabitants had probably fled into the nearby Argent Heights for some reason or another.

Across the room, to the east, stood the map of the world as the king's forces saw it now. There was no Redwood Valley Eyrie on this map either.

The scholar limped to the map, pointing at the southeast corner, near the Crackling Sea Eyrie. "It's an offshoot of Reevesport from the previous king's final visit to Belamuria."

"Oh good, more peafowl," Hi-kun commented. With the king secured and safe, nurses saw to the commander's injuries.

"It's all rumors," the scholar continued, "but there's been a trial of some sort that ended in the scholar's banishment. Our contact paid a forger to make copies of his books. Reading through them, he seems to know the secrets of changing one's biology... for eggs."

Emin considered this. "Only eggs? Not adults?"

"He doesn't have the salts," the osprey explained. "If we gave him access, perhaps he could find a way."

Emin looked at the ceiling. Hanging from it were the bones of the stranger, her six wings spread out. Ever since meeting her on the beach, he'd dreamed of returning to the homelands, of reclaiming them from the ash.

The only issue with his dream seemed to be the northern ocean itself. No matter how many ships he sent north, none returned. The stranger's map already hinted at this. She was part of a fleet of ships, the only one to get past the dangerous waters where the creatures of the depths waited to attack passing travelers. Then there were areas of deadly algae blooms that transformed swaths of the ocean into poison for opinici.

It would take a body well-adapted to crossing oceans to make the journey north and see what was there, whether anyone had survived. It would take a body like the seraph's.

"What is this scholar's name?" the king asked.

The osprey pulled a book from the shelf. "Mally, it says. During the trial, the locals referred to him as the Nighthaunt. Apparently, there was an issue of him kidnapping pregnant opinici and eggs to experiment on after he was expelled from their university."

Emin's eyes were on the skeleton hanging above him. While she'd referred to herself as an opinicus, in her papers and books, she'd included a study of the evolution that had led to his present shape. One of the distinctions proposed by the book and rejected by the old king was 'seraphic opinicus' and 'gryphonic opinicus,' so Emin had labelled the stranger as a 'seraph.'

"Is there enough of you left?" he asked the skeleton. "Could we reverse the effects Belamuria has had upon us?"

"Your Majesty?" Hi-kun prompted. He was already fitting his armor back on. "I can have the army prepared for the trip by nightfall. We will take this... Redwood Valley Eyrie. Find their scholar."

Emin shook his head. "No, I need you to take Reevesport. We've been too lenient. Find their sweetest orchards and burn them to the ground. Then kill everyone who worked there. They should know the price of rebellion."

Hi-kun bowed and left, leaving Emin alone with the osprey.

"I can reach out as a scholar," she added. "I'm not sure where he's gone since he was banished, though. He could already be dead."

The king stood, stopping in front of a mirror. He'd need to find black and grey dye. Over time, he could make it appear that his markings had faded with age, and no one would be any the wiser.

"Fetch Piprik," he ordered. "He's my eyes across this continent. Let him find the Nighthaunt. If this banished scholar can really do what you say, we can offer him anything his heart desires."

The Seraph King stood inside the hidden workshop he'd built for Mally the Nighthaunt on the southern border of his territory. Until the scholar achieved his purpose, there was no point letting the rest of the kingdom know what they were up to.

Mally's early experiments had shown promise. The scholar's black eyes were another reason Emin was happy to keep the Nighthaunt so far from civilization. Several soldiers nearby sported the same black eyes. They'd become a necessity as the attacks from the nearby abyss gryphons increased. Hi-kun had seen to it that opinici were trained to fight in the dark, and that their biology had been altered to accommodate.

Vats stood on platforms, filled with the purple salts. The largest one was being prepared now. The bones of the seraph had been ground into a powder and added to the mixture.

The king took off his harness and crown. This was what he had waited for. He just wished he was certain it was going to work. All the previous experiments required blood. They hadn't been able to get it to work with bone dust, and there were limits to the Nighthaunt's alchemy.

Gryphon, opinicus, and bird blood all seemed to work to trigger the change. While Emin had found a catalogue of creatures the seraph called *mammals* that seemed to match the back halves of most gryphons and opinici—though not the seraph herself, oddly enough—there were no *felines* on the continent. It appeared the algae blooms had killed off most of Belamuria's native mammals. Even the escaped squirrels and capybaras had gone into hiding along the southern coast and jungle, as though afraid to approach the blood coasts.

There was no proof the seraph's body would allow him to

create more like her. Yet, Emin could taste that he was close. He had to be. According to his scholars' calculations, he had but one change left before his body gave out.

To the north, another of Mally's creatures slammed its beak into a tree trunk several times, warning that their enemies drew near. Creating a set of woodpecker gryphons and opinici hadn't been Emin's idea. He'd never have recommended creating a gryphon at all. It was antithetical to his goals. Mally had come up with that proof of concept on his own. Both woodpeckers, imperial and ivory-billed, were extinct, but specimens remained frozen and preserved in several universities.

In creating his gryphons and opinici, in changing the Seraph King's old wounded guards into them, Mally proved that not even death could keep him from his goals.

Turning the Nighthaunt to their side had been a win, but it had come with costs. Many soldiers died evacuating Mally from a Blackwing Eyrie exploratory camp in the Emerald Jungle. Piprik himself was among the missing, and the king would need to assign a new spymaster.

"It's time," the Nighthaunt said. "We're at peak potency. For a change so drastic, the temperature needs to be hot. The salts need to be concentrated. You'll feel both heat and chemical burns this time. And you need to stay in as long as possible. Bones are... not ideal."

The king nodded. He stepped to the edge, but Hi-kun stopped him.

"Your Majesty, this is too dangerous. I can't let you do this." The armored opinicus looked down at his talons, afraid to correct royalty in front of others. "It's the Nighthaunt's mixture. Let him take it. If it works, we can get more blood from him. Isn't that right, Mally?"

The scholar shifted uncomfortably. His black eyes were unreadable. "Yes. If it changes one of us to a seraph, after time, we can draw out that blood and use it on the others. In theory."

The Seraph King sighed, but he allowed himself to be led away from the vat. While he dressed, his soldiers forced Mally in his stead.

The Nighthaunt, usually unreadable, let out a loud cry once the salts took effect. The cry of the abyss gryphon whose eyes he had taken, a cry that echoed across the pits of the Abyssal Naze.

The depths of the earth shouted back. The cave gryphons spilled out of every hole and crevice, forcing Hi-kun outside to join the fray. All along the edges of the workshop were cages that had once housed cave gryphons. Someone had been careless, and one of them had escaped, opening the other cages on his way out.

That same gryphon had rallied the others, and increasingly large forces had spilled out of the caves north of the Emerald Jungle. The easy solution would be to gather up the goliath birds, pack up the supplies, and ride for Duckbill. Unfortunately, the first scholars who attempted to do that discovered that the road was no longer safe when it collapsed into a cavern and they were all eaten.

Nasty things, cave gryphons. They always hold a grudge.

As all of their essential salts were in this workshop in heavy, metal containers, there was no real way to transport them out while under attack.

More shouting came from the vat where Mally's feathers floated to the top, echoed by the cries coming from outside as a mix of woodpecker and alabaster opinicus troops tried to hold the line against a flood of cave gryphons. They'd repelled attacks by the abyssal gryphons in the past, but something was different this time. The king's forces were losing ground.

An hourglass counted down its final sands, and Emin gave a nod to his bodyguards, who pulled Mally out and laid him on a towel. Several assistants approached, drying off their mentor and seeing to his wounds.

The results were... disappointing.

The Nighthaunt's body had stretched, but not nearly as long as the seraph's. His tail, a short, peregrine falcon's tail, was now long and split at the end. His back legs showed a little feathering, his front legs more so, but he was a far cry from the beauty of their forbearers.

"It failed," the guard next to him said. "He did not acquire ascension."

The Nighthaunt coughed, water dripping from his body. "It was not fresh enough. I need blood. I cannot do this without blood."

"So be it," the king said. "Your Redwood Valley spy reports there are some desiccated remains in the bog. And before Piprik died, he was following reports that a frozen seraph had been found in the eastern mountains."

The screams came from inside the workshop now. Apparently, the cave gryphons had burrowed beneath one of the storage areas without a stone foundation and come in behind the royal guard.

Hi-kun burst into the room. "We have to leave. Now."

"This will set us back." Mally looked to the vaults, now being sealed up, where the salts were stored. "We'll need to acquire more."

"Send me to Crestfall. I will make the pink reeve see sense," Hi-kun said.

The king nodded. His energy was low. He needed this last regeneration. If too much time passed, he'd need to decide between extending his life a few more years or getting his ascension.

It wasn't an easy decision. No one else held his faith, his conviction. No one else saw what he did, a way to reclaim the old lands, to return to their home. If he died, his dream died with him.

"It's time." Hi-kun gathered the last of the guards, who opened the roof exit. Several cave gryphons tumbled in, but the royal guard protected both Emin and Mally as they flew away from the chaos.

The screams of opinici and cave gryphons followed him north, but the king thought little of them. He'd searched the sea for shipwrecks, never finding another live seraph. A few more artifacts from the old world had washed up along the northern blood coast, but the Reevesport natives had burned the boat and its occupants, then tossed the bones into the sea.

If just one of these reports of preserved seraphs was right, however, that would change everything. With their wings, he could go north. He could take his rightful place again.

He was so close.

1

THE SILVER REEVE

The Argent Heights were a place of contradictions as Foultner quickly discovered. The temperature at the peaks was cold, but it grew hot along the base of the mountains. There was no rain this time of year, but there were still hot springs of undrinkable water nearby. It was as remote as any eyrie could be while also having comforts of civilization that even the Redwood Valley Eyrie had lacked.

The peaceful farming eyrie was nestled on a mountain between a barracks housing the Seraph King's reserve army and the largest prison on the continent. It was the most stressful place Foultner had ever lived, and somehow Henders was having the time of his life.

"Hey Foult! Come see what Tilly did!" the ex-Reeve's Guard, now espionage-inclined rancher, shouted.

Foultner grumbled. She was tired and dusty, and she wanted to soak in the hot springs. She didn't really want to be out here with Henders guiding the birds around. Of course, that was her *job,* and she needed to avoid looking suspicious, so she crawled over to where her mate was situated.

From a distance, the mountains around the heights all appeared fairly uniform. Sometimes they were rocky, sometimes they were covered in scrub brush. They never revealed their secrets unless she landed. In this case, it was a goliath bird with an armored head clearing out a thin but deep canal cut into the earth.

Clean, farmable, *drinkable* water was the most valuable resource this high. Come spring, she'd been told, they would get flooded with water for a brief rainy season. Then it would stop raining for the rest of the year.

Judging by how long she'd been here without so much as a sprinkle of snow, that felt about right. But there was no easy way to store that much water inside the cramped eyrie. So instead, the argent hawks had figured out a way to get nature to do the heavy lifting for them.

When the rains came, the runoff naturally formed several rivers, flowing down into the farmlands and out in the direction of the ocean or Crackling Sea. Most of them evaporated once they reached the heat at lower elevations. The moisture from the rains came fast and furious, and it left in much the same manner.

Except that the silver eyrie had built deep, thin canals to siphon off the water from the raging flood and divert it down other parts of the mountain. They weren't really storing the water so much as they were delaying it. Instead of taking days to travel from the peak to the lowlands to evaporate, these canals redirected it through a series of cushion peat bogs that slowed the current and fed it through limestone to keep it drinkable.

Supposedly, the Argent Heights had once had a university,

and its scholars had created *cushion maps* of the water flow, taking special care to track the speed of the currents. Some canals started the water down a path of peat and limestone so slow the water took weeks to reach its destination. In other places, months. In a couple of places, the drinkable water used on the farms had first arrived via raincloud two years prior.

Foultner shook her head. Opinici were crazy like that, determined to live in locations they weren't meant to be.

Leave these places to the gryphons. Let them build their Hoarfrost Catacombs or Owlfeather Highlands here.

Henders pointed proudly to a pile of muck and dead tumbleweeds. "Look! She's getting much better cleaning the canals."

"It's slime and dead plants," Foultner said. "I'm proud of you, Hends, for teaching her. But it's hard to get excited about."

He shook his head at her. "If the goliath birds weren't doing this, it'd be up to us. So every bit of slime she brings out is some we didn't have to do by talon ourselves."

Foultner tried to look happy. He was right, of course. And before domesticated goliath birds had reached the Argent Heights, they'd really had a team of opinici whose sole job was to keep the canals clear. She was just feeling... morose. Depressed. Anxious.

Months had passed, and she hadn't been able to get word home. She hadn't even seen another Redwood Valley opinicus, except a quick glance when some captured opinici from the Crackling Sea were brought to the prison mountain.

No matter how subtle and persistent Foultner had been, she couldn't get Silver to tell her about the prison or garrison.

Instead, asking about the prison earned her more stories about the Duckbill Murder Hen.

I'm about to go full murder hen if I hear that story one more time. She only killed twelve opinici. Blinky's killed more than that. And she used a spike while Blinky just had her claws.

In addition, Blinky had managed to kill the blue reeve, or so the stories went. Jonas's unconscious body had been brought through here before the prisoners, and he hadn't been seen since. If he was alive, the Seraph King had him in hiding. If he was dead, Foultner wanted to confirm it and spit on his grave.

Instead, even for the little information she'd been able to gather, she hadn't found a way to pass it along to the Ashen Weald. And she didn't have a good way of finding out about her homeland while she was up here. Officially, she and Henders had been described as fisherfolk from King's Reach.

She had no idea where King's Reach was located. She sort of knew it was on the far corner of the world, but she couldn't name a single city there. If she'd been pressed about her cover story, she'd have caved immediately.

Thing was, nobody else knew anything about King's Reach, either, except that it was part of the kingdom. Some sort of port city near Alwren. Not the sort of place anyone wanted to go, though. Too close to the starlings. Going to fall off into the sea one day, the poor dears, and nobody would notice they were gone.

Foultner sighed. "Come on, Hends. Let's pack it in. Another day of honest work finished, and I'm ready to be warm and fed."

"After we brush down all of the goliath birds," Henders added. "You said it yourself, you need to look like a real rancher. You can't keep leaving me to do the work."

"Of course not!" she said. Of course, she really wanted him to do all of the work, especially the parts of work that required physical labor. Even at her laziest, she was somehow building muscles out here she didn't know she had. Not as fast as Henders was, which was nice, but she'd never felt so strong before.

She thought back to when they were carrying Silver's broken body out of the bog and across the sawgrass flats to safety. That felt like an eternity ago, but they'd both been surprised at just how strong Silver was for such a small hawk.

Having lived out here for a few months, Foultner was starting to understand how that happened—against her will, which wanted to soak in the hot springs and sleep all day. Her one saving grace was that she wasn't really a rancher, she was a spy, so she had things to do that kept her mind occupied while she stared at the hundredth canal this month.

She whistled for the goliath birds. Tilly perked up. The others ignored Foultner, so Henders went to get them.

"Hey there, ya big bird," Foultner said to Tilly. "We've had quite the journey here, haven't we? Travelled the world, you and me. Let's get you some food so you can take a nap."

Tilly let out a loud *mronk* and waddled back to the ranch.

Oh, to be as happy as a goliath bird running to dinner.

THE ARGENT EYRIE had a lot of rocks. Not precious gemstones or metals. Maybe it had those, buried deep beneath the mountain. Mostly, however, it just had stone living quarters, stone tables, and little stones for lying on that meant everyone carried around their own cushions to place atop them.

Foultner sighed, running back to her room to fetch *her* cushion. She couldn't leave it behind and steal someone else's. Well, she could, but not without making Henders upset. He'd sewn this particular cushion for her, and it had two opinici on the front she thought were supposed to be her and Hends hugging a large goliath bird that was definitely Tilly.

The cushion smelled like goliath bird. She didn't know if it had goliath feathers inside. She didn't want to ask. She just tossed it on her back, balancing it between her wings, and went to dinner late.

Usually, the dining hall was busy. *Bustling,* even, with opinicus activity. It was a good place to hear the latest gossip, word from the front, and even rumors of what was going on south of Duckbill. Supposedly, the royal fleet was parked nearby, and the king was in attendance.

Staying up late to brush down the goliath birds and feed them meant that Foultner was now here alone. A fire was going, always pleasant, but it required a little encouragement to give off warmth. She located some cold food and went to put it next to the fire to heat up, then curled around her cushion, not bothering to sit on it.

Her food would probably burn—*again*—but Henders would wake her up after he finished his bath. He liked to read in the bath, so that could take hours. Not exciting books like *What Does Your Plumage Say About Your Personality?,* but boring books about canals and irrigation. He was, honestly and truly, a born rancher who had only now found his calling thanks to her spy missions.

She was just dreaming of eating an oscillated turkey when a voice woke her.

"Looks like your meat is getting a bit crispy there," Reeve Silver said, moving Foultner's bowl away from the fireplace.

"Mmm, kills the worms," Foultner replied. "Sorry, I must have dozed off."

Silver smiled. "Canals are hard work. I used to do them as a fledgling with my sister. Good, honest work, but it doesn't leave much time for anything else."

Despite her instincts, Foultner had never been able to get a read on Silver. When she said things about *not having time* or about *honest work*, Foultner wondered if she knew about what Henders and Foultner had been up to. But Silver seemed to speak about honest work and such to everyone, so it could be Foultner's imagination.

"It is what it is," Foultner said, trying to sound like a rancher. "We've got a lot more to do before the rainy season. Otherwise, we won't have crops come summer."

Silver waited for her bowl of stew to warm. It had seemed unthinkable at first that a reeve would come down and eat with the members of her eyrie, but Foultner had grown used to seeing the hawk down here. In the early days, when they weren't sure they'd get the canals done on time, Silver had even stripped off her harness and waded naked into the canals, pulling out a blockage of sticks and tumbleweeds that threatened the whole operation—tumbleweeds and weather were the two most popular topics of conversation up here.

Once things were back on track, Silver was able to go back to leading her government or whatever it was reeves did.

"How goes the reeving?" Foultner asked. "Keeping everyone in line?"

Silver shrugged. "The Argent Heights runs itself. Everyone knows what they have to do, and they do it. Even when things go wrong, it's not particularly spectacular. Speaking of which, there's a new bark beetle outbreak. I'm going to need you and Henders to take the birds down there for a few days and help carry away the lumber to be burned."

"Again?" Foultner asked. This was the fifth outbreak. They weren't severe, but they required cutting and burning out sections of the forest. Foultner liked trees, and she hated to kill them for any reason. The lumber would have eggs in it and couldn't be used for building things, so it just became a kind of pointless bonfire.

"It is what it is." Silver echoed Foultner's words back at her with a smile. "I asked the alabasters at the garrison if they'd come down to help, but they said they're 'awaiting orders and need to be combat ready.' As though they're ever doing anything other than sleeping, drinking, or playing dice. Waste of space, they are. Thankfully, we're not the ones feeding them. Reevesport is."

There was a strange rivalry between Reevesport and the Argent Heights, both of which had formed the dangerous front line against the Blackwing Alliance before Whitebeak was established. They were philosophically opposed. The Reevesport opinici, as best Foultner could intuit, thought of the argent hawks as being poor and unconcerned with the finer things in life.

Hot springs feel like one of the finest things in life, if you ask me.

The argent hawks believed that the Reevesport opinici were spoiled and lazy. Spoiled because of the large amounts of cider and apple pastries they ate. Really, though, working on a farm wasn't easy work, so she didn't think working an apple orchard would be much better.

Especially when Reevesport orchards seemed to be ninety percent giant cobras and ten percent apples. At least nothing in the Argent Heights was actively trying to kill Foultner, except for the occasional rattlesnake.

Sorry, 'rattler.' Gotta sound like a native.

"We'll head down tomorrow. The lumber mill has stables, doesn't it? We can leave the birds there," Foultner responded.

"Are you still looking for interesting places to visit?" Silver asked. Foultner had spent their first month here getting the lay of the land, in case she needed to make a map later. "There're some old mining towns in the area. The mines have mostly closed due to, well, let's just say they dug a little too deep. But if your beak's hard, you should try some of their food. Rock candy, stuff like that. I'll make sure you and Hends have the nights off together for the rest of the month."

Foultner perked up. "Thanks! That'll be nice. Henders is always looking for things to eat."

Silver finished her goodbyes, leaving Foultner to pick at her stew, now both burned and cold. Henders showed up soon after, and once they were done eating, they retired back to their quarters.

Most of the beads Silver had paid them had gone straight back into her coffers when they purchased these quarters, but they were worth it. They were spacious—really, everything in the Argent Heights was wide open—and there were several different rooms, mostly empty. Foultner just didn't know how you filled up more than one room.

There was even a room where the undrinkable but pleasantly warm spring water fed into, letting her take a bath in the comfort of her own home. And, courtesy of the stone walls, so long as the door was closed, she didn't have to listen to her neighbors.

It was nice. If everything in the world went wrong, this would be a good place to hide. Which was why, as she drifted off to sleep, her thoughts—the same thoughts she'd had every night for several months now—were so disturbing.

There was nothing special about the Argent Heights except that its ruler kept track of the supply lines of an entire continent. The only thing special here was Reeve Silver, and Foultner had no way of getting that information back to the Ashen Weald. No way of getting *herself* back to the Ashen Weald, wherever they were hiding, which was another part of her problem.

Because if Blinky couldn't get here, that meant it was up to Foultner to assassinate the argent reeve and give her friends a fighting chance.

And because there was no way out of here, she didn't know what would happen to Henders when she made her move.

2

ALABASTER EYRIE

Emin sat atop one of the large towers overlooking the Alabaster Eyrie. The city sprawled out before him, buildings rising into the sky. When he took over as its reeve several lifetimes ago, the skyline had been very different. Buildings rose even higher, obscuring the view of the palace. He'd sent his scholars to search through the archives, attempting to reconstruct how the city had looked in the old days.

Then he'd slowly used his political and financial power to reshape it, rooting out the buildings that ruined its shape and 'growing' new ones in their place to match a painting from hundreds of years ago. He'd come to think of himself as a gardener of cities.

The palace back then had lost part of its beak and a wing. However it had been constructed out of stone, the massive opinicus with its spiked crown had been through a lot. The exact techniques were lost before Emin became reeve, so he'd pushed his considerable wealth into rediscovering them.

Not all of the old methods were still usable. The large, stone opinicus had been restored, but the archives spoke of a fleet with stormcloth sails. While the actual technique for making stormcloth had been recovered, Belamuria lacked the trees to make it work. Plant fibers had to be processed into a thin, translucent state and combined to create them. His mistake had been in thinking the *technique* was what mattered. Five years in the archives and his scholars had worked it out again.

What had actually been lost were the trees from the homeland needed to make it work. The cloth his scholars made was opaque and far too heavy for sails.

When we return home, we can build a fleet of stormcloth ships, stormcloth eyries.

Still, they'd figured out enough stoneworking to fix up the giant opinicus statue. That was something. And he'd regulated the building sizes down to let the palace shine again. Getting the eastern hills free of buildings to restore the botanical refuge had taken some doing. Ultimately, he'd been forced to wait for several opinici to die, then he'd purchased their land and donated it to a trust he secretly controlled. The trust transformed a section of the city back into a nature preserve.

The trees and animals wouldn't be the same as they were hundreds of years ago, but did that really matter? He had nearly achieved his vision of restoring the Alabaster Eyrie to its former glory. Of restoring the opinici to their former glory.

The last part of his plan was nearly complete. It would require the greatest sacrifice, but all glorious things did. Part of tending to a garden was pest control.

THE KING WALKED through his palace. The flight over here had hurt more than he cared to admit. His body was old. It was a situation he had been in several times before.

Just a few more days, and I'll be back to new.

For the last time, for the final time. But that was all he needed. A few more years of youth would give him time to grant the opinici his greatest gift: ascension. That was what his skyline was truly missing. It needed seraphs to fill its skies, not these devolved opinici.

The words of the stranger echoed in his mind. *Gryphon,* she'd spat at him. An insult. Devolved, fallen, no longer worthy of the title *opinicus.*

He shook his head. Not anymore. Soon, they'd earn their wings again. Soon, they'd return to the homeland. He just needed a little more patience, and he was nothing if not patient.

The entire continent had stood against him. Nature itself forced seraphs into opinici, opinici into gryphons. The gryphons could not be saved. It was too late for them. Their bodies could be fixed, certainly, but not their brains. They were too far from opinical enlightenment. They'd need to be purged.

He paused near his throne, looking at the banners of the eyries he had conquered. The glass chimes and trinkets of Crestfall transformed the light into rainbows. Losing the pink palace had been his greatest defeat yet. With unlimited salts, he could have transformed all his followers into seraphs. With its loss, he'd been forced to adjust his plans.

He made a solemn vow: Next year's chicks would all be born as seraphs. He would make it happen. He could give them a brighter tomorrow. He could pave the way for them, terraforming the future the way he had this eyrie, this continent.

"My King?" Hi-kun's voice echoed across the throne room. As Emin's health faded, he'd ceased allowing large numbers of opinici into this room. It had become his sanctuary, open only for special occasions. If his subjects needed something, well, that was why he had so many opinici in his employ.

"Is it time, old friend?" The king only used the term of endearment in private. When the salts had flowed freer than they did now, he'd blessed his greatest champion the boon of youth.

If the Nighthaunt's old workshop still has its salts, I can grant ascension to Hi-kun and my other reeves. A fitting gift for such loyal servants.

He allowed Hi-kun to lead him down the gold carpet, white marble framing either side of the room. Many of the banners were pristine, but the one from the Crackling Sea had been pulled out of that wretched city and was in need of repair. As did the eyrie itself. It was too bad Jonas hadn't named a successor.

The doors to the throne room were opened by several of the royal guard, their red crests held high, and the king adjusted his gait to something more regal.

Outside, on the steps to the palace, were hundreds of his elite guard. More patrolled the air. Several opinici sounded their musical voices in song.

The king took it in stride. He didn't look out at anyone, though the few reeves who were in the city, such as the portmaster, were permitted to come and bow before Emin. He acknowledged them with a glance only.

Moving his flagship across the continent had not been

easy, especially with his old enemy, the blackwing reeve, having spies in every port.

Officially, their expedition against the glacier gryphons had been part of a celebration for his hundredth birthday.

It was all nonsense, of course. He'd been born before the Connixation, after all. But it was the pretext they needed so they didn't arouse suspicions from his enemies, or his allies, some of whom were getting restless.

Let us see if they remain restless after my ascension.

Hi-kun gave some sort of speech, repeated by several particularly loud and lyrical opinici across the courtyard. The king had stopped listening long ago. Kind words were used by enemies as often as friends, and he had no need of someone else's puffery. Not when he was already so sure of himself.

Cheering erupted from the tiers of the buildings around him, and the king, bones aching, took a moment to rear back, wings in the air, mimicking the opinicus statue behind him.

No one alive would remember it, but the Alabaster Eyrie crown had originally been a small, blocky, simple thing with a jewel in it. That old crown still existed, tucked away in a vault somewhere. But when the statue had been repaired, Emin had given himself a new crown to match it.

He allowed himself a single smile. Then, bones protesting, he lifted into the air to fly south to continue his... birthday celebration.

Hi-kun and the royal guard flew with him. They were flashy in their own right, but the real reason they were here was to mask Emin's own weakness. His bones ached. His mind ached. Even his armor felt heavy, and it was a lighter set he'd had forged just for ceremonies.

Once they were out of the eyrie, the king landed on a

cushioned platform lined with gold. The royal guard each grabbed a rope of shining white, then lifted him in the air to carry him the rest of the way to Duckbill.

The king settled in, the cushions designed to make it appear he sat upright, and dozed on the trip.

3

LEI

Lei let out a big yawn. The ride from The Wrecks north to Ashfoot and onto Sandpiper's Dune was a long one, and while he wouldn't want to fly it, he got bored on ships.

Pip slept below decks. They'd both enjoyed the past few months exploring the island, cataloguing the different types of ships dredged from the reef and learning about the inhabitants. As fun as it was, both 'salt traders' felt a calling to come north again. Word had reached The Wrecks that the Seraph King's armies were pushing around the Crackling Sea, up towards Blacktalon, and Pip seemed determined to find a way to make sure his family was safe, not that they'd recognize him.

Lei had his own plans, though they didn't go so far north. Ellore's words in the desert had taken root in his soul, and he needed to know who had killed his father. He'd borrowed some of Orlea's books about the night of the fire, courtesy of Naya, and he thought he knew who he needed to speak with.

With the war on, the trick was finding them and getting them to talk to him.

He worried at a talon. The first two of those conversations were waiting for him at Luminaire, and he wasn't ready. His soul ached at what he might learn. He couldn't let this go on any longer, though. He'd come to terms with Zeph and Kia's part in his mother's death. Now he needed to know what had happened to his father, Larren.

Cielle, one of the islanders from The Wrecks who was descended from the Williwaw Pride of taiga gryphons, led Pip up to the top deck. "Hey, Lei. We're close enough now, you're better off jumping ship and heading east if you want to reach Luminaire before sundown."

Lei nodded. He'd packed lightly, just essentials and some food. A few of his more sentimental items were stored back at The Wrecks, and anything they had of value to trade was waiting for them north of Poisonmaw.

First, though, Luminaire.

Pip and Lei said their goodbyes to Cielle, then hopped off the boat and soared east. The fisherfolk shore settlements would make tempting targets, but after the Seraph King's original attacks on the glacier pride and the Ashen Weald's counterattack by Bogwash, the king's forces had withdrawn from the south. No one was sure if they'd return, but several observation posts had been set up on islands to keep watch, stocked with a team of two fantails.

Lei loved this stretch of ocean. Schools of flying squid shot out of the water below him. They looked happy, and he took them as a good sign until several sharks appeared, chasing after them.

Pip pointed down to Luminaire, and they descended. While his medicine opinicus mentor went to check on an old hut on the other side of the island, Lei went looking for two legends, two fisherfolk who had taken him in when he was having the worst year of his life.

It was time to ask Tresh and Rorin if they'd murdered his father.

LEI CAUGHT up to Rorin first. The large crane opinicus was sharpening spears in the beak-shaped bay of Luminaire. Down below the rocky cliffs, crates of food were packed up to go out to The Wrecks. The ship would swing by here before making its return trip to the deep ocean in a few days.

"Rorin!" Lei called, thankful to have found him alone. "Do you have a moment?"

"Can't say that I ever do. But why don't you grab a knife and help. What's on your mind?" Rorin asked.

Lei sat down and got to work. There was always something to do in the fishing villages. It wasn't that the inhabitants here never took time off, it was just that time off was an event to be savored. As Lei had finished his studies with Pip, he'd learned to be useful around The Wrecks. Among the skills he'd picked up, he was now a competent swimmer. He'd never be Turresh the Shark, but he no longer worried about drowning if he fell in, either.

He watched Rorin to see how he wanted the tips shaped, then started on his own spear. "I have a question to ask you. I don't mean any judgement by it, I just need to know."

"Mmm." Rorin gave a noncommittal response without looking up from his knifework.

Lei cleared his throat. "Did you kill my father?"

Rorin's knife stopped. He turned to Lei, a look of concern

on his face. "I don't know what it says about the past few years that I can't answer that question, but between the rangers, the wingtorn, and everything else... I really don't know. Who was your father? Why do you think the answer might be yes?"

It had been a long time since he was a scared chick at the Redwood Valley Eyrie, but Lei had never forgotten his father. He explained to Rorin how Larren had been a Reeve's Guard captain who had been put in charge of leading the wingtorn south. How he'd disappeared sometime around the attack on Swan's Rest. Then he waited for Rorin's answer.

"I can't say for sure," the crane answered. "There were skirmishes for a couple of days after the attack. But I spent the big, initial battle with Jun the Kjarr. Then I mostly fought wingtorn before working to secure Luminaire in case their allies found us. I don't think it was me."

"Was it Tresh?" Lei asked.

Rorin stood, stretching his long crane legs, and put away a finished spear to grab another. "You'll have to ask her. She's in the shallows, fetching clams. Just... be careful with how you proceed. Talking about Swan's Rest is hard for her. You weren't the only one who lost family that night."

"What about Quess?" Lei asked, but Rorin just grunted and went back to sharpening. Out of respect, the peafowl finished another few spears before he travelled north to the stretch of water between Luminaire and Swan's Rest that the fisherfolk called the shallows.

IT TOOK Lei some searching to locate Tresh. She had a way of resembling any other sea creature beneath the surface, and what finally gave her away was a nearby raft with several buckets of clams already on it.

Lei settled onto the water next to the raft and waited. Around twenty minutes passed, then he felt something under the water tug at his tailfeathers.

"Hey, Tresh." He turned to look at her, but no one was there.

Her voice came from across the raft. "Hello, Lei. Welcome back to the shore. How are you and Piprik?"

Another tailfeather tug sent him leaping onto the raft, but once he was above the water, he saw Quess beneath the waves.

She surfaced with a grin. "Weren't expecting two of us, were you?"

He laughed. "No, I can't say that I was. May I borrow Tresh for a little? I wanted to ask her a few questions. I can carry the buckets of clams back later, if it'll help."

"No need," Quess said, and several more shapes rose. There were around twenty petrel fisherfolk here, some just past fledged. He remembered how strange he'd felt as a young fisherfolk, how the adults treated him like he would shatter. Most of Crane's Nest had been made up of petrels, and very few of these young fisherfolk would have older friends or siblings who looked like them.

They were staring at him with confusion. His first thought was of his feather dye, but then he realized he had always looked young for his age. They probably thought he was one of the eggs from the lost generation. He did his best to appear reassuring, but he was glad when Tresh suggested the two of them head to the other side of the shallows so she could check on a few traps.

"Is everything okay?" she asked Lei. Her harness sported

new carvings of eels, pumpkins, and one that was very stylized but looked like a petrel and taiga gryphon intertwined in a sea of jellies. "You seem... unhappy. Perhaps you would rather talk to Rorin about this? He is better with feelings."

Lei laughed, though Tresh didn't seem to mean it as a joke. He just kept thinking of Rorin, sitting there like a giant while he sharpened deadly weapons to throw at opinici, making noncommittal sounds now and then.

"Perhaps a Carru, then," Tresh amended. "Though I do not know where he has disappeared to. Maybe Hoarfrost."

Lei settled down on a new raft, this one not full of buckets, while Tresh pulled up the trap lines. "No, this is personal, and it's about you. Did you kill my father? I heard that at least one opinicus was pulled under by a petrel during the conflict at Swan's Rest. Was that you?"

Tresh pulled up a trap with a small rock crab in it. She hissed at it, but it was too small to eat, and she tossed it back. "I do not know. If he was at Swan's Rest that day, and he flew out over the water, then yes, I did. There were four jailors controlling the wingtorn. I killed one, but the other three were on the shore."

"Four?" Lei asked. He'd known of two: his father, Larren, and one named Maurle. "Did they survive?"

Tresh put a wet paw on his shoulder. "These are questions for the Ashen Weald. I cannot answer them. If I killed your father, I am sorry. I was all panic and worry. We were still searching the shore for lost eggs. Still shouting for our children. It was... not a good time."

"It's okay." Lei didn't feel okay, but he'd told himself that whoever had killed his father, he was here to forgive them. There were Redwood Valley opinici who had done nothing wrong during the days of the conflagration, even those who had aided the gryphons. Lei's father was not such an opinicus, and Lei had resolved himself to that fact.

"It does not seem okay." Tresh looked towards the weald shore. "I tell myself those days are behind us. I tell myself I will not need to kill again like that. Yet the Seraph King feels so near, and Rorin believes he will return. There will be more killing. I do not believe there is any way to kill which does not leave scars on the soul. But I cannot flee. It is not in my nature."

When Turresh said *scars,* Lei's gaze went to her beak. Pip claimed it was healing up nicely, but it still looked jagged, like shark teeth.

Lei had never seen it as ferocious, but even now, he wondered if those same grooves had killed his father. "May I ask a favor? We've been down at The Wrecks, and I don't know where anyone is located anymore. Both you and Rorin pointed me at the Ashen Weald. Do you know where Thenca is staying?"

Tresh finished with the traps and led Lei back to Luminaire. "I do not know where the Ashen Weald hides. Satra changes locations often. But Soft Paws is at Sandpiper's Dune. If you ask, she will take you to Bogwash. The city looks abandoned, but the witches have individual dens in the nearby bog. If you sit and wait long enough, one will come find you."

Lei thanked Tresh for her time, then changed direction to find Pip. The bog witches had seemed scary at first with their skeletal paint, strange attitude, poor social skills, and tendency to create peculiar brews. Oddly enough, there was one who wintered at The Wrecks, Cielle's mate. Though his face paint was less skeletal and more... pumpkin, hence his name.

Lei and Pip had enjoyed their stay at The Wrecks, but

Pumpkin had fallen in love—first with Cielle, then with Cielle's moms, then with Cielle's moms' cooking, and then with the volcanic island itself. He was prone to seasickness, so he'd stayed home on this voyage to shore, but before snow had taken over the island, he'd built up a treasure trove of new pigments and paints.

In fact, Lei had brought some with him, both for personal use and as a gift for Naya. A lot of Lei's confidence after coming out had come from Naya's deft makeup work allowing Lei to change the shape of his face. At first, the goal had just been to hide the last of Reeve Brevin's heirs. Brevin was widely and incorrectly known to have had seven daughters. Giving Lei, who at that time had been going by Mi-Lei and Levin, a new name and obscuring his gender had seemed like a good way to keep the assassin Rybalt Reevesbane from finding him.

It had worked. It had worked so well that Lei had realized at that moment that his gender had been wrong the whole time. There had been hints along the way, talks about the difference between a peacock and a peahen that raised questions, but in the end, his disguise as Lei the Salt Trader had proven more true than his previous identity as Levin, Heiress to the Redwood Valley Eyrie.

Now, only a few opinici knew of his previous life. And the more time that passed since the Redwood Valley's destruction, the less important Lei felt. He'd done the best he could for his mother's subjects, but he'd abandoned her metal talons and the infamous snake necklace of his family. Instead, he was happy as a fisherfolk.

But he had questions he needed answered. His mother had always put a barrier between Lei and his father, and Lei wanted to know why. And he wanted to know if he had any siblings on that side of his family. And… he needed to know where his father had died. Just so he had a place to visit.

It shouldn't matter to him, but it did. Or maybe it didn't, but he couldn't be sure until after he knew. Either way, it looked like he was headed to Sandpiper's Dune.

THERE WAS a time when Lei could never tell what was going on in Pip's head. After all they'd been through, after the assassins, immolations, hidden laboratories, and pretending to be salt traders or apple growers, Pip had finally opened up.

His medicine opinicus hut on Luminaire was in shambles. It was too easy a target, and assassins had come after him here before. And, in fact, it was those same assassins who had left him a message.

"What's it say?" Lei pointed to the sealed letter. The symbol wasn't one he knew, but he suspected it was probably a gryphon pride and not an opinicus eyrie, so the most likely suspect was Iony.

Pip stood, taking a few boxes off the shelf. Concealed within crates that looked like they contained basic medicines were smaller jars that held the last of Pip's personal things from when he had been Khalim. Broken promises and a terrible trip to the jungle had made Khalim one of the first opinici to experience the effects of the purple salts.

Once a Blackwing Eyrie scholar, he and his other apprentices had been betrayed and made to look like traitors by Mally the Nighthaunt, then left for dead. Khalim had murdered a high-ranking Alabaster Eyrie opinicus, Piprik, the Eyes of the Seraph King, and taken his identity.

Not just his identity, also his appearance. Where Khalim's

best friend Wendl and the other scholars had transformed themselves into starlings to escape, Khalim had used the blood and remaining purple salts to turn himself *into* Piprik. There was no going back for Khalim, now Pip, but he worried about his family often.

"It's what I was hoping for," Pip said. "Thanks to owing Cielle a favor, Iony was willing to set things up for us. It's going to be risky, but we still have one final edict with the Seraph King's seal on it. Assuming the seal hasn't changed, assuming no one is onto us, I think we can go home."

Lei was happy to hear the words *us* and *we*. He'd been worried his mentor would abandon him. While he knew Pip had his own family, and Lei often experienced bouts of jealousy, he thought of Pip as almost like a father to him.

Not quite a father. More like... a father-in-law? An uncle?

"Are you still okay with me coming?" Lei asked. When Pip nodded, he followed with, "My search for my father won't slow you down?"

Pip finished packing his things. "The war moves slowly. The Alabaster Eyrie is building new outposts, ports, and fortifications as they go. It'll be a while before they reach Blacktalon. I want to get there before they do. I just... need to make sure my mate and son are okay."

"Know what you want your edict to say?" Lei asked. Inside Mally's workshop along the edge of the desert, they'd discovered the royal seal. There had only been enough wax for three scrolls, and they'd used up two of them already. The third scroll could be incredibly valuable to the Blackwing Alliance or the Ashen Weald, so neither Pip nor Lei had mentioned its existence.

As important as the war was, Pip's priority was keeping his

family safe. His family, whom he hadn't seen in years now, who believed he died a traitor in the jungle.

"Not yet," Pip said. "I'll think of it on the way. Where are we headed?"

"Bogwash by way of the dunes," Lei explained. As they left Luminaire, only stopping to pick up a few rare supplies, Lei pondered the other mystery Khalim kept in his harness: a single vial of the purple salts. While there was no way for Pip to use it to return to his original appearance—he'd have had to freeze his own blood before changing for that to work—Lei wondered if Pip could use it on a random dying blackwing. It wouldn't be quite the same, but at least it'd be closer. If nothing else, Pip wouldn't have to see the face of his enemy every time he looked into the water anymore.

Such things were not Lei's place to ask or suggest. Instead, he was happy he'd get to go north. First, however, he had one last mystery to unravel. How had his father died, and who had killed him?

4

DUCKBILL

The Nighthaunt hated the sunlight and resented being forced to work in it. The water table around Duckbill was too high to allow for much in the way of basements or hidden underground workshops, which was a pity. What he really wanted was the kind of place he could make his own. A den or perhaps a lair.

Oooh, a lair. That would be nice.

The darkstalker by his side felt similarly. While the cave gryphon's vision worked in the light and dark, something about the process of stealing their sight had made both Mally and his top lieutenants sensitive to daylight.

It was the early days, after all. I didn't yet know what I was doing.

He escorted his black-eyed assistant from the abandoned inn they'd taken over to the Reeve's Nest building where the more presentable members of the king's entourage were situated.

The citizens of Duckbill stared at the Nighthaunt and his

darkstalker. Mally had let his whiskers grow. He was already uncanny by opinicus standards, and he found it reassuring the local opinici were afraid of him. It meant they'd leave him alone.

His darkstalker had not adjusted to life as a monster nearly so easily. She trimmed her whiskers, and she wore the polished armor of the king's guard when she was out in public. Technically, she was still on their payroll, and she had some sort of enlisted rank Mally had never bothered to learn.

Oddly enough, the waddling duck natives were more afraid of her than him. Monsters happened, of course. That was just a fact of life. What seemed to truly frighten them was that Mally had turned a normal, respectable alabaster opinicus into a monster, too.

Her pristine white feathers and fur shone to his sensitive eyes. There was some sort of light dust she sprinkled in that gave the sparkling effect. He'd forbidden her from wearing it out in the field, but every time they were in a city, she glowed.

And, in fact, she attracted a fair number of glances. Sometimes, another opinicus would rush up and ask her where she purchased her feather sparkle. Then they'd look into her eyes, her black eyes, and see the way the markings around them dripped down to her cheeks and would back up, frightened.

Would you volunteer again for my experiments, knowing where they've put you?

They reached the main building. Hi-kun waited for them. With all of the talk of the assassination attempt on the pink reeve, and the actual assassination of the blue reeve, the guards were anxious. Hi-kun didn't want any misunderstandings, so he led Mally and his darkstalker inside, making it clear they weren't to be murdered.

It was very kind of him.

The king sat on a cushion. Mally had been around the dying long enough to see how poorly off Emin was. They were cutting it close. For all the promises of youth and a new life the elixir held, even on a healthy opinicus, there were diminishing returns.

The alabaster guards, with their brown eyes and clearly defined *non-dripping* markings, backed away from Mally and his minion. The royal guard showed no fear of him, which fed into the narrative that they had no fear.

It wasn't true, of course. He'd seen the terror in their eyes when he transformed them into their current shapes. They were fully capable of fear. They just believed he'd already done his worst to them.

It wasn't an unreasonable thought. For the ones who hadn't had offspring, it was true. For the others... they were starting to discover that a strange, new strain of bloodbeak had spread throughout the land. The king planned to claim the next generation of opinicus-spawn as seraphs. So be it. Mally had claimed the last two for his own purposes.

Already, he was flooded with letters from physicians across the kingdom asking for copies of his research. Copies he had made years ahead of time and packaged up, ready to go. Fortunately, the scribes who managed the efforts had been killed by a 'wild animal attack,' so they couldn't tell anyone Mally had known this was coming.

A wild animal with black eyes.

He was, for now, above suspicion. And he'd rallied the entire continent to search for a cure for him.

He smiled. Then remembered he was supposed to be bowing to a king and adjusted his attitude. "My dear King, we come with good news!"

That was his sign for the darkstalker to step forwards. She knelt, giving the impression that her black markings might drip down onto the floor, and put a small vial of salts on the ground in front of her. "I infiltrated the workshop. The cave gryphons didn't get into the vault. The salts are still there. What's more, most of the equipment is still functional. Once the opinici evacuated, the gryphons abandoned it."

The king nodded to Hi-kun, who picked the vial of salts up. "Then we shall have the ascension there."

"My king?" Hi-kun asked. "You put me in charge of your safety. Allow me to retrieve the salts. Then we will hold your ascension back at the palace."

Mally shook his head. "The palace is full of spies, your Majesty. All eyries are. I see the wisdom of what you're saying. The only place we can be sure there are no *reevesbanes* waiting for us is here."

"The Emerald Jungle—" one of the commanders began, but Mally interrupted him.

"My spies say the starlings are docile, content," the Nighthaunt said. "The glyphs are holding. A pact of a hundred years, but they still cannot cross. It's only the cave gryphons we need to worry about."

The commander balked. "How can anyone have a spy among the starlings? It's impossible."

Mally didn't respond. Everyone in this room knew he had a way of checking on the starlings, but they didn't yet know how... or why. *Why* was the much more important question, and not everyone in this room needed to know it.

Not yet.

"My assistants," he gestured to the darkstalker next to him when he spoke those words, "are taking care of our other problems. The cave gryphons seem without end, but we can hold one small workshop long enough for the king's purposes. Until then, we've caused as much chaos as we can to buy us time."

The commander grumbled but gave in. The king issued his orders to Hi-kun and the others, and they rallied the forces. Military matters weren't Mally's concern. He'd already weighed in on the importance of transporting the salts safely and explained what supplies they'd need to bring with them during the acquisition and subsequent defense of his workshop.

The king waited until the room was empty except for Mally and the royal guards. "Are there enough for two vats, Mal? I can see how bloody you've become. You don't have much longer than I do."

"A gracious offer, my king." Mally paused, pretending to consider it. "With the new bloodbeak disorder, there's been a lot of scholarship floating around. Nothing about the seraph biology suggests they'd help me. I would rather wait, see what comes of this. A change now would grant me three years at most. A breakthrough in the disorder could grant me thirty."

The king nodded. "Strange thing, that outbreak. Do iron disorders just... evolve like that? Under normal circumstances. Even my spies in the Blackwing Eyrie report cases on the rise, the old treatments not having worked."

"How odd." The Nighthaunt kept his voice neutral. "I'm certain we will have a new treatment before next year's eggs hatch. Nothing that would interfere with *your* plans, of course. You have my word on that."

Emin was still looking straight at the Nighthaunt. "Make sure that's the case. You're dismissed. Go crawl back into your den. If everything goes as planned, I'll see to it every scholar and hospital redirects its efforts into helping cure you."

"Very kind, your Majesty." Mally slipped away from the king's gaze. He'd known he'd be found out eventually. He didn't trust the king's promises, but at least for now, it appeared he wouldn't face justice for his crimes, so long as the ascension went off without issue.

5

BOGWASH

The trip from Sandpiper's Dune to Bogwash was uneventful. While any rafts caught on the ocean were out of luck if a storm or ship hit, teams of fantails kept a close watch along the coast. That wouldn't stop a particularly crafty serpentine whale, but it gave Lei some peace of mind.

Much the same way Pumpkin's paint was skeletal but also had that hint of carved pumpkin to dull the scary edges away, Soft Paws was a mix of skulls and flowers. She wore the traditional bog blossom blue and left her claws out and painted. According to the gossip on the dunes, and Naya's fisherfolk were nothing if not talkative, being a gryphon with non-retractable claws was a trait she'd acquired from her mother, rumored to be Ari, the kjarr den mother.

Where Lei was currently obsessed with finding out about his father's family and Pip was determined to save his own, Soft Paws seemed unconcerned with seeking out her mother.

"But... don't you just want to say hello?" Lei pushed. "She's your mom and all. That's gotta be important. My mom used to read me snake tales before I went to bed."

Pip nudged Lei, a reminder to be careful. Certain things about how Reeve Brevin treated her offspring were common knowledge. Problem was, Lei didn't actually know what life with a normal family was like. Did most opinici not teach their children about snakes? That seemed like an oversight, considering the number of venomous snakes in the valley and bog.

Soft Paws remained indifferent. "She laid an egg, but that's all she did. It doesn't matter much to me now. Maybe things are different for opinici. I know some weald gryphons seem very concerned about being parents. That's just... not what I care about."

The raft arrived at Bogwash, giving Pip and Lei an opportunity to use their talons to secure it to the docks. There were a few rangers on the raft, but they unloaded the supplies, unconcerned the city was unpopulated.

Lei and Pip wandered around. There were a few barrels of drinking water, a bit of clean nesting material, but otherwise, Bogwash was empty.

"I've never seen an abandoned nesting grounds before," Lei told Pip.

The old medicine opinicus's eyes were on the forest around them. "I'm going to guess the hidden entrances are over there, by the bent palm bush. Then right next to the mangroves, where the ground is worn down a bit. Then maybe just off the boardwalk. What do you think, want to make a wager?"

"My wager is... you're wrong on all accounts." Lei grinned.

Soft Paws went to the edge of the camp and let out a

sound that echoed. She stayed silent, standing there, until the hiss of an angry monitor returned.

Lei and Pip stepped back as bushes shook and trees moved.

Then, from the direction of the docks, Thenca appeared. "You brought guests, Soft Paws. Is Bogwash accepting tourists now?"

The witch shrugged. "Lei wished to speak to you. It is my city. I thought you might be lonely."

"We don't need to follow you to the bog," Lei pressed. "I just wondered if I could sit down with you for a few minutes and ask some questions?"

Thenca shrugged scarred shoulders. "Sure. I need to check on the raftworks. Want to come with me?"

Lei followed along. The raftworks was farther west, on the river. It was a bit of a walk, but he was happy to stretch his legs. And unlike with Rorin or Tresh, he wasn't worried that Thenca might be the murderer.

"I've been trying to figure out who killed my dad," Lei said. "I talked to Rorin and Tresh, thinking it might have been them. I think he died during the attack on Swan's Rest. Rorin didn't kill any opinici that day, and Tresh says she pulled one under and drowned him. But she doesn't know the names. She suggested I should ask you since you were in charge."

Thenca froze for a moment, and Lei rushed to reassure her.

"Oh, don't worry!" he hastened to add. "I know you and my dad were on the same side. I'm not accusing you. I just... want to know how he died. His name is Larren. He was in the Reeve's Guard, I think."

Thenca turned and looked at Lei, sizing him up. Her eyes had a serious streak that worried him. Her feathers and fur were dark with her winter coat, and she wore a kind of leather armor that covered her scars. "I wouldn't say we were on the *same* side."

"Oh, I didn't mean... I'm sorry. I wasn't thinking of it like that." Lei felt his nares flush red with embarrassment. Unlike his sisters, he wasn't cut out for conversations like this. "I just meant you weren't actively trying to kill him at the time. I know... I'm sorry."

They'd reached the raftworks, and Thenca circled around it, hopping up to the roof to check the storm shutters, then landing beside him to return to Bogwash.

"Look, fisherfolk," she began. "We've all had bad parents, bad friends, bad siblings. The opinici were there to make sure we killed every last fisherfolk chick, much like yourself. I don't know their names anymore. The best I can offer is that the opinicus with the map's name started with a *Mau* sound. So if your father didn't have a nickname or something with a *Mau* at the front, Tresh didn't murder him. Good?"

Lei nodded. "I'm sorry to have brought all of this up. It's just... I only knew my dad a little. I'd feel better if I knew where he was buried. I know you said you didn't know the names of the opinici with you... do you know where they ended up? Did they all die?"

He was careful not to mention what had set him down this path—the opinicus who had asked him if he knew how his father had died. There were rumors Ellore had returned to the bog and assembled a team of some sorts that were harassing the Seraph King's supply lines. While Ellore, once Ranger Lord Ellore, had been kind to Lei growing up, her own crimes were numerous. In fact, those same rumors that said she was back also stated she was helping the Ashen Weald to work years off her prison sentence.

Rumors or not, Ellore was rightfully hated by most prides and eyries in the Ashen Weald. She had few friends here, and those were looked at askance. Drawing attention to his relationship with Ellore would raise too many questions that he couldn't easily, or even *safely*, answer.

Lei and Thenca neared Bogwash, and more wingtorn had appeared with supplies for Soft Paws's next stop. Thenca paused while they were still out of earshot and offered some advice. "I don't think you should follow this path, but yes, there were two survivors. At first, they stayed up at the Strix Plateau, watching the kjarr gryphlets. Later, they moved to the kjarr nesting grounds. When those were evacuated, they disappeared. I don't know where they went."

Lei thanked Thenca, then followed Pip back to the raft. Their original plan had been to backtrack a little and follow the taiga north, but Lei convinced Pip they should take a short detour and follow Soft Paws to the Heart of the Bog. While Thenca's comments made it seem like the opinici with her father had disappeared, she'd given Lei an idea.

If the surviving guards had travelled with the kjarr gryphlets across so much distance, it was possible they were still with them now. Or whoever was with the gryphlets might know where they'd gone. It was worth a try.

Soft Paws gave the final shout. The rangers pushed the raft away, raised the sail, and headed farther west, into the unknown.

6

THE SUNKEN EYRIE

There was no abandoned city marking Lei's second stop. Instead, there were simply a few glyphs painted on a tree. It took the most eagle-eyed among them to notice the signs, but once they saw it, they located the small river nearby.

They secured the raft and followed the waterways inland. When Lei asked about how they'd get the goods north, Soft Paws explained that some wingtorn would tie a rope and pull their craft upstream later.

"We just need to let them know we're here," the witch said. She seemed more at ease than Lei had seen her before. She even stopped to sniff a few trees and scratch them with her paws. "Thistle is doing well. I have been worried about her. She leaves me news of the other violet bog gryphons."

'Violet' was a polite way of saying the gryphon pride who had previously attempted to assassinate leaders of the Ashen Weald. There were no hard feelings, and, in fact, the 'violet' boglings had reverted back to the light blue paste of their other pridemates, but the term was an easy way to distinguish between the two groups.

Every so often, Soft Paws would lead her companions away from the river. The glyphs in the trees, more chalk paw print than any actual glyph, were tracking a very large matamata who had been liberated from the sunken eyrie ruins. It now haunted this section of the river, raising some safety concerns.

"Turtles don't seem scary to me," Lei said to Pip.

He just shrugged. "Believe me, you don't want to see what can happen to you in a bog. I paid a smuggler to get me through this bit, and turtles are some of the nastier things out here."

They hit some ruins of a tower or bridge, then Soft Paws led them up and over. One side had a massive, collapsed sinkhole with pieces of an eyrie inside of it. Waterfalls came down the other side.

"Remember last time we were here? We had fish," Lei said.

Pip nodded. "We should check in with Black Mask. See if he remembers us."

At a glance, the eyrie appeared abandoned. The stone floors were covered in lichen. Spider webs did a healthy trade in dead moths. A flock of territorial swifts had taken over the skies above, their silky nests dotting the decrepit pillars. But a few steps down a passage revealed an entire population of kjarr and bog gryphons living here.

While Soft Paws and her rangers went to report to Urious, and Pip went to talk to Black Mask, Lei slipped away and tried to locate the kjarr children. The ones from the day of the fire had fledged and were all around him, but there were a new set of gryphlets and fledglings being taken care of somewhere in the eyrie, and he was determined to find them.

As fond as he'd grown of gryphons, and as much time as he'd spent with Zeph and Tresh, there was something different about talking to a gryphon in a fisherfolk village or opinicus eyrie than here. While Sandpiper's Dune wasn't an eyrie, the fisherfolk huts felt opinical, which had a grounding effect on him.

He didn't feel the same here. This was a *gryphon* city, even if half of the floors were underwater. Glyphs, scents, and the general layout defied everything he'd learned growing up in the Redwood Valley and Swan's Rest. He was an outsider here.

This is probably how Satra felt at the Redwood Valley Eyrie. He banished the thought from his mind. He was a guest here. The kjarr pride had not been guests at the red eyrie, no matter how his mom had portrayed it. His conversation with Thenca had made that much clear.

Pip had always said travel was good for the soul, which was a strange thing for him to say considering that everywhere he went, opinici tried to kill him. But Lei understood what Pip meant. The horrors of Mally's workshop, the horrors of the bog: These things were paired with a sense of wonder. The desert had been magical. He'd never forget the giant megapedes feeding on an overturned sour apple cart. And even the bog was full of interesting flowers. While the moss gave it a creepy appearance, it was also so vibrant, so alive.

Lei channelled that feeling of wonder as he walked through the different corridors. He could fly, of course, but this was a city that housed a lot of wingtorn, and it would be disrespectful to do so. It had even been reshaped for paw traffic. Where rocks had collapsed or new tunnels had been dug out, soft moss had been prepared and laid down to make walking easier. In other places, there were opinici scrubbing down the old stone roads of the eyrie, buried under an era's worth of grime.

One of the rangers saw Lei, and for a moment, he worried he'd been recognized. He'd done his best to modify his feathers. His natural green plumage had been dyed to make it appear closer to blue. His eye shape had been changed, too, and he'd managed to get the stripes of yellow around them changed to an aquamarine.

The ranger who ran over, however, wasn't looking for the heir of the Redwood Valley Eyrie. Instead, he offered a vial of pumpkin.

"New here, eh?" the ranger said. "While everyone is welcome at the Heart of the Bog, those of us who aren't kjarrlings or boglings have to use a buddy system. Find someone to check your eyes every morning, and if you're feeling the least bit weepy, you take this, got it?"

Lei nodded. It was strange, but he'd actually forgotten about the parasite despite having been there for the starling horde's assault on New Eyrie. "I've come with a couple fisherfolk. I'll make sure we do that. Thank you so much!"

The other ranger, still clearing out the floors, looked up at them. Maybe it was a trick of the light, but there was a slight pink sheen on his blue heron plumage. "Hey Jer, you gonna keep yapping your beak or you gonna help me clean?"

"Yeah, yeah," Jer said to his friend before turning back to Lei. "One more thing. You see those stripes there along the edges that face the water?"

Lei nodded.

"Where you find the sky glyphs, that's where it's safe to land or fly away from. Otherwise, it ain't polite, got it?" Jer didn't wait for an answer, instead heading back to his cleaning. "Dunno what you're complaining about, Xalt. You've been polishing that same square inch for the last two hours."

"And I'll keep polishing it 'til it's clean," Xalt grumbled back.

Lei left the two rangers to their work, excited to finally get to explore the inside of the Heart of the Bog.

THE SKY GLYPH had been so obvious and clear that Lei had mistakenly assumed all of the writing and markers inside the eyrie must also be literal. If the sky glyph was for flight, and he saw a watery glyph near some of the pools that were set off from the main area, perhaps all of the glyphs made a kind of sense.

His theory was quickly proven wrong. Most of the other glyphs were more metaphorical in nature. The glyphs marked with a tiny, angry turtle seemed to actually denote an area of hot water for bathing. He stood in front of the turtle for a long time trying to work out if turtles represented cleanliness or if maybe the lines of anger were meant to be heat exhaustion.

This is the seahorses thing all over again.

He was still staring at the lines when a familiar face appeared.

"Well, I do declare," Black Mask said. "You enjoyed your last trip so much, you've come back to say hello. What was your name again, fisherfolk? You were with Blinky, weren't you?"

"Name's Lei. You're Black Mask, right? I'm having a hard time figuring out what these glyphs mean. I get swimming and flying, but what does bathing have to do with turtles?"

The wingtorn laughed. "Sorry, that's on me. This stretch used to be full of turtle eggs. I guess the glyphs here are more like the names of the different parts of an eyrie. Or perhaps merchant stores? I'm sorry, I haven't seen the nicer parts of an eyrie, just the dregs."

"Oh, I get it!" Lei perked up. "So this is like... the Angry Turtle Bathhouse? And the sailfins there are like the Merchant Quarter of the Redwood Valley Eyrie."

Black Mask nodded, leading Lei around this floor. "Redwood Valley Eyrie is quite a ways off. You seem a little young to have visited there."

"I come from a salt trading fisherfolk village," Lei explained. "Since we look like peafowl, I'd often accompany them. It's really just the merchant quarter where fisherfolk were allowed, you know. But we had the best salt."

Black Mask accepted that explanation without asking further questions. "For the most part, the winged quarters are up near the top for easy access to the ledges. The wingtorn are farther down. If you're not living here, it's probably best to let those be. Not that we're unfriendly, mind you. Just that unless a wingtorn has invited you there, it's mostly bog and kjarr nests."

"Actually, I'm looking for the kjarr nests," Lei explained. "Oh, that's probably a strange sentence coming from a fisherfolk. I know the kjarr gryphons are protective of their children. I wanted to speak with two of the caregivers down there."

Where the paths leading up were easier to find, full of stone and cleanliness and markers, the way down to the bog and kjarr quarters were a little different. It made sense they wouldn't want them to be obvious in case of attack, but Lei had walked past the woven murals on the walls a dozen times in his wandering, and it never once occurred to him that there were passages behind them.

Black Mask pushed one aside and guided Lei into the depths. "The tunnels go below the water line, but the stone keeps this section dry, at least for now. We've been trying to add in our own layer of protection."

"If it's stayed dry for a hundred years, it seems weird that it'd fail now," Lei commented.

"There haven't been hundreds of gryphons crawling all over it until the last few months." Black Mask reached a divider in the darkness. He started to go left, towards a glyph marked with long green spines, then turned to go the other way, towards the black and gold crest. "Sorry about that, I'm used to going to the bog side. You said the kjarr nests, right?"

Lei nodded. The corridors here were smaller, but even as deep as they were, some light made it down. The stone walkways above used braziers from time to time, but as best Lei could tell, someone had set up mirrors and stormcloth in such a way that light somehow reached even these depths. Once his eyes adjusted, it was just enough to see by—most of the time.

Black Mask chirped greetings as he went. "Since we're not kjarr, it's important to announce ourselves, but without disturbing anyone's sleep. Lots of trauma all around, and you really don't want someone to turn a corner and see someone unexpected. That's a good way for *mishaps* to happen."

The emphasis on *mishaps* suggested that perhaps there had been injuries or deaths. In a way, the glyphs kept newcomers safe, though as they walked through some of the common areas, Lei realized he and Black Mask weren't the only non-kjarr gryphons here. In fact, where dividers were open, he saw there were a lot of different gryphons and opinici living in the kjarr section.

A feathermane and wingtorn played some sort of game while a Crackling Sea opinicus served as the referee. Groups of parrotfaces ambled around in long lines. Lei had often thought of that pride as only concerning itself with caring for others or providing food, but when Lei and Black Mask passed through a much larger area, he watched a parrotface spar with one of the hooked-beak gryphons who looked like Carru.

The parrotface came away the winner.

"The Night Parrot," Black Mask explained. "My mate's been giving him lessons. Turns out, he's not just good at sneaking, he's also a bit of a brawler. He just didn't know it 'cause nobody had given him an opportunity to learn. They're not really big about hunting anything other than fruits and berries in his pride."

Lei nodded, wide-eyed.

"Blinky calls him the Terror Parrot." Black Mask paused here, but Lei didn't respond. "Well, just trust me, that's hilarious in owlish."

They soon reached the end of kjarr nests, entering into an open area full of spongy moss and mushrooms which housed around a hundred gryphlets and fledglings.

"Here you go!" Black Mask said, disappearing to go talk to the mysterious Night Parrot.

7

THE DEN MOTHER

Lei looked around the room. When he was a chick, he was kept under constant guard. He only really got to play with his sisters, most of whom were much older than him. And most of that was less *play* and more learning about reading, writing, or the history of Belamuria and the Redwood Valley Eyrie.

For these children, it looked like being a gryphlet meant learning to be fast and mobile. Lei stood in what amounted to the middle of an obstacle course. Where the ceilings down here were fairly low, this was one room where they went up, and some of the older fledglings leapt from pillars and learned to glide.

Not just the fledglings—the gryphlets were doing it, too, with much less success. Suddenly, the soft ground and cushions everywhere made a lot more sense.

Was I like this when I was young? Or if I'd had this opportunity, is this what chickhood would have been like?

While he was thinking of this as a *gryphlet* versus *opinicus chick* distinction, that wasn't entirely true. There were a few opinicus chicks in here. Some had gryphon fur and feather patterns, suggesting they'd had both gryphon and opinicus parents. Others were just heron chicks from some of the Crackling Sea opinici who had come down here to help clean up the sunken eyrie.

A particularly angry-looking opinicus chick ran up and tried to stab Lei with her beak. Thankfully, the den mother had the foresight to wrap the tiny spear in soft material. After she'd poked Lei a few times, she ran off again and attacked a hide-wrapped monitor toy.

Lei shook his head and looked around, spotting two opinici in Redwood Valley harnesses. They looked a little like Henders, more peregrine falcon than the flashy northern quarter opinici like Lei, but they now wore Ashen Weald badges.

He made his way over to them, trying to think of a way to break the ice. Instead, they did it for him.

"Is one of these yours?" the first guard asked, holding up a gryphlet.

The second guard chimed in with, "I don't remember any peafowl in this bunch, so your gryphlet must resemble his mother."

Lei balked a little at the implication he was old enough to have chicks of his own. "Oh, no, actually... I was wondering if I could speak to you two? I've been trying to find *my* father, and I think you two served with him at the Redwood Valley."

The guards shared a look, but one of them got the attention of a yellow, spotted wingtorn and made a gesture they were going on break. The den mother nodded, and the guards led Lei past a battered, dubiously gryphlet-proof gate to an area with a hard floor, food, and no children.

"Your father was a guard at the Redwood Valley Eyrie?" the first opinicus reiterated.

The second guard chimed in much like he had the first time. "You must not look like your father, then. Didn't have any peafowl serving with us. Your lot were usually up in the heights."

Heights, in this case, referred to the higher levels of the Redwood Valley, the tops of the platforms and the higher altitudes. There was a saying Lei had heard but hadn't understood as a fledgling, 'the sun don't shine on the underbough,' which referred to how only the wealthy could afford to have a nest on top of a platform instead of underneath it.

And, of course, the building of more northern quarter homes ended up blocking even more light from reaching the depths. All of which were privileges Lei had been unaware he possessed at the time. Living among the fisherfolk, learning from Pip and Kia, had done a lot to teach him about how the world worked, specifically that everything had a cost.

Rorin was very fond of saying, *You can't eat a fish until after you catch it.*

"Well, not *at* the Redwood Valley Eyrie, specifically," Lei admitted. "I understand you were one of the guards who were sent to keep track of the wingtorn who attacked the fisherfolk villages. My father was Larren. I think he was with you there."

The guards shared an unhappy look. Clearly, they didn't want that part of their history remembered.

"Please," Lei said. "Nobody can tell me what happened to him. I just want to know where his body is."

The first guard sighed. "Look, kid, I'm sorry. I knew Larren had a daughter with the reeve, some spoiled brat locked away outside Reeve's Nest, but I didn't know he'd had other chicks. Your father died on the shore. That's the best I can offer."

"But *how* did he die?" Lei pressed.

The second guard shrugged. "Who knows? It was chaos. The cranes rained spears down on us from above. One of them sharks pulled Maurle under. Accursed wingtorn killing us left and right."

"Oy, watch your tone," the first guard said. "Mind your audience."

The second guard shook his head. "It isn't a secret. The den mother knows, she was there, too."

"Look, fisherfolk," the first guard said, assessing Lei's outfit. "Anyone could have killed him. But at the end of the day, you know who the real murderer was?"

Lei shook his head.

"Reeve Brevin," both guards said together.

"It wasn't a secret," the first guard continued. "She hated that Larren was trying to use their shared daughter to try to become the reeve-consort. Brevin's daughters all had different fathers, see. And where the fathers were nice and quiet and *absent,* there was no problem."

"And where there was a problem, those guards were assigned out to the waystations," the second guard added. "Larren, though, thought he could boss around Snakey Brev, so she assigned him to the shore, knowing that if the fisherfolk didn't get him, one of the wingtorn would."

Lei blinked. On the one talon, the fact that these two guards were speaking so candidly of his mom meant they had no idea who he was. On the other talon, he'd never stopped to consider his parents' relationship. Both had loved and spoiled him. And if they were rarely in the same place at the same time, he hadn't thought anything of it. That was just being a reeve.

Honestly, he hadn't actually given any thought to the fact

he didn't share a father with any of his sisters. He'd heard the rumors that Ivess's was Impir, but he'd sort of assumed that was a one-off thing because she was blue. Lei hadn't considered who the fathers of his other five sisters were or what had happened to them.

"I see," Lei said, still a little dazed by the revelation.

The first guard offered him a piece of jerky as way of consolation. "Look, I know how it is. You lose someone, maybe you've made mistakes yourself, and you need someone to blame. Well, I can give that to you. Captain Larren would have been alive if he hadn't had that daughter with Brevin. You want someone to blame, you blame Brevin and her brat. They're the ones who set him on the path that ended at the shore."

"'Course, they're both dead!" the second guard laughed. "It's convenient to hate the dead. Then it's only up to you to get over it on your own. Useful thing, that."

The spotted den mother poked her head next to the gryphlet gate. "You two about done gabbing? Stabby managed to get her beak protector off, and somehow, she's climbed up to the ceiling. You're on."

The guards mumbled something consolatory to Lei, then left. The fisherfolk just stood there for a long time. Of all the things he thought he'd hear on this journey, none of this was what he'd expected.

He'd had a clear idea of what he thought would happen. He knew his parents loved each other, and that Kia and Zeph had killed his mom. And his dad had probably died to a stray spear, maybe from Rorin, and then Lei would have to learn to forgive Rorin.

It would never have occurred to him that both he and his mother would be what most opinici considered the cause of

Larren's death. His heart had broken into eight pieces, one for each dead family member, and he'd assumed it couldn't break any smaller than that. Yet somehow, it crumbled to dust with each new revelation.

My mother hated my father, wanted him to die.

My father used me to try to become reeve-consort. Did he really love me?

My existence is what started the events that led to my father's death.

Lei left through the gryphlet gate, almost forgetting to latch it again, and went through the downy forest of baby gryphons to reach the other side. Once he got to the opposite hallway and was on his own, tears spilled from his eyes, blurring some of the paint he used.

One more thing in a long list he hadn't considered: the need for waterproof feather paint. He'd thought he was done crying. He didn't think he needed it anymore. Maybe there was no end to the tears. He should see if Soft Paws could help him with a feather dye that wouldn't run but worked on his small facial feathers.

He quickly and carefully wiped away the tears when the gate opened. He turned, expecting it to be the guards, but instead it was the den mother.

"I'm sorry, but I overheard your conversation with my assistants," she said. "My name is Ari."

Lei nodded. He'd been caught up emotionally with the other parts of the conversation, but now that he'd had a few moments away, he remembered them saying Ari was one of the wingtorn who had been on the beach that day.

"If you're really interested in finding out what happened to your father, you should ask Urious," Ari said.

Lei shook his head. "But Urious was attacking the other city, wasn't he? He wasn't at Swan's Rest."

"That's... not entirely true," Ari explained. "When Thenca found Jun's body, she called out for Urious, and he led the other wingtorn back across the delta. They joined us by the end of the evening. All four of our jailors were still alive at that time. They stayed back, hidden, while we were forced to kill the children. It was only when everything went wrong that they found themselves dying in the following days."

Lei looked down the hall, towards the common areas and kjarr nests. "I guess this is the place to find him. Do you know which nest is his?"

"Well, he spends entirely too much time in *my* nest," Ari said playfully, "but his quarters are up top, near Kjarr Satra's. He's probably busy right now, but if you visit his nest this evening, I'll make sure he's there."

Lei's voice broke a little when he spoke, but he managed to say, "Thank you. I appreciate it. I... don't know what I expected to find out, but it wasn't this."

"You don't have to go on, if you don't want to know." Ari groomed away some of the salt, leaving a hint of blue paint on her beak. "But some paths must be walked in their entirety or you can't leave them behind."

"Is it true that Soft Paws is your daughter?" Lei wasn't sure he should ask, but he still felt bothered by the witch's dismissal of her parents.

Ari turned to leave. "That's what they say. I've had a lot of daughters over the years. Soft Paws has had an unusual life. As den mother, I think of all of these gryphlets as my children, one way or another. I'm the one who has to raise them. Thankfully, I have a lot of help."

Lei knew a dismissal when he heard one, so he reiterated

his thanks and disappeared into the corridors. Before they'd gone into the depths, Black Mask had mentioned there was a place offering free food, and Lei planned to eat away his emotions with freshwater shark as soon as possible, then decide if he was going to visit Urious or not.

8

KJARR

Lunch had turned into a much longer affair than expected when Lei ran into Blinky upstairs. As it turned out, she was Black Mask's mate this season, and the owl gryphon was determined to make sure Lei tasted one of everything.

Lei was full of knife fish, eel, a type of freshwater shark Blinky called 'minnow,' and strange witch brews by the time the sun descended. Only a few braziers were kept lit this late, and each one had a firekeeper next to it. Owls patrolled the night, keeping watch for the Seraph King's scouts. If any came near, they notified a network of wingtorn who could project their voices like birds, signaling that all light was to be extinguished from the Heart of the Bog.

It was a strange system, a reminder that the Ashen Weald was in hiding. For the moment, the Seraph King's eyes looked north. But a time would come when he might decide he wanted the rest of the south, too. In a way, the destruction of the Redwood Valley Eyrie, Lei's home, was probably what kept the king from pushing southeast. He didn't think of any land without an eyrie as civilized.

Does he know about the sunken eyrie? Lei wondered.

He climbed up to the top story, then went through a winding corridor into the area where the important gryphons and opinici were stationed. There was a time when places like Reeve's Nest or the throne room felt comfortable for him. He'd played at both such places as a chick. Yet as he walked through the sunken eyrie's version of them now, he felt more like a fisherfolk and a salt trader.

There were a lot of factions an opinicus couldn't just join. He didn't know how to become part of the Fantail Pride, for example, and he couldn't imagine the Strix Pride taking him in. Being fisherfolk was different. At first, he'd hid as Mi-lei, pretending to be the drowned daughter of a peafowl islander family. By the time he'd come into his own as Lei and learned about trading salt, he decided it was time to finally join the fisherfolk in an official sense.

However, all of the fisherfolk assumed he was already one of them. He ate and fished with them. He talked like them. He lived with them. So the ceremony was held in secret, with only the gryphons and opinici who knew his identity. All of the usual faces were there—Zeph, Tresh, Rorin, Kia—with the addition of the gryphon prisoner from New Eyrie who had actually saved Lei that day when everything went horribly wrong, Askel the Phoenix.

Askel and his mate, Triddle, had joined the party at Luminaire. It was the first—and after their Crestfall-colored fireworks got out of hand, probably the last—time they'd visited the fisherfolk villages.

Lei'd gone back and forth on inviting them, but in the end, he really wanted an opportunity to thank Askel. Both he and his mate had promised to let Lei join them for the summer and learn about fire and water. It sounded dangerous, but Lei was looking forward to it.

Assuming things don't go wrong with Pip when we go to check on his family, that is.

Lei reached the ring marking the Ashen Weald's main chamber. There was a room in the center where all important meetings were held, but a circular hallway ran around the outside, and the outer ring of that hallway included the quarters.

He started to the left and made his way around. A particularly skilled artist had drawn along the walls, creating murals that told the story of the bog pride who made their home here. Though they'd opened their doors to the Ashen Weald at last, it was clear this would always be their true home.

Though that hadn't always been the case, Lei mused as he arrived at a point on the ring where the mysterious artist had yet to reach. It had been transformed into a gryphon eyrie, yes, but beneath the thick paint, where the walls had been scrubbed clean, there were hints of the original owners. This had been an *eyrie*, after all, so presumably, it had been full of opinici and ruled by a reeve at one point.

Lei put his head on the wall. It felt cool against his stress-heated body. When he looked up again, he was surprised to see that the tops of this hallway had been decorated with seraphs.

He put a talon up to trace the design. *My mom would never have let me grow my talons so long and sharp.* If Lei had been the sculptor and was asked to design a gryphon-themed chamber, he'd probably just take the idea of a gryphon, create one template, and repeat it as needed. At most, he might include a fantail or feathermane to mix it up.

Some of the boats out at The Wrecks had a six-wing emblem, stylized, that was repeated over and over again in the older ships.

The seraph carvings along the top of this hallway, however, weren't like that at all. Every seraph was different. It was possible that no opinici had ever lived here, not as Lei knew them, but instead, this had been a… what?

Did seraphs have eyries?

He shook his head, but he couldn't shake the feeling that each of these carvings hadn't been drawn from the imagination of the sculptor, but instead, they'd been based on living seraphs.

Lei had nearly gone around the entire ring when he reached Urious's door. Though most of the Ashen Weald thought of him as being second-in-command to two generations of Kjarrs, the glyph by his name was the same as the one at Bogwash. That made sense. Thenca was supposed to be his sister, after all. It was just strange to think that after all the bog pride had gone through to become independent, several had chosen to stay with the kjarr gryphons.

The peafowl fisherfolk knocked. A sound came from the other side, muffled by the strange wooden door, and Lei took that as a sign to enter.

He opened the door and was surprised to see that it wasn't Urious waiting for him.

It was Satra.

"I believe you've been looking for me," the leader of the Ashen Weald said.

"Kjarr Satra?" Lei stuttered. "I think there's been a mix-up. I'm looking for whoever killed my father at the shore. I'm looking for a wingtorn or fisherfolk."

Satra motioned for Lei to come inside and sit down. The room was empty except for a small, fishy brazier and a nest that appeared not to have been slept in, lending credence to Ari's comment that Urious spent most of his time with her.

"Guard Captain Larren was best known for catching poachers at the reeve's personal hunting grounds and having them executed," the leader of the Ashen Weald stated as though reading it out of a book. "He was cruel to both his underlings and those under his care. He had little self-control, but one night, around when word of what happened to the Crackling Sea's ruling family reached the Redwood Valley, he found himself as the very last in a long line of opinici waiting to report to the red reeve.

"Commander Wolden, several of the other guards, and even her advisors had long since gone to sleep. Brevin continued seeing opinici because she didn't want to think about what might happen if the same assassins came to the Redwood Valley. I don't know if she was interested in Larren. I don't know if it was just because he was last in line. By all accounts, they were never alone together again.

"Once Brevin knew she was pregnant, she used her trade contacts to get a jade peacock brought down from Reevesport, not an easy thing to do in those days. I believe it actually came from Crestfall, though I'm not sure why they had peacocks. Not really desert birds, as far as I understand it."

Lei was wide-eyed. He'd spoken briefly to Satra a handful of times, always a few words about trading salt. He wasn't sure what he'd done to earn this many words all at once.

"That bird's blood gave Brevin's seventh child his green

plumage, now iconic for the red reeves. Of course, this is where the two of us enter the story. I'd seen Larren's cruelty with my own eyes. And I'd seen you, Lei, as you were growing up, though always from a distance. While Jonas believed himself in control of the kjarr pride, your mother was much smarter, and she never risked putting me close to her children.

"The day of the fire, I had one thought: set the kjarr pride free. That meant getting the gryphlets and fledglings to safety. That meant killing Jonas, something I failed at and has hopefully been remedied by our mutual owl friend. But that also meant going down with two of the young kjarr gryphons who had just learned to fly, intending to show my father and the wingtorn army that they were free and that he didn't have to hurt the fisherfolk.

"I was a little late. It's not easy to plan a rebellion. So many things could have gone wrong. So much of what happened that night was beyond my control, such as the fire. I only learned later what had caused it, and I worry the blood of the opinici who burned that night is on my paws."

Here Satra hesitated, looking down at her claws. Lei had never really given the Kjarr a good look. Her golden crest, her mix of brown, black, and grey plumage. Her impressiveness came from the way she held herself. Lei himself had only gotten glimpses of her through the windows of Reeve's Nest when Jonas brought her along. Lei hadn't spoken to her then or considered what life was like for her in the depths of the Redwood Valley Eyrie.

"Of course, I was speaking metaphorically there about having blood on my paws," she continued. "When it comes to your father, however, I am not. When I arrived at the shore, I saw the destruction my pride had wrought. From the skies, I saw where the nests had been destroyed, where the sands were stained with blood. And when I landed, I was overcome with rage.

"I gave the opinicus jailors who survived one opportunity to surrender. You saw what happened to the two downstairs. A third had died before I arrived, killed by Tresh, I suspect. The fourth, your father, didn't bow before me. I wish I could tell you that he tried to kill me, that it was self-defense. Or that I did it to avenge the poachers he'd killed. Or even that he said something particularly horrible.

"I don't think he did. I think he just failed to bow his head, and so my claws hit his throat before it even occurred to him the gryphons he believed he could order around like pets might turn on their masters."

Satra adjusted herself on the cushion slightly without ever taking her eyes off Lei. "I apologize I've chosen to ambush you here. Once you talked to Thenca, she sent a warning ahead that you were looking for me. She thought you were perhaps the half-brother of Brevin's youngest. But your age, your look, your desire to know what had happened to him, the faint blue paint on Ari's beak after she groomed away your tears... I knew who you were."

"Who told you I was still alive?" Lei asked.

"No one," Satra answered. "Oh, it wasn't any one thing. It was more the culmination of one too many rumors. I know we talk about your sisters like they were afterthoughts, but as the Jonas loyalists became a problem, Merin sought the fate of all Brevin's children. He could only account for five. Ivess was easy. Bario killed another four. That left the eldest and youngest still missing."

This was the first time Lei had heard any of his sisters

might have survived the Blackwing's assassins. "Is... what happened to the other...?"

Satra shook her head. "I don't think she survived. By all accounts, she was right next to Bario's explosives. It's more likely her body was thrown out to sea or that there was nothing left. But for you, I had accounts from Henders and Foultner about where you were that day. Your body was very specifically missing from New Eyrie *before* the starlings and fire started, before Blinky and Foultner came looking. I don't need to know who helped you survive, so please don't tell me. I've already guessed that you're the reason Zeph disappeared in the middle of battle, only to turn up at the shore several days later.

"Now that you know the truth, what would you like to do about it?"

Lei shook his head. "What do you mean?"

"Well, you could challenge me to honorable combat," Satra said. "I hear fisherfolk don't fight fair, so you've got a sporting chance. You're welcome to bring it up in the courts. I realize you may not trust the Ashen Weald, but one of the free prides could arbitrate. You could even try to take over as leader of the Redwood Valley refugees. They're mostly part of Grenkin's lot, now, but a few might like to see a familiar face."

"I'm not a reeve, nor part of that eyrie anymore." He hadn't forgotten his attempt to meet with some of the red refugees near Whitebeak and how that had gone. "I'm not that opinicus anymore, either. I'm a fisherfolk named Lei. I just needed to know what had happened to my family, where my dad's grave is located, so I can mourn him properly."

Satra nodded. "I realize with everything going on, there are no certainties. But if you ever want to ask me any questions, you know how to reach me, Fisherfolk Lei."

Lei stood to leave, his legs shaking. Unlike Ari or the others, Satra didn't reach out a talon or attempt to groom his tears. She just let him stand and make his way to the exit.

"One last thing," Satra said. "In the wake of losing the Crackling Sea, the fisherfolk sent over the remains of my father and the non-fisherfolk dead from Swan's Rest. If you head north, then east, you'll find a large grave. Your father's resting place should be marked."

9

LARREN'S GRAVESTONE

Lei was too tired to tell Pip everything that had happened. The emotions of it all were too much to bear, and he spent the night crying and sleeping. He was already awake when morning came, and he went to find the graveyard.

Gryphon burial grounds were a little different from what he was used to at the Redwood Valley. There, often a large memorial was built first, and the bodies of the dead were interred around it. The individual names were rarely recorded, so visiting their resting place was a matter of knowing what statue to look for.

The kjarr and bog had their own way of doing things. Perhaps this was due to their attempts to stay hidden from the Seraph King's scouts, but the 'graveyard' was just a thicket of wild purple flowers sprouting from mountain bee plants. They grew so tall, he had to rear up on his hind legs and stretch his neck to see over them.

Lei wandered the living maze, unsure if he was in the

right place until he stepped on a rock. When he looked down to see what he'd chipped a talon on, he saw there was a name written on the stone. That started him moving among the flowers, trying not to trample them, looking for where his father had been buried.

The space between the branches buzzed, and bees of every color and size parted for him. He was nearly at the northern edge when he found what he was looking for. The flowers stopped here, though he saw a few old markers that continued on into the tangle of cypress. Lei sat down and stared at the word *Larren* etched into the stone.

This was the moment he'd expected to be overcome with emotion, but none of that came. Instead, he was numb, paralyzed. He couldn't move. He felt stupid. He'd already known his father was dead, why did this part matter? But, of course, it mattered a great deal.

Just past midday, the flowers nearby parted, and Pip showed up to put a talon on Lei's shoulder and offer him water.

Lei drank deeply of the flagon. Little green bees landed on his beak when he pulled it out and sipped at the moisture.

"Family's a funny thing," Pip said. "Sometimes it matters a lot. Sometimes it doesn't seem to matter at all. I don't know if my mate and son are waiting for me. He'd be an adult now, not much older than you, but he's unlikely to remember me. And I've been gone so long, I almost hope Vilessa has found someone new."

Lei had never heard Pip say his mate's name before. It was strange that such a mythical opinicus even had a name that could be spoken aloud.

"You know, I was a lot like you," Pip continued. "I came to the fisherfolk under an assumed name. I gave away my past to stay there. I thought I was just waiting for a chance to kill Mally the Nighthaunt, but there was more to it than that. Rorin and Tresh gave me a home. They gave me a new kind of family. Fisherfolk are great that way, huh?"

Lei nodded, still crying.

"It's okay to love your mom and dad. It's okay to mourn them, even as you learn they weren't who you thought they were." Pip paused to drink. "But all of that baggage isn't on you. Your responsibility is to the family you create for yourself. Friends, gryphons and opinici you look up to, mentors, lovers. That's the family to worry about. Those're the connections you're making now."

"You've always been like family to me," Lei said. "Nobody has looked out for me more than you have."

Pip looked like he might be a little teary-eyed, too. Perhaps it was the pollen from the flowers, or perhaps he'd been stung by one of the bees. "Look, Lei, you're always going to have a home with the fisherfolk. And I'm not going to lie. The Wrecks are probably the safest place for you right now, considering what's coming. But if you still want to come with me north to find my son and mate, I want you to know they're not going to replace you because I consider you part of my family, too. And if Vilessa and my son are anything like they were years ago, they're going to love you just as much as I do."

"I'd like that." Lei looked at Pip, realizing that he'd finally grown just as tall as his mentor. He still had a lot of emotions to process, but those could wait for later. "We've come too far from the water. There are no shrimp to release his spirit. I don't really know how the Redwood Valley dead wish to be treated."

"Buried, so he's already taken care of," Pip said, "though he's in bog territory now. They celebrate their dead with a kind of feast. The idea is that the souls of the dead sometimes hide within the bones, so it's the job of the living to show them the afterlife is a good thing. By feasting and singing, the dead see that they're starting a new chapter of their existence, and they're able to leave the mortal world behind."

Lei thought back to the lessons on the beach. Pip always said that belief was part of every culture, that you couldn't fight like a pitohui without understanding what they believed. Here in the bog, perhaps it was time Lei embraced their beliefs, at least on his father's behalf. "I wish we could do that for him."

Pip managed a smile, then guided Lei to look behind him. Just outside of the field of bee plants, Soft Paws and a wing-torn with a missing eye and a green, thorned spiral design were setting up barrels of flavored water. The rangers cleaning the tunnels and the ex-Reeve's Guard who were now assistant den fathers started cooking food, though some of the raw strips of fish disappeared down Blinky's gullet.

Even Satra made an appearance. She visited the burial site of Jun the Kjarr, her father, where she whispered to both Urious and Thenca, who must have spent all day running to reach the Heart of the Bog by paw.

Ari led a small group of gryphlets and chicks to visit the graves of their lost loved ones. Though young, they didn't seem afraid. A little sad, perhaps, but not overcome the way Lei had been.

Once the food was ready, Pip left Lei's side, providing Satra an opportunity to show up again.

"I hope this is okay," Satra said. "This is more Soft Paws's doing than anyone else's. Bog witches are very big on honoring the dead."

In the distance, Soft Paws and Ari were finally talking

while the den mother's assistants took the children back to the eyrie.

"It's... okay," Lei admitted. "I'm okay. Not completely okay, but I think I understand who I am now, and who I want to be."

Satra reached into a harness pocket, pulling out an old Redwood Valley captain badge. "I'm not entirely sure this is your father's, but I don't believe there were any other captains there that day. It's yours now, if you want it."

Lei took the badge, and Satra disappeared into the field of flowers. Several fantails landed, presumably reporting on whether or not there were any argent hawks searching the bog. Since the celebration continued, Lei assumed that meant the Seraph King was preoccupied elsewhere.

The wingtorn kept their distance, only nodding at Lei if he made eye contact. As the celebration ran long, fewer and fewer gryphons and opinici stayed. Owls appeared to take up the watch, and the cooking fire was doused. The last gryphon to search out Lei was Soft Paws.

"It must be strange to celebrate the dead for you," Soft Paws said. "I hope I have not overstepped my bounds."

Lei shook his head. "No, it's good. And I'm glad you talked to Ari, even if nothing comes of it."

Soft Paws shrugged. "She has had so many gryphlets, I did not think she would remember me."

"But she does?" Lei perked up.

"No." Soft Paws laughed a little as he deflated. "But I will still keep talking to her so she may learn about me as an adult, if she wishes."

"You're so... relaxed about that," Lei said. Then he realized that his disappearance the last few days might have delayed the raft schedule. "Oh! I'm so sorry. Did this celebration slow us down?"

Soft Paws stretched her wings, their blue flower design dislodging the purple flowers of the plants. "Only the rangers worry about schedules. And I took the opportunity to test out a new brew. You know how gryphmint affects gryphons?"

Lei didn't know firsttalon, being an opinicus, but he'd heard what it did and said so.

"There is a particularly rare type of mint that only grows at the Heart of the Bog which I have nicknamed opinimint. It... appears to be working."

They looked over where the opinici were drinking their bowls of water or had been a few moments ago. Three of them were now passed out snoring, and the other was talking to a tree.

"Strong stuff, opinimint." Lei made a mental note to stick to unflavored water.

Soft Paws shook her head. "No, they are just not used to feeling its effects. Soon, such a small dose will be like nothing. They thought themselves brave, trying gryphmint. But I will have to be careful to keep my supplies of opinimint secret. I do not want them overharvesting it. Not until I find a place to grow it away from the eyrie."

"If we were heading back tonight, I don't think that's happening anymore," Lei said.

Soft Paws slow-blinked. "That was the plan. In fact, I do not believe our ranger friends will be ready for the return trip until tomorrow afternoon. I thought you could use a little more time to be alone."

"Oh no, I've had enough of being alone." Lei stood and stretched his legs, wings, and tailfeathers. "Being around friends is much better."

“Excellent. In that case, I hear you are adept with feather dyes. I would like to trade information, see how you do yours,” she said.

Part of Lei wanted to stay here, among the flowers and the dead. But he had to admit, sharing feather paint tips with a bog gryphon also sounded like a good time. “Okay, let’s do it. I didn’t bring much with me, but I have a few back in my room.”

Soft Paws led Lei to the eyrie, where they picked up his supplies and then descended down to the bog quarters to paint away the night.

10

THE PLAN, AS HORRIBLE AS IT MAY BE

Satra awoke the next morning to find a note that said Erlock was looking for her. The Kjarr's head and heart ached from the funeral celebration the previous night, but she felt like she'd done a good thing in talking to the fisherfolk. And her assessment of Zeph had gone up a bit. She'd spent a long time wondering why he'd disappeared during the assault on the Ashen Weald. Finding out he was saving Brevin's youngest made more sense than the other theories she'd heard.

Her morning grooming routine complete, Satra went to see if Erlock had eaten yet. She tapped her beak on Erlock's door, and a familiar feathermane answered it.

"Oh, hello," the Kjarr said, but the mismatched feathermane only offered a fluffy headbutt of greeting before rushing past her and slipping out into the hallway.

Satra continued inside, where Erlock was still preening her tail. "I didn't mean to interrupt you and your mate."

"Nothing to apologize for." Chartail looked up. "She was

late for her rounds, and while I don't think we're as vulnerable to spies as an all-opinicus eyrie might be, I'd rather keep our relationship a little secret and risk hurting her feelings rather than turn her into a target for the Seraph King's assassins."

Satra let Erlock lead her to a private dining area. Since Askel and Triddle spent most of their time in the weald or fixing the water situation at Crestfall, their quarters had become a secret snacking location.

"It's not really the Seraph King's assassins I'm worried about right now," Satra admitted between bites. "It's the Blackwing Eyrie's."

Erlock had to enter the room in a kind of circle, bringing her tail around the outer rim so she could face the food. "I won't tell you that you're not making a mistake. But what options do we have, and what's the worst that could happen? Getting Rybalt across the desert is our best hope. The Seraph King is building ports on the Crackling Sea. There's no giant sea monster preventing him from doing so, thanks to us. Any day now, he could turn his sights from the north to the south and decide we're too dangerous down here."

"I know, I know." Satra waved a paw. "I just feel like we can't trust Rybalt. And I *know,* that's because we can't. I just... don't know what will happen when he reaches the Argent Heights."

Erlock's ears perked up. "Oh, you're worried about Foultner and Henders. I invite you over for strategy and tactics, but you're too caught up with friendship."

"Rybalt is a precision weapon until he kills his target, then he explodes," Satra said. "There are going to be a lot of innocent lives lost if we go through with this. Not just Foultner and Henders."

"Foultner always lands on her feet. And Silver's not innocent in this. She enabled Jonas's victory," Erlock countered. "I'm also not sure about your use of *if we go through with this.* It's already happening. Even if you sent your fastest messenger north, you couldn't reach every sand gryphon in time to stop it."

Satra sighed. It was true, but it didn't make her feel any better. "That brings us to the second part of our plan."

"The one you didn't tell Rybalt about," Erlock added. "Don't you think he could work better if he knew what we were up to?"

"Honestly? No." Satra stuffed her harness full of eel jerky for the upcoming journey. "If he knew what our plan was, he'd use it for his own purposes. I'd rather he see this as a kind of happy accident. A strange coincidence."

Erlock led Satra out of the Ashen Weald chambers, up and out of the sunken eyrie. "You're putting a lot of trust in the free prides. Is there no one else we can send?"

"You don't know these three," Satra replied. "Zeph and Kia are Reevesbanes in their own right, and Cherine is... a problem for others wherever he goes. I'm just grateful he's not my problem this time. If you trace back the events that led to the creation of the Ashen Weald, you're going to find their paw prints all over them. They're free pride, but they're very good at what they do."

Erlock shook her head. "And the cave gryphons don't seem to be willing to work with anyone else. I still get shivers thinking of them crawling through the tunnels of the weald under my pride. I've had to rethink every story of monsters stealing gryphlets out of nests in the night."

"Stop," Satra commanded. "Look around you. The bog gryphons faced that same kind of talk from my pride. It's what led my ancestors to try to conquer them. Cave gryphons aren't monsters any more than Thenca or Urious are. The one cave gryphon that stayed with Hatzel's pride gave us an entire network of connected caves to hide gryphons and opinici in. You may find yourself living in a cave sooner rather than later if this goes wrong."

"Kinda feel like I'm living in a cave now," Erlock laughed. "I liked it better when you were the hot-headed one. I'm not sure how I feel about being told to calm down and think rationally by a Kjarr."

Satra joined the laughter, but she had more thoughts about this plan of theirs. She just wanted to wait until they'd reached Poisonmaw before she spoke them aloud to give her trio of cave explorers a chance to weigh in on the consequences of what they were about to do.

Thankfully, she had a few days of ground travel and night flights while skirting the Seraph King's new outposts around the Crackling Sea Eyrie to convince herself of the necessity.

Also, she and Erlock weren't entirely correct when they said they only had two plans in motion. There was also the matter of a certain ex-ranger lord and her team. No one was depending upon them, per se, but Satra had seen in the past what happened when Ellore was given free rein.

WINTER STORMS RAGED over the Crackling Sea. Without the storm curtains to protect it, the balconies had become death traps, and the infirmary was full of opinici who had slipped and broken paws or talons. While the Seraph King's forces looked askance at the so-called Jonas loyalists who had helped them lower the defenses and take the eyrie, Jonas had insisted they all be treated with the utmost respect, right before an owl pierced his insides and his unmoving body was sent to the Nighthaunt's workshop.

Thus, there were a good number of Crackling Sea opinici working around the eyrie, many of whom had been forced to live in secret amongst the Ashen Weald population, not interacting with each other. It was a setup which made it very easy for several new herons to suddenly appear on the list without raising suspicions.

Bruen led a goliath bird down to the stables. "Oy, Llore! I need help detaching the bird from the wagon. The metal bit is stuck."

Llore, whose name once contained an extra letter at the start of it, came over to help him. Her long list of betrayals and parasitic warfare had made her unpopular with fisherfolk and Ashen Weald. Bruen's association with her had forced him to stay on Luminaire with Quess, who had thrown a fit when she found out Bruen had volunteered for such a dangerous mission under Ellore's command.

At the same time, he knew Quess understood. This was his chance to help Ellore atone for her crimes, many of which he'd helped her commit. This was both of their chance to return to their home eyrie and, if they played their cards right, free it from the grip of the Seraph King.

Ellore slammed a hammer against the metal spike connecting the bird's harness to the wagon, knocking it loose. There was no meaningful glance between them signifying their friendship or acknowledging that they were both spies who would certainly be killed if anyone figured out they were working for the Ashen Weald. No, the only time they talked was once every other week, when they'd meet in one of the secret passages off the butchery that the Alabaster Eyrie's goliaths hadn't been able to sniff out.

These public moments of indifference were here to give an excuse as to how the two might know each other should they be found. These interactions just helped reassure Bruen that he'd made the right choice. It was one thing to serve with someone, but Ellore had disappeared after the bog, turning out to be a Blackwing traitor and getting locked up in a prison in Whitebeak, where her infection spread and nearly brought about an outbreak. Then she'd been up north near Blacktalon doing who-knows-what.

She was his friend. But she was also a traitor, and she'd hidden the extent of their plans from him when they were both assigned to the kjarr nesting grounds. They'd lost many of their friends fleeing from the kjarr into the bog. Eaten by starlings, gutted by fisherfolk like Quess, and then tormented by Vitra. When Ellore had put out the call for a team this time, many hadn't opted to join her.

Not until Bruen stepped forwards. The advantage to hiding out in a fishing village and having been presumed dead a dozen times over was that no one knew about the good or evil he'd done as a ranger. He was just one more nameless, faceless blue heron working the stables and docks. Which was exactly what they needed.

Ellore brushed his talons, putting a vial into them before she led the bird away. At their last meeting, they'd talked for ages about the best way to slow down the Seraph King's advance. They'd come up with a dozen methods, but all of them were high risk, low reward. So they'd waited, figuring out where each box went, figuring out what they could poison now that might not show until much later.

Fish from certain areas contained trace amounts of toxins,

which were deadly in higher doses. The Seraph King's forces didn't understand that an opinicus would have to eat fish for every meal over a course of decades to see any ill effects, so it was a simple thing to add a much higher dose of toxins to the shipments heading north without it being traced back to Bruen or Ellore.

Bruen yawned, making his apologies to the stablemaster and explaining that he'd had a hard time getting the birds here from New Eyrie. The stablemaster, a flamingo, waved an idle talon and let him go.

Unlike the intruders, Bruen enjoyed the rain. He walked along the balconies, feeling the sleet and wind against his feathers. Ellore was right about one thing: it was good to be back. He just hoped he survived long enough to return home to Quess.

He used his walk to check the progress on the dock. The Reevesport opinici were used to working with the ocean. Most eyries tended to be built where nature was kindest, where it was easiest to construct docks or goliath trails or homes. Whoever had built the Crackling Sea Eyrie had taken a different approach, seeming to have chosen the one place on the sea coast where both the summer and winter storms were at their worst.

The first two docks had been swept away. Many of the docktalons had fallen into the water and drowned after being stung by jellies. Even more had been surprised when the large waves washed the jellies up onto the bottom levels of the eyrie, causing even more harm. It was almost laughable how bad the non-blue opinici were at living here.

Maybe I'd feel the same way in the desert. I shouldn't be too hard on them.

A howling sound erupted from the sea, and Bruen braced

himself. Some of the previous, Ashen Weald occupants had carved holes into the cliffs, so when the wind hit the eyrie, it howled like the spirits. What had started as a bog witch's practical joke had doubled as an early warning system. This particular gust of wind knocked the weather barriers off several nests. Upstairs, he heard a *crash*, then a shattering sound and a lot of swearing.

After Jonas's owl-fueled absence, the pink reeve had been sent in his place. The Crestfall opinicus, happy enough in pools of toxic, boiling liquid in the desert, didn't seem to know how to deal with the constant rain and wind. He kept trying to put up glass chimes or stained glass windows, but so far, nothing had survived the storms.

There was a reason the founders had used stormcloth and not glass to secure the eyrie. Cloth didn't shatter.

Bruen sat along the edge of a balcony, holding on tightly, watching and waiting until no one else was around. Then he took a waterproof scroll container, tied a heavy rock to it, and tossed it off the side for one of the jelly-immune petrels to pick up off the sea floor and return to the Ashen Weald for him.

Ah, Quess, just how are you faring out there? I miss you.

11

CAVE EXPLORERS

Kia looked up from writing a letter to her siblings. The owl guard around her had all suddenly woken up and looked south, an indication that someone was arriving at this small grove where she, Zeph, and Cherine were hiding out.

This was the same grove that had served as the location of Cherine's past exile. It was west of Poisonmaw, just down the mountain where the aneda forests gave way to the plains and then salt marshes. Some of his things were still here, and after he'd been pardoned, he'd offered it up to any Ashen Weald who may need a place to crash this far north.

Several owls went back to sleep, a sure sign that whoever was coming wasn't spoiling for a fight. Zeph climbed up a tree to look out, chirping down that it was Satra. Kia hurried to finish her letter.

Olan, her brother, had always been understanding about her wanderlust. He didn't have any questions for her about why she was going to explore caves as he lived out the last of his life afflicted with bloodbeak by Mally the Nighthaunt.

Kia's sister was not nearly as kind in her assessment. Mia thought Kia should stay here. And when Mia found out that Satra was sending them on a special, dangerous assignment, it didn't make her feel any better.

"I'm going to lose my brother and my sister to this stupid war," she'd said.

Kia understood the pain. She remembered seeking out her family after the fire, finding out Mia was in a bog full of infected starlings, and despairing. She'd travelled to the desert to get her brother back. What Kia knew that Mia didn't was that Mally the Nighthaunt had put plans in place to force others to find a cure for him.

Gryphlets and chicks from both the Seraph King's and the Blackwing Alliance's eyries for two generations had been afflicted with bloodbeak. If those eyries didn't find a cure—a cure Mally also needed to save his own life—their children would die.

The southern eyries and gryphon prides had been spared, but both she and Cherine had spent weeks rallying the remaining Redwood Valley University scholars to join in the research. The original egg treatment had come out of the red eyrie, after all. The disorder had been common in the south before a preventative was found. Now they just needed to figure out how to stop it in an opinicus that had already hatched.

But there was another reason Kia had wanted in on this expedition. She and Zeph had poisoned the pools of essential salts that allowed the Nighthaunt to reset or alter the biology of gryphons and opinici. Then Pip and Lei had taken his stores and given them to the starlings, where they'd disappeared under Wendl's care. That meant there was only one place left that still had the salts Kia needed to buy Olan more time.

Mally's original workshop, the one where he began his experiments on the gryphons of the abyss, the one he'd been forced to abandon when the cave prides rose together to destroy it.

While the Ashen Weald didn't have spies among the king's eyries, Rybalt Reevesbane did, and he'd passed along that knowledge: the reason the main armies of the king hadn't come east was that they were all amassing at Duckbill, near the Abyssal Naze, to take and hold the final workshop long enough to transform the Seraph King into an actual seraph.

Which means there are salts there. One vial could buy years of life for my brother, enough time to find a cure.

The waking owls stood and formed a line. Where once the leader of the Ashen Weald would have flown down escorted by fantails, times were now too dire for that. Instead, the Kjarr snuck in from the aneda forest, Erlock Fantail in tow.

"Ah, good, we're all assembled," Satra said. "We've arranged a delay in the king's caravans for tomorrow, so the grove of trees your cave gryphon pointed you to should be clear for most of the day."

Kia and Cherine put away their writing, and Zeph hopped down from the tree branch where he'd been hanging upside-down.

"We appreciate you doing this," Erlock continued, "but we still wanted to give you a chance to back out. I know there are... ethical considerations here."

"And those are?" Pink Paw arrived with her mate, Xavi, and their eldest son, Xin, in tow. While the cave gryphons remembered Cherine from his time in the desert and the gifts he kept leaving in caves for them, Xin had struck up a surprising friendship with them after his sight had been damaged by an explosion. It was unlikely Kia or the rest of them would be allowed into the secret tunnels of the cave gryphons without Xin coming along.

Satra spoke with the owls, and they disappeared from the grove. They'd probably still hear the conversation, but it served to emphasize the need for discretion.

"Mally the Nighthaunt and the Seraph King are located in a rather peculiar location," Erlock explained. "They've brought an army they believe can hold off the cave gryphons. It's an impressive army, and one of Rybalt's spies called it the largest force of opinici in the region."

Satra took over. "His spy is correct, but only because she said *opinici* and not *gryphons.* See, the workshop isn't just along the edge of the Abyssal Naze. It's also perilously close to the Emerald Jungle. The starlings, not the would-be king, are the true rulers of that part of the world."

"But the starlings can't cross the glyphs," Xin said. "That's what I learned from the cave gryphons. They put up glyphs to block their side the same way you put up glyphs to block your side. Right?"

"Not just that," Xavi added, "you're also asking the starlings to fight for us. Once they're in a frenzy, they're no longer in control. You'd be using them, and they'd face the worst losses from that kind of conflict."

Pink Paw added, "Not to mention the fact that you'd now have a swarm of starlings roaming the countryside, eating nests and eyries as it goes, lost to their frenzy until they're all eventually killed. You can't get them back in the Emerald Jungle when they're like that."

Satra nodded to Erlock. "Tell them what Nighteyes said."

"When we first spotted the Seraph King's armies

marching on New Eyrie, Nighteyes offered to send her swarm to aid us," Chartail explained. "I'm going to take that as consent. And, as best I can tell from my time in the jungle, we're probably going to get her swarm and the jadebeaks, who already seem pretty happy crossing borders and causing chaos."

Pink Paw shook her head in disbelief. "Even if so, what about the glyphs?"

"Bark beetles." Kia held up a drawing. "Nighteyes told a story about how the Abyssal Naze and Argent Heights don't get along, so their glyphs have a gap between them. If we remove several glyphs, we can use that same gap to funnel the starlings to the workshop."

"Xin won't be a part of this," Cherine hastened to add. "He'll stay down in the naze. And Kia's quick-thinking got us searching for the ruins of the old botanical gardens in the Redwood Valley. There, we found enough yolkbloom to make us all immune to the starlings' altruism, at least long enough to remove the glyphs on their side."

"Won't the king just renew his glyphs?" Xavi asked.

Satra stretched a paw in painful memory. "Not if he's in the vat, mid-change. Plus, you need the scent of the paste to go with it. He'd also need to know of our plan, which only those of us here do. We also expect the Argent Heights to be... incapacitated by that point. But this means you're going to need to work quickly if you want to get both the king while he can't fly and the Nighthaunt."

Pink Paw and Xavi were clearly unhappy with the decision, and Kia felt their pain. Their son was excited to live with a new pride, a pride that had been teaching him to echolocate. All parents needed to learn to let go of their children at some point, but it was harder when they'd become his caretakers after he lost his sight. Seeing him on his own, independent, must require some time to get used to.

But it wasn't just that. Zeph and Xavi were best friends, and Pink Paw had taken a shining to Kia and Cherine. They were all friends, and if this went horribly wrong, there was a chance they'd lose their eldest and their support group in one fell swoop.

While Satra claimed that only the gryphons and opinici in this grove knew what the plan was, Kia was pretty sure Zeph told Hatzel. It was the only way to explain her behavior. She'd been cold and distant, then clingy, neither behaviors Kia expected from the saberbeak pride leader.

Then again, judging by Mia's response, maybe it was the right reaction.

"Well, I'm ready," Zeph said. "I can't wait to see where the cave gryphons live. I'll bet there are interesting bugs to eat underground."

Kia thought back to the strange creatures of the desert. "I'll just be happy if nothing down there tries to eat us."

"Could you pass these along for me?" Cherine handed over a stack of letters to Satra, making them her problem. "Because of how the cave gryphon explorers work, it'd be a month before you find out if things went wrong. If everything goes off without a hitch, however, we'll be back as soon as we can. I just don't want anyone to worry."

Four of the letters had the Strix Pride glyph on them, letting Kia know exactly who Cherine was thinking of. Ninox had expected that by having offspring with a scholar, her gryphlets and chick's father would always be safe and out of harm's way. Unfortunately, she'd chosen Cherine, not realizing his propensity for getting into trouble.

Though, judging by how the blackwings and pitohui call him the Pink Reeve's Daughter, I suspect he doesn't have anything to fear from them.

Zeph and Satra talked while Kia and Cherine went through the supplies one more time, making sure everyone had what they needed. Most of that was travel rations, but the scholars both had journals where they'd written down important information. Then there was the matter of gifts.

Hatzel's agreement with the gryphons of the abyss was that she created a room where supplies were left, and cave gryphons would steal things and leave payment. Based on what disappeared and what remained, Kia had worked out what things she thought cave gryphons would be most interested in.

The answers included a few surprises. Sure, there was tasty food. They weren't as keen on salt or sweet, but they enjoyed dried rimu olives. And, beyond food, they adored ground parrot feathers and never got enough gold mint. It had taken some negotiating with the Parrotface Pride, but Kia had secured a stockpile of parrotface gryphon feathers, much larger and more majestic than the simple ground parrot variety, and the olives and mint.

Unlike gryphmint, gold mint had medicinal properties. While rare on the mainland, the fisherfolk seemed to have an unlimited supply available for trading. Now that the weald had regrown a bit, Kia had included one more thing she wanted to deliver to the leader of the cave gryphons personally: red fern.

Different eyries and gryphon prides had their own methods of contraception, but none was as effective as the red fern. The catch was that it was impossible to grow in most locations. Poisonmaw and the Redwood Valley were the prime sources, and the Redwood Valley had burned down. It was starting to bounce back, but most of Kia's source had come from the botanical gardens. Without opinici around, some of the experiments there had taken root.

She'd brought along seeds because the cave gryphons fit into a very interesting niche. They were able to travel the continent, above land and underground, and they might be able to find more valleys where the fern could flourish. If those valleys were unknown to the other prides and eyries, that might give the cave gryphons something else to trade with the surface world.

"Okay, that's everything. Let's go!" Cherine declared. While the four cave explorers were ready, it appeared Pink Paw and Xavi weren't yet. The goodbyes dragged on, and even once they'd left, Zeph kept commenting that he could hear Pink Paw tracking them through the aneda forest.

Once they'd left Cherine's old hideaway behind, walking along the aneda forests for an hour before heading into the tall grass to check on the roads, Xin apologized. "Sorry about my mom back there. She's having a hard time. I'm glad you two are here, though, Kia and Zeph. And you, too, Cherine. You've become very good at clicking."

Kia ruffled Xin's feathers, then remembered she was dealing with an adult and smoothed them back down. "Sorry. I'll try not to embarrass you in front of your cave friends."

Xin laughed, the sound of a black-billed magpie. "I think I'm more likely to embarrass you three. You should hear the tales Hatzel tells about you."

Kia and Zeph shared a look. For all the impressive things they'd done over the years, there had also been a lot of stories they didn't really want Hatzel to tell.

"She didn't mention bees, did she?" Zeph asked. Before Xin could answer, Zeph crouched down and hushed them.

Out of the forest, along the Seraph King's new goliath trail, a caravan had broken down. There was a small fire and blood, and only two survivors.

"What is it?" Xin asked. His sight only allowed him to see things right in front of him or listen for the sound his clicking made.

"I don't know. I think those opinici are in trouble, though! There's fire and blood and..." Zeph stopped himself.

Kia looked closer. "Is that Pip and Lei?"

12

SALT TRADERS

"Spikes in place?" Pip asked. His assistant, Lei, nodded. It wasn't easy to slip onto the goliath bird path that came up the eastern edge of the Crackling Sea, but they'd pulled it off with a little help from above. Namely, from Iony and the glacier pride, who had made use of their own flechettes and caltrops to spike the entire path and kill several goliaths and all surviving opinici.

Then it was up to Pip and Lei to slip their wagon in next to a dying bird, add in a few scratches and blood, and wait for someone to find them.

In this case, *someone* was a very unhappy Crestfall soldier. As soon as Lei spotted the next caravan of birds, both he and Pip played dead.

"What's going on here?" the flamingo shouted. "Hello, are there any survivors?"

Pip managed a realistic groan of pain courtesy of being stuck out in the sun waiting for someone to find him for so long.

There was no medic with this group, so the best they could do for Pip and Lei was water and bandages. They had brought a spare goliath bird with them, fortunate for Pip's wagon, which really was full of salts and other things to trade.

Once they were alone in the sleeping wagon in the back, Piprik pulled out his sealed document to show the lead flamingo. "Thank you for saving us. We were on a mission for the king, but somehow, the blackwings got word and sent their assassins to kill us off. It's a miracle we survived."

The flamingo's eyes widened as he read. "It says here you're going to pretend to be a doctor up north. Do you have medical training? Our medic was washed off the docks in last night's storm, so we had to go on without him."

Pip nodded. "All of the spies dispatched to the east work in teams, one as a medic, the other as a trader. My assistant here handles the salt and other goods, but I've had some medical training. I'd be happy to keep watch with you on the way up."

Once the flamingo had left, Lei shook his head. "I didn't think it'd be that easy."

"Shhh," Pip scolded him. "No talk like that for the next few days, at least. We're not in the clear yet. There's always a chance they check the logs on arrival and see we don't belong. Then we'll see how much good our piece of paper does us."

A Reevesport opinicus came back with water, and Lei's make-up was put to the test. In theory, Reevesport had jade peafowl. In actuality, most of them had peahen plumage, regardless of gender, and they all belonged to the trade families. There was too much Pip didn't know about how Reevesport worked, so they decided to dye Lei blue to help disguise him until they reached their destination.

In a sense, even if someone spotted his blue dye, it might

serve its purpose. Supposedly, the infamous children of the trade families sometimes colored their own feathers blue to try to fit in with the general populace. So even if someone guessed Lei's true colors, they'd just assume he was slumming it and didn't want to be recognized.

Though the peahen who came back now seemed suspicious. "The captain said you're something to do with trading, but we're to treat you right? Sounds fishy to me."

Pip and Lei shared a look, then Lei spoke. "I used to be in the apple business, but there was a bit of a mishap. You remember the one. Let's just say I've put my fortune in salts as of recently. No sense letting the fisherfolk monopolize the market, not when such new and interesting opportunities have arisen."

Lei looked out at the sea, and she seemed to catch his drift. The northern coast's toxic algae blooms made it a poor location for a saltworks. The Crackling Sea, however, was far enough inland its southern coast had several small saltworks.

"Well, anything you need, you just let me know." She tapped her beak knowingly and winked at Lei. "I'm always a friend to the trade families, even those who're down on their luck."

"Oh, er, thank you," Lei responded. When she leaned over and kept batting her eyelashes at him, he added, "I'm sorry, I'm not really interested in female opinici."

"Ain't no shame in it. I've got a brother on just about every caravan out of the sea. Just take your pick." She tapped her beak knowingly again, leaving Lei at a loss for words.

Pip stifled his laughter. "Do you know how long it'll take until the roads are clear?"

"Half a day if it's an hour," she said on her way out. "Might have to ride the night. Nasty going, that, with the blackwings about. Also hear there's some sort of giant owl in these parts, feeds upon opinici. Bad luck being out at night. Hear they're bringing in one of Mally's dark-eyed lot to sort it."

As she left them alone again, Lei looked up at Pip. "That's okay at Reevesport, right? Male opinici liking male opinici? I never stopped to think what it might be like up north."

"Sounds like it is," Pip replied. He had no idea. The Blackwing Alliance was just as accepting as the southern eyries, but he'd never had to ask about the Alabaster Eyrie and those it had conquered.

While Lei took a nap, Pip left to go check on the medical supplies. Already, a second caravan had come up behind them and was asking questions. Pip had specifically asked Iony to hit a wide swath, killing a dozen caravans along this route. He did this as a favor to the Ashen Weald, though they hadn't explained what they were up to. Just that a few of Pip's old friends would need a break in the supply lines to sneak across.

13

LOWLIGHT DEPTHS

The tall grass hid the cave expedition's approach. Zeph knew this particular grove of trees well—they'd spent the night here on their ill-fated trip to check on the glassworks. It was a good place to nap, but any grove of trees suggested fresh water, which meant that some of the traders would stop to rest their goliaths and refresh their supply.

Though when Satra and Erlock had said they had a distraction planned, Zeph wasn't thinking of Pip or Lei.

"Do you think they'll be okay?" Kia asked. "I'm just thinking of last time. That was a bit messy."

Zeph sniffed around the spring. The ground was rocky in parts, but he hadn't found his way down into the tunnels yet. It all looked like normal plants and soil. "I'm not sure, but they managed to free the refugees of Whitebeak with only an apple cart. They probably know what they're doing."

Xin and Cherine conducted their own search. While the grove was full of birdsong, Xin practiced his echolocation, clicking around. Despite their reputation, the cave gryphons, with their oilbird eyes, whiskers, and plumage, weren't blind. They lived in areas without light and travelled overground at night. So even though they could see, they never depended solely upon their eyes. As such, their paths were detectable by the clicking sounds Xin made.

In theory.

Zeph hoped that was the case. His nares certainly weren't getting them anywhere. Nothing about this spring smelled like a cave. All he could smell were crawfish and oscillated turkeys. *Maybe I should have eaten something before sniffing. My stomach is getting the better of me.*

"Over here," Xin called. He faced a large tangle of moss and thick scrub brush.

Zeph sniffed but didn't detect any strange smells. If the cave gryphons came through here, they either hid their scents or didn't come aboveground to drink from the spring. "Do we clear away the brush?"

"I don't think we should, not if it reveals to the enemy there's a cave here," Kia countered.

Cherine practiced his own clicks. He'd spent most of the autumn learning some basic echolocation. Zeph and Kia had, too, but unlike them, Cherine was pretty good at it. None of them had the oilbirds' special adaptations, but the right clicking sound could still tell them a lot about their surroundings.

"I can hear it, too. There's something hard the sound reflects off of near the top of the tangle." Cherine reached up through some dead vines and pulled out a stone talisman. "Looks like cave gryphons to me."

Zeph sighed, already knowing they were going to ask him to go into the mess of plants. He was going to come out of it with ticks or fleas, he just knew it. Still, he put aside his personal feelings, crouched low, and dug his way through the bottom, where opinici wouldn't think to look. He'd only gone ten paces into the thicket when he suddenly dropped down with a small screech.

"Found it," he shouted back up. "It's a long drop, though. Too small to fully extend your wings, so be careful."

Cherine followed, then Xin. Cherine was tall enough that he was able to catch Xin and lower him, then do the same for Kia. The lesson was clear: Cherine should always go first if a tall opinicus was required.

The little light from the hole was enough for Zeph's blue eyes to see. Kia shifted nervously. Cherine did the auditory equivalent by running his mouth. Only Xin exuded calm. The brazier in his room back home saw almost no use except when his family visited, so he probably felt at ease here.

Zeph took advantage of his winter sight to search around. Unlike echolocation, which worked in the darkest of places, his eyes needed some light to see by. In the darkest night, there was always a little light that slipped through the clouds, even if it was only starlight. That was all he needed.

Down here, down in the depths, there were places without any light at all. When that happened, he'd be unable to see. It was a scary thought.

"Is there a place I can set my things?" Kia asked. Xin and Zeph went to either side of her and guided her down the passage into a large meeting area. It was currently empty, but tunnels went off in all directions. Xin's cave gryphon friend had been hesitant to tell them about the wonders of the Abyssal Naze and how its inhabitants moved across the world, but the tunnels heading east and south made Zeph curious. Were they dead ends? Or was there a fully underground path that led into the weald that the cave gryphons didn't wish to share?

"I think I hear three passages, is that right?" Cherine asked.

"Four," Zeph replied.

"Six," Xin countered. "I can hear six."

After Xin pointed Zeph in the right direction, Zeph was able to locate the other paths. They hadn't been visible, another reason why echolocation was so valuable. On the other paw, they'd been warned about stretches where echolocation sometimes failed, places the cave gryphons took advantage of to ambush the Nighthaunt when he moved underground.

"Am I safe to light the lamp?" Kia asked. They'd been told that in certain places like this one, it was okay to hang a light. It would help the cave gryphons know friends were waiting. Zeph hadn't considered that cave gryphons might have friends before being told that. But they were very particular about what type of lamps were acceptable.

No explanation was given, but neither the Crackling Sea nor fisherfolk fish oil lamps would do. And the ones used by the Alabaster Eyrie were considered anathema. In the end, they'd had to rely on Satra to find a few of Bario's old scentless braziers.

After getting confirmation, Kia struck flint to tinder fungus, then used it to light the brazier and hang it. "Ah, much better."

Zeph looked away from the flames, down the dark corridors. The deep places of the world scared him ever since the incident at Hoarfrost where he'd had to lead wounded fisherfolk through the catacombs of an abandoned taiga nest as more and more infected starlings flooded in after them. Only the timely arrival of a sparkling pink Younce had saved them.

He wasn't expecting starlings here, but he also wasn't about to go exploring until the cave gryphons arrived to guide him around.

In the end, it was after nightfall when their escort arrived, from the same hole Zeph had fallen down.

Kia tended to the fire, Zeph asleep at her feet, when the cave gryphons arrived. Xin and Cherine perked up first.

"I hear someone echolocating above us," Xin said. "Oh! I think that's Chert."

A long-whiskered, grey face peeked down the hole. "You have good ears, Xin!"

She dropped into the cave, followed by twenty gryphons of varying shades of mottled white, grey, black, and brown. They naturally congregated along the sides of the walls, where they vanished against the stone. Cherine always claimed he'd stared at the walls of Crestfall's guest cave many times, never once seeing the gryphons hiding there. It was only when they had their black eyes open and reflecting light that he spotted them.

Chert was the cave gryphon who had spent the autumn with Hatzel's pride, showing them the local cave systems. With her help, they'd had no trouble finding homes for all of the refugees from the Crackling Sea Eyrie. She was, according to Xin, amazing.

She also seemed quite fond of the magpie, and while it wasn't on Kia to speculate, she suspected he was the real reason Chert had stayed, and possibly the reason she'd agreed to bring everyone along to the Abyssal Naze.

That, and their unflinching hatred of the Nighthaunt.

"Weald gryphons! In my tunnel." The largest of the cave gryphons made his way forwards. Like all of his kind they'd met so far, he spoke with an opinicus accent. "Get lost taking a sip and decide to take advantage of our hospitality?"

"Not at all! We were just looking for a place to leave your gifts." Kia had been told to expect this. She pulled out the parrotface feathers and other goodies, setting them in front of the leader of this cave gryphon team.

The cave gryphon sniffed them, his whiskers wiggling with the effort. "Ay, I think this'll do nicely. Know just where I'll put these feathers."

"I'm Zeph," the copper hawk said. "This is Kia and Cherine. I think you already know Xin. We're members of Hatzel's pride, more or less."

"Fancy names," the leader said. "You already know Chert. She won't shut up about your magpie. You can call me Slate. We don't have the time to introduce the rest; you'll have to figure it out on the way. We've had a bit of a hitch in our runabout."

Some shouting came from outside, including a few screams, and even what sounded like the echolocation of a cave gryphon. Yet Chert was already helping the others pull out a small barrier to block the way down into this tunnel.

"Your Nighthaunt friend has sent out some of his darkstalkers to guard the supply lines in the night," Slate explained. "I suspect it's something to do with your owls."

Zeph shook his head. "It's not just that. The taiga pride's blue eyes mean that even though it's dark most of the time now, we can still see at night. It's definitely made avoiding the Seraph King a lot easier than it was in the summer."

Slate put his black orbs up close to Zeph's blue ones. "Go on, put out that fancy lantern of yours."

Kia obliged. The barrier wasn't completely up yet, so Zeph took one last look around the room, studying where everything was. Once Chert had the boulder in place, the copper hawk wouldn't be able to see anything.

"Blue eyes are pretty for your mate to look at, but they ain't much good down here," Slate said.

Chert remained positive. "He'll be useful when we need to make the run overground."

"It's... very dark here," Kia said. "Will we be able to use the brazier later on?"

Slate sighed. Then repeated it louder in case anyone had missed the first one. "I expected one of you lot would ask that."

"Not me!" Xin said.

Slate seemed to pat Xin on the head, or so the movement through the darkness suggested. "No, you're a good hopper, you are. I didn't mean to lump you in with these light-glutted laze-abouts."

"I'm not sure if I should be offended or not." Cherine made clicking sounds.

They must have made some sound reflecting off Zeph's harness, because he reached forwards and a moment later, Zeph said, "Hey, watch your talons and paws."

"Sorry, sorry," Cherine replied.

Kia tried clicking, but things were still perfectly dark. Some of the cave gryphons moved around her, helping guide her, and they began their journey into the depths.

"Was that a cave gryphon I heard outside?" she asked. "It sounded a bit like you."

Slate's voice came from behind her. "No, that's the dark-stalker. They share our eyes."

"At first, they came into the tunnels with the Nighthaunt, trying to track us down," Chert chirped. "Over time, we managed to kill most of them. There's only a pawful left."

Kia thought about the limited remaining salts. "He probably can't afford to make more. I wonder if they pass their eyes on to their offspring?"

"We've been careful not to let him catch more of us." Slate's voice came from far in front of Kia, making her wonder if the passage was larger than she was thinking. She expanded her wings a little, feeling them brush against the sides of the tunnel. "They got smart, though. The last three *usually* stay out of the caves. And when they're not needed, the king keeps them hidden inside the Alabaster Eyrie, where we can't get to them."

"Least not yet," Chert squeaked. "The inverns team is working on that. There are a few eyries that have caves leading into them, so we're holding out hope. But mostly, the old tunnels into the king's eyrie have collapsed."

Cherine's voice came from farther ahead, near where Slate had been a moment ago. "I'm so sorry if this is a rude question, but are you digging these caves? Or do you just find them?"

There was some chittering between the group of cave gryphons ahead of Kia and the ones behind her.

Eventually, Slate stepped in. "Hey, heya, in common for the opinici. They're gonna think you're no better than starlings."

"Sorry," came a voice right next to Kia. "It's going to be

hard once we're back home. A lot of the younger ones like Chert speak common, but the older ones don't. You'll be able to tell them by their accent. They sound more like Blue Eyes. But no, the tunnels mostly predate us. We just clear them out or prop them up a bit if they look unsteady."

They continued talking in the depths, occasionally going silent when Chert or Slate, currently at the front and back of the line respectively, gave the order. From what Kia could gather, some of the tunnels came close to the surface, so there was a chance they might be overheard. In other cases, wild animals were the cause of the forced quiet. And when they hit a section that absorbed the sound of their footfalls, someone explained it was another trap for the Nighthaunt.

Here they slowed, causing Kia to run into Zeph. At least, she thought it was Zeph she'd slammed into. His feathery tail wasn't like Cherine's. She couldn't remember if any of the cave gryphons had feathered tails.

The careful pace allowed her guides to maneuver her through a series of traps. Every so often, the paw of a stationary gryphon hiding near a trap would reach out and pet her as she walked past. That was her only indication there were other cave gryphons down here. Since no one spoke, she didn't know if there'd been just the talonful who tapped her, or if there were hundreds lying in wait.

Time was elusive without light, and it felt like hours later before they were allowed to speak again. One of the unnamed cave gryphons chittered, earning a response from Chert.

"They know the others can't see down here. I don't think they thought it was rude," she said.

"Thought what was rude?" Kia asked.

Slate's voice came from above her this time, suggesting the tunnel had opened into a cavern with several paths. "When you pass in the tunnels, you tap the other gryphon to acknowledge each other. Next time they come home, we'll explain that you didn't know."

"And couldn't see them," Zeph added.

"I tapped them all!" Xin announced.

"That's right you did," Slate said. "You're a good wealder. Gonna make you a solid cave gryphon yet."

Zeph's tail swished the way it always did when he was sad, forcing Kia to swat it out of the way. "I miss being praised like that."

"You have very pretty eyes," Cherine said from below.

"Thank you!" Zeph replied. He was now located above Kia, making her wonder when that had happened. She reached out for his tail but caught the long, fuzzy tail of a cave gryphon.

Chert purred back at her.

"Er, sorry," Kia said. "Thought that was someone else's tail."

"Oh my," Chert chirped.

"Oh my," Cherine added.

"Oh my!" Zeph said, but his was an exclamation of surprise, and the sound started above Kia and quickly plunged down below her.

Slate shouted, "Gryph overboard!" and the sound of several cave gryphons flying past Kia caught her off guard.

Chert slowed, forcing Kia to slow with her. "You can hold my tail if it'll make you feel better until you get your other tail back."

"I'm perfectly fine, thank you," Kia replied curtly.

Chert nudged her. "You could also light a brazier here. We should be far enough out of the way, and I can hear camp just ahead."

Kia didn't need to be told twice. She lit her brazier. Chert grabbed it and flew through the cavern, hanging it in a small perch away from the dripping water.

Kia looked around. It felt like she was in a large university hall back at the Redwood Valley. Long stalactites hung from the ceiling, dripping water from their tips. Looking back at the path she'd travelled, several levels of pawpaths that twisted and turned around each other, she was surprised she'd stayed dry.

Cherine was ahead of her, blinking his eyes as they adjusted. The way they'd been led went past a waterfall, and water had filled the depths beneath them. Coming in had been claustrophobic when Kia thought there were walls on all sides. Now she saw just how much room there'd been.

Chert motioned for the two opinici to fly up after her. Across the river, nestled on a ledge, there was a dry spot off the main path.

"Wait, is Zeph okay?" Kia asked.

Slate appeared next to her, still a thing of darkness. "We'll get him out of the water. No need to worry. And we'll make sure that doesn't happen again. The tykes get excited when they're near a place we can rest and forget their responsibilities."

"Welcome, new friends, to the Lowlight Depths!" Chert called down.

Zeph yelped as the path beneath his paws vanished, and he fell into the darkness. Frigid water went over his head, and he clawed his way to the surface just in time for brazier light to fill the cavern, letting him look around.

Down at his paws, several white crayfish wiggled towards him. He swam back, grabbing hold of the bank, flapping his wings, and getting out of the current. He'd disturbed a few pale salamanders who looked for new places to hide.

"Doing okay?" a cave gryphon asked. "It's better if you don't run off. Much safer."

Zeph looked at the crayfish and salamanders. "Can I eat those?"

"You'll have to ask Slate," the voice replied. "I don't know if they make wealders sick or not."

Zeph groomed himself dry. The caves here were full of strange bugs and pale creatures in the water. He'd never seen such an interesting place before. If they were lucky, maybe Slate would let Kia draw a few of them.

"Up here!" Xin called down to Zeph. The copper hawk flew up, landing in a small camp site, full of strange opinicus artifacts. A wooden sign read: *Lowlight Depths.*

Kia offered Zeph a fish bar. "Strange name, especially if you don't bring your own braziers. Why'd you call it that?"

"Wasn't us." Chert shook her head. "Some opinici came this way once, had a camp here. It didn't last long."

"Another ambush, like the ones you use to try to get Mally?" Xin suggested, but Slate arrived to set them straight.

He was wet with the water from the waterfall. "No, we're not sure what got them. The thing about cave gryphons is that we make a lot of noise. The sounds tend to scare away the larger predators, causing them to set up shop away from our paths."

"Mostly," Chert added. "Don't go wandering off alone. The reason we move in such large groups is that when you're down to five or six gryphons, you can hear things chasing you in the dark, staying just past your echolocation. Scary things."

"Hey, don't frighten the wealders. Look, by the time you get to the naze, it's all sunshine and rainbows." When no one responded to Slate, he added, "Is that not what you wealders say? It sounded like a thing you'd say. Same way you say 'Oh, it's so dark down here,' even though you're in a cave, so of course it's dark.

"Look, the point is that the closer you get to our home, the more it's safe to be alone. But until then... stick close. There're two things you've got to watch out for around here. The things that come at you from above, the diggers, and the things that come at you from below, the skulkers."

"And darkstalkers," Zeph added. He looked to Slate for praise but received none.

"Those come from above, so they're diggers, Zeph," Xin explained to him.

Chert purred.

Once they were done eating and settled in for the night—or was that day now?—Slate insisted they extinguish the brazier, turning everything dark again. Zeph wondered idly if this was what it was like in the fisherfolk's afterlife, voices in the endless void calling out for one another.

He curled up with his paws over his beak to keep it safe in case the crayfish climbed up after him. While it was still pitch black, he recognized the smell of Kia as she curled up the opposite way, facing him so their faces nearly touched. He adjusted himself so he could put a paw over her beak, too, to keep it safe from crayfish.

Better safe than pinched, just like Xavi says.

14

THE CALCITE TEMPLE

Morning, or what passed for morning in the Lowlight Depths, came too early for Zeph. They'd slept with the brazier off, but Slate permitted the opinici to light it again so everyone could eat and clean. Zeph volunteered to help with the small camp so his opinicus friends could glide down to the water and sketch the albino newts, crayfish, and other exciting creatures. Where the water came down a slow, rocky slope, there were tiny fish with hooked fins who clawed their way up, sometimes hopping from rock to rock.

Zeph had been warned not to eat anything without asking permission first. It was like he was staying with the fisherfolk again. He rolled his eyes, but cave gryphons set the rules here. Zeph helping out with camp provided Xin and Chert an opportunity to run off together.

Not that they ran far—really, flew far. Chert and Xin chirped and clicked back and forth, the magpie on the path across the river, Chert up at their base camp ledge. Then Xin would launch himself into the air and try to fly up, using his clicks and memory to find his footing.

After a few repetitions, he glided back down to take a break, and Zeph came over to Chert.

"I don't think I've seen him fly since he lost his sight," Zeph said.

Chert was busy cleaning her long, oilbird whiskers. "I noticed he wasn't doing much back home. I can understand that. The world is large and scary, and his clicking back then wouldn't have done a good job of letting him know who was flying nearby."

"Why encourage him, then?" Zeph asked.

"He's going to need to fly down here." Chert clicked at Xin to tell him to resume his practice. "There are places where the stalagmites are too sharp, and there's no walking path. He'll need to trust his wings and senses."

Zeph nodded sagely, only later realizing that her comments implied that he and the opinici were also going to have to fly through the dark. *Maybe we'll get to use the brazier.*

Xin was getting comfortable with the simple flight to and from the base camp when Slate said it was time to get moving.

"We're about to enter the fun bit." Slate's grin was the last thing the 'wealders' saw before the light went out. "I hope you taloned scholars can keep up!"

Zeph turned to give Kia and Cherine a look. He thought he could feel them returning it, though it was too dark for him to see. The afterimages of the fire still danced in his sight, giving form to the unconscious worries hiding in his mind. Saber beaks, peafowl fisherfolk, even flashes of pink and blue.

"Grab my tail, Xin," Chert said from somewhere ahead of Zeph. "And get ready to run like your life depends on it."

"Wait, what does that mean?" Kia asked. She let out a

squawk that quickly faded into nothing as though she had suddenly started moving at high speeds.

Did they pick her up? Zeph wondered. A moment later, he felt a sharp peck on his haunch and let out his own squawk, then started running.

"Faster, wealder, faster!" Slate was on one side of Zeph, one of his friends on the other, and they were guiding him as he ran.

The floor was free of loose rocks for this stretch. He felt like he was running through the sky during a new moon. Darkness on all sides, dashing forever into the void. "Are you sure this is safe? What happens if I fall?"

"Nothing good!" Cherine shouted from behind him. "I think I'll trip if you fall, based on where I'm hearing you from."

Into the darkness, for an hour at a time, Zeph ran. He was panting by the time things slowed down, and he was allowed to eat and drink. He missed the walking from the previous day. He was starting to think they were going to have him run across the entire continent.

Sometimes, when he got bored, he tried to echolocate as Chert had taught him. At first, it all sounded the same. They were in some sort of cleared-out tunnel meant for running. But over time, he started to feel like someone had scratched something into the walls of this stretch.

It didn't just seem to be in his head, either. As the scratches became more common, the cave gryphons slowed their pace. Up ahead, Kia asked Slate if something was wrong.

"We need to be mindful for this next part," Slate said. "Tread very carefully."

Zeph tensed, but more clips of conversation came from next to him, Chert talking to Xin.

"No, nothing like that," she replied to an inquiry Zeph had missed. "It's just that the temple is delicate."

Xin asked another question, lost in the running and sound-absorbing fluff of the cave gryphons, and she offered more of an explanation. "Nobody made it. It's always been there. Just a few moments more."

The cave gryphons slowed. Zeph's clicking didn't tell him anything other than the texture, and he was grateful when Kia asked if they could light the brazier.

Most cave gryphons seemed against it. Through the hints of common, he got the impression this was a place that never saw light. While Slate wasn't willing to let them use the brazier, he produced a few rushlights.

"It sounds like the others don't want us using light?" Cherine ventured. "We don't want to offend anyone."

Slate laughed. "I'm in charge here. If they're going to be mad at anyone, it's me. Besides, they're all too young to remember what this place looks like with even a little bit of light. I think they'll be quick to forgive."

"First, a few ground rules!" Chert paused, as though waiting for a response.

Xin chuckled. "Oh, because we're underground!"

"Exactly!" Chert continued, sounding much more pleased. "Stay on the path. Don't touch anything. Paws are like acid, so talons probably are, too. But most of what's beautiful under the earth can be melted away by touch. When we reach the naze, you'll find the gryphlets have done that work for you. But out here, in the depths… it's important to be respectful."

Zeph turned to look at Kia and Cherine again but couldn't see them in the dark. "May we strike the rushlights now?"

Slate's voice came from farther up the tunnel. "You may."

In what was quickly becoming Zeph's favorite part of the

journey, Kia and Cherine both lit their rushlights, transforming the darkness around Zeph into a beautiful corridor of cave paintings.

"Did you draw these?" he asked, not knowing if the cave gryphons could draw in the dark. There was also a texture to the corridor, carved in, and based on the way Xin kept clicking at different parts of it, it must be like the auditory equivalent of artwork.

"Slate did," Chert chirped. "That's why he's seen this corridor in the light and we haven't."

But Slate shook his head, his whiskers wobbling. "We touch them up every so many years, but they were here before cave gryphons found the corridors. Nobody knows their origins. We just preserve them as another wonder, keeping them safe."

Safe from whom? We're beneath the earth. Surely, there's no one else down here.

Zeph marveled at the paintings. There were few colors down here, mostly white, black, grey, and a rusted brown color. With just those few, however, birds and other beasts came to life. There were drawings of at least ten types of bats. Some had leafy noses and long fangs. Others looked like fuzzy-faced squirrels with strange wings.

There were also pictures of goliath birds. Many looked familiar, though not all, leaving Zeph to wonder if they were still living. Kia and Cherine both had their notebooks out already and were whispering about bats until Slate opened a panel into the temple proper.

Outside, the wonders were all gryphon or possibly opinicus made. Inside, nature had done the painting. The room was coated in crystals like they were snow. Stalactites hung from the ceiling, a perennial favorite of Zeph's cave adventures, and stalagmites rose from the ground to meet them, creating columns that sparkled in the weak light.

Even the cave gryphons were impressed. But that wasn't what was wondrous about this strange temple. It opened into a room about the size of the medicine gryphon caves. There was a footpath between the columns, like a trail through a crystal forest, and between the calcite 'trees' were the bones of strange animals.

After years, decades, centuries, and whatever was longer than centuries that Zeph didn't know the word for, the calcite had covered the skeletons, causing them to sparkle like they were made of gemstones.

Many were too far away to inspect properly, but the trail went right past a skull sitting on top of a rock, and he was able to get a good look at it. There was no beak on the face, no hint of wings in the skeleton. Instead, it looked like a capybara's skull, except with long, predatory teeth. The body was far too long for a capybara, as was the tail. The creature looked *sleek.*

"What would something like that be doing in the desert?" he wondered aloud.

Cherine and Kia had decided to split up, Kia going back to draw the cave paintings and Cherine taking over the skeletons.

"We don't know if this was a desert back then," Cherine said. "I've never seen it firsthand, but we know the Connixation transformed parts of the continent. Ecosystems collapsed. There's even reports that some of the farming in the king's lands had a similar effect."

Something itched in the back of Zeph's brain. "The weald fire. Brevin was trying to make fields to grow things in, wasn't she?"

"That's right." Cherine touched his metal beak, a quick

check to make sure it was there. It was a habit he had when he was anxious or unhappy. After the trial in the weald, he'd discovered the Redwood Valley Eyrie had been using a lot of his research to justify purging the gryphons and fisherfolk from the weald and shore. He'd been acquitted, but Zeph had noticed a change in his friend. Cherine was much more careful both with what he studied and who he shared his knowledge with.

As the scholars sketched with the limited time Slate allowed them, Zeph moved back and forth, trying to help match the crystal skeletons with the paintings. It was kind of fun, really, and he said so out loud.

"Maybe I should apply to be a scholar," he said next to the cave paintings.

Kia looked up from her sketches. "You're not allowed to eat what you're studying."

He frowned and wandered back to see what Cherine was doing, but their time was up, and they needed to keep going.

"You said you wanted to rendezvous with the sand gryphons, right?" Slate asked as they prepared for the next part of their journey.

Kia doused her rushlight after they exited the tunnel. "Right. They're headed north to meet the other part of our plan. It'd be good to speak with them first at the guest cave, just to make sure there's no... confusion about the timing."

More clicking, then Chert spoke up. "It'll be close, but these three wealders don't wobble much when they run. I think we can make it before the week mark."

Zeph didn't have time to weigh in. One of the cave gryphons had already pecked his haunch to get him running again, and once they started, they liked to keep going for hours.

It was the *week* comment that caught him off guard, though. Had they really been down here for a week? They'd paused several times to eat, drink, and nap. But they'd only stopped for a long period of time once, by the waterfall with the crayfish he hadn't been allowed to eat. In that sense, it felt like it had been two days.

Without sunlight, without any frame of reference, he had no real way of knowing what was going on above. If it really had been a week, how much ground had they traversed? He knew how long it took to fly from Poisonmaw to Crestfall, but he'd never walked any long distance if he could help it. He preferred stalking and pouncing.

Within the running pack of gryphons, he smelled Kia's familiar, berry-like scent and whispered her name.

"Oh, hey Zeph," she said. "How did you know it was me?"

Zeph clicked his beak. "Good sense of smell. I was wondering, have you and Cherine checked your talons? If we've been running for a week, we should make sure they're okay."

"Chert took care of us," Kia replied. "Had us rub this stuff on our feet, and then we trimmed down our fighting claws."

Fighting claws was how the more scholarly opinici referred to the set of talons they didn't trim or dull to help make writing and using tools easier. It was different for each opinicus, left-taloned or right-taloned, and the northern quarter merchants used to keep a set of metal talons to use on their *scholar talons* foreleg.

Zeph was grateful once again for being a gryphon. His retractable claws stayed sharp even while he was running. It was a useful adaptation.

They spent the rest of the day running and stopping to drink. The cave seemed to stretch on forever, and in the darkness, Zeph was able to imagine the cave paintings and crystal skeletons of the depths. He was spending so much time in his mind's eye he almost missed when he could see.

"We must be getting close. I can actually see what we're running through now. Oh wow, that's a big bug!" he said, motioning with his beak up at a tailless scorpion crawling on the ceiling.

"Don't eat it." Chert poked Zeph again to keep him running, which he didn't appreciate now that he could see.

He hurried, wanting to find Kia and Cherine. "Is it poisonous?"

"No, we're just in a hurry. We'll eat at Crestfall," Chert explained.

It was a good plan. But the scorpion looked meaty, and Zeph wanted to get to eat at least one interesting cave bug before his journey ended.

In watching the cave gryphons, however, he had a realization. While they said they could see at night, his blue eyes seemed to give him sight before the others. And Kia and Cherine couldn't see at all until they'd come upon the guest cave.

Not that the light lasted long. They spilled out of the cave and into the southern entrance of Crestfall Eyrie right as the sun was setting.

Zeph tried to bury himself in the cool, refreshing fluff of the nearest sandgrouse gryphon—his absolute *favorite* part of visiting the desert—but the closest one happened to be Sponge, and she was already flinging herself at Cherine.

"Guests!" Hoppy shouted from the stone arch into the eyrie's canyon. "And metal opinicus! Come, come, have food!"

15

CRESTFALL UNRUINED

Cherine was so used to running and trusting the way would be clear that when a fast-moving Sponge hit him from the other direction, he just collapsed.

She cooed at him, a mix of what seemed to be anger, love, concern, and a noise as close as a coo could come to sounding amorous.

The cave gryphons had been good about keeping everyone hydrated, but out of respect, Cherine sipped Sponge's feathers.

It was still weird.

The sandgrouse gryphons were all essentially mobile ponds. Every morning, they flew out to the few watering holes in the desert that had fresh water, soaked them up in their feathers, then flew home again. That was how the Padfoot Pride was able to spend hours at a time in the heat. They always had water with them.

He let Sponge lead him through the canyons. Gryphon homes, once opinicus homes, dotted the rocky cliffs. During his last visit here, colored scraps of cloth had hung down from them, marking which home was which. Now, there were bits of metal and chimes hanging up there, though no glass.

"Don't those attract giant teratorns?" He pointed to some metal chimes.

Sponge cooed at him. It had taken some practice, but while he wouldn't say he could speak sand gryphon, he had a feel for understanding it.

"Oh, that's the idea?" He looked out at the large cooking fires. Several Ashen Weald opinici had come north to help upgrade Crestfall Eyrie. They were tending to the original pits he'd used to cook the teratorn bird he'd been kidnapped to bring down.

They were cooking a new one now. Where once, the thirty-two-foot wingspan birds seemed like creatures out of the old tales, even more so for the tiny sand gryphons, it appeared the Padfoot Pride had mastered the art of killing them.

Sponge cooed again. Since Kia and Zeph were nearby, Cherine helped translate.

"She says they're not killing all of the teratorns in the desert," he explained. "Just the ones that attack the eyrie. They like having the giant teratorns out there because they keep dumb opinici out of their desert."

The sandgrouse cooed something else.

"Oh, no offense to you, Kia," Cherine said. "You can't help being an opinicus, after all."

The parrot scholar rolled her eyes at Cherine, whom the sand gryphons had adopted as one of them. Or, at least, all except Hoppy had. He liked having a *metal opinicus* of his own as a counter to Hi-kun, the Metalworks. The sandy leader thought that if both he and the Seraph King had their own metal opinicus, they were of the same prestige.

Reeve Hoppy Padfoot, the tiny ruler of Crestfall Eyrie, was busy taking care of the cave gryphons. There were foods and goods to trade, stories to tell, and napping to do.

With their escort in good paws, Cherine let Sponge continue with the tour. While even the flamingo opinici had abandoned Crestfall before the sand gryphons moved in, there were some new Ashen Weald transplants trying to eke out a living here.

Surprisingly, many were Redwood Valley opinici, uprooted after the night of the fire. They waved at the newcomers, welcoming them.

"Is that a flameworks harness?" Zeph asked, pointing at one of the opinici. "This seems like a terrible place to hide saltpeter."

Kia shook her head. "The university had a school devoted to eyrie maintenance and improvements. They've come out to make Crestfall a little more... habitable. Turns out, the flamingos did pretty well in the heat. But for most of us, there needs to be water and a cool area for the day."

Cherine listened. "I think I hear running water. What is that, Sponge?"

She cooed a response and led them down a corridor and into the stone. Thankfully, unlike the cave, this one had braziers set up to light their way. Though the pink opinici had a palace in the desert—at least, before it had shattered into a million pieces through absolutely no fault of Cherine's—the eyrie kept its own throne room and a kind of miniature Reeve's Nest.

If he understood the cooing correctly, Hoppy thought it was dumb to sleep here, so he'd set up his own quarters elsewhere, closer to where his shiny treasures were stored. That meant the coolest part of the eyrie, the safest part, was fairly empty. Or it had been empty, before the arrival of two gryphons.

"Zeph!" Askel shouted.

"Cherine!" Triddle added in. "It's so good to see you! You should see what we've done here. We've been finding ways to store fresh water. I don't think we could house an army, but it should be enough to let maybe a hundred opinici or non-sand gryphons live here."

While their excitement was contagious, Cherine did his best to honor their new station with a bow. "Pride leaders, it's good to see you two again!"

Askel wore two metal bracelets on his forelegs, and Triddle's forelegs were similarly decorated, though he had a third on his tail. Those bands had a morbid history to them. They'd originally been worn by the commander of New Eyrie. He'd died fighting Zrim Feathermane, and Merin had retrieved the bands, though there were only four at the time.

Satra the Kjarr had searched out a matching metal and had the metalworks make a fifth band for Merin. Most opinici had feathered tails, but Merin had long despaired of not having a band for his tufted, gryphon tail. Her Blue-eyed Festival present to him had fixed that.

Moments before his death, defending a hospital from giant monitor lizards, he'd declared Askel and Triddle his successors as co-consorts. His sons and daughter had decided to pass along the bands to mark the change of station. It was a kind move, considering most of them had probably expected to take over after Merin's death.

Cherine let Triddle lead him around, showing him how they were storing rainwater, purifying it, and keeping it from going bad. Sponge weighed in several times, expressing her displeasure.

"Oh, I'm sure your water is much nicer than this water," Cherine reassured her. "This is just for emergencies. I mean, they can't take this water with them out into the desert, right?"

She purred.

Kia laughed. "You should maybe lay off a little if you're not intending to winter here. I'm starting to see how you get yourself into these problems."

Cherine's nares blushed red. He didn't have to ask what *these problems* were. Though it just now occurred to him that the reason Ninox might have been upset he was coming this way was because she knew he'd be stopping off at the Crestfall Eyrie.

"Oh, that food sure smells nice!" he said to change the topic. "Why don't we go get dinner?"

GIANT TERATORN WAS AN INTERESTING TASTE, not quite like anything else. A touch of frost chicken, a dash of kakapo, and a kind of tough texture that worked best with patient chewing. Cherine was happy to see the cooks were still using his recipe. He took a few minutes to talk with them. Of all his pet projects, and there were many, food preparation and safety had always been the most important to him after he'd lost his brother to a foodborne pathogen in monitor meat.

"No gifts for Zeph or Kia!" Hoppy said after Cherine returned to the eating circle. "We give gifts last time. You understand."

Zeph nodded sagely, but Kia looked a little disappointed.

"Lots of cave gryphon gifts," Hoppy added.

Chert clicked towards Sponge, who cooed the message up to Hoppy. From the little Cherine understood, he gathered that teratorn jerky was a big hit back at the naze. Thankfully, the birds loved remote nests in inhospitable wastelands and were happy to try to murder anyone who came near them, so they shouldn't face the same overhunting problem the ground parrots had after the weald fires.

Several prides that had, well, *prided* themselves on their parrot-hunting ability in the past now protested the Ashen Weald's laws forbidding the killing of a ground parrot for food. The kakapo population was recovering well, so it was just a short-term protection, but it had definitely made some gryphons mad.

"Oh!" Hoppy shouted to get Cherine's attention. "Sponge have gift for Cherine. Triddle, too."

Cherine stood up and was approached by Sponge, Triddle, and Askel.

Sponge's gift was a new beak.

"Last one fake!" Hoppy explained to the circle. "No react to magicnetic rock. New one real."

Sponge cooed.

"That what I say: magnetic. And fancy, yes!" Hoppy agreed. "Fancy beak. Good name. Maybe use that, yes?"

There was a medicine opinicus on staff at the Crestfall Eyrie, and she took the time to carefully remove Cherine's old beak prosthetic. He'd grown used to it since his savage beating at the paws of Merin's offspring. Where once he'd missed the tip of his beak, he no longer thought about it.

His original replacement beak had been a gift from Orlea, whom he'd spent hours arguing with in the medicine gryphon caves after his injuries. It was basic but functional.

The new beak was a copper color that better matched his plumage. It also had designs etched into it.

Cherine recognized the patterns sand gryphons would scratch into sandstone, now engraved upon the copper. He'd seen Sponge come south to speak with the metalworks, owned by Orlea, but he hadn't given it much thought. The sand gryphons' theft of Crestfall Eyrie had included its massive stores of metal, weapons, and armor, buried by a sandstorm and lost to their original flamingo owners. It hadn't occurred to him that Sponge might have also been planning this.

"And these here are from Askel 'n me," Triddle added. They were metal bands and beads meant to go over some of the leather straps and bits of his harness. Some were buckles, much fancier buckles than he already had. "We heard some of the Darkfeather University scholars say that a scholar's harness is their armor, so we thought we'd give you a bit of an upgrade."

Cherine took off his harness, removing a few of the inkwells he didn't want to get smashed by accident, and let them attach the new additions while the medic checked to make sure his new beak was secure.

"Look at you, all fancy." The medic's comment earned her an angry coo from Sponge. "Alright, paws off. I get you. Don't bite."

Kia laughed at the exchange, earning herself a glare from Sponge. "So, how're things going with, uh, your chicks?"

"Chicks?" Zeph asked, looking from Cherine to Sponge. "Oh! The... I understand, now."

The reason the sand gryphons had kidnapped Cherine—really, they'd kidnapped Cherine's beak and forced him to work to buy it back, even though Cherine was still attached to his beak at the time—was that they wanted to kill a giant teratorn. Their religious beliefs mirrored Mally the Nighthaunt's theories on gryphon evolution. They believed the sand gryphons who resembled Hoppy had evolved by eating all the hoopoe birds in the area.

Thus, Sponge reasoned, if she could eat the giant teratorn birds who haunted the desert, her offspring would evolve into giant gryphons.

Unfortunately for her, as Cherine explained now, he'd come by long after mating season. So while Sponge was still eating raw teratorn meat, there'd been no results suggesting her theory was correct or incorrect.

"You're going to have to hope that the egg isn't the size of a giant teratorn's egg," Kia added. "I'm not sure I'd take that risk. You're a tiny gryphon."

Sponge puffed up angrily, and Kia recanted her statement.

By the time Cherine's armor had been fixed up and Hoppy had declared him the sand gryphon's diplomat to the Abyssal Naze, it was just about time to sleep. For Cherine's own safety, he opted to take a nest at the far side of a small room with Kia and Zeph closer to the door just in case Sponge stopped by.

Their actual late-night visitor wasn't a smitten sand gryphon, however, but Chert. "Hey you three. A bit of a change in plans. We're going to head out before dawn and fly for a bit."

"That'll be a lot faster than walking," Zeph said. "Are we *running* behind?"

There was no response to the pun, but Chert shook her head. "No, we're doing fine. It's just that Hoppy's roadrunner scouts found the bodies of several cave gryphons who came before us dead in the desert."

"Shouldn't that mean flying over the desert is less safe?" Kia asked. "If they died flying there, I mean. I'm thinking of the teratorn birds specifically."

"They were scheduled to go through the tunnels, but they're Silkmouth Pride..." Chert trailed off, then seemed to realize no one here knew the cave gryphon prides and clarified. "No echolocation or night vision with that bunch. Terrible whiskers, spiked tails. They're more builders than explorers, and they were supposed to fix a bridge you three are going to need to get across.

"Slate's being careful, figuring they ran into an animal. But I think something killed them down there and dumped the bodies up top so we wouldn't know what tunnel they were attacked in."

Cherine looked up from his journal writing. "Mally the Nighthaunt? I thought he was near the naze, not in the desert."

"Maybe? But some feral goliaths or large monitors will hunt underground, then pull the bodies topside to eat them," Chert explained. "Gryphon-eating animals are just as dangerous as an opinicus. So flight it is. There's another, less-travelled tunnel system we can pick up farther out, past the bridge. There's a small satellite nest of silkmouths out there we can notify about their kin. If we leave before sunup, we should get there before it's too hot. It's just... not as easy to bring guests through those caves, so be ready for a couple of rough days."

Cherine already ached all over, but he reminded himself that he'd spent months trying to talk with the cave gryphons again, and it was an honor to get to see their home.

Plus, he was a diplomat now. A sand gryphon diplomat.

"Of course, there's no problem. We'll do our best. We trust you to keep us safe."

Chert left them alone again to sleep.

"It can't be Mally, right?" Zeph asked. "Everything we've heard says he's near his old workshop."

Cherine shrugged. "I'm sure we'll be fine. Remember what Slate said? They're the ones laying traps for Mally under the earth, not the other way around."

"I, for one, am looking forward to flying," Kia added. "Getting to our destination early will buy us some extra time to scout and plan."

Cherine checked to make sure the ink was dry, then slipped his journal back into his harness. "We'd better sleep. This might be the last time we get a nest for a few weeks."

Though he was tired, his brain continued going through his questions from the day. What had happened to the dead cave gryphons, and why were they called silkmouths? And if there were several cave gryphon prides, which were they travelling with now?

16

BLACK TALONS

Reeve Rybalt Reevesbane of the Pitohui Eyrie looked out upon the citizens of Blacktalon and took pity on them. Today, they celebrated him and the largest army the east had ever seen on their doorstep. They believed Rybalt had come here to save them, to stop the Seraph King and the pink reeve from destroying their farms.

The soldiers accepted the gifts of food, the aerial parade, the lodging, and the affection of the locals. Some had done so only under protest, for they'd all been ordered to do so.

Tonight, the locals celebrated hard, but the soldiers had been warned to limit their drinking and have their packs ready to go. Because when morning arrived, the entire army would be gone, leaving Blacktalon to fend for itself.

"It feels cruel," Stripes said. "We should evacuate them to Mothfeather."

How he'd come to have such a kind-hearted sister, Rybalt didn't know. In better times, she'd have made the perfect reeve of their eyrie. But these weren't better times, and so

Rybalt prepared his army to disappear into the desert and leave the farmers to their deaths just to fool a king into thinking he'd won a victory here.

"Sister, dear, remember the rules. Quiet beaks and no trouble," he repeated.

She bristled. Some opinici knew how to act contrite, but that had never been Stripes. No, when she screwed up—like failing to assassinate Impir the Mad—she became less sweet. Angry, even.

Not that Impir had been her only mistake. She wasn't used to the front lines, and she wasn't used to being around opinici who weren't pitohui and gryphons who weren't motmots or Iony.

My long-eared friend is running late. I wonder what 'favor' he had to do down south. It hasn't been easy covering for him.

"Look, *he* was flirting with *me,*" Stripes said defensively. "How was I supposed to know he wasn't immune? It seems like a very simple thing! Don't shake your tailfeathers at a pitohui if you don't want to be shaken."

Rybalt sighed. This wasn't really Stripes's fault, not as much as she thought it was. While, yes, she shouldn't have nuzzled Bario, poisoning him unconscious, she had no way of knowing that Rybalt had slowly been slipping chemicals into the phoenix's food to make him more vulnerable to pitohui toxin just in case Rybalt needed to kill him later. After Impir, he wasn't taking any more chances with scholars.

However, the brother's machinations and the sister's simple nuzzle had sent their top phoenix unconscious for several days. Unlike the farmers and a handful of local soldiers, they couldn't leave *Bario* here to die. So he was being transported home.

As punishment for her amorous misdeeds, Stripes had

been assigned to help the main army instead of coming along with Rybalt.

"Do you just not like pitohui and motmots?" Rybalt asked. "It seems a fairly simple thing to only poison your enemies, not your friends and lovers."

Stripes was in the middle of listing every mistake Rybalt had ever made since they were chicks when Iony arrived, forcing the siblings back to the pretense of civility.

"Sorry for the delay," the glacier gryphon said. "It's a bit harder to find caltrops and flechettes this side of the desert."

Rybalt raised an eyecrest but didn't comment. He had no idea what good delaying the Seraph King's march on Blacktalon would do, but he trusted his old friend had a reason for wasting time on this. "Nice to have you back. Our little sand envoy wouldn't talk to us until you were here, too. It seems that, using both the titles reeve and pride leader, Hoppy Padfoot would not speak unless one of each were present to bow before him."

"What?" Stripes asked. She was the only one of the trio who had not met the sand gryphons yet, and she was in for a treat.

Iony snorted. "You'll enjoy the Padfoot Pride. Just tie down anything you don't want stolen. Part of the cost of doing business is finding your harness pockets full of sand by the end of the journey, and emptied of treasure."

Stripes shook her head, but before she could ask more questions, the blackwing commander called for her. "I guess that's me. We're all counting you, Iony. Don't let Rybalt screw up."

Iony laughed as Stripes flew away, a small escort of brightly colored gryphons coming with her. The motmots weren't strictly necessary, but since Stripes had a tendency to poison her allies, it was best to give her an honor guard immune to pitohui toxins to serve as a buffer between her and the blackwings. They'd also kept her safe from assassins while Rybalt was in prison.

"I think she missed me," the gryphon said to his opinicus friend.

"My sister?" Rybalt asked. "I don't know, she seemed interested in our fiery companion. It would be nice if she'd settle down with someone she can't kill with a nuzzle."

Iony fluffed up a bit.

"Alas, it's too bad we don't know anyone like that," Rybalt finished. "Shall we go meet our sandy liaisons?"

Iony shook his head, ears moving back and forth. "Rybalt, sometimes I don't know why anyone likes you."

The Reevesbane laughed. "I'm very pro-active. Everyone loves an opinicus who can get things done. The murder thing is just one of my fun personality quirks."

THE SUN SET on the desert, transforming it from a heat-blasted wasteland to a void of cold and sand. Crawly things came out of their burrows to search for opinici to sting and gryphons to bite, and tonight was their lucky night as Rybalt had provided them with just that.

"Ow!" Iony swore, swatting something off his leg. "This whole desert is an anthill. No safe place to stand."

"Mmmm," Rybalt agreed. To the north was the bulk of the army. Mostly blackwings with a few others mixed in. And Stripes, of course.

Here to the south, the Pitohui Eyrie's reeve led a smaller force of pitohui, motmots, and glacier gryphons. Everyone who didn't play well with others. While the blackwings were going to conquer cities, Rybalt's targets were smaller, though no less defended.

Something small dashed across the desert in front of him. Iony crouched, ears back, nub tail wiggling.

"Iony," Rybalt warned. "Don't eat our friend."

The glacier gryphon relaxed. The desert prides were a bit of a mystery, but Rybalt was fairly certain an actual roadrunner wouldn't be coming *towards* a group of gryphons and opinici.

And, indeed, the roadrunner gryphon ran up to Rybalt, giving everyone a look at her long legs. "Pride Leader Reeve Hoppy Padfoot, Ruler of Crestfall Eyrie, will see you now."

The roadrunner sprinted away, leaving Rybalt and Iony to fly after her. While they were gone, the army would divide itself into small teams. That's what the sand gryphons had insisted upon. They'd been able to hide caches of water and food across the desert, but no single place had enough for an entire army. So instead, groups of ten and twenty would each have one or two sand gryphon guides to lead them, then they'd converge again on the other side.

Or so the theory went. Rybalt wasn't entirely sure he wasn't about to be betrayed. Not deliberately. The Ashen Weald seemed sincere. The sand gryphons were being well-compensated for their time and without guile in their deals, though they had philosophical issues with the idea of property rights.

It's a good thing I ordered all the pitohui to carry extra anti-toxin with them. I suspect at least a few sticky paws will lead to unconscious sand gryphons before this is over, and it's no good killing our guides.

Mostly, he didn't want the bad karma on his soul. His deal

with the sand gryphons didn't include an escape plan. If things went wrong, the Blackwing Alliance was in a severe amount of trouble. There were exactly enough supplies to get them across, then they were on their own.

"It's called motivation," Iony had said when some of the soldiers complained. "You'll just have to succeed."

Not the most reassuring pep talk the glacier pride leader had given, in Rybalt's opinion, but it did the job. If things went horribly, terribly awry, he thought his personal force had the best chance of getting home.

Of course, what the Blackwing Eyrie reeve will do to us if we come home and his army does not is another matter.

A bonfire marked the meeting location, and Rybalt flew down to allow the roadrunner to announce him.

"Rybalt Reevesbane and his friend, Iony," the small running gryphon said, earning a sigh from Iony, who stepped forwards.

"Iony, pride leader of the glacier pride," he corrected. "And this is Reeve Rybalt of the Pitohui Eyrie. I recognize a few of the faces here. Pride Leader Reeve Hoppy Padfoot, we owe you a great debt, which we have paid in metal and food. The Feathermane Pride leaders, Askel and Triddle, nice to meet you under less murderous circumstances. And Sponge, Champion of the Desert. Always a pleasure."

One of the sandgrouse gryphons, the wettest of the bunch, cooed and said something in owlish to Iony that Rybalt couldn't understand.

"Oh dear," Iony replied.

Hoppy Padfoot didn't speak to the two opinici, instead remaining perched on a stone that put him above the others. His crest was up, orange with black stripes, and all around his feet were metal coins. He wore a magnet around his neck.

Askel, perhaps the first gryphon phoenix, spoke next. "You're going to need to break the trip up over several days. Each team has three camps. There's a fire so you can cook, and there'll be food nearby. Mostly, though, you're moving at night. The fire is just to give you warmth when you wake up. There're also the tents you're bringing with you. They'll help hide you from the teratorns. Each group will have two guides, just to be safe."

Askel's mate, Triddle, joined in. "There's more water than there are camps. We've been filling barrels of rainwater and hiding them in the desert. Be aware, though, that once you leave a location, sand gryphons will come in and clean it up. So you can't go back the same way, and even if you memorize these routes, you won't have supplies at them. This is a one-way trip."

Bario would have been able to get more information out of Askel, but as Rybalt and Iony had started the sequence of events ending in Merin's death, neither of his pridemates seemed willing to talk to the Reevesbane.

Hoppy whispered something to Sponge, who translated it into owlish for Iony, who then had to translate it yet again for Rybalt.

"She says depending on how many shiny things we find, we might be able to negotiate a fee for a trip back," the glacier pride leader explained. "But she says it takes time to prepare, and the rainy season isn't for months yet, so water will be limited."

"I see," Rybalt said. "Thank you, Hoppy Padfoot and the Ashen Weald, for your assistance in this matter. Tell your Kjarr that we'll do our best to destroy the enemy's supply lines. When we do, however, be aware that the Seraph King will already have begun his attack on our lands. Once the supply line is cut, I need Satra to apply pressure to the Crackling Sea so they withdraw their forces."

"If supply stops," Hoppy said, "will keep promise."

Rybalt bowed and allowed himself to be led back to his troops. As much as he hoped crossing the desert would be the easy part, he wasn't so naïve. He'd seen legions from both sides attempt a crossing just to become bones for the giant teratorns. In fact, he expected to lose at least some of his soldiers before they reached their destination, and then they'd need time to recover.

With my luck, a freak storm will spread the red algae inland and kill us all.

There was a cheerful thought. He gathered his small group of twenty. The blackwing commander had insisted Rybalt include two particular blackwing opinici with him on this trip. It was a strange thing to do, especially considering what had happened to all the blackwing opinici sent south with him last time.

In an amazing coincidence, all of them had been killed by the Ashen Weald or Mally the Nighthaunt.

Strange, that.

Rybalt had included his own odd addition in the form of a pitohui stargazer, what passed for a scholar on his home island. This opinicus's job was to track their path across the desert, taking note of the landmarks. All their sand gryphon aid would dry up, so to speak, once they crossed. But if they happened by any drinking water or oases, Rybalt wanted to know where they were for future desert expeditions.

It was a long shot, but if things went wrong, he'd need a long shot to survive.

The first day in the desert was miserable. Rybalt sweated out all of his batrachotoxin, large drops of poison landing on scorpions who twitched and curled up. Something he hadn't considered was just how many scarabs he needed to bring with him. Even for a pitohui, he couldn't just down a vial of toxin and become poisonous. It took time to digest. And if he was going to kill the silver reeve, he'd need to save some of his scarab snacks for later.

Which meant he'd be striking Whitebeak with a team of pitohui at their least poisonous and most sweaty. When he brought the matter up with his roadrunner escort, asking if there was a place for them to bathe on the way, she just shook her head.

"No! Poison bird no bathe in oasis. Bad thought." Then she'd run off, forcing them to hurry to catch up to her in the night.

Before their journey, Iony had spent the flight to Blacktalon talking about how taiga fur was layered in such a way he wouldn't feel the desert heat nor the desert cool. It was a long speech about fur that only the stargazer seemed interested in, and as impressive as it had been, by the time the sun came up, he was begging to be shaved.

There were few sights sadder than a shaved gryphon. One of those was a shaved, sunburned gryphon, and after the second day, Iony had turned as pink as Younce.

Thankfully, the stargazer had brought a type of ointment that kept the sun at bay. It wasn't something pitohui normally used, but sometimes, the motmots would put it in their feathers, and Iony was so grateful, Rybalt was worried he might be losing his spot as the glacier gryphon's best friend.

And that was before the incident with the burned paws

came up, teaching them they needed to wait a little after the sun went down to emerge from their caves.

The opinici and gryphons ate, the two blackwings staying back from both, and Rybalt went to talk to their roadrunner escort. She seemed to enjoy the heat and resented being forced to move only at night.

Rybalt would have given her some free food, but he'd sweated over everything he owned. He hadn't realized opinici could sweat so much, outside of their paws. Somehow, this was a new experience for him even after his past excursions into the desert.

"Are we close now?" He knew the answer, but he wanted to keep the roadrunner talking instead of sulking.

She shook her head, shaking the lizard in her beak, then swallowed. "No, long while yet. This is why you no cross before. Impressed you get to palace to blow up. But would not have made it across. Too far."

He stayed to chat, waiting for the world to cool down, but he couldn't help but notice that the lizards the roadrunner was eating were slowly retreating towards a cave for the night. He waited until his sand gryphon went off to mark the nearby rocks with her scent, then he called for Iony to join him.

The cave was small, and it didn't seem to be part of a larger system, but it had a strange smell to it. He lit some rushlights and was rewarded with the discovery of a large sand swimmer. Iony dispatched the lizard for him.

"This way, we can let our guide eat it." The glacier gryphon dragged it out of the cave, away from Rybalt's deadly talon prints.

The Reevesbane didn't know what he expected to find in the cave. He just wanted something to break up the monotony of the desert run. So when a familiar, chemical scent reached his nares, his eyes pinpricked in anticipation.

"It can't be," he whispered to Iony. "Fetch the stargazer. Don't let the blackwings know."

The scholar arrived moments later, carrying with him a brazier. Inside the cave was a pool brimming with small, purple shrimp.

Using a single talon, the stargazer brought one to the surface and nodded. "It's the same type as the palace. The explosion must have sealed off this section so Ellore's poison didn't reach them."

Rybalt and Iony shared a look. This presented some fascinating opportunities. "How much salt can we get from this pool?"

The stargazer used a measuring stick with a small scoop on the end. "Not enough. It takes decades for the creatures to build up, die, have their bodies worn to sand, and for those 'essential salts' to be usable. I'm impressed this group survived at all, but it isn't going to let you do much."

Rybalt frowned. That wasn't what he wanted to hear. He'd already had plans for his salt supply. He didn't have time to wait decades.

"What if we... use the pool itself? If we dumped two bodies in?" Iony asked.

"You'd kill the shrimp. Their ecosystem is delicate," the Stargazer said. "But you could probably trigger the transformation once before they all died."

The little creatures, sentient but not sapient, swam around their pool, oblivious to the opinici plotting their demise above.

"One death. One change. It... could work," Iony said. "It would just need to be the right death."

Rybalt already had someone in mind. Getting *that* opinicus dead, and then getting them all the way out into the desert without anyone suspecting, would be quite the magic trick. But he'd often said that the right death could change the world for the better.

"Stargazer, I need you to search the skies. Memorize how to get back here again," Rybalt ordered. "Can you promise me that? Are you certain you can?"

"Of course." The stargazer bowed his head. "That's why I'm here, isn't it?"

Iony looked out of the cave, back at the camp. "I'll make sure the blackwings don't report this cave to their leaders. It's unfortunate they stumbled across such a large sand swimmer, which got the best of them. Thankfully, I killed it right after."

The stargazer shivered.

"Oh, don't *you* worry," Rybalt said. "You just became the only opinicus on this continent I am devoted to keeping alive."

17

THE WRITHING DEPTHS

Soaring through the night air felt wonderful to Zeph, who enjoyed visiting the desert but didn't particularly care for the heat. The light of the moon was bright enough that the cave gryphons were able to see again, and only Xin needed a little help flying in the open air.

Not that he was slowing anyone down. He seemed determined to impress Chert. She seemed just as interested in showing off how well she could guide them, so they flew close, clicking back and forth as she led him through the sky.

Down below, Zeph watched small creatures scavenging for food in the night. Beetles, scorpions, snakes. He even caught sight of a strange gryphon, presumably one of the other desert prides, who resembled a roadrunner. She dashed out, saving a small bird from a snake.

He resisted the urge to chirp a greeting. The cave gryphons had warned him they weren't to trust anyone. At least two gryphon prides had allied themselves with the Blackwing Alliance, and while none had allied themselves with the Seraph King, that didn't mean there were no gryphons in this territory.

"Just 'cause there are no prides, doesn't mean there are no gryphons," had been Slate's explanation. "Alwren's fisherfolk gryphons count as eyrie citizens if they're married to an opinicus. And there are gryphons around, they're just—"

"Sad and broken," Chert finished for him. "You'll see some families, but they tend to live in the spaces between the eyries. And if they're caught by the opinici, it's not good."

Slate nodded. "Some of the dumber eyries still use caves as prisons, so we've broken out some gryphons in our time. That's how we met the Silkmouth Pride originally, on a lampworks raid. Half were being used to construct outposts for the Alabaster Eyrie while the others worked the textile mills. If they have nowhere to go, we help them relocate."

Zeph wondered where the gryphons were relocated to. Maybe the roadrunner below was one of those same gryphon prisoners, freed by cave gryphons. Or perhaps there was some hidden gryphon paradise.

Or maybe they're all living underground at the Abyssal Naze.

The lands ahead of them were a mystery. Thanks to Kia's books, a bit scorched after the fire, he generally understood that the southwest corner of the continent was all Emerald Jungle, with a few small opinicus settlements on the other side. And he'd seen maps of the Argent Heights and where they were going past it. But it looked like the rest was just farms and grasslands, the same kind of place Brevin had hoped to transform the weald into once she removed the gryphons from it.

The morning sun lightened the sky, and Slate gave the order to land. Giant teratorns wouldn't be out yet, but they were nearing the new road system that connected Reevesport to Whitebeak to New Eyrie, and it would be guarded.

They crossed several dunes by paw before stopping in a patch of sand that looked no different from the rest. It took a little digging, but when they dislodged the right rocks, it was like pulling the plug in a rainwater collection barrel, the sand spilling down into a desert canyon.

For the first time since their journey began, the cave gryphons sniffed nervously, sometimes licking the cave walls. Slate, always confident and gruff, softened and let his pridemates chitter instead of insisting they use common.

"We sealed up this cave for a reason," he explained. "Whenever small groups came through here, they felt like something was watching them. I say small groups, but even groups as large as seven or ten felt like there was something living here."

Chert looked up from reassuring Xin. "If it's been starving since we sealed up the cave, it might be willing to attack us. It's important to stay together. We also didn't bring enough antivenom. The desert is a poisonous place, and the path from the guest cave west goes deep enough that we usually skip most of that, thanks to the bridges."

Despite their nervous disposition, the cave gryphons didn't detect anything wrong, and they began their descent. Unlike the cool, sometimes frigid temperatures of the caves east of Crestfall, Zeph found himself sweating through his paws. There was also some light from time to time, which meant they had to be quiet so they weren't overheard, but even a little light was enough for Zeph to see.

That made him feel better up until he actually looked around. The same small cracks that let light and sound into the depths also allowed snakes in.

Slate kept them walking on rock where possible because the sands down here, away from the hot desert sun, were alive with sand swimmers and sidewinders.

"They call this place the Writhing Depths for a reason," Chert whispered to him when he gave a wide berth to a tangle of snakes.

From just behind her, led by cave gryphons, was Kia. "Wait, *why* do they call this the Writhing Depths?"

A pair of blue eyes shared a knowing look with a pair of black eyes, and Zeph whispered back to his unseeing friends, "Oh, because the path is so winding. That's why we keep swaying back and forth. Don't want to fall into the sand."

"That's nice," Cherine said from ahead of them. "I was worried it was worms or those weird tailless scorpions you keep trying to eat. Or giant spiders."

"Nothing like that," Zeph mumbled, watching as a small sand swimmer ate a tailed and venomous scorpion. "Definitely no tailless scorpions down here."

They reached the edge of the desert, and the sandstone and light faded into the darkness again, taking away his sight. The cave gryphons alternated quiet clicks and loud ones, raising questions from Kia whose answers didn't make any of the guests feel better.

Slate called for a halt. "There's something following us."

"Could it be a wounded silkmouth?" Kia ventured. "Maybe it survived the attack."

Chittering from the cave gryphons, then Chert said, "No, I heard high-pitched echolocation, not just clicking. The silkmouths can't do that."

One of the cave gryphons Zeph didn't know spoke up. "There are always tales about voices in the dark. We all hear them. We know not to go to them alone. They're why we travel in groups. It's just one of those."

A long pause before Slate spoke. "There are over twenty of us here. I've never heard of one of the voices following a group so large. They only attack when they can get us alone."

"It may not be a silkmouth, but their pride isn't far from here." Chert's words lacked her usual cheer. "We should warn them, maybe leave one or two of our own to help search, then go. You know what the convocation said. Stopping the Nighthaunt is our priority, and these wealders can make that happen."

This was the first time Zeph had heard about a convocation. In fact, he'd never stopped to think about what had gone on from the cave gryphon side of things. He'd assumed they were being allowed in because of the jerky and because Chert wanted Xin to see her homeland. The Ashen Weald had been upfront about their ultimate target, the Nighthaunt, but he hadn't considered that they'd been brought in as weapons.

Or assassins. I'm a hunter, Kia and Cherine are scholars, but that's not how Hatzel introduced us. She introduced us as the Bane of the Red Reeve, as the ones who destroyed the pink reeve's palace. Zeph shifted his paws, his ears and tail both down. *Is this what I've become? The Rybalt of gryphons?*

Opinici killed each other all the time. But gryphons killing opinici, killing reeves, destroying eyries? That was something new.

"Fine." Slate gave the orders, and they continued moving, though they used less echolocation and discouraged the 'wealders' from clicking lest they attract the strange sound in the darkness.

The pace picked up, and a couple of times Zeph felt his paws slip on the sand, narrowly avoiding going over a ledge as the cave gryphons around him tried to keep him on track. In fact, at one point, he leaned a wing out on a turn and discovered there was no cave gryphon on his right. She'd flown off the ledge, beating her wings, and caught up again.

That didn't make him feel better about not being able to see.

Wherever we're going, at least we'll get there fast, I suppose.

From his left, a mass of snakes hissed in the sands beneath him.

KIA'S TALONS ACHED, and for the first time in her life, she wished she were a gryphon. Bird feet were just not built for this kind of running. At least, not talons like hers.

I wonder if there are goliath bird gryphons. Oh, we wouldn't know because of their paws. Well, goliath... opinici?

The thought made her laugh, startling the cave gryphon next to her. Still, goliath bird feet would feel pretty good for these long walks. The bit of flying before sun-up almost made it worse, reminding her that if the world were peaceful, she could be flying this route instead of walking it.

The cave gryphons running alongside her were quiet, and they seemed to have a system where Slate would do the echolocating and guide the others, keeping their audible impact on the caves at a minimum. Unfortunately, that meant the cave gryphons were guessing about the path now and then, which nearly got them killed when another bridge was out.

Slate slid to a halt, sending the cave gryphons and wealders behind him into a crashed bundle of wings, paws, and beaks. Several cave gryphons latched onto Kia to keep her from falling down the sandy side, pushing her against a cave wall to their right. To the left, she heard the sound of wind on sand, perhaps, as it hissed through the cave. She wasn't sure.

"One bridge might collapse on its own," Chert said from ahead of them. "Two is strange. The silkmouths are good builders. I've never heard of anything they've made failing, not ever. Most of their bridges survived the earthquakes, even."

Cherine chimed in from the back, also against the wall with Kia to keep from sliding down the sandy side. "I can feel a wooden plank here next to me. We're pretty handy with our talons. If the building materials are still here, we can probably make it work."

The cave gryphons laughed, and though they didn't elaborate, Kia got the impression that the silkmouths brought special materials with them into the caves.

If they can't echolocate, do they bring braziers or rushlights with them? I don't know of any gryphon prides who regularly use fire beyond the taiga pride.

Next to her, Zeph poked the plank. "I wouldn't pull this out. I think it's how we're not sliding down into the pile of snakes."

"The pile of *what?*" Kia asked. The hissing sound suddenly made a lot more sense. "When did the snakes appear?"

"Oh, um, since the beginning," Zeph replied. "Sorry. I forgot you can't see down there. Don't fall. Definitely *do not* fall."

"Wait, can you see here?" Kia asked. "Is there light?"

A pause from Zeph, then he turned her head towards where she heard Chert and Slate talking about the bridge. It was mostly black, but in the distance, she saw what appeared to be strings of light hanging from the ceiling. Every so often, a tiny blue light pulsed from the top, going down. They were far enough away that their illumination did little to reveal the path, stone wall, or snakes.

"That's useful," Kia said.

"It's a problem," Chert said from right in front of her. "You don't want to get tangled up in glow worm goo when you fly across, and without a bridge, that's our best option. That, or go back and find what's been chasing us."

More chittering from the cave gryphons, then Slate made the call. "Waiting here is doing us no good. It's too far to go back. We need to push forwards. We'll just have to guide you across carefully."

"Is it very deep?" Zeph asked.

"No, it's shallow, and that's worse," Slate grumbled. "Glow worms and spikes up top, a short drop to spikes down at the bottom. I'd rather it be a long drop. That gives you time to recover. Here, it's going to get messy if you go too high or low."

Chert chirped, an almost upbeat sound despite their predicament. "We'll take good care of you. Don't worry! I'll go across with Xin first. I'm used to guiding his flight, so I don't think we'll have trouble. Then Slate can bring Cherine across. Then we'll give the all-clear."

"Has our loquacious cave monster been following us, still?" Cherine asked.

Chittering, then Chert: "We haven't heard him. But we're about to get really loud to see all of those stalactites and stalagmites, so he could come for us."

The slip from 'it' to 'he' wasn't lost on Kia.

A flutter of wings, some echolocation loud enough for Kia to hear the squeaks, and she assumed the first group was off.

A sound came from far, far away, and Cherine was led past her to the front of the line. Judging by how many more wings and squeaks there were, it seemed they'd brought several spotters to keep him safe.

"Oh, I should have gone first," Zeph said. "I forget they need more light than I do to see. It's a weird feeling."

"Will your eyes be okay when we're back in the daylight?" she asked, reaching towards the sound of his voice to try to find him. "I've never asked what the winter sun is like for you."

He caught her talons and put them on his head. "It's fuzzy. But there's so few hours of sunlight in winter, it doesn't matter much. In the taiga, we'd just nap in the sun, so no need for good vision. Then we'd hunt at night."

The all-clear sounded from across the bridge, indicating half of their troop was over the abyss.

And then the rocks from the ceiling fell.

Small ones at first, then a few larger. Kia didn't want to risk the spiked pit or the sand snakes, so she pushed back against the cave wall.

With a crash and a bright flash of light, a dozen armored Alabaster Eyrie soldiers burst from the rubble. The cave gryphons reacted quickly, but they'd been just as surprised as Kia. Even with her poor eyesight, she'd been blinded by the flash of light.

A talonful of gryphons died before they found their footing. The opinici were adept at fighting cave gryphons, but they weren't expecting Kia and Zeph.

"Zeph, darken the sky!" she commanded. She had a wall of cave gryphons around her, and she prayed they figured out what she was doing. She reached down to find the loose plank holding the path together, and when Zeph kicked the attacker's brazier off the cliff face, their tunnel returned to darkness once again.

Kia yanked up the plank, and their section of the path collapsed, sliding into the den of snakes.

She leapt into the air, trying to guess where she could fly without hitting anything. She heard screaming and hissing below her and shivered.

Few opinici and fewer gryphons could hover, and the few that could required winds to steady themselves. There was only a slight breeze in the cave, not enough to shake the glow worm's shiny threads, and Kia was trying to circle, guessing at what she was seeing.

Glow worm threads. Her eyes had adjusted enough that she could see them in the distance. She couldn't keep flying in circles here, not without hitting someone, so she tried to go towards the light, staying below it. There must be enough room to cross since they'd gotten Cherine to the other side.

She felt a paw grab her harness from above, and Zeph said, "Up a little here, there's a spike. Okay, now down. Wait, to the left. No, don't beat your wings, we need to slow down. I'm going to fly in front of you, grab a tailfeather with your beak and follow in my wake, okay?"

Together, they traversed the pit, Zeph guiding her. Only once the cave gryphons chittered the all-clear did Slate ask Cherine to light his brazier.

The pit of spikes and writhing snakes had all been after-images from the alabaster opinici's attack. Looking back now, Kia was amazed any of what they'd done had worked.

"Sorry about your path," she said. "I didn't know what else to do, and you seemed to be in trouble."

Chittering, then Slate spoke for the others. "We'd have lost more than four if not for your quick thinking. The bodies were all white-tailed kites, the king's favorite fighters. There were no darkstalkers with them."

"How did they ambush us?" Chert worried at her whiskers, recleaning them again and again. "We were quiet on the approach. Once we arrived, sure, we were loud, but not loud enough for them to sneak up on us. I didn't hear a tunnel above. I... didn't hear them hiding. And look at their metal armor! *They* should have been loud."

Kia inspected the ceiling from across the pit. It looked as solid there as it was here. "I'm sure I felt rocks falling before they came down. Maybe they were up top somehow? I mean, they jumped down only after word came that half of you were too far away to help us."

More chittering, and this time, even Chert had stopped using common. There were strong feelings on both sides, and this group had probably run these tunnels a hundred times together. The four dead cave gryphons weren't just comrades, they were friends.

"We can't send word back. It's not safe," Slate said. "But we'll make sure other groups know not to come this way. We'll have to clear the tunnels and find new ones, now that the opies know about them. This... is going to be a mess to fix."

Kia was more worried about who had led them here, setting the trap. Chert was concerned about sound, but Kia was more concerned about the scent. "Could you smell their braziers?"

"No, there was no scent," Zeph said. "Not until after the attack. The brazier hadn't been lit ahead of time. I'd have smelled it."

Cherine looked up from where he was trying to sketch the

glow worms. “That’s not so strange, right? Bario has scentless braziers.”

“Scentless to opinici, maybe,” Zeph snorted. “I can still smell if one has been lit. Unless they’d been in there for weeks, there was no brazier or rushlight used until the attack came.”

Slate sighed. “Chert, you’re in charge. There’s water ahead. Be careful of another ambush but wait there for me. I’m going to fish the alabasters out and check their eyes. Maybe there’s a darkstalker we missed.”

Chert nodded.

Normally, this is where Kia and Cherine were ordered to douse the brazier. This time around, they were allowed to keep it burning as they began their ascent. The ground here was wet, and a stream with a strong current ran alongside them. Unlike on the sandy side of the pit, there was no need for a wooden path.

Kia managed one look back at the spikes. She couldn’t see the broken bridge, just lots of some white, threaded substance in the bottom, maybe a strange gypsum or calcite formation.

18

CHRYSALIS

While they waited at the waterfall, which Kia was assured was safe to drink, she sketched some of the strange little fish that crawled up and down the rocks. Four long fins, both climbing claw and fin, led to her nicknaming them *serafish.* She didn't know aquatic life any better than she knew cave life, but she'd long maintained that the new Darkfeather University should reach out to the fisherfolk and see if any of the diving petrels were interested in becoming scholars if peace came.

When peace comes, not if. I know it has to.

Kia had spent a lot of time anxious and worried when the old university and eyrie burned down around her. The guilt of knowing she'd set events in motion by finding Satra and the wingtorn hidden in the underbough had weighed heavily upon her soul. Yet every time she went back through the events of the conflagration, those weren't among her regrets. The alternative would have been the death of every weald pride. Not that the underbough opinici, who had taken the worst of the flames, had deserved to suffer any more than the gryphon prides had, but Kia would rather err on the side of trying to save those in need than sitting back and hoping for the best.

Which was why she was here, of course, trying to stop the Seraph King and Nighthaunt once and for all. She was anxious about a lot of things. Haunted, perhaps, like the voices in the depths. She worried about her brother, Olan. She worried about what would happen to the starlings when they removed the barrier. But she did not worry they would fail, that peace would not come.

It might take a while, but we'll get there. Kia Reevesbane: optimist. It has a nice ring to it.

Slate caught up with them an hour later, nursing a few snake bites. They didn't slow him down, but that meant their limited supply of antivenom was gone. Zeph was already looking at everything askance, especially after finding out that there were snakes who enjoyed hanging down to catch oilbirds flying in and out of the caves.

"Should we douse the brazier?" Cherine asked. "Just to be safe?"

Slate agreed but assured them this next section wouldn't be so dark. They'd crossed into the maple forest, and there'd be holes from above letting light seep in. That was more useful for Zeph's blue eyes than Cherine or Kia's, but at least it meant she might get to draw something now and again.

I should've brought a second notebook.

They crawled through the caves, mindful of the water. Twice, she heard Chert talking to Xin, reassuring him that, unless the rainfall had been particularly unseasonal, they wouldn't need to do any swimming.

"Do you have a waterproof pouch on that fancy harness of yours?" Kia asked Cherine.

He shook his head. "I guess I knew caves are often formed by water, but I didn't think of it. When we get back, we should visit Sandpiper's Dune, see if they sell something."

Zeph trailed along behind them, and every so often, he'd tell them to watch their footing. The sections of the cave where the ceiling gave way and light spilled down were full of plants, not exactly normal cave ecology, but it was still pleasant to pass by some friendly ferns or see the flies coming into the cave to become lunch for the glow worms overhead.

Kia's first hint that something was wrong came from Zeph, who whispered the two words she really didn't want to hear.

"Are there… giant spiders, by chance?" he asked Chert.

Giant… spiders? Kia shivered.

"In general?" Chert replied. "Or in this stretch? I don't think there are any big bugs for this section. Except megapedes. Some of those may come down, but I could really go for one of those to eat."

"You and me both," Zeph agreed.

Another hour passed before he began asking more questions that made Kia wonder what it was she wasn't seeing in the dark sections. "So are there maybe giant butterflies? Or…?"

"Just dragonflies," Chert chirped.

At this point, Kia'd had enough. She pulled him aside to ask, "Zeph, what're you seeing? No gryphon just keeps asking about giant bugs. What's going on?"

"There's just a lot of spider silk here, and, uh, it's making me nervous," he admitted. "Maybe it's one of your fancy rock formations, but it looks… gooey. And there are things in it."

The next time a hole opened above and light spilled

down, Kia looked back the way they'd come. She could see white spots on the walls but couldn't make out what they were. For all she knew, they were swiftlet nests. There was a small colony east of the Redwood Valley Eyrie that had taken over an old saltpeter mine. She knew little about the small grey birds with their white chins and stomachs, but she'd heard their nests were pure white or a rusty red. Some of the merchants paid a hefty price for the nests, using them in soup.

Another hour passed where Kia's worry had turned to wonder at the strange silk cocoons along the walls. Like Zeph, she was now imagining giant moths and butterflies. She'd heard rumors of dragonflies the length of sand gryphons in the desert during the rainy season, and she was curious just how big flying bugs could grow after seeing the megapedes on her previous northern adventure.

Her wonder turned to dread when the next patch of light hit, and she saw what was definitely an opinicus skeleton trapped in a web of silk.

"That's... not a chrysalis," Cherine quipped. "I don't think that opinicus is going to hatch into a beautiful, colorful gryphon."

Zeph crouched down, which Kia had learned was his way of preparing for a fight. A smaller target was harder to hit, and he stalked his way across the ground now. Not for the first or last time, she was grateful for his blue eyes.

Kia turned to ask Chert if she knew what was making the webs, but Slate hushed them all.

"We're getting near their pride," he growled back. "We don't want anyone following us through the entrance. They're a favorite target of both the darkstalkers and Reevesport's trade families."

The scholars kept their beaks shut, though sometimes, she heard Zeph hissing at random bugs, daring them to spray silk at him.

Ultimately, Slate's warning had come too late. When they turned the last corner, entering a room that looked like a trap-door spider's home, the alabaster opinici were ahead of them.

19

SILKMOUTH

A single brazier gave light to the cavern, around the size of Hatzel's new cave. The walls were covered in the sticky substance, and skeletons of opinici hung from the webbing. More than that, many live opinici, Alabaster Eyrie armor shimmering in the light, had cornered a small, black-and-white gryphon.

The way split in this cavern. Zeph and the others came in from the east, and the obvious exit proceeded west from here. But a section of the strange webbing had been torn down to reveal a path north.

An opinicus with a small circlet, something Zeph still associated with the Reeve's Guard captains of the Redwood Valley, was tormenting a beaten, bleeding, and bruised gryphon. She let out the occasional wet hiss but was otherwise unresponsive.

The cave gryphons crouched down, using the shadows and darkness. With the element of surprise, they stood a good chance of winning.

Zeph's attention wasn't on the alabaster opinici. The flickering brazier light interfered with his vision, but he saw something in the western passage, staying out of the light. Its body was white, much like the white-tailed hawk look of the Alabaster Eyrie's residents. But its face looked wrong.

The firelight glinted off the white and orange eyes of the other alabaster opinici, but not the one in the dark corridor. White-tailed kites had dark facial markings, well-defined circles or ovals with a clean, round shape. But their eyes were always bright and colorful.

Whoever, *whatever* was in the cave had black eyes. And the large markings around those eyes, or where Zeph assumed there must be eyes, looked like they were made of running ink, dripping down its face. Almost as if the creature had been melted, as if something hot had been applied to its face.

Hot... and salty. Mixed with blood.

The desert smuggler who had led Zeph and Kia to the palace in the desert had a similar look on the part of his face pressed into a vat of the essential salts. The reason this creature in the cave looked the way it did could be the same.

"Darkstalker," he tried to warn to Chert, but Zeph was a moment too late. Slate charged the alabaster captain.

As they attacked, the cave gryphons let out a screech that echoed in the small room and deafened their opponent—and their allies.

The captain turned his back on the small gryphon he'd been tormenting, and Zeph got his first look at the creature that had been killing opinici and wrapping them up.

The tiny, helpless-looking gryphon opened her beak, which dripped white gooey liquid, and latched on to the captain's wing. She was so small that, when the captain swore and kicked her as hard as he could, Zeph fully expected the little silkmouth to go flying.

And she did. Though not nearly as far as he'd anticipated, since her sticky mouth pulled out every feather it had latched onto.

The captain screamed in pain. He charged, trying to vivisect her with his metal talons.

Zeph was mid-dash towards the darkstalker in the far corridor, but he was close enough to reach out and grab the captain's back leg with both of his forepaws, claws springing out.

The captain's slash missed the little silky, and she immediately bit at his metal talons, something that would have been silly for another gryphon. No beak could stand against metal.

Except that once she got her mouth around them, she pressed the talons, still gooey, against the cave wall. The captain struggled with Zeph, finally dislodging him, but by then, the silkmouth was gone. She seemed to know exactly how long she needed before the goo set.

When the captain turned his attention back to her, she'd already disappeared, leaving him to try to free his webbed foreleg. He swore, using the long but non-metallic talons on his other foreleg to try to liberate himself. While he did that, the webbing along the wall had a small shape moving behind it. It seemed that while the fresh silk was wet and gooey, it didn't retain that stickiness after it set.

There was a slender break in the white wall that Zeph would never have known about had the little cave gryphon not burst through it. Her mouth opened wide like a snake, latching over the opinicus's head.

Zeph thought she was going to eat him, but she pulled him against the other webbing, letting the new goo bind his head there before she disappeared back into the wall, then out the other side, helping her oilbird friends with the others.

By the time Zeph got to the far corridor, the darkstalker had disappeared. Out of instinct after days of wandering caves, he clicked into the darkness. From so far away that not even his blue eyes could make it out, he heard the high-pitched echolocation sound come back to him.

Slate said not to follow the whispers into the caves alone.

Zeph opted to follow Slate's advice and returned, finding the opinici had all been wrapped up. While a few were dead, most had just been incapacitated.

The silkmouth gryphon wiped her beak on the walls, spitting a few times to get the silk out, then thanked Slate. "I'm glad you came when you did. They'd had enough of being led down the wrong corridors. I think they were about ready to kill me."

Slate groomed her face, a common gryphon response to meeting a friend, but she didn't return the gesture. "We found some of your pridemates in the desert. Seven of them. The sand gryphons took care of the burials. Are there others out there?"

"No, that's all of them." She shook her head. "If you go by the glow bridge, be careful. They had me create a light wrapping around a few of their fighters so your echolocation wouldn't find them."

Chert chirped her own greeting. "We took care of those. They killed four of us, but one of our guests pulled out the plank and sent them down into the snakes."

"I guess I should send a team in to fix the bridge. I'm afraid I'm a bit out of spit at the moment." The silkmouth gryphon laughed, a wet sound despite her claim of being out of saliva. "Guests, though? Are these new rescues? I've never seen anyone like them. Magpie sure is pretty."

Chert moved protectively in front of Xin.

The silkmouth sniffed at Zeph, who sniffed back tentatively. After being around the cave gryphons so much, he'd become used to their extra-long whiskers, fuzzy feathers, and black eyes. The newcomer had normal eyes, a white underbelly, and a mix of black and brown feathers and fur over the rest of her. The only thing unusual was her long, black tail and paws that seemed adept for climbing. She had a fan of feathers over the top of her long tail, but the feathers ended in sharp spikes.

I wonder what those are for? I guess they're a nice way to say 'stay away from my tail.'

Zeph's friends introduced themselves without sniffing, instead speaking out loud the way opinici always did.

"I'm Kia, formerly of the Redwood Valley Eyrie, currently... unattached," she said. "Friend of fisherfolk, Ashen Weald, and Hatzel's pride."

"Oh, an opinicus. You can just call me Silky. That's probably easier for you." She sniffed at Cherine's beak, tapping its designs with her paw. "You're some sort of sand gryphon?"

He nodded. "You can call me Cherine. I'm their diplomat to the cave gryphons. Friend of Hatzel's pride, the Strix Pride, and formerly of the Redwood Valley Eyrie."

"And I'm Xin," the magpie added. He clicked to find her, then did his best bow. "Member of Hatzel's pride but going to stay with the cave gryphons a season."

"Such strange names," Silky said, "and words. Cave gryphons. How... monolithic. How very opinicus-like. Can you vouch for them, Slate?"

Their leader did his usual grumbling. "Yeah, I can. Or at

least Chert here will. Look, it doesn't matter, though. If the darkstalkers are this close, you're going to need to pack up and head to the naze for your own safety."

Silky shook her head. "This is our home. The naze is so... crowded and dark. My pride isn't going to want to leave."

"We'll help you clear out the tunnels and find a home like this one," Chert reassured her. "But there were more bridges out. You're being hunted."

Silky climbed the silk walls, finding another hidden gap in the ceiling. It seemed the path north was just a ruse. "Well, the darkstalker's hunting all of you now, too, so I guess you can come spend the night with us. Come on up!"

Zeph climbed up on Cherine, then carefully put a paw against the webbing. It was soft.

"It's not sticky," he shouted down.

The cave gryphons let out their chitter which he'd come to recognize as meaning more-or-less, "Yes, we know."

Kia was grateful and climbed up Cherine and Zeph and into the dark passage. When Slate had said they were nearly there, Zeph had been thinking that meant a few more hours. But in no time at all, they came out of the passage and into a small valley.

There was still some daylight, so the world was fuzzy to Zeph. He expected maples, but there was heavy vegetation overhead, likely the reason this little valley, more of a crevice, wasn't visible from above.

Below the trees were many large silk nests. Little black faces with white chins stared out at them, chirping curiously. Against one side of the valley, he could just make out a silk-mouth creating a new nest. It was fascinating, but also a little gross.

How do they groom themselves?

Silky shouted, gathering everyone down below, and explained what had happened to the others. "Pack up everything you can. We're headed back to the naze."

Most of the gryphons groaned. The one building his new nest looked upset he'd finished most of it just to be told it was time to leave. He wiped his mouth against a leaf. "Not the naze again. It's not safe to go out during the day there. Basically the king's lands, at this point."

"These three are going to take care of that for us," Chert said.

All eyes were on Zeph, Kia, and Cherine, who made their introductions again. Kia and Cherine out loud, but Zeph went from gryphon to gryphon, sniffing them. He only came away with a little goo stuck on his fur.

Something seemed to click for Kia when she saw the nest. "Swiftlets. A pride of cave swiftlet gryphons. That's fascinating. I never thought about where the silk for the birds' nests came from. I just... assumed it came from somewhere else. Bugs or something."

While everyone settled in and the silkmouths found opinicus-appropriate food, Zeph sought out Slate. "I saw your darkstalker in the far passage, staying away from the brazier. Is that what led the alabaster opinici into the tunnels? And was it the same one you were fleeing from when we first caught up to you?"

"Yep. Still three of them left," Slate explained. "Mally got my eyes, but the others got the eyes of my friends. It's hard to look into the face of a stranger and see my loved ones staring back at me. We made a promise when we escaped the Nighthaunt's dungeons that we'd hunt down every one of those darkstalkers and put an end to them."

Zeph shivered.

"Don't look at me like that," Slate said. "If they'd just stay out of our caves, they'd be safe. But they were created for a very particular purpose. The king wanted to be able to hunt through the darkness. He fears us the way we fear the Nighthaunt. Once the last of his darkstalkers and the Haunt himself are gone, we can take back the night and be free again."

"Should we go after the darkstalker?" Zeph asked. "His alabaster friends are all dead."

Slate shook his head again, a motion he seemed to do quite often. "No, they're a crafty bunch. You can't follow 'em without falling into a trap. Best to stay as far away as you can if you don't have an army with you. Come to think of it, I think we're going to have to go through the forbidden caves to avoid this one."

Chert looked up from where she'd been helping Xin with his clicking. "That's... not a good idea. We won't last more than five minutes in there."

"That's why they won't be expecting it." Slate led them to a dead megapede and a small collection of purple-skinned apples. "If we cross there, we'll hit an abandoned mine that cuts all the way through the Argent Heights. Opinici broke through to the forbidden caves long ago and had to seal it off."

Chert preened Xin nervously, though he didn't seem to mind. "Let's say you can get across it without dying. How do you even get inside?"

Silky joined the conversation. It looked like she'd been showing Cherine where he could set up a fire to cook the megapede. "We're the ones who sealed it up on this side, back before Slate freed us. We can bring it down without much trouble. The opinicus mine on the other side will be trickier, especially with the heat."

Slate pointed over to the opinici. "If we can get them saltpeter, they can blow the door, right?"

"Where are you going to find saltpeter in the forest?" Zeph longed to fly up out of their hideaway and get the lay of the land.

"Whitebeak," Silky said. "The alabaster opinici have it, and they're not watching the old workshop. That's a huge risk for a little saltpeter. Is it worth it?"

Slate grinned, which looked strange on his gruff beak. "Oh, the saltpeter is secondary. We're going to have to break into Whitebeak for the first part of my plan anyways."

As Zeph listened to the strange plan, he felt his eyes growing wider and wider. He'd heard a lot of crazy plans in his time, had come up with a few of his own. These cave gryphons took planning to another level.

Without consulting Kia or Cherine, Zeph said, "Count us in!"

Surely, with a plan this exciting, they'd want to be a part of it.

20

BLUE APPLES

Reevesport was not prepared for the armies of the Blackwing Alliance. All their soldiers, both the normal blue-plume variety and the dyed-black berserkers, were currently across the desert marching on Blacktalon, if they hadn't already taken the city.

Which meant that Reevesport—this port town, this trading capital of the north—was woefully undefended when the blackwing forces arrived.

The first peafowl defenders to sound the alarm died quickly. There were so few of them, far too few to hold the city. Most of the opinici who rose to protect their homes were farmers. The merchants saw the oncoming storm and fled. Some of their bodyguards went with them. Others looked at what a few beads were worth, then abandoned the merchant lords and turned instead to help defend their families and loved ones.

Stripes and her motmots had been ordered to sneak around to the far side of the city and lie in wait for the fleeing merchants. It was the only place the blackwing commander felt safe using her. She was offended but also relieved. She didn't have to wade into the worst of fighting. There was this assumption she often fought against that any pitohui who left their island was some sort of assassin.

That wasn't her, though. She'd only left because, as acting leader with Rybalt in jail, she'd been ordered to the mainland by the blackwing reeve. And while performing her duties, she'd discovered why trade had broken down between her home and the continent. The blackwings just plain didn't like her brother and were taking it out on the entire Pitohui Eyrie.

Well, she couldn't fix Rybalt, and she couldn't change the blackwing reeve's vendetta, but she *could* instigate trade with the merchants directly. The artificial gatekeeping the Blackwing Port provided could, she learned, easily be bypassed by working one-on-one with the representatives of other eyries.

Her people had gone without staple foods and supplies for months. They were about to enter winter missing some very specific things they needed, and she'd been able to make that happen. And then she'd been caught up in more of Rybalt's schemes, ordered by Iony to assassinate the egg-sabotaging war criminal, Impir. Which she failed to do.

And now she was here, in the midst of a desperate spearhead assault, a vital part of a war she wanted no part of.

I just want to go home. Am I really doing my eyrie more good on the front lines than I would be writing letters and giving orders? I don't think so.

Her motmots ambushed a lone merchant, killing him and attracting the attention of a better-guarded set of traders nearby. Their family looked terrified. Stripes commanded the motmots to ignore the little ones.

When she ordered around some blackwing lackey, they

obeyed her because they were afraid of being poisoned. The motmots were different. They fed on the same teal scarabs she did, but unlike a pitohui, the motmot gryphons didn't become poisonous from doing so.

Most days, Stripes wished she'd been born a motmot. Today, however, she was tackled by an angry peafowl who wanted to murder her and was only saved when he started twitching and collapsed.

The large temples, their paper walls on fire, turned to cinders. Several ships fled, but saltpeter bombs solved that problem. Stripes did her best to kill anyone who could fight and reined in her motmots from killing fledglings or the wounded.

Once the main fighting was over, she went to find the blackwing commander. She was tired of death, tired of fire. She'd only thrown up once, but she'd done so out of view of the blackwings, so her reputation was intact.

Not that this is the kind of reputation I want.

A red-shouldered scout flew past, nearly barrelling through her on his way to the commander, which would have been fatal for him. "Sir, the city is burning down. We've secured the main holds of the merchant families. There's a lot of beads, but also food and supplies. Enough to last us on our march west. No sign of their leader. The portmaster must be with the king or managing the Alabaster Eyrie docks."

Stripes settled down next to him. Taking Reevesport was a risky ploy on her side's part. They'd assumed—hoped, really—that it was undefended and full of food. Had it been a trap, their offensive would have been over before it began.

Looks like the gamble paid off. Too bad the reeve—rather, portmaster—wasn't here, too.

The blackwing commander stood atop the gate of the city.

Below him, his soldiers were leading away several goliath birds, trying to figure out which were friendly enough to commandeer. North, the port burned. And in the heights, his armies worked to stop the fires from consuming the nicer homes so they could use them as a base of operations.

The commander took a bite out of a blue apple, letting the juice run down his beak. "Head out to the fields, find where they grow the Reevesport blues. Then put fire to the entire orchard."

"What good will that do, sir?" the messenger asked. "Won't they just regrow them from seeds once we're gone?"

Stripes knew the answer to that. "Apples have a sort of built-in defense against being pollinated by themselves or closely related trees. So the apples that fall from a tree will never grow into the same apple trees, no matter what you do. They'll all taste different than the famous Reevesport blues."

"Then how do you get a field of them?" The scout noticed her plumage and took a big step back. "Pardon me, reeve-sister. I didn't recognize you."

Reeve-sister is not a title I ever thought I'd get called.

"Clippings. You can grow a new tree from them," she explained. The commander seemed impressed by her knowledge. "The catch is that the trees are all completely identical, so one bad bout of disease can take them all out. You remember what happened to the starberries and bananas."

"Teach you that in assassin school, did they?" the commander asked. "Our reeve's orders were clear. If they care so much for their apples, that's what we'll take from them. This is how the false king brought them to heel originally. Let them reconsider their actions in the future. Grab some soldiers and see to it."

Stripes waited for the messenger to depart, then slipped

away to leave the commander to eat his barrel of expensive apples and watch the port city burn. While there was no assassin school, she had learned a bit about war by watching her brother. This was one of those battles that served to boost morale, but it was a false indicator of victory. If any messengers escaped, the next city would be ready for them. And if they weren't careful, the eyrie after that would probably have a full army.

That wasn't her real concern, except that she didn't want to die. She'd leave warcraft to the military and spycraft to her brother. There were a few things she knew, and one of those was what went into agriculture. She also knew how gryphons and opinici expressed themselves as individuals and communities, and how art took on a different form depending on who created it.

Below her, below the open buildings with their sliding paper doors, were some of the most beautiful gardens on the continent. In some, that beauty was visual. From the sky, she saw how the paths through a particular orchard created a stylized peacock feather, how those feathers spread out from a building that rose like the bird's neck.

The motmots who flew by her, their bright plumage and beautiful tails catching the eyes of the blackwing arsonists spreading out through the fields below, also valued things that were pretty to look at. They nested by flowering trees. Their mating ritual saw them flying high, dropping petals, and then flying through them in an increasingly elaborate dance.

Seeing how the Reevesport opinici looked, their magnificent peafowl plumage, it would be natural to assume they felt the same way. But the truth wasn't in the gardens that looked beautiful from the sky, it was in the smaller, more personal ones. All the opinici here were beautiful, and so none stood out. But within those gardens were a mix of edible and fragrant plants, and *those* were how they expressed true beauty, through taste and smell.

Stripes ordered one of the motmots to watch for the commander's messenger, then she sliced through the paper walls and into the farthest building, the one that had stone walls to keep wild goliath birds from getting at the apples inside.

A peafowl rose, her feathers dyed black with red circles. Behind her were several assistants, all fairly young.

The berserker looked at Stripes. "I know why you have come. I won't let you burn this orchard. I will defend it with my life."

Stripes's escort bristled, their long beaks glistening. Though Stripes herself wasn't a great warrior, they were. And because they were immune to her poison, they could slide their beaks along her feathers until they glistened, lending them a bit of her toxicity.

She wasn't here to fight, however. "Good. Then try to stop the soldiers coming this way now. They're going to burn down every tree."

The peahen's eyes narrowed.

"If you can hold them off long enough, we'll help you cut as many clippings as possible in the short time we have, then send them with your assistants to hide in the hills. Plant them across every hidden grove you can find so they're not caught. That's the only hope for your apples."

She didn't know if the Reevesport opinicus would trust her or not. There was no reason to. But the peahen finally unfanned her tail.

"So be it." The berserker ordered her assistants to begin

getting the clippings, then she turned to Stripes. "When fifty pots have been hidden, come find me. I will not stop until you perform the killing blow, pitohui."

Grim.

Stripes fled into the fields, doing her best to help while also not appearing suspicious. The few times one of the blackwings looked down, she pretended to chase down and 'kill' an assistant. She was careful not to drip on him, urging him to lay prone until the scout passed overhead.

It worked pretty well. Though one of her motmots accidentally touched her glistening beak to a different gardener and had to quickly lead Stripes over to administer the antidote. They finished the fifty clippings and evacuated the orchard staff and their precious cargo. It was time to see what had happened to the berserker.

The peafowl was inside the main building, surrounded by blackwings. They were toying with her, or so they thought. She had a few superficial wounds, but she'd held them off long enough.

She caught Stripes's eyes and the pitohui nodded. The berserker suddenly rushed forwards, killing five of the soldiers before they realized what had happened. All the others quickly followed, not used to facing a foe with such long talons. She was closing in on the original messenger when Stripes caught her from behind.

The berserker slashed back with her shorter talons, driving them into Stripes's chest before the poison took hold.

The pitohui stood there, shocked, staring down at her own blood. She'd never been hurt like this before. She didn't know how serious the wound was and had no frame of reference to know if it were fatal or not.

The scout was stunned for a different reason. All his

soldiers had been killed by a single peahen. He looked down at the dead berserker's body, then up at Stripes and swore. "I'll... I'll get you a medic! I'm so sorry, I didn't realize you lot could be hurt. Thank you for saving me. Don't die!"

His eyes were mixed with both relief and fear. Relief that he'd survived, fear that if she didn't, Rybalt would hunt him down.

Stripes collapsed onto her side. Her motmots rushed in, reassuring her that the gardeners had escaped. To most opinici, their reaction would look cool and distant. These same four had stayed with her since Rybalt's initial arrest, tasting her food, fending off all manner of attacks by gryphons and opinici trying to get revenge on her brother by hurting her. She'd eventually traded in her small opinicus nest for one large enough to fit all five of them in it together when they wouldn't let her sleep alone.

So where most opinici heard indifference in the motmots' voices, Stripes saw the worry in their ears, watched their long, feathered tails twitch with agitation. She saw the way they kept extending their claws into the ground and knew that this was the most emotion they'd ever showed around her.

"Was it worth it?" one asked, trying to apply pressure to the wound. "Nearly dying for an apple?"

Stripes's beak shivered a little when she spoke. "I don't think she was trying to kill me, just... not to raise suspicions. I just..." she paused to gather her thoughts. "This is going to sound stupid, but I didn't realize it hurt so much to be stabbed."

"You'll get a pretty scar," a motmot said. "It should help you find a mate next season."

Not having four gryphons in my nest every night would do a lot more towards that goal.

"That a proposal?" she asked, trying not to think of how it felt like her insides were on fire. Her vision greyed as a medicine opinicus rushed in.

He looked from the glistening beaks of the motmots to the dead berserker to his patient. He must have been treating wounded soldiers all day because he didn't stop to consider the orange mixed in with her black plumage.

He reached out to touch the wound, then fell back, twitching.

The motmots looked at each other, then one used its long beak to grab the antidote off Stripes's harness. The vials weren't intended for gryphon use, and it was all Stripes could do to get the stopper out of it so her gryphons could help the doctor.

This is going to be a long night.

STRIPES WOKE up the next morning on her back, her wings spread out. It was her least favorite way to sleep. She shifted to adjust herself and felt an intense pain across her chest.

Oh, right.

She sighed, and one of the motmots sleeping around her perked up. "I can get you anything you need. You have been ordered to rest until midday, then catch up to the army."

"Am I safe to fly?" Stripes asked. The answer didn't reassure her.

"I do not think the blackwings care," another motmot said. "They just wish to keep you close so your brother will not betray them."

Stripes rested for as long as she was allowed, then ate. The medicine opinici had all followed the army west, along the coast, to clear out the fishing towns and boats. There were a few apprentices taking care of the worst of the wounded, and one came to check on her. Unlike his predecessor, he was much more careful about touch. Which was too bad because he was kind of cute, in a red-winged blackbird way.

"Let's get you on your feet," he suggested. When none of the motmots responded to his orders, mostly pretending not to hear him or increasing the volume of their fake snoring, Stripes cleared her throat.

"May I have a little help, please?" she asked. They grumbled but helped her right herself. "Am I safe to fly, Doc?"

The assistant shrugged. "War has its own rules. There's a large grain distribution center inland. You're expected by nightfall."

She grumbled but got moving. The apprentice gave her some medical supplies they'd found in the local hospital, along with directions on how to do her own stitches, and let them be.

"I do not like him," one of the motmots said. "He is not a good medicine opinicus. You shouldn't fly."

Stripes shrugged. "Great, so are you going to carry me, then? Is there a goliath bird fast enough to reach the distribution center in time? I don't think I have much of a choice."

Despite their grumbling, the motmots were, as always, happy to help her. It was strange. Among the entire northern forces marching with the blackwing commander, there were only these four gryphons, but they didn't seem to feel out of place. They seemed almost content here by her side.

Back home, motmots and pitohui were always arguing. It was the nature of things. The pitohui wished to develop the eyrie, build it out, create new fields. The motmots were trying to preserve the tropics and resisted encroachment.

Rybalt hadn't been as willing to listen to them as his sister was. Not that she thought her brother disliked the motmots. It was more that he saw himself as speaking for the entire island, the final word, where when he left Stripes in charge, she wanted to hear what everyone had to say. Unlike him, she never assumed she knew what was best for someone else.

Well, we'll be home soon enough, and I can go back to arguing with these motmots about trees again.

21

WHITEBEAK

Kia did not like the plan nearly as much as Zeph. She did not want to be part of the team breaking into Whitebeak. She'd already broken into the Whitebeak military outpost once in her life, and the first time had gone poorly. She'd ended up in a cage with Zeph, who had chatted the entire time, and only the arrival of Pip and Lei with a key from the nearby jail had let them escape.

At least this time, they'd be coming in under the fence. With so many crates piled up between the walls and the workshop, and with Mally across the world from them, the building should be easy to infiltrate and escape from. She and Zeph had been put in charge of finding the saltpeter. The others were searching for large quantities of something even rarer this close to the desert.

"Ice," Slate explained. "We're going to need a massive amount of ice to survive in the forbidden caves. Normally, it kills a gryphon dead in five minutes. We need more time than that to cross safely and blow the door on the other side."

Kia shook her head. She understood they couldn't take the normal routes through the blackness with the darkstalker plotting against them, but this seemed extreme. "Does that give us enough ice to retreat if something goes wrong?"

Chert's black eyes were unreadable, but her tail swished back and forth. "We'll see what we find, but I doubt it. Whoever goes in there and explodes the door, the others need to be right behind them. You can't really keep ice cold for that long. This is going to be a mad dash."

Below them, the Silkmouth Pride had closed as many tunnels as they could to slow down the darkstalker and waited to open the door into the burning depths. Once they heard the plan, Silky had ordered them not to carry more than two sentimental items, no food or water. "No extra weight. We'll drink the ice if we need to."

The silkmouths created a hideaway for the things left behind, including the weald's gifts to the naze. The scholars took a moment to explain about the red fern seeds in case they didn't come back this way, so the knowledge could spread among the cave gryphons.

While Zeph was overly enthusiastic about infiltrating Whitebeak and running through a fire cave, he did have one fashion-based complaint: he didn't want to leave his hat behind. Cherine was trying to talk him out of keeping it. Zeph made the case that not only would it serve as an excellent disguise in case he needed to impersonate an opinicus, but the merchant who sold it to him had promised the hats were all the rage at Duckbill.

"If we end up at Duckbill and we need you to impersonate an opinicus, things have already gone horribly awry," Cherine countered.

Zeph clutched his blue feathered hat. "Have we ever had a plan that went perfectly?"

Kia did not find out whether Zeph was allowed to keep his headwear. She half-expected her copper hawk friend to wear it into battle against the Seraph King himself in the days to come.

With the preparations finalized, they waited until nightfall, then Chert led Kia through a maze of wagons and crates to the workshop and squeezed both of them behind a box. The Redwood scholar worked the door open while the cave gryphon listened for hostile echolocation.

It'd be just our luck to break into the workshop and find all three darkstalkers there.

While Chert's plumage blended into crates, stone, and dirt as well as it had the cave walls, Kia's bright green, blue, and red coloring left her vulnerable. She could hear the goliath birds nearby, the sounds of patrols circling the city, and the clanking of someone's poorly fitted metal armor as they made the rounds.

The Ashen Weald had been collecting keys, and they'd gifted her one of each they'd found. When the one she'd used to escape Whitebeak the first time failed, she wasn't too concerned. She figured they'd change their locks sooner or later. When she made it through the entire keyring without hope, she realized she was going to have to pick the lock.

Thank goodness Orlea was willing to teach me how to do this.

While the ruler of the ruins of the Redwood Valley Eyrie had taught Kia these skills in case they needed to rescue Foultner, a lock was a lock. Following the ex-poacher's advice, Kia had left one talon a little long. She grabbed some quill pens and bits of metal and got to work. The Alabaster Eyrie made better locks than the Redwood Valley ever had, but she thought she was getting the hang of it.

Then Chert gave the signal to hide.

Kia slipped into the bottom box of a pile as the alabaster opinicus in his clanking armor came by. He stared at the crates, sensing something was awry, while the Redwood Valley scholar held her breath.

"I know you're there," the patrol said. Kia assumed that if he knew someone was there, he wouldn't have called out. Still, he took a few steps in her direction, and she wondered if the other cave gryphons could hide in time without her being able to warn them.

The guard was nearly upon her. "Go ahead and show yourself!"

To Kia's surprise, she heard a familiar voice above her.

"How'd he spot us?" the cool voice of a gryphon asked.

The reply was smooth with a slight rasp to it. "My dear Iony, even a bad guard gets lucky once in a while."

As the guard reached for Kia's crate, Rybalt Reevesbane pounced from above, killing the unfortunate opinicus. "I suppose we'll never know the answer now. They've filled the outpost with empty boxes and left the wagons full of food and supplies outside. I think they're just asking us to bomb the city. Let's go."

Kia decided to gamble and whispered through the slats in her crate. "Reeve Rybalt, a word, please."

Iony's grey owl face pressed up against the box. His sunburn was visible beneath his light plumage. "Must be a reunion tour. You're one of the reds, aren't you?"

Rybalt made his way around the box. "My dear Kia Reevesbane, how have you been since the swamp? And why do you smell like a spelunker?"

Kia resisted the urge to look at Chert, who remained hidden. "You said you're bombing this town. I need an hour to clean out Mally's workshop."

"Is that so? What do you hope to find in there?" the pitohui reeve asked. "More of our purple salts?"

All around her, the shadows churned as orange and black opinici crawled out of the mountain of discarded crates.

There was only one place to hide in Whitebeak, and we all hid in it.

She shook her head. "No, those will be long gone. But my brother's blood is here in the cold room. I need it for my work on a cure."

It wasn't the whole truth, nor was it entirely a lie. It was a mixture of half-truth and prayer. The Bane of the Crackling Sea Reeve and so many others moved closer to her, glistening with poison in the slight light of the braziers around the camp. She needn't have worried, however, as Iony was here with him.

"Rybalt," the glacier pride leader said. "Give her the time. It's not just her brother who will be helped by this."

The reeve paused, withdrawing a little with a bow. "You have one hour, Bane of the Red Reeve. Use it wisely."

Before they left, Kia offered one last piece of information in exchange for this boon. "Mally created three more with his black eyes and echolocation. Darkstalkers, they're called. They can see you even if there's no light. There's one based in this city. I don't know where the other two are at, but... be careful. If he'd been here, he'd have spotted both of us via sound."

"Hmm," was all Rybalt said, but Iony inclined his head in a bow. She could see Chert bristling, but she didn't think there was harm in letting them know. It wasn't like she'd told him where Mally had gotten his black eyes from, and for once, Kia actually wanted Rybalt to succeed at his goal.

She turned to go back to working on the lock and found a glistening key on the ground, left by one of the pitohui. She pulled a torn rag off a crate, wrapping it around the key several times since she had no antitoxin, and put it in the lock.

The workshop door swung open.

Chert gave the signal. Zeph and the other cave gryphons followed her path through the maze of crates around the abandoned Whitebeak workshop, slipping through the open door. Inside, the walls were lined with books. One passage led up, another down.

Down to where Olan was experimented on.

She longed to see it, however painful it might be, but that was for the cave gryphons. There'd be ice there to preserve the blood, and she'd swing by later to grab some of the vials. She went upstairs with Zeph, trusting his blue eyes in the darkness.

In a sense, finding the upper quarters lit would have been better. A burning lantern would have let them know that if anyone was up here, they weren't one of the darkstalkers. Without any light, they had no such certainties.

"It's better to know," Zeph whispered as he led them into the domicile. There were empty bunks in long rows, all formerly occupied by Mally's followers. Down at the back was a thick curtain, heavy enough to block out light. They crawled past rows of beds, Kia careful not to click her talons against the stone floor.

Except for her makeshift lockpick, she kept her other talons dull. It was a hard decision. What it had come down to was this: she was a mediocre fighter compared to the gryphons, but she could work a lot of opinicus tools they couldn't if her talons didn't get in the way. Orlea had offered her a pair of metal talons after the wingtorn all had their own prosthetics, but Kia had declined. That just wasn't her way.

She pulled the curtain aside, and Zeph sprang through the door.

"It's empty." He sounded disappointed. "But there're nests here for three darkstalkers. And they've gone to great lengths to keep it dark here. Their only lamp is covered in cloth."

"Let's steal it." Kia reached in to take the lamp from Zeph, then lit it, peeling off the dark adhesive dampening the light. The scent was uncomfortable, but she couldn't quite place it.

Zeph could. "It's... the oil cave gryphons have in their fur. How did they get so much of it?"

"Poachers," she mused. "The darkstalkers are... poachers, but not for animals. They were collecting the silkmouths to use the silk the way we sometimes steal nests from swiftlets. They must have been using the cave gryphons for oil. That's why their lamps smell so strange."

Zeph looked as disgusted as she felt. Neither were under any illusions that the cave gryphons who 'donated' their oil had survived the process. All of the sudden, their strong feelings about lamps made a lot more sense.

Kia and Zeph searched the rest of the upper floors but didn't find anything of interest. They brought the lamp downstairs, earning some ghastly looks, but explained they were still trying to find the saltpeter.

The cave gryphons, both oilbird and swiftlet, formed two lines coming in and out of the ice room. Inside, Cherine chopped the ice into pieces, making it easy to move.

Kia slipped past him, making her way into a room full of animal pens and the scent of blood. She read through an abandoned logbook, finding her brother listed as Subject 429-7341.

"Not here," Zeph said. "They wouldn't want explosives near their test subjects."

They turned back down another corridor, entering a fancy, well-stocked study. Considering the entire workshop was full of books, that was saying something. Rare volumes of a dozen varieties filled the shelves, and Kia desperately wished she could take them all.

She found a list of supplies and went through it, searching for saltpeter.

Zeph sniffed at the paintings on the wall. "There's something wrong here. I smell caves."

He nuzzled his way around the edges, peeling them back to reveal passages into the darkness.

"This must be how the darkstalkers are getting around." Kia located the saltpeter and tossed it in her harness. It wasn't much, but she didn't want to cause a cave-in. Assuming the door at the far side was as Slate had described it, this would be enough. "We should leave them a parting gift."

They reached the line of gryphons coming in and out of the workshop and redirected a few of the stickier swiftlets. From the cave side, it would look like the usual back of the painting. But from the workshop side, three silkmouths slathered the walls with gooey strands to form a saliva barrier.

"Think it's enough?" Kia grabbed the vials of blood labelled 429-7341 before following her cave gryphon allies as they evacuated into their own tunnels before the ice melted.

Slate nodded. "No way to know for sure, but caves are a

dangerous place. If they're expecting safety and find their escape sealed off, sometimes that's enough to get someone killed. Here's hoping."

Caves are a dangerous place. It was true. And what came next might be the most dangerous leg of their trip yet.

22

THE FORBIDDEN CAVE

The plan was simple. Insane, yes, but simple. Zeph sat in front of an ominous seal made from stone and secured with swiftlet spit as a team of cave gryphons directed Cherine on how to burn away the webbing.

Carefully burn away the webbing. Meanwhile, the other Silkmouth Pride were using their own spit to wrap up gryphons and opinici in ice.

"This is very chilly," Zeph said. "I can't feel my undersides."

Silky looked at him, silk dripping from her beak as she spoke stickily. "Can you run okay?"

He went around in a circle a few times and shook his tail before nodding affirmative.

"Great, that's all you're going to need to do," she said.

The silk gryphons finished with the oilbirds and wealders, then got themselves going. Once the seal had been weakened, they wrapped up Cherine, too.

Slate stood in front. "I'll lead the way. The two opinici will set the charges, twenty second fuse, and blow the door. At that point, it's a mad rush. Get through, get safe, and make room for those behind you."

"The old maps say there's a well the miner's left on the other side," Chert added. "Do not, *do not,* go straight into it. If your body temperature drops that quickly, your heart will stop. You will die."

Slate nodded his approval. "That's a good point. We're all going to be miserable. It's going to take us a few days to recover. Just assume we're spending all night lying down. I've got a little food to tide us over until we're strong enough to hunt. And we've got the ice for water. It'll heat up to a safe level, but don't drink too fast. Sip, don't gulp."

Silky nodded to her pridemates pushing against the door, which radiated heat. "We're coming in last and fast, and we're bringing this door with us to seal the other side once we're through. We're going to have to close it behind us. Just remember, once you hear the explosion, it's time to go. Be quick, but be careful, too. We don't want anyone dying of heat exhaustion. Good?"

"I like it when we have a good plan and it comes together without any problems," Zeph said. "It makes even the craziest things seem really easy and possible."

Kia and Cherine shared a look that suggested they did not feel the same way as Zeph. Possibly because he was just support and they were going to have to blow things up.

Chert's ears twitched, and she kept looking behind them. Zeph followed her gaze but didn't see anything. She opened her beak as if to ask a question, then reconsidered. Zeph could feel his own ears tingling now, and her hackles were up. She started to issue a warning, but it was too late.

Silky and Chert pulled off the door, and even here in the

corridor, it felt like Zeph had stuck his head too close to a bonfire.

They'd all decided that it was better to have the light, so a few gryphons held braziers in their mouths, illuminating the inside of the forbidden caves. They were long and tall, and there was no visible stone. Every surface inside was made of white crystal larger than many opinicus pillars Zeph had seen in his time.

They scrabbled for purchase on the crystal, and several times, it seemed like a gryphon was about to fall to their death before a quick beating of wings or help from others saved them.

Zeph's instinct was to latch his claws into the ground, but that didn't work with the crystal. Some of it was softer than others, but he got the best grip by just using his paw pads.

The temperatures were unlike anything he'd ever experienced. It was hotter than the hottest day of summer. It was a heat he hadn't known existed, and the ice felt woefully inadequate. He wished they'd dunked him in a giant pit of water, flash froze him, and slid his ice cube through this tunnel.

It had been minutes, and he was already feeling sick. He turned to look back, putting a little room between him and the opinici holding the saltpeter, and he saw that the others weren't waiting for the sign. They were rushing forwards.

Chert shouted in oilbird, and Slate translated. "She says the darkstalker caught up to us. He's afraid of the cave, so they're coming in fast. Just stick to the plan, we're going to be fine."

Silky and another gryphon held the seal on their backs, secured to the makeshift ice harness with extra silk. They were the last ones inside, and an alabaster opinici leapt after them, landing on the seal.

To their credit, they didn't lose their footing with the extra weight on top of them. The alabaster opinicus was pulled deeper into the forbidden caves and panicked. His armor scalded his skin, and he flung it off. He tried to fly back to the entrance, but he was already wobbling and hit a crystal, collapsing.

Two of his friends came in after him, barely managing to grab his body before the heat overwhelmed them.

The darkstalker stood at the cavern entrance. The distortions from the heat made his face look like it was melting even more than before.

"Boom!" Cherine said. "Or whatever you say when you light a fu—"

The explosion was bigger than expected, and while the mine door shattered into rocky pieces, the cave gryphons were flung off their paws. Zeph leapt down after Silky, catching her before he landed on a blade-shaped slice of crystal. He helped with the door, and took one look back, seeing the darkstalker coming after them.

Slate helped everyone through the far side of the passage. Gryphons were passed out everywhere. Kia was gasping, and Cherine lay limp. One of the silkmouths crawled towards the sound of water, but Chert grabbed his paw and held him back.

"It's death," she whispered.

Zeph and Silky pulled the seal in, and using pieces of the mine door, the silkmouths began fixing it in place. Their thick, sealant-like goo dripped from their beaks like spit, too hot to seal. And for a minute, Zeph didn't think it would work.

He tried to crawl away from the heat, but his paws had lost their strength. Then, the heat lessened, and it seemed the silkies had managed to seal one side.

A moment later, the temperature reached what it had been on the other side before they opened the passage. He still felt like he was going to die, but it would be a slightly cooler death.

"Puncture... the silk... drink... a little... of the hot... water..." Chert said between gasps, but Zeph didn't have the strength.

Kia used her hooked parrot beak to do it for him, and he held his face against the water.

"Thank you. You've saved me," he gasped.

Kia tried to laugh, but it was a dry sound, and there were tears coming down her eyes. He reached up and realized he was doing the same thing. They all were.

The seal pounded, and the silkmouths desperately crawled to double the sealant. On the other side of the door that, if opened, would kill them all, there were opinici pounding for their lives.

The sound lessened. Then stopped.

"The darkstalker," was all Chert could say.

There were still two left, but it seemed they'd killed this one. Zeph didn't know how he felt. Every part of his being had wanted to open that door and let them through, even knowing the heat would finish him off.

Yet no part of his body was capable of moving. He tried to keep sipping as Kia helped him puncture more of the silk-sealed ice, now hot water, so he didn't dry out.

Eventually, however, he felt himself losing consciousness.

We made it to the Argent Heights. We're so close.

He whispered a small prayer that he would open his eyes again and this wasn't the end.

23

BEES

Word that the king had sent out three of his darkstalkers was both good and bad, to Rybalt's thinking. Good because if there were only three left, the Abyssal Naze had been effective at thinning the enemy's numbers. Bad because they complicated his own plans.

Hunting an opponent with impressive night vision and echolocation was a tricky proposition. There was nowhere Rybalt could hide where the creature couldn't find him. And once alerted to Rybalt's presence, it would flee and return with an army.

Before the salts were gone, the Nighthaunt had been freer with his darkstalkers, sending them across the world to serve as his assassins. In a sense, Rybalt had a kind of professional relationship with his colleagues from across the desert. He respected their capabilities, and they respected his.

Respect between assassins was measured in how many contingency plans Rybalt created before they next crossed paths.

After Crestfall, the few remaining darkstalkers had been withdrawn. Or, if not withdrawn, moved out of reach of the Reevesbane's talons. He'd long suspected there had been one hiding around the Crackling Sea to help minimize deaths from owl gryphons. Though once the taiga gryphons' eyes turned blue, the smart thing would have been to evacuate the darkstalker north.

Night vision is much more useful when a large number of your enemies don't share it.

Kia's intel suggested the king was using them defensively now. If Rybalt were in charge of managing the darkstalkers, he knew where he'd place them. He'd keep one close at all times. He now knew they'd sent one to clear out the cave gryphons, probably thinning out all gryphon prides along the plains. But that third darkstalker would need to be guarding the supply lines.

Hence his current plan. While he and Iony chatted and ate, he'd set a very peculiar kind of trap.

Not far away, there was an abandoned mining camp. Inside it were two motmots who could manage a fairly reasonable Argent Heights accent. They sat in the dark, their paws hidden under a blanket, and followed a long script Rybalt had written himself. In it, they talked about a rebellion within the enemy's ranks. They talked about certain opinici under Reeve Silver who would lead the rebellion.

It was all nonsense, of course. But they'd been ordered to sit and read the script to each other all night, every night, for the past few days. The information was vague enough Rybalt hoped it would attract the attention of a lone darkstalker and not, say, a small army. So far, it had not borne fruit, but he was a patient opinicus.

Iony, however, was not a patient gryphon. "Why are there

so many bees? I can't sleep anywhere during the day with all of that buzzing about."

"It's a forest, Iony." Rybalt sighed. "There are going to be bugs. Just be grateful they sleep at night."

The glacier gryphon's unhappiness was visible on his face, and the rest of him. Shaved, sunburnt, slightly singed from saltpeter. He wasn't a happy gryphon. Bees were just the latest problem.

They sat in silence, waiting for word on their trap. Or Rybalt sat in silence. Iony continued complaining.

"Here's what I don't get," his sunburned ears wobbled when he talked. "The buzzing is enough to send any of us running for the hills. Why bother stinging?"

"Professional pride?" Rybalt ventured. "Dedication to their craft?"

The gryphon guffawed. "But it kills them! The queen sends them out to die, and they do it willingly. You can bet I'd reconsider my line of work if the reeve ordered us to die."

There was no need for Rybalt to ask which reeve. *The reeve* always referred to the Blackwing Eyrie's master. Despite the council, he was always there, pulling the strings. Only survival held the alliance together. Even then, Rybalt wasn't entirely certain they *hadn't* been sent to their deaths.

He sighed. "Bees don't know they're going to die when they sting you."

"Can't they see their dead friends, guts ripped out, stingers still pumping venom into me?" Iony groused.

"That's the thing," Rybalt said, "bees don't normally die when they sting something. It's only the thick hide of an opinicus or gryphon that catches their stinger. So when the queen orders them to go out and attack, they believe they're going to survive. They don't know we're fatal to them."

That quieted Iony's complaining. "Huh. Never knew that about bees."

They sat in silence until well past the middle of the night when a scout appeared. "Reeve Rybalt, there's… something in the mine."

THE REEVESBANE casually walked into the long chamber leading to his two loquacious pieces of bait. They waited for the trap to be cleared out before exiting.

Inside was a lone white opinicus twitching on the ground. The entire floor in this section had been filled with nettles of the type that grew near mountain towns. The sorts whose long needles became lodged in opinicus talons and paws.

This particular crop of deadly flora had been picked by Rybalt himself, coated in his poison, then placed down after the motmot bait was in place. It was a nice trap if he said so himself.

"Ah, hello, Tinkt," Rybalt said to the darkstalker. "It's been a long time since we last met, hasn't it? I didn't realize you were one of the darkstalkers. I'd have killed you earlier."

Despite the large number of nettles sticking out of his skin, 'Tinkt' wasn't dead yet. It was a surprising development, and Rybalt relished in it.

He ordered several of his pitohui to clear out the nettles and escort the two gryphon actors from their den at the end of the cave to safety while Rybalt lit a lantern and chatted with his old colleague.

"I always wondered, do you lot volunteer for your black eyes, or were you ordered?" He pulled out a journal and flipped through the pages. Many of the names were crossed out. Some in red, indicating he'd personally killed them, others in black, killed by circumstance, fate, or another's talons. "I'm very excited I get to cross your name off myself."

The opinicus, white with dripping black marks, stared up at Rybalt. It was hard to read black eyes, but there was a spark of something in them.

"Oh dear, that vitriol. Do you mean to say they were punishment from the last time we met?" The Reevesbane shook a bottle of ink to stir up the particulates, then looked for his favorite feather pen. He was going to savor this moment. "Ah yes, I see my talon marks on your face now. I suppose old Mally offered to fix you right up and got creative with the cure. Well, all's well that ends well."

The white opinicus continued twitching, resisting death, glaring up at his assassin.

"What do you mean, it's not well?" Rybalt laughed. "My dear friend! You got your eye back, better than before. And I've always felt a pang of guilt for not murdering you that day. So now I get to rectify that. You have your sight. I can cross your name off the list. It's a reason to celebrate for all sides."

The darkstalker remained in the throes of death while Rybalt watched. Assassinations were often such brief affairs. Even when he poisoned someone, he usually disappeared out the balcony before they passed. It was fascinating to see someone survive so long. Was his poison fading, or had Tinkt built up a resistance to it? Perhaps the desert crossing had affected him more than he realized.

"I must say, I expected you to have died by now. I even started crossing out your name." Rybalt had, in fact, already crossed off one of the entries that read *darkstalker*. He just hadn't managed to finish the word *Tinkt* yet. It was nice crossing off two names from one killing. "I should have brought snacks."

Iony appeared in the entrance to the cave a second later, looking for nettles, then came in holding a basket in his beak.

Rybalt thanked him, then waved him off. Iony didn't care much for murder. "That was sweet of him, don't you think? Ah, honey tarts! Delicious. Though I suppose this explains why we've made enemies of the bees."

The twitching grew less intense, though whether that meant the darkstalker was finally dying or recovering was still up in the air.

"When you put together your own assassin teams, do you include one opinicus who can cook?" Rybalt asked. "Because my cook is an excellent assassin but he's a killer chef."

He paused, then laughed. "I am so sorry the last words you hear will include puns. I'm usually more professional than that. This is just such an exciting moment for me. Would you like a taste?"

He drizzled honey on Tinkt's beak. The opinicus—*not dead, finally recovered*—slashed up with his claws at Rybalt's face.

Rybalt jerked his beak back, dropping the tart and splattering honey across the cave, then kicked with his back paw as hard as he could.

The metal talons he wore over his hind paws went up and under the darkstalker's ribs. Then Rybalt cut his neck, a strange moment of mercy considering the past few minutes.

"I'm glad you got that last bit of fight, Tinkt," he said. "We should all go out fighting."

He used the darkstalker's white fur to wipe off his back feet, then used straps of leather torn off Tinkt's harness to get the blood out from between the metal claws. Most opinici preferred having metal talons for their forelegs, and those could be useful. But when Didi reported that the metalworks in the weald was producing paw prosthetics for the declawed wingtorn, then metal paw weapons for the other gryphons, he knew he wanted a pair for himself.

She'd sent them as a parting gift, though they both knew Didi was only on break until Rybalt needed her services again. Until then, she was hiding out among the fisherfolk of Sandpiper's Dune, eating fish and looking for an ex-lover.

"Now, where was I? Oh, yes." He flipped back a few pages in his diary. Here, he had a page of opinici he hoped to someday kill but didn't expect he'd get the chance. He went past several names, including the reeve of King's Reach and the starling pridelord, past the Blackwing Eyrie reeve and even his own name, finding the one he was looking for.

With his red ink, he crossed the name *Tinkt* off his list.

Another day, another murder.

When Iony arrived later, Rybalt was just finishing the remains of the honey tart not covered in dirt or nettles.

"Ah, Iony!" Rybalt said. "Send in the cleanup crew, give my regards to the chef, and tell everyone the Argent Heights has been blinded. Er, deafened. Just in time, too. It's time to put our plan into motion."

Honey dripped from his beak when he grinned.

24

ARGENT HEIGHTS

Foultner and Henders led the goliath birds as they took piles of lumber away from the lumberjacks. A few nature scholars of some sort looked over the wood, searching for signs of bark beetle eggs. It didn't seem to matter if they found eggs or not, the lumber went into the fire afterwards, burned to a crisp, and then the ashes were disposed of in a large cavern.

Caverns of ash, under the ground, wasted trees.

It made Foultner sad. But what didn't make her sad was getting a break from the canals *and* getting to spend the evenings visiting the little mining towns sprinkled across the farmlands from the eyrie. That was fun, and it gave Henders a chance to do something other than talk about birds.

They finished up their work for the afternoon, took care of the goliaths, and used the last of the light to visit a new town. This one was fairly small. An elderly couple lived there, receiving supplies from the eyrie and keeping watch so no one wandered into the mines and died.

Foultner and Henders agreed to fly their dinner up to them, then sat around eating and hearing the old stories. There were paintings of crystals that looked impossible. A room made of crystal, pillars taller than an opinicus. It was amazing.

"Sadly, you can't go in there," one of the elderly couple said. "That room burns hotter than the hottest day in the summer. It eats away at your soul, wearing you to nothing. The old name for it was the Chamber of Hungry Crystals. Though, of course, scary names are just a fanciful way of keeping opinici out!"

"Not that it worked," the other half of the couple said. "It had the opposite effect, really. Every few years, someone manages to break the seal. Sometimes, they come crying to us, apologizing, and Reeve Silver sets them right. Other times, they go inside, and we only discover them after they've died."

Foultner shook her head. If there was one place even she wouldn't go, it was underground. Creepy crawlies, stories of cave gryphons, more creepy crawlies, possibly bats, and then death crystals?

No, thanks!

Henders, however, wanted to see the door to the Chamber of Hungry Crystals, so the elderly couple gave them a lantern and showed them the two-bead tour.

A mine shaft looked like, well, a mine shaft. It was boring. There was a route they used for tourists and fledglings, and Henders was delighted to follow it. They were even happy to lead them down to the seal, though something surprising waited for them.

"Oh dear," the elderly matron said. "There's some kind of build-up on the barrier here."

"Hmmm," her mate responded. "Cave silk. Haven't seen its

like in years. Weird to have it build up so thick around the heat. Maybe the sealant had failed. If so, the goo kept us all safe. I'll send word to the reeve to come fix it."

They went upstairs for Foultner's favorite part, rock candy, and then said their goodbyes, leaving the elderly couple. Foultner was just about to fly back to the eyrie when she heard a rustling in the trees around the mine.

Another opinicus might have investigated, but not Foultner. She got out of there, taking to the sky.

Not today, weird cave beast!

Unfortunately, Henders stayed on the ground, forcing her to come back for him. When she landed, he was talking to a hole in the ground.

"Foult! You're back," he said. "It's Zeph."

Of course it's Zeph. Was it too much to hope for Blinky?

"And Cherine!" came a voice from in the hole.

Another chimed in with, "And Kia!"

Foultner sighed. "Well, it's about time you came to rescue us. I have a ton of information that needs to go east. Does this hole of yours go back to the Ashen Weald? What's going on there, anyways?"

Zeph crawled out of the hole, startling her with his bright blue eyes. "Actually, we're going west. Things aren't so great back home. The Seraph King took the Crackling Sea Eyrie. He's ignoring the weald and bog for now, but his armies are marching north. And... more bad news, we're not here for you, or to go back east."

"We heard you and Henders making noise in the cave and came to investigate." Kia poked her head out of the hole. "We're heading west, to the Abyssal Naze, to meet with the cave gryphons. We just, well, needed a favor and couldn't pass up a chance to say hello."

Henders was practically purring like a gryphon. "This is so fun. I wish we could show you where we're staying. It's nice! And warm. Oh! And Tilly is here, the goliath bird. Did you meet her? We're having a great time."

"Spying isn't easy, but we're doing our best. I guess it was too much to hope you were here for us." In truth, Foultner had hoped they'd brought assassins with them. For a moment, she saw a way out. Even now, she considered sending Henders with them, though that would probably clue in the king's forces. "Oh, in case there are more of you down there, mind the mountain east of here. It has the king's reserve army. They're just keeping it back in case they're attacked, the pink reeve runs into trouble from you lot, or the king comes under siege."

Zeph and Kia looked at each other. "That's good to know. And it might be a problem. Here's what we need from you, though: bark beetles."

Henders perked up again. "Oh! I can get you a lot of those!"

"Really?" Kia asked. "I thought this'd be more difficult. Well, that's... one problem solved. We need them in something that'll keep them alive while we transport them underground."

Henders stuck his head in the hole. "What's down there? Are there roads between eyries? What's the weirdest thing you've seen down there? Zeph, what's the most interesting bug you've eaten in a cave?"

"Hends, it's just a hole in the ground," Foultner began, but even in the starlight, she saw a dozen black shining eyes staring out at her. "Oh. Hi, uh, cave gryphons, I guess? Probably. Nice to meet you. You in the back with the light eyes, you've got something sticky on your face."

Hends reached into the group of cave gryphons to tap Cherine's face. "Your new beak looks great!"

"Look, we're in charge of dragging the lumber around." Foultner kept a tight grip on Henders's harness so he didn't fall in. "There's a huge fire pit, but the grass is pretty tall near it. 'Ol Sneaky Zeph can probably get close since everything is brown and dead. We'll put the lumber that doesn't seem to be crawling with beetles on the east side, the infested lumber on the west side. If we can find some containers, we'll leave them nearby. Just grab what you need, but be careful."

Henders stole hugs from Zeph and Kia. "You two smell really terrible, but it was good to see you. Did you know there's a huge cave full of death crystals near here? Oh, you did. Well... we'll catch up later, okay? After the war. Good luck with your bugs!"

Foultner shook her head. It was nice to have some real spycraft to do, but collecting bugs? Just what was the Ashen Weald playing at?

In the dark of the night, the cave gryphons flew to the next cave. The closer to the Abyssal Naze they neared, the cleaner and less interesting the caverns beneath the earth became. Some of that was simply a matter of safety. They may be close to the cave gryphon home, but they were also in the middle of territory owned by the Seraph King. It wasn't a good idea to build homes here.

Once the cave was determined to be uncompromised, Zeph and Cherine went out to collect the bugs. Kia was too bright and colorful, and while Cherine was tall and scholarly, his plumage didn't stand out in a field of grass.

"This is fun," Zeph said. "We don't get to do things together."

"Oh? I suppose that's true," Cherine replied. "We should do this more often. I guess I just get caught up with everything going on. The Darkfeather University is trying its hardest to find a cure to bloodbeak, but we're just spinning our wheels. I'm hoping we find a tome or something in Mally's old workshop that at least tells us what he's already tried."

"Mmm." Zeph crawled through the grass, towards the pile of lumber. He got a little too close, and a goliath began sniffing and honking in his direction, but a familiar voice calmed the bird down.

"Hey, be sweet, girl!" Henders said. "It's just grass. Yeah, you remember grass. Nothing to worry about."

Zeph chirped back, and Cherine crawled forwards after the goliaths had left. They found a little area where the bark beetles seemed to be pretty bad and grabbed what they could. Foultner had left a box of glass vials here. They were surprisingly large, and Cherine tried wrapping the tops with a piece of paper with a little hole poked in it to trap the beetles inside.

They chewed themselves free almost immediately, as paper wasn't much heartier than bark. Finally, he sacrificed his spare strips of leather, putting tiny holes in them, which successfully secured the vials. He included a bit of bark to help the beetles survive the trip, then they retreated back into the forest.

Kia was excited to see the bugs, sketching the adults and asking for a detailed description of the larvae. "Well, this'll be good to know if they show up in our section of the woods. It'd break my heart to burn down redwoods."

Zeph's hackles rose out of reflex, and Kia shook her head. "Sorry about that. I wasn't thinking."

"It's not you," Zeph reassured her. "It's just a touchy subject, I guess."

Chert poked her head out of the far end of the tunnel. "We're going to have to take another detour. We found a dead body near the entrance to the main tunnels. It might be the work of another darkstalker."

The three wealders shared a look, then packed away the bark beetles and mentally prepared themselves for another cavern of spikes, strange cave gryphon prides, or impassable crystal furnaces.

25

THE ABYSSAL NAZE

What awaited them, however, was none of those things. Zeph listened while the cave gryphons explained they'd just have to go over the land for a bit at night, then enter the Abyssal Naze the old-fashioned way. From the sky.

It sounded too good to be true, which was why he wasn't surprised when they listed off everything that could go wrong. Not that he was listening. Everything they were talking about was just the usual problems gryphons had in the air: large birds, opinici, wind currents, finding places to land and stay that wouldn't lead to attacks at night.

Oh, and wild animals. There were apparently some small variants of the goliath birds called cassowaries out here who had a nasty kick and liked to pick a fight. Well, that wasn't much of a problem for Zeph.

He looked back at the Argent Heights, wondering if Foultner and Henders were okay. Henders seemed happy, but that was his disposition. If everything went right, the king's forces would be in disarray, and Zeph could swing by and get Foultner and Henders on the way back.

Assuming there is a way back. I'm not going through the forbidden caves again.

The heat exhaustion stuck with him even now. He felt like part of his being had burned away, melted, and it would take some time to reform. But he was glad he'd gotten to see the crystal spires deep within the earth, something no other weald gryphon had seen. This was why he liked hanging around Kia and Cherine. They always found the wonders of the continent, the things he'd never have experienced if he'd stayed home.

Despite the grim purpose of their trip, Zeph felt surprisingly content. Happy. Good friends, exciting places to visit, a strong purpose, and new things to eat.

Well, I could use more cave bugs. How is it that I've crossed so much of the continent, and I haven't eaten any yet? Maybe when we reach the naze.

One of the oilbird gryphons let out its call, and it was time to go. It was hard to describe the cry of an oilbird. While they spoke common like an opinicus and chittered in a friendly way when speaking among themselves, their cry was like the sound of a monster deep beneath the earth that hungered for death and destruction.

That does explain why the myths about cave gryphons are so scary. But it's funny once you get to know them. They're so happy and friendly!

Chert kept close to Xin again in the air. Pink Paw's son was nervous about flying outside of the caverns, where the open air made him doubt his clicking. Chert, however, had given him back much of his confidence, and that made Zeph happy. He couldn't wait to see what kind of gryphon Xin grew into after he'd lived in the naze a few years. Hopefully, by then, the cave gryphons would have cleared out the darkstalkers so Xin could visit his family again.

They'd already killed one darkstalker. If Slate was right, there were only two left. If Zeph were the Seraph King, where would he want them? It was a tough question. He just didn't know enough.

Far below him, the maple forest gave way to new types of trees he hadn't seen before, wind-twisted things that perched on the spires of eroded limestone jutting out of the earth. The worn limestone sometimes made large spikes, sometimes blocky pillars, and sometimes small needle-like points.

Their journey, made only at night and with an abundance of caution, took a few days. When it was dark, they scouted, then flew from spire to spire, avoiding the forest floor. During the day, they napped, which Zeph was very good at.

His opinicus companions, however, were not. They spent too much time awake, cataloguing bugs and plants, and then they were tired when they flew at night. Zeph understood their sense of wonder. This was a new forest with new things to eat!

At the same time, there'd be plenty of time to eat bugs and plants on the way home. They had a set timetable, and they needed everything in place when the day came to release the starlings from their jungle.

The starlings here in the west, Rybalt's attack on the Argent Heights, and the Ashen Weald's attack on the Crackling Sea all needed to happen according to a time frame Satra and Rybalt had agreed upon. It was going to be close.

But if it works, the war could be over. Everything could go back to the way it was before the king marched on the Ashen Weald. In a month's time, I could be back home, hunting parrots and talking with friends, happy as an axolotl.

Zeph shook his head. There was a lot of work to do. It was nice to dream about a plan gone right, but plans were like floodwaters, they tended to get out of control quickly.

Especially around Triddle.

Chert detached herself from Xin's side, letting him glide on his own a little, and flew over to Zeph. "We're going to stop early tonight. The Abyssal Naze isn't far, but we haven't seen any scouts. We should have seen someone by now. One of the smaller nesting grounds was also empty, though there were no signs of a struggle."

Slate gave the order, and everyone flew towards a spire to rest while the oilbirds scouted on ahead.

WITH ZEPH'S BLUE EYES, he was allowed to join Slate and Chert as they searched the way ahead. The ground near the naze was interesting. According to the maps, there was a large lake somewhere north of them where Duckbill was located. Rybalt's secondpaw reports suggested the king's army was there, likely guarding the frozen seraph until the workshop was reclaimed. If they flew far enough west, they'd hit another ocean coast. And every so often, to the south, Zeph could see the various Emerald Jungle trees encroaching upon the rocky forest beneath them.

While the limestone spires were impressive, there was another reason he thought of it as a *rocky forest*. Though the tops of the trees resembled other forests he'd flown over, they were growing out of a crust of stone that sometimes collapsed. Every so often, he'd look down and see a stone hole in the ground with waterfalls disappearing into it. It made him wonder how often new holes opened, if the ground was hungry.

Slate led them south first, hugging the border with the starlings. That made sense to Zeph. If there was one place he'd normally keep far away from, it was the Emerald Jungle. He wasn't looking forward to sneaking in with the bark beetles to remove Reeve Silver's glyphs.

While the previous holes in the rocky forest had been large enough to swallow a nesting ground, Zeph's first distant glimpse of the Abyssal Naze looked like it could have eaten an entire eyrie. The ground had collapsed, creating a giant crater, and one side of it had a massive cave entrance. Rivers flowed into the crater from all directions, cascading over the walls and disappearing into the mists. The largest waterfall emerged from the mouth of the cave. It was a wondrous sight.

Just north of the naze, a stone opinicus building sat perched atop a high overlook where at some point the ground had crumbled away to form a sheer cliff. The design wasn't anything Zeph had seen before. They'd just taken white stone and built it up. His closest comparison would be the waystations along the mountain path between the old Redwood Valley Eyrie and the Crackling Sea.

Those had been built to withstand a rockslide. This one looked like it was designed to stand against... well, an army of cave gryphons.

"It's so close to your home," Zeph whispered to Slate. "How did they build it without you noticing?"

The cave leader snorted. "We did notice. My predecessor just didn't think anything of it. Something you're going to quickly learn if you keep travelling is that every pride has a blind spot. The fisherfolk think in terms of water rights. For opinici, they think in terms of eyries. You surface gryphons enjoy your trees and the area above ground."

"But for us, we kind of forgot about the surface," Chert continued for him. "It's a little fuzzy where our pride ends, but most of our caves go east of here. If someone wants to build a tiny nest on top of those cliffs, it doesn't really affect us. Or so we thought."

Zeph had heard the rest of the story on the way over. Once the opinici had a fortified location away from the prying eyes of other eyries, Mally had captured and experimented on cave gryphons, trying to unlock the secrets of the essential salts. His twisted form, both rotten seraph and cave gryphon, had come from here. As Slate had previously mentioned, the black eyes of the Nighthaunt and his darkstalkers had been stolen from Slate and his friends.

"How did you take the workshop the first time?" Zeph asked. "Does it have any weaknesses?"

"Sheer numbers," Slate said. "And we had a few ways in. Most they found during the fighting, but we still have one path just west that they never found. We attacked so fast they didn't have time to call for help."

Above the workshop, a patrol of alabaster opinici flew down. Their armor shone in the moonlight to Zeph's blue eyes. Where there was a break in the trees, he could see armored goliath birds patrolling a bridge leading to the ridge that housed the overlook and workshop.

"We're too late. The Seraph King's armies are already inside the workshop," Chert said. "There were barely enough cave prides to siege it when they *didn't* know we were coming. But just... look at all of that."

Zeph wasn't concerned. He and his opinicus companions had remained tight-beaked about their plan in case any of their escort were captured. Once they were inside the naze, they'd explain it to their allies. For now, all he said was, "When the time comes, we'll be able to match their forces."

"We should go," Chert warned. "There are too many scouts here. We're going to have to find a back way into the naze."

WITH THE SKIES over the Abyssal Naze controlled by the opinici, a new route was called for. Zeph listened intently while Slate told them where they were going.

"You know those holes in the ground full of water?" the oilbird asked. "Well, most of those eventually go through the naze. So we just hop in one of those."

"Sorry," Kia interrupted. "We're flying down over the water into the naze? There's enough room between the water and the rocky ceiling?"

"Not... over," Chert chirped. "We're definitely going to get wet. But if we find the right entrance, it shouldn't be more than a quick swim."

Silky nuzzled up to Kia. "Do you need me to seal your harness pouch so your paper doesn't get wet?"

"Er, yes, that would be good, thank you." The expression on Kia's face as Silky began chewing sticky silk all over her harness was not one of gratitude. Another of the silkmouths sealed up Cherine's pouch.

"This is useful," Cherine said. "I wonder if the university

would let me hire one of you as an assistant. Just think of the places we could go, Kia."

"The places we could go?" She shook her head. "We're there, Cherine. Look around us. These are the places we could go. Take good notes."

He reflexively reached for his pouch, stopping before touching the white goo. The black and white swiftlet gryphon looked up at him, her mouth dripping. "Oh, sorry. Carry on."

"There's probably air to breathe," Slate said, letting the word *probably* do a lot of work. "We might have to swim under a little, but it'll just be in short batches. How full of water the caves are depends on how the rains have been over the winter."

"Is there light?" Kia asked. "Or are we swimming in the darkness."

Chert looked at Slate, and they both shrugged. "This isn't how any of us usually goes home. In fact, it's strictly forbidden. We're just out of options. Maybe it's the alabaster opinici, but the other cave entrances along the way were sealed up. If you saw the little white glyphs on the trees, they're a warning."

"Is it more darkstalkers?" Zeph asked. "Or... do you think the opinici have already taken the naze?"

Slate didn't look worried. "Opinici fear the dark. The cave entrance is so large, they've tried to bomb it closed a few times without success. The rubble just gets washed down into the waterfall and swept away, and the entrance to our home grows. That's why their darkstalkers haunt the far tunnels. Even they fear the pitch black of the naze itself."

"I definitely share their fear of the dark," Cherine added. "And water. I'm not really good in underground water cave situations. I have a bit of a history."

It was Xin who wasn't willing to let Cherine off the hook. "You're going in there able to see. I'm not. And I don't know if clicking works underwater. You think you're scared? Sheesh. Think of how I feel."

The tall, golden opinicus reconsidered his stance. "I get what you're saying, but I think it's okay for anyone to be scared about doing something like this. Think of your dad, right? He's terrified of snakes, but that doesn't stop him from going out and helping your mom hunt sometimes, right?"

Xin nodded.

"Scared and brave aren't opposites. They're complements," Kia added. "It's okay to be frightened. I can't think of anything I've done that didn't start with me being terrified. That's just... how it is. Bravery is going forwards regardless of how, well, big the snake is."

Chert interrupted. "Can we stop saying snake? You're going to jinx us."

"Jinx us from what?" Zeph blinked.

He didn't get his answer, however, because Slate gave the word, and the oilbirds descended into the forest and crawled to the closest hole.

I really hope they didn't just pick one at random.

Unlike around the naze, there weren't waterfalls feeding into this hole. The ground just dropped fifty feet, and at the bottom, he could hear running water.

"Oh! That's fun," Cherine said. "There's two layers. Limestone, which the water can eat through, then a second type of rock it can't. Hence the weird underground rivers. Isn't that exciting?"

Zeph reserved his judgement until he actually got in there and saw what types of bugs there were to eat.

Silky went first, crawling to the edge, then slipping down.

Around three quarters of the way, she opened her wings and glided to a small ledge over the water and called back up. "The current is going this way, so I think we're good. Come on down!"

Chert and Xin followed, the oilbird guiding the magpie carefully to the entrance. His flying had greatly improved over the past few days, or perhaps the stone walls gave him a better feel for his surroundings, because he did a little twirl around Chert before landing perfectly.

"Xavi's going to be so proud of him," Kia said.

Zeph twitched his feathered tail in preparation for his own jump. "He already is. Pink Paw, too."

The copper hawk felt his stomach drop as he plunged towards rocks and icy water, then he opened his wings to glide over to Silky. Using the spikes on her tailfeathers to help her cling to the stony surface, she'd already created a few silk nests for gryphons to perch on since there wasn't enough space on the ledge for everyone. This way, they could rest before they went into the river. She worked much faster than the cave swiftlet birds in the weald, her silk drying in moments.

Once everyone was gathered just above the water's surface, Slate took the lead. He ordered Zeph to stay close just in case the light was minimal. Oilbird eyes were excellent at night, but they needed echolocation when the light was nearly gone, and no one seemed sure how well that was going to work for their current plan.

With two of Silky's friends holding him steady, Slate stuck his head under the rapids for a few moments to try echolocating, then the silkmouths pulled him up, and he shook off the water. "There's too much noise, too much moving water. I can't get a reading on it. It'll be calmer the farther we go."

One final check and a little extra silk on Kia's packs, and it was time for an exciting water adventure.

At least, that's what Zeph told himself. He kept casting glances at Chert, and she did *not* seem happy to be coming this way, leaving him to wonder what had been left out of their briefing.

26

HENDERS

Foultner sat alone in her room again, looking over her scant belongings. She had a knife, true, but she thought that would be too obvious. She needed a weapon that would be unexpected.

The barnacle scraper sat there, taking up her vision. She wasn't sure how to kill someone with a barnacle scraper. There was probably a way. Then again, would that point the talon of guilt at her? Did the opinici in King's Reach have barnacle scrapers?

She sighed. She'd come up here to spend an hour alone plotting, and she'd wasted all of it. She didn't know how to kill a reeve. She knew how to kill turkeys, but even then, not a specific turkey. She just used traps to lure them in, then checked the traps every day.

The silver eyrie was not particularly well-suited for traps. It was sparse. Everything here had a purpose, and Foultner was often clueless as to what that purpose was. It was hard to trap something if she couldn't tell what it was doing.

She reached up to the clay trinket hanging around her neck. Inside was the vial of pitohui antitoxin. Henders wore a matching vial. She figured they could claim it was each other's blood or something creepily romantic if it broke and someone noticed. That was the only way she knew to keep it on her.

There was a bit of a commotion in the hallway, and she'd left her door open, but she thought she heard the words "goliath bird." She packed away her things, then went to check on Henders.

Where the Crackling Sea Eyrie had balconies and open walkways that faced the sea, the Argent Heights only had a talonful of ways in and out. There were no storm curtains here to keep enemies and weather at bay. Instead, they used the mountain as their fortress. The only adornment visible from the outside was a massive bell that could be sounded in case of emergency.

She stretched and glided out to where Henders was supposed to be clearing trenches now that they were done with the bark beetles. No one was there, but she saw some blood along an old canal.

Well, that's not good.

Her first thought was that Henders might be hurt. She flew towards the ranch and saw that her guess had been incorrect. *Tilly* was lying there, scratching and biting at anyone who came near, nursing a broken leg. Some other opinici were working to get a rope around her beak while they tried to sedate her.

Nearby, Silver reassured Henders. Foultner slipped close enough to overhear them, but back enough that they didn't notice her yet.

"I promise we'll do everything we can to get her okay

again, Henders," the reeve was saying. Seeing the leader of an eyrie take an interest in a goliath bird was a strange sight. "We've got some of the best animal doctors living near here. They'll get her back on her feet again, I promise."

Henders sniffled. He did this thing where he didn't cry, but he clearly *wanted* to when something sad happened. It was a very different approach than the one Foultner took, which was to be angry in the moment, and then cry later when she was alone in her nest.

"Promise you won't put her down?" he said. It was a big request to make of a reeve.

One Silver had no problem making, apparently. "I promise. Now, I need to go send a messenger to fetch the doctor. Are you okay here?"

That was Foultner's cue. She rustled a little as though she'd just landed, drawing attention to herself behind them. "Hends! I saw what happened to Tilly. Are you okay? Is she going to be okay?"

Silver bowed out, and Foultner let Henders talk about all the good Silver had done. Foultner didn't really go in for jealousy, not on a personal level, and she was grateful that Silver had made him feel better.

Though that will make her even harder to kill with a barnacle scraper than she was before.

Foultner's jealousy was often on a societal level, instead. She'd resented the northern quarter. She resented reeves, or so she thought. It was surprisingly hard to resent Silver. She was just too nice, too disengaged.

Though disengagement is a kind of harm. She's sitting back here supplying the seraph king's armies with food, weapons, and reinforcements while they perform the real cruelty.

That strengthened Foultner's resolve, but only a little. In

her heart, she knew that if she were in the argent reeve's position, she'd do the same. Survive.

Once Henders was asleep—he'd insisted on staying with Tilly until the doctor took over—Foultner was able to slip away and get some food. She asked someone in the kitchen if the reeve was around, but Silver was only just arriving back from an issue over at the garrison. Apparently, she'd raided the Seraph King's reserve forces and stolen their goliath veterinarian, and whoever was in charge had taken umbrage at the fact.

The ex-poacher considered her options, then ordered two bowls of stew. She warmed them at the fire, passively listening to the chatter from the messengers. Thanks to Tilly's misstep, Foultner was finally getting to hear the gossip.

It was fairly boring, except for word that the king was ready for something called the ascension. It seemed silly to her, so she ignored it. Faith was something she'd never understood, and she didn't know enough about the king's religion to comment.

More interesting was the fact that there was a gap in the trade caravans coming down from the north. This happened from time to time and was nothing to worry about, the scouts said, except that this time, even their messengers hadn't arrived back. Both Hi-kun, the military commander of Whitebeak, and the peafowl reeve had been recalled west to aid the king. Silver hated dealing with their underlings, but enough days had passed that they were out of options, so the plan was to gather some soldiers from the garrison and head north in a few days to make sure the Padfoot Pride wasn't causing more issues.

Foultner put lids on both bowls of stew, tied a string between them slowly so she could absorb the gossip, and carried them in her beak. She'd never gone up to Reeve Silver's rooms before, but she knew they were near the bell tower, so she continued walking up ramps until she found a lone guard blocking the way to the highest hallway.

"Rancher Foultner, bringing Silver some food from the kitchen."

Shoot, should I have said Reeve Silver?

The guard didn't notice or didn't care. "That's sweet of you. Go right in. She just got back from bathing."

Foultner continued. The hallway had room for a large reeve family, but most of the doors had been boarded-up. In fact, when she went to the fancy door at the end of the hallway, the only one with a silver veneer on it and ornate decorations, no one answered.

She backtracked, finding one of the small bedrooms meant for a fledgling, and saw drops of water going into it. She knocked and Silver answered.

"Oh, is that food? You're a lifesaver," the reeve said.

That is literally the opposite of what I'm trying to be.

Foultner allowed herself to be guided inside. She'd brought two bowls on the hope that she could convince Silver to let her stay and eat.

As it happened, Silver just assumed Foultner would be eating and invited her in without any fuss. "Going to sit? There are some spare cushions behind you."

"Thanks, I was so busy with Henders, I forgot mine." That part was true. Foultner was terrible at remembering her cushion, and an eyrie of opinici carrying around pillows was hard to adjust to.

She settled in and took a few bites. "Thank you for taking care of Tilly."

"Tilly or Henders?" the reeve asked.

Foultner shrugged. "It's kind of the same thing. She was the first goliath bird that warmed up to him when we started, er, working at the ranch."

"I get it," Silver replied. "I took care of goliaths growing up. They're like pets. They're smart, and if they like you, they're really friendly. You get attached."

"We can pay for the cost," Foultner reassured her. They'd been saving money. They didn't really have anything to spend it on out here.

Silver laughed. "She's my bird, remember? That means I need to cover the vet costs. You tell Henders he can come visit her any time. This'll get him in."

The reeve fetched a small badge. It wasn't one meant to be worn on a harness, but it denoted someone on reeve's business. "Just tell him to bring it back once she's better. And hey, in the mean time, you can use it to bring up food here whenever you want. I'll let the guard know."

Foultner accepted it graciously, surprised at her good fortune. When she'd seen the guard, she'd assumed there was no way for her to come up here to kill the argent reeve. Now she'd been handed a pass that would grant her access anywhere.

All over a bowl of thick soup.

She took a look around the room. It was small for a reeve but still a comfortable size. A very fancy harness and crown sat in the corner, collecting dust. The outfit didn't look like it had been worn since the day Silver was made reeve. Nearby, several identical leather harnesses hung from pegs in the wall. Those had seen more use and were of a practical design. Bits of metal sat discarded on shelves.

"Hoping to find something to borrow?" Silver asked. "I'm afraid I'm hopeless when it comes to harnesses. I just wear whatever my guards set out when I'm in the field."

Foultner looked at the reeve and really took stock of what she was wearing in the privacy of her own chambers for the first time. The reeve's outfit was a mix of vibrant blue, lime green, and a shade of orange that looked like a greased pumpkin in the sun.

"That looks... comfortable," Foultner ventured. "I guess I never thought about what a reeve wears in the privacy of their own home."

Silver laughed. "It *is* comfortable. My ex made it. I guess I ended up liking the shirt more than her. This is my one act of rebellion against the kingdom. Within my chambers, not even the king can stop me from wearing whatever I want."

Foultner found herself laughing along, too. It was impossible not to like Silver. She was just too charming.

Oh depths, what if I walk in to assassinate her and she's wearing that outfit? You can't stab someone wearing that. That's... that must be an assassin faux pas.

Foultner put thoughts of murder from her mind, just enjoying the stew and chatting with a friend until it was time to return to the nest and check on Henders again.

Why does murder have to be so hard?

27

BLACKTALON

Blacktalon was less of an eyrie and more of a military outpost. It owed its existence to the founding of Whitebeak across the sands. In the early days, teams of blackwing and alabaster opinici would attempt to traverse the desert. Rarely, a small contingent of them reached the other side, dehydrated and near death. Then the opposing faction would capture them.

Unlike Whitebeak, Blacktalon also served as a base of operations to monitor the northern shores for invasion. Many scholars who looked at maps remarked upon how strange it was to have a city watching a body of water from far inland. None of them had experienced the storms off the northern blood coast and the toxic blooms of the algae there the way Khalim had.

He huddled in his wagon, trying to use his wing to shield Lei's eyes from the fighting. He'd heard through his contacts that the Blackwing Eyrie's forces were headed west. Iony had given him that information when they'd met.

What Iony had left out was that Blacktalon had been left woefully undefended. The soldiers inside the fortress fought their hardest, but they were quickly dispatched. The forces the pink reeve sent up from the Crackling Sea had expected a much larger fight. They'd expected to need to burn down the farms, starve the blackwings out. They'd expected this to be a long campaign.

Instead, it was over in a day. And while it was no consolation to the soldiers inside Blacktalon, it had spared the citizens and their fields from death.

When the screaming stopped, the leader of the king's forces called out for the supply lines to be moved forwards. "I'm not sure why we brought you lot. We now have farms to grow our food for us."

"If you trust them not to poison it," Khalim said. "You'd probably do best to let them feed themselves. At least that way, you know they're not going to put anything funny in the food. Safer if we stick to our supplies for now. That's why you brought us merchants, isn't it?"

"Mmmmm," the commander said. He seemed to be taking it under consideration. "That's a good point. That way, we're not worried about feeding prisoners."

There was little concern about opinici escaping to send word of the assault. They were in Blackwing Alliance lands now; it was a certainty their enemies would figure out the king's forces were here.

Khalim had spread rumors of the might of the Mothfeather Eyrie. While he was playing the part of salt trader, there was no reason he couldn't perform a bit of subterfuge. The commander ordered the defenses of Blacktalon rebuilt. Little did he know the Sleeping City posed no danger this time of year.

Khalim spread his lies for several reasons, but one was to give them a fighting chance. If the Blackwing Eyrie could hold the king back until spring, Mothfeather could be evacuated. Once the residents of the Sleeping City had entered their hibernation burrows, there was no way to easily relocate them. He owed Wendl that much. Coming back without her felt like a betrayal, though he knew she'd understand.

Where in the jungle are you now, Wendl? What are you doing with all those salts we gave you?

Lei handled the wagon, taking most of the supplies to the quiet front. Strange for a conflict between two large eyries, the victory had been complete. There were no pockets of soldiers attacking. Even the farmers had given up.

Once they arrived at Blacktalon's fortress, Khalim waited for another opportunity to speak to the commander alone, though it took an hour. "Commander, you know my orders. I need to set up in one of the northern farms and await word from my spies. Once they report in, I'll let you know about the enemy's forces."

"Excellent," the commander said. "I'll let everyone know that... Well, I'll tell them something. I'm not used to this espionage business."

Khalim bowed his head, then grabbed Lei and a smaller wagon to head north. He brought along as many supplies as he thought he could get away with, including salt. While it was still expensive, he didn't trust the commander not to salt the fields if he saw he had enough to pull it off. The farmers could use it for food preservation if they needed to.

"This is horrible," Lei said. "They didn't stand a chance. Is it true the king is unstoppable?"

Pip shook his head. "It's not like that. It's just that, in war, there are sacrifices, and this was one of them. We're lucky it didn't become a siege. The opinici here will suffer less than others. The inhabitants of the Blackwing Eyrie won't fare nearly so well if the king reaches their terraces."

The wagon went past the carnage, onto old roads no longer familiar to him. He noted the names of the farms, hoping to spot some he recognized.

Not that I'm going to be familiar to any of them.

It appeared some of his siblings had formed their own farms, and he wished them well. He couldn't reveal his identity to them. They'd never believe, and he'd never been close enough to them to persuade them of the impossible.

Instead, he was saving his energy for Vilessa and his son. If he could convince her to let him stay there, he could use his cover story to keep the blackwings from hurting them. He had to trust.

The journey by wagon was longer than he expected. Frightened farmers watched him from their homes. They saw his plumage, saw Lei's plumage, and didn't know what they were up to. Had this been a normal battle, there'd be teams of soldiers attacking the supply lines. He prayed the farmers didn't take it upon themselves to do the same.

When they finally reached his childhood farm, no one was there. He looked out at the fields, scant because it was winter, and searched for the capybaras and goliaths.

He heard a *mronk* from the forest. "They must have released the livestock so the soldiers didn't get them. That's smart thinking. Though it's tough to wrangle capys back into their pens."

Lei remained silent and wide-eyed. Khalim wished there was something he could say to the wayward opinicus, but he suspected his young charge still needed time to process the revelations about his father.

Khalim opened the door to the main building. "Hello? Is anyone home?"

Because so many families lived together and worked the same land, the buildings were many stories high and had several different nesting areas. Everyone wanted their own privacy. There was still a main, open area in the center so opinici could fly down and eat together. Only the bedrooms were really private.

No response came. Khalim tried again. "Hello? We mean you no harm. We've brought supplies."

Nothing.

He asked Lei to carefully check upstairs as the doors were open. That wasn't unusual during the day, and hopefully, it'd let Lei see down to the nests.

Khalim went into the kitchen. There was still food, enough to last the winter. There used to be a storage cellar here somewhere. *Storage cellars aren't the sort of thing you can just misplace.*

He rifled through the crates, trying to remember where it was. The heaviest boxes had been piled in the corner, which made sense if someone were trying to keep something beneath them hidden.

He pushed the boxes aside, removed several rugs, and found himself staring at the entrance to the old cellar.

He took a deep breath, tried to think of everything he wanted to tell his mate, and opened it.

Lei poked around the upstairs nests. None of this had seemed real until a day ago, when they reached the first of the farms south of Blacktalon. It had felt like a small journey, like they were really salt traders. Now, he was overcome with anxiety. They were part of the war.

He moved from room to room. No living quarters had just one nest. It appeared everyone here had a mate or was young and living with their siblings. He'd never really given much thought to farm life, though he saw his privilege reflected back at him. He'd had a room to himself at the Redwood Valley Eyrie. Only during his mom's more paranoid episodes would she force them to stay together under guard.

He looked at paintings hanging from the walls. Or, in one common area down a nesting wing, someone had painted flowers *on* the wall itself. He smiled. That was nice. He should do that in his fisherfolk hut back home.

Back home.

It was weird to think of the islands as his home. He'd lived on several now, and while he didn't feel strongly that Luminaire was better than Ashfoot or The Wrecks, he felt at peace on all of them.

"I should really settle down," he mumbled. "Find a mate and a place to live, paint on the walls."

Creaking came from another floor, and his hackles rose. He slipped across the common area, wishing his wings were quieter and his train of tailfeathers less wide. He listened, and he thought he heard a scratching sound down the hallway, just out of sight.

Oh, a squirrel then, probably.

He relaxed but took the time to explore this section of the building. The first room he checked, a rare single-nest room, had all sorts of interesting designs woven into the cloth dividers. There was also a pile of books about culture, religion, and everything Piprik had taught Lei.

He opened one and saw why that was. Inside the book

was a place for each new scholar to list their name. These had been Khalim's books from university. Beneath Khalim's name was one other, Lemmy.

I guess that's his son's name. He never said.

The peafowl continued down the hallway, seeing the fuzzy rear end of a capybara sticking out from behind a nest. It was nibbling on some snacks.

"Capybaras are the same wherever you go," he grumbled. "Let's get you back in the pen."

He walked inside the room and was shoved into the wall. He let out a scream, then ducked as a large book crashed into the place his head had just been located.

"Stop! I'm not your enemy!" he said, but his assailant looked as terrified as he was.

The blackwing's talons were dull, his book expended, but he was looking for anything to use as a weapon.

Just as his opponent's talons grasped a particularly heavy gemstone, Lei shouted, "Khalim sent me!"

The blackwing, not much older than Lei, looked stunned. "What? What did you say?"

Lei looked at the book on the ground. It was about pitohui grapplers and how religion informed their style of combat. "Your father sent me. He's downstairs."

The blackwing hesitated. "My father is dead. I'm not going to let a Reevesport opinicus lie to me."

Before he could grab his rock again, shouting came from downstairs, followed by alarmed yelling. Lei and the young blackwing rushed to the common area where another blackwing opinicus screamed and slashed at Khalim.

"Stop!" Lei shouted, leaping down to try to fend off the angry opinicus. "Khalim didn't mean any harm!"

The new blackwing, her harness suggesting a medicine opinicus by trade, stared at Lei. "What did you call him?"

"It's me, Vilessa," Khalim said. "That's what I'm trying to tell you!"

"I didn't marry an alabaster opinicus," she retorted. "Why tell such a poor lie?"

Khalim leaned back on his haunches and held his talons up to show he had no weapon, then very slowly opened his harness and pulled out several artifacts, including his old eyrie badge.

"How do you have my mate's things?" she asked. "What happened to Khalim?"

Khalim sighed. "It's… a long story."

While Vilessa tested Khalim's knowledge, shouted at him, cried, demanded to know why he hadn't come home earlier, and everything else under the sun, Lei sat upstairs with his son.

"That story is crazy," Lemmy said. "Why would you two think we'd believe it?"

Lei pulled out a salted fish bar and offered it to the blackwing. "Because it's true. I didn't really believe it, either, until we saw Mally the Nighthaunt. That's when I realized everything must be true."

"You met the Nighthaunt? Who are you?" the son asked.

Lei considered relaying his entire history but wondered if that was wise. There'd be time to tell the long version later. "Just an orphan who was saved from the starlings and wound up in a fishing village. Your father has been tutoring me."

The son shook his head. "How does a Reevesport opi end up near the Emerald Jungle?"

Lei pulled out a spare feather he kept around for imping,

one of his old plumage. "I'm dyed blue to fit in, but I'm not from Reevesport. I'm one of the reds."

Khalim's son had never heard of 'the reds' or 'the Redwood Valley Eyrie,' so Lei found himself facing his own barrage of questions, though none nearly as harsh as what his mentor faced downstairs. He remained purposefully vague for his own safety, but he explained about the reeve's plan to kill all the gryphons, leaving out that she was his mother. Then he talked about the blue opinici's plans to tear off the gryphon wings and turn them into an army.

Khalim's son hadn't heard of the Crackling Sea Eyrie, either, leading to more explanation. In the end, Lei summed it up as thus: "I had a mom, dad, and six sisters. They weren't perfect. Most of them died doing the wrong thing. But I loved them with all my heart, and I was broken for a time. Then the fisherfolk found me and made me whole again. That's why I'm here with your dad. I wanted to see him made whole, too."

When the depression set in, Lei asked the blackwing questions to pull himself from it. They could still hear shouting and arguing downstairs. Vilessa seemed to believe it was really Khalim and not an alabaster spy, but that had made things worse.

"Khal, how could you have stayed away?" Her anger spent, her voice only contained hurt. "How could you let your son believe you were dead? And who is that peacock you brought with you?"

Khalim deflated. "Everywhere I go, I'm hunted by assassins. Rybalt, Iony, but also the Nighthaunt. That's why I stayed away. But once Mally realized who I was, everything changed. It became too dangerous to leave you alone. I thought he was going to come after you. It just took me a while to figure out how to get up here."

Lei gave the son a hug. "I know it's impossible to believe, but it's true. This was the first time he could come home to you. I'm so sorry you've been without him. I know how much he loves you."

Lemmy didn't respond, but Vilessa found her voice, and the shouting below continued.

By the time the farmers hiding in the cellar ventured out to see what had happened, the worst of the anger had faded. Lei was still upstairs with Khalim's son, comforting him in the bedroom. Vilessa had reached some sort of agreement with her old mate, crafted some sort of lie to tell the others, and called a meeting.

Khalim and Vilessa's family had grown close after his death, and everyone in the building was related to Khalim by marriage or blood.

None of them could be allowed to know it was really him. Not now, not when any could be taken and tortured. Not when none of them would believe it.

Instead, she told them Pip was an alabaster eyrie opinicus who had been assigned to their farm. He'd been there when Khalim had died and had promised the dying opinicus that he would attempt to do what he could to protect his family.

That raised even more questions, and the real Khalim, back to going by Pip, spent hours relaying his death, a modified version of the starling story that didn't include downing salts and transforming. He also left out that Wendl was alive.

As the questions downstairs began, Lei and Lemmy retreated to the bedroom. Lemmy wanted to hear all the stories of their adventures. Lei told everything he could, figuring Khalim would want his son to know the truth. He told the real version while everyone was distracted downstairs by the cover story.

Vilessa came to fetch Lei partway through, pulling him back to the far bedroom with the wayward capybara and leaving Lemmy on his own for a few minutes. "Lei, Khal— Sorry, *Pip*—told me to ask you who you were. He said he'd leave it up to you to tell me."

Lei hesitated, but he knew Pip trusted this opinicus more than anyone else and told the truth. "I'm the last living heir to the Redwood Valley Eyrie in the south."

Unlike her son, Vilessa had kept up with world politics through other medicine opinici, hoping for word of what had happened to Khalim. "Reeve Brevin, was it? I thought all her daughters died. I thought she had only daughters."

"No, but it's safer if everyone thinks that," Lei said. "There are a few who know who I am, mostly those who saved me. Well, and a few who tried to kill me, like Rybalt. And I can't remember if Wendl knows or not."

Vilessa froze. "Wendl is alive? She's a fisherfolk, like Khal... Pip?"

"No, she's a starling." Lei wasn't sure what he was seeing in Vilessa's eyes. A little jealousy, maybe, or deep concern for an old friend. "She's trapped in the Emerald Jungle with more of Pip's friends. He became an alabaster opinicus to try to stop the Nighthaunt, but the others became starlings knowing that both sides would want them dead. We met her on the border a few times 'cause she can't leave the jungle. Altruism and all. She's trying to help the starlings Mally experimented on. They didn't have the egg treatments, so bloodbeak is spreading among the Nightsky Pride."

Vilessa mulled this over, then looked down and saw the

anxiety on Lei's face. "Sorry, there's a lot to think about. And Rybalt Reevesbane knows who you are? But didn't kill you? I'm sure there's a story there."

Lei nodded. "Rybalt has the red crown and peacock talons. That was the deal."

"Here's what we're going to do," she continued. "Khalim and you will stay here. We have a cover story. You're safer than he is, because there's a black-market trade with Reevesport, so we're used to seeing opinici who look like you without them murdering us. I'm going to put... Pip... in the spare room up front. You can stay in Lemmy's room for now. I think it's better if we keep you in this wing. Be careful where you go, though. You're always going to be in danger here."

Lei nodded. He'd never shared a room with anyone his own age. When he'd stayed with Mi-lei's family, it had just been one fishing hut, so there was no privacy. But they were older and tended to ignore him out of grief.

Vilessa dismissed him, and he went back to make sure Lemmy was okay having him here. Now that Lei had explained who he was to Vilessa, he also felt obligated to tell Lemmy.

Down the hall, Khalim and Vilessa argued again, though it didn't seem as angry as it had been downstairs. They started with Wendl, Khalim telling her everything they knew about the scholars hiding as starlings. But it ended with an interesting tidbit Lei hadn't considered.

"It's not the alabaster opinici finding out about you that I'm worried about, Khal," she said. "It's the Blackwing Eyrie. Do you think the reeve will let this stand? What happens when they retake Blacktalon?"

Lei blinked. Iony had told them the army wouldn't be

there when they arrived, but he hadn't given the fisherfolk any more information than that. What would happen if the blackwings retook the city?

28

THE SUBTERRANEAN TANGLE

The water nearly filled the underground cavern, leaving only a small pocket of air along the top. That section wasn't empty, however. The long roots of trees above burst through the ceiling, giving a strange roof to Zeph's aquatic journey.

In his mind, it felt like there were octopodes hanging from the ceiling, letting their tentacles drift in the water. Not a particularly reassuring thought. He'd hoped his blue eyes would reveal a large, open, safe space. Instead, small fish darted between the roots, and their long strands made it hard for him to see.

Judging by Slate's navigation, those same roots were interfering with his echolocation.

The start of the journey featured many small holes above them where acidic rainwater had cut paths deep into the earth, providing a little light to see by. They also gave access to bugs and small lizards. Zeph kept a close eye on those. If they were just little lizards, that wasn't a problem. But sometimes, baby monitors hid in the root systems of cypress or mangroves while the large, adult monitors lounged nearby. Fighting a weald monitor in the water was a tricky proposition. He wasn't Tresh or Quess, killing sea monsters on their home turf.

Mostly, however, the lizards and fish were just curious about the fuzzy creatures floating through their home. Sometimes, they swam at him, kissing his fur with their fish faces, then darted back to hide in the roots.

So far, there was enough room to breathe—if he didn't mind the feeling of muddy roots on his ears, which he did not. In fact, after they'd drifted down river for about an hour, Zeph started to calm. He liked little fish. River fish, stream fish, they were all cute. Sometimes, he'd make faces at them under the water when they approached.

Where the light was dimmer, he could see adult cave fish swimming near the bottom. They were much larger, but when they opened their mouths, he didn't see any nasty teeth. They were just... fish. Doing fish things.

I'm doing fish things, too, he thought as he swam by. The current was doing most of the work. They had a good amount of air. Everything was pleasant. He kinda hoped they'd get to do this again sometime.

"This is fun, isn't it, Kia?" he asked.

She didn't seem to be having as much fun as he was. Nor did Cherine. Clearly, they were caught up on the part of the plan where the river plummeted deep into the earth and spilled out inside the Abyssal Naze.

"I'm having fun," Xin said. "I've been afraid to swim ever since the night of the fire. But... this is just like floating."

Zeph sent a happy chirrup Xin's way, which the little magpie returned. "You should see the hot springs at Snowfall.

They're underground, and they're warm. Plus, there's a shallow end. Just always bring a friend. The heat can be a bit much. Though not compared to those death crystals, I suppose."

"I wish this water was hot," Cherine started saying, but the top of the cave dipped, and everyone gasped for breath before going under.

There was a strange, muffled sound of moving water that Zeph always got when his ears were beneath the surface. It was pleasant. He could see a spot of sunlight ahead, suggesting he'd be able to catch his breath soon. He braced himself.

Silky slipped past him and Slate, swift bird that she was, and surfaced.

She must not be able to hold her breath for very long.

Beneath the water, Zeph could just see her lower half as she stuck her head into the light to breathe. A moment later, something splashed down, catching her in its mouth and pulling her out of the water.

A few cave gryphons tried to backbeat their wings, but Zeph and Slate pushed forwards, climbing up into the large crack in the earth to see what had happened.

A titanic boa hung down from a fallen tree, the swiftlet in its mouth. The only thing that had kept her alive was that its head was large enough that she fit comfortably inside. Her claws dug into the roof of its mouth while her tail spikes impaled its tongue. Nothing had been bitten off.

The reptile attempted to swallow her whole, but Silky stuck herself to the roof of its mouth and sealed it closed so the boa couldn't hurt any other gryphons.

The snake shook its head back and forth, and Zeph caught onto some roots, trying to pull himself high enough to get lift. Slate beat him to it, flying at the snake, which let out a sticky hiss.

Zeph caught the beast's tail, shouting for help below. Silky had fused its mouth shut to keep it from hurting anyone else—with herself inside—and the snake was beginning to wind away, trying to escape. More of the silkmouths found their wings and joined in, sealing off the crack in the ground above it while the oilbirds latched on weighed it down.

"Go on without me!" Silky's shouts were muffled by the *chrysalized* snake.

Zeph wasn't having it, though.

"Cherine, up here!" he shouted.

The scholar was waterlogged and needed some help, but the swiftlets had given him a path of silk nests up. He looked dubiously at the giant snake, still writhing in the mess of webbing. "Er, what did you want me to do?"

"This!" Zeph's claws were ineffective against the desperate goo Silky had flung, but they weren't made of metal. He pushed Cherine's beak against the snake's mouth, cutting open a hole for air to go in. Silky was still moving inside.

"You two!" Kia shouted to the swiftlets. "Bind the mouth *open* so we can get your leader out!"

Slate and Chert used their strength to slam the boa's head into the side of the cave, facing down, while the swiftlets stuck one side to the wall and tried to get the other side open.

The length of the snake up top still thrashed, starting to pull down logs and break the silk. A huge tree dropped past Zeph and into the river below, but Slate managed to get the snake's mouth open once Cherine slashed the last of the webbing with his metal beak.

Silky dropped out of the mouth, falling towards the water.

Some of the others caught her, and Xin helped hold her head above water while she recovered.

"Thanks," she stuttered to the magpie. "I've never been eaten before. That was... terrifying."

Xin groomed her feathers free of snake spit. "It happened to my dad once. He doesn't really like snakes now."

Silky stared, then laughed. "Maybe I'll go meet your dad sometime, and we can share war stories."

Xin grinned. Then part of the crack in the ground collapsed, sending rocks down after them as the snake began freeing itself.

"Okay, cave gryphons, it's time to go!" Slate shouted.

Everyone took a large breath, then descended back into the watery depths. The silkmouths had created enough of a latticework to make it hard for the snake to follow them, giving the cave expedition a chance to find the naze before they were pursued.

29

DARKHOME

Kia shivered in the water. They were past the point of light, past the point where roots still dangled overhead. She missed the little fish and, well, being able to *see* the little fish.

Chert took this as a good sign, however, and her mood improved. She chirped every time they went up for air.

"Without the roots and water falling down, it's easier to echolocate," she explained. "I can sort of hear where we're going now, where the air is. I think we're getting close."

Kia trusted as best she could. This was the end of their wet cave journey, so there was nothing else she could do. She certainly wasn't about to swim back past the giant snake.

She ducked under the waves again, letting the current carry her. She spent two hours in the darkness, trusting others' sense of hearing, until they reached a new section of roots, and Slate sounded that they should climb up and take a break.

They'd just passed an air pocket, and it took some doing

to get back against the current, but their entire expedition clung to the bubble-like break in the rocky ceiling.

"We've got a small problem." Slate was still partially submerged. A silkmouth used her tail-spikes to hold them both in place. "Seems some bright bird had the thought to put a grate on this part of the river."

Kia wasn't as harsh on whoever the gryphon had been who put up the grate. Presumably, it was large enough to keep giant snakes from swimming into their nests. "Is it made with silk, or was it stolen from opinici?"

"Both," Chert said. "The metal isn't anything we can make, but it's secured with layers and layers of silk. Must've been put in during the last dry season."

More chittering among the gryphons. Zeph wanted to try to claw through it, but it was hard to expend energy underwater like that. Biting had a high cost. What Kia really needed was a knife.

Zeph plus *knife* was an easy equation after their adventure with the snake. She knew what she had to do.

Kia turned to Silky. "Is it dry enough up here for you to make a rope out of spit? One large enough to reach the grate?"

The silkmouth nodded. "It'll be tricky. We can't really make things underwater, not with any strength. But if we use the air pocket and only drop it into the water after it's set, sure."

"Is that going to be strong enough to pull the grate up?" Slate asked. "Just how strong is a silk rope?"

"I doubt it," Silky replied. "It works best if we use little bits, extra gooey, in a dry climate. It'll snap before a secure, reinforced grate will. I'm not sure how feasible it is to make a bunch of ropes, but we could try?"

Kia studied Cherine's beak. "That won't be necessary. I didn't think to bring a knife with me, but we do have one metal weapon we know works on the silk."

"Wait," Cherine protested, then he sighed in resignation. "Okay, fine. Just... don't lose it, okay? Sponge took my old beak to sell."

Kia carefully removed the metal tip of his beak. She would never have thought of using it against the snake like Zeph had, but she hadn't seen how sharp Sponge had made it. Cherine was a scholar, but his beak belonged on a warrior's face.

"Okay, once the spit sets, tie it around my middle," Kia said. "The first time, wait about fifteen seconds, then pull me back. We'll need to figure out the right length of time. This'll take a while, but I think we can pull it off."

Once the silk was ready and secured around her middle, she gripped Cherine's beak in her dull talons, waited for Silky to give the word, then let go and drifted until she hit the grate. She couldn't see it, but she felt along its edges to find where the silk was.

The cold, moving water had hardened the webbing, but if she scratched hard enough, it gave way. She'd just made a dent when she was pulled back.

"This is going to be slow, but it's working," she said.

Slate gathered everyone together for warmth. Now that they weren't swimming, it was easy to lose body heat to the cool water. "Do you think you can stay down longer?"

She laughed. "No, fifteen seconds is good. You don't want me to drown and drop the beak. I'm a parrot, not a petrel."

Kia went back a dozen more times, slowly chipping away at the goo. The grate was still lodged in place by virtue of having been here for so long, so the next time she went up, she suggested the silkmouths create more ropes.

"Once we get the goo off, I think we're going to have to try pulling it away," Kia explained. "It shouldn't take too much, just enough to dislodge it a little."

She spent the better part of two hours scraping away ten seconds at a time, then getting pulled back to the air pocket. By the time she'd removed the last of the strange sealant, she could feel the grate shift a little with the current.

That was her sign to go back, fetch the four ropes, and secure them to different sections of the grate. Then, while she took a break in a makeshift swiftlet nest, the others pulled as hard as they could.

A few silk strands broke. The others held, and the grate lurched forwards before getting pulled downstream by the river.

"The way our luck is going, it's going to lodge further down, and we're going to have to do this again," Slate grumbled.

Chert was much more upbeat. "Are you kidding me? We survived the forbidden cave! And the giant snake! Could we be luckier?"

"I know I feel lucky," Silky called down from her little silk nest, where she and the other silkmouths were making ropes and taking naps. Several of the feather-spikes above her tail were gone, having lodged in the base of the boa's mouth.

The oilbirds did a little echolocating on strands of silk, and it seemed that while the grate had wedged itself against something new, it was sideways, so they could all squeeze through.

"We'll go one at a time so no one gets stuck," Slate ordered. "The current picks up right after, so I think we're close. If you feel yourself falling down a waterfall, try to slow your descent with your wings so you don't hit the bottom too hard."

"Any idea where we're coming out?" Chert asked, but none of them ventured a guess.

Turns out, no cave gryphon has attempted to take the waterways into their home.

Kia watched as a dozen oilbirds entered the water, then it was her turn. It was hard to reattach Cherine's beak in the dark, but Silky had offered help, which would be a problem when he needed to take it off again to clean it.

"We didn't think to bring any with us, but there's a solvent you can make from ground loquats that'll fix you up right as rain," Silky explained. When the last oilbird disappeared under the water, she turned to Kia. "By all means, go right ahead."

The parrot scholar sighed, then returned to the freezing depths.

Kia hit the grate sideways, bruising her ribs and leg. She tried to go around the left side, but it was all rock, so she squeezed around the right. It would be easy to panic and drown down here, and it was a miracle they hadn't lost anyone.

The current pulled her, and she thought she saw a glimmer ahead. *It must be a trick of my eyes. Unless this comes out above ground?*

It was not a trick, and it did not come out above ground. Instead, she spilled out of the earth and down a waterfall that opened into a chamber bigger than any room she'd ever seen. A chamber with several large bonfires in the center.

She spread her wings, but her mind was already playing through a dozen scenarios where things had gone wrong. Cave gryphons wouldn't need a bonfire. Only opinici would.

But that wasn't quite right. The swiftlets couldn't see underground or echolocate any better than Kia could. Chert chirped a greeting to her, and she flew over to see what was going on.

The river cut the cavern in two. On one side, there were small nests built into the rocks. *I hope I don't end up having to sleep in one of those. They'll have to have Silky stick me to the nest so I don't roll out of it.*

On the other side were smaller chambers and bonfires. Someone was cooking food, a decidedly un-gryphon-like behavior. While she saw the glistening obsidian orbs of oilbirds across the river, near the light were gryphons of a dozen varieties she'd never met before.

Woodpecker gryphons with long, black fuzzy tails huddled together. Kia was a naturalist, and while they looked like the royal guard the fisherfolk had fought off the bog coast, their pattern was distinct in several noticeable ways. The white and black were in different proportions, the tails long and gryphonic. They seemed to be cousins, two sides of the same badge, one gryphon, one opinicus.

Other gryphon species filled the cavern. Some she could tell at a glance had been the offspring between opinici and gryphons: Alabaster Eyrie markings, Crestfall, Reevesport peafowl, even some duck-shaped gryphons.

For others, she couldn't even begin to guess at the bird. Osprey, certainly, for one couple. Another set looked like the cassowary she'd glimpsed running beneath them in the woods.

Vibrant colors, dull colors. At least two could possibly be cave gryphons, based on their plumage and how comfortable they felt down here, but they didn't look like oilbirds or swifts.

"What happened here?" she asked after Zeph, Xin, Cherine, and Silky joined them.

Silky didn't wait around, running off after some friends and showing off her broken spikes.

It was Chert who responded to Kia's inquiry. "The Seraph King declared war on all gryphons. Guess he was worried about losing the workshop again and decided to take preemptive action. The pridemates living at the mouth of the cave had to flee deeper. More gryphon refugees kept showing up, so we kept finding hiding places for them. Now they're all stuck here at the very back of the caves."

"The attack on the Silkmouth Pride wasn't an isolated event," Slate grumbled. "Darkstalkers have led teams to try to track down all of the gryphon prides beneath the earth while roving bands of Alabaster Eyrie forces swept the forests, fields, and cliffs where gryphon families might have been living."

One of the osprey couple spoke up, "We were living in Alwren, but we got word that they could be coming for us next. Some of the gryphons mated to opinici stayed, but all the others fled north. We're not considered citizens of the empire."

"Can you feed this many?" Kia had faced this kind of problem before. An army, a pride, an eyrie, they were only as good as the food in their belly.

Slate hesitated. "Short-term, yes. Everyone brought food with them, we have clean water, and the local prides have been attacking farms and stealing food stores."

"Can you cook grains?" Cherine asked. "As a gryphon, I mean?"

The other osprey spoke up, "Some of the Alwren fisher-folk came with us. They're cooking anything that might go bad."

Cherine disappeared to help oversee the cooks. It was strange, of all their scholarly knowledge, these two things had proven the most important: Cherine knew how to keep food safe and preserved, and Kia knew how to ration and distribute it. That knowledge more than any other had saved lives.

"Who's in charge here?" Kia asked. "This is something I can help with. We saved the weald and kjarr from their food problems after fire and war."

Slate chittered something at the wall of obsidian eyes, and they chittered back. "Well, dang. I am. The king caught one of our prides off guard with explosives, killing the ones normally in charge of the naze itself. Then one of the dark-stalkers came in and led an attack on the gryphons who would had taken over. That just leaves my pride while they sort out their new leaders. Whatever you need, opinicus, just shout. We'll make it happen."

Zeph had finished grooming, something she'd noticed he needed to do before speaking, and joined in. "Don't go just yet, Kia. They need to know our plan."

"In four days, the Argent Heights and associated supply lines will come under attack," she explained. "When that happens, the Ashen Weald will retake the Crackling Sea. The Blackwing Eyrie is going to handle the border eyries and create chaos. That's when we'll attack here."

Chert looked around. "This isn't enough to stop an

opinicus army, let alone the Golden Sky, the king's elite forces."

"The starlings are joining us." Everyone looked at Zeph like he'd grown an extra pair of wings. "With their altruism, it's a tricky matter. But when we last talked to Nighteyes, she said to lure the alabaster forces into her swarm. We're taking her at her word that this is okay."

Green Wing Altruism was a term that needed a little explaining. Everyone here, especially those who had come from Alwren and King's Reach, were aware of the starlings' peculiarities. It was just the phrase itself they hadn't heard before, prompting some questions about the use of the word 'altruism' to describe it.

While Zeph explained, Kia had a silkmouth help her open her packs, where she checked on the bark beetles. For all their adventures, the bugs were doing pretty well. Thankfully, they'd been acquired after the fire cave. "We can remove the argent reeve's glyphs. There's a corridor that funnels in this direction. I recommend you reinforce the glyphs at all entrances to the Abyssal Naze so they can't get down here. But we're going to flood the area with starlings, the only army the Seraph King fears."

The cave gryphons looked incredulous, but none of them contradicted her. They were aware of the event Nighteyes had told the Ashen Weald about, where a starling made it through the same gap in the glyphs that had later been shored up.

"You said there's one last western cave that comes out near the workshop, right?" Zeph asked Slate. "Make sure it's glyphed up tight so the starlings can't cross. The starling's path is taking them up from south of here, around the east side of the workshop. Add some glyphs to make sure that happens. Meanwhile, if you attack from the west, there shouldn't be any... confusion."

"This plan is absolute madness," Slate, the gryphon who had led them through the forbidden caves and down a giant-snake infested river said. "If I'd known this was what you were going to do, I'd have left you in the weald."

"I like it!" Chert chirped. "You've never seen fear until you've seen the look on an opi's face when they hear a starling chitter."

"And you?" Slate turned to Silky. "Are you okay with this?"

In the dark of the cave, it was easy to forget what Silky had been through. Now that there was the light of the bonfires to see by, the silkmouth really had been through hell. "Do you even have to ask after the things we saw at the lampworks? I've got a bone to pick with the Nighthaunt for coming after my pride. We'll be there, on the front lines. And I want Chert with us, listening for Mally and his darkstalkers. If we can get rid of them, the caves should become safe again."

Kia tilted her head to the side.

"Except for the snakes, fire, heat, death crystals, and everything else, I mean," Silky amended. "You know, the normal levels of dangers you get every time you take a stroll to visit a friend."

Zeph puffed up. "Great! We don't have much time to get organized. Let's get to work!"

Kia followed Slate to check on a crate of scavenged weapons. She and Cherine could put armor on the gryphons, but any tools or metal talons they found would probably be wasted. Still, there were a handful of osprey fisherfolk from Alwren who could make use of them.

In most opinicus-gryphon conflicts, the opinici tended to assume they could shut the door and the gryphons wouldn't get through. As the Ashen Weald had proven, all it took were a few opinicus allies—like Kia, Cherine, Orlea, Quess, or Foultner—to seriously mess up an anti-gryphon strategy.

This also wasn't a war, not really. For all the starling hordes, cave gryphon armies, Blackwing Alliance forces, and Ashen Weald, this was really the most coordinated *assassination attempt* anyone had ever made with the king as their target.

What does it feel like to know an entire continent wants you dead?

Kia pulled out her notebook. The first step to every great plan was to figure out what you have at your disposal.

Fifty fisherfolk, five opinici, forty-five gryphons, mostly osprey.

Twenty silkmouths (cave swiftlet morph) able to fight.

Two Redwood Valley scholars, opinical, one with a metal beak.

One particularly determined parrot hunter, copper hawk morph, with pretty blue eyes...

30

DRESSED TO KILL

Stripes spent a few days waiting in the grain belt of the Seraph King's lands while her stitches healed. In that time, she poisoned no fewer than six medicine opinici, and she was starting to run out of antitoxin.

The commander had ordered her to wear the *trashbird coverings,* as he called them, but she hadn't brought any with her. It wasn't like pitohui dressed that way on their island. Even Rybalt had been known to take off his weird leather mask and bindings while at home. After some arguing—he was the commander, after all, but with everyone calling her the reeve-sister of the pitohui, she figured she had some clout to push back—they'd given her access to a seamstress who had been captured at Reevesport's textile mills.

"So you need a harness?" the peafowl asked. "But it needs to cover... most of your body?"

Stripes nodded. "The oil on my feathers and fur is poison, so the commander would like me covered while I'm around his troops."

The peafowl shook her head. "Normally, I would say that it cannot be done, that if it could be done, you couldn't afford it. But you've stolen everything of value from my home, so let's see what we can manage, shall we?"

The Reevesport opinicus reached out to measure Stripes, then stopped. "If I touch you, I will die? Right now?"

"Yes," one of the motmot bodyguards said. "If you show us how, we can measure."

That was partially true. They didn't use a measuring tape the way the seamstress did, instead holding it in their beaks, but they managed to stop Stripes from poisoning a seventh opinicus.

Ultimately, the first outfit proposed was beautiful, ephemeral, and useless. Whatever it had been spun from, some sort of thin material, it didn't stop the poison from coming through.

Stripes knew this because she'd gone outside to flirt with one of the guards, and he was now twitching on the floor.

One of the motmots stayed with him, and the peahen went back to the drawing board, coming up with something new. A type of silk that didn't come from caterpillars. When Stripes inquired further, the seamstress just said it came from swiftlets.

"The cost is unimaginably high, but at least this way, someone will get to wear it." She drew out a great length of it, placing it on top of Stripes like a sheet.

"Not very elegant, but I suppose this works," Stripes grumbled, but the seamstress wasn't done. She found places to secure it to the pitohui's harness and armor, letting it cover Stripes's wings. The seamstress added in a little hood, perhaps as a nod to the rumors of what Stripes's brother looked like, but instead of straps of leather prison bindings hanging down, there were silver strands ending in teardrop crystals that caught the light.

"Did you steal my mirror, too?" the peahen asked, sending the guards to look for it. They didn't find that particular mirror, but they'd found a store of Crestfall glass that included an even more ornate one.

Stripes stared at herself. "I don't look like me, but I like it."

The motmot gryphons circled her. They loved vibrant colors and beautiful things, and they were always stealing flowers from the eyrie gardens. She could see in their eyes that they didn't know what to think.

"It is... pretty," one said. "But it is white. That is not your color."

Another *tsked.* "We are among the enemy! Looking white is useful. It is called camouflage."

"She is not going to *fight* wearing that outfit! It stops her poison," the third motmot protested.

The fourth used her long beak to pull up the hood and look at Stripes. "It must be red. The silk comes in red, yes? That is better."

The seamstress sighed. "It's going to use up all the red cave silk I have. I know, I know. I'm a prisoner. I suppose it's better used than sitting in a forgotten crate, likely to get ruined. I'll get to work on it. Let me take that one off you to use as a prototype."

Stripes tensed, fearing she was about to poison an eighth opinicus, but the silk was thick enough that her poison didn't go through it. "Be careful, please, when you touch the underside. I'm... a lot more potent than I would normally be. You know, with the war and all."

The peahen made some noncommittal sounds and went back to work, leaving Stripes and the motmots to depart. They'd nearly made it back to the nests when they ran into the blackwing commander in the halls.

"Ah, the *reeve-sister,* so good to see you," he said.

She struggled to keep her hackle feathers down. "The seamstress is working on a covering. It'll be done soon."

This pleased the commander, though it didn't stop his news. "I need intelligence from inside the Alabaster Eyrie. We can't get any closer without tipping them off. We need to know if they've figured out we're here or not. I believe we've caught everyone who fled west and forced the others to hide and wait it out. But I need to be certain."

"So send your spies?" Stripes wasn't sure why she was part of this conversation. "What does this have to do with me?"

"You're pitohui. You're an assassin. If you can sneak, you can spy," he said. "My scouts are making sure no one tips them off early, and they don't blend in with a city."

And I do? I'm black and orange. You're black and red.

She started to protest again, but he brought up reports from the messenger at Reevesport whom she'd saved from the berserker.

"If you can kill a peafowl, you can kill an alabaster kite." Those were his final words.

Stripes grumbled, then went to find a pair of metal talons to borrow. She'd fill up on scarabs this afternoon, then fly out at night, under cover of darkness. She wasn't sure what she was looking for, but everyone here seemed to think pitohui had magical senses for these sorts of things.

The motmots were excited to get to do more flying and volunteered to come along.

She took one look at their bright plumage and shrugged. "The more the merrier. You're about as sneaky as I am."

"Sneakier," one of the motmot whispered from behind a crate, causing Stripes to jump.

31

GARDEN OF THE FORBEARERS

The Alabaster Eyrie was built on a peninsula, with some rocky cliffs on all sides, a well-developed port, and walls so tall Stripes was having trouble getting close enough to see over them.

Spying was not going well. Though the motmots were excited. They chirped encouragement and showed her how to move through the cover of darkness and foliage. Sadly, the *darkness and foliage* ended at the walls.

Well, 'walls' was a bit of a misnomer. It was more like the buildings had grown close, then gardens rose up, and finally fences had been constructed around the gardens to keep goliath birds and emus from stealing the fruit—or so it went in Stripes's mind. The end result was the same: a tangle of stone, foliage, and lanterns that blocked the way into the city.

"Do you see the garden ahead? I want to eat it," one of the motmots said. While they were known for enjoying bugs like the teal scarabs, they weren't above stealing fruit.

"Later," another hissed. "We need to finish spying. What if we... go around?"

Alabaster opinici in armor patrolled the skies, and it appeared that the arch over the main goliath road into the city was a popular place for the city's Reeve's Guard to hang out. There was no going in that way.

"Okay, follow my lead," Stripes ordered. "Let's crawl to the shore, see if it's clear, and head for those hills. They seem less populated."

Several fishing boats were out, but there was less light pollution this far from the city, and Stripes decided to risk flying. The capital of the empire had a lot of different opinici, and she hoped she wouldn't stand out.

They kept close to the cliffs, coming up upon the thick trees marking the... gardens? Wildlife preserve? Stripes didn't know. This didn't feel like a garden, but along the southern strip there was a sign that read *Garden of the Forbearers.* She had no idea who the forbearers were or why they'd decided to name this section a garden, but she was grateful for a place to hide with a view.

While the motmots kept watch, she took out her journal and tried to mark the different sections of the city. The giant crowned opinicus statue was probably the palace. Considering it was made of stone, it wouldn't be easy to siege. But maybe they could use saltpeter to blow up the main entrance and trap someone inside.

The real target was the port. According to the commander, it was the true prize of the Alabaster Eyrie. With Reevesport and the Alabaster Port out of commission, life here would grind to a halt.

It was far from the front gates, however. They'd need to come in from the side. Night fighting was tricky, but a black and red target was harder to hit than a white one in the dark, she supposed.

She was struck by the sheer size of it all. Sure, the Blackwing Eyrie, with its terraces of flowing water falling down the mountains and into the ocean, was impressive. It felt eternal, immutable, part of the mountain itself.

Yet it was small in comparison to the city before her now. The Alabaster Eyrie's beauty came from its size, scope, and planning. The water flowing down the blackwing terraces was liquid chaos, but every part of the architecture here was precision and order. The blackwing homes were built where the mountain had been worn away. The alabaster nests were built upon solid rock.

In fact, she couldn't tell quite how big the city was. It stretched south and west beyond her vision. She knew the Golden Sky was away guarding Duckbill, but the sort of Reeve's Guard that could handle a city of this size was an army in its own right. She'd seen so many patrols flying about that she wondered if her side was outnumbered.

And the buildings were of a style she'd never seen before. With gold rooves and white stone walls, they rose in square shapes with terraces on each level to allow opinici to roost in the shade.

She took a deep breath. She was supposed to be finding out the weaknesses here, but she didn't see any. With even a relatively small number of defenders, this city would be invincible. Even void of its Golden Sky army, she didn't feel confident in the blackwings' chances. Not when she couldn't bring an army anywhere near here without alerting a patrol.

The motmots behind her began sniffing. "We are not alone. Reeve-sister, prepare yourself."

"Whatever happens, follow my lead." Stripes put away her

journal, leaned against a tree, and slipped on swirled metal talons. They felt strange over her own dull pair.

"Hello? I haven't seen gryphons like you before." An elderly opinicus, his white feathers mostly replaced with grey, stepped out from behind a trail none of them had seen. "Well, don't just stand there. We've got more than enough food for everyone."

The motmots didn't wait to see what Stripes did. With the promise of something to eat, they dropped their defensive postures and padded after the stranger, who led them deeper into the foliage.

The tall trees in this section of the garden hid a valley that stretched the length of the small range of hills. And in that valley were at least a thousand gryphons.

"What... is this?" Stripes asked.

The greyfeather laughed. "What you were looking for, I assume. The Nest. Now, let's get you some food. Been some good scavenging tonight, let me tell you."

Stripes wished she'd brought her white silk garments. As it was, most of the gryphons and the few opinici here were all in a pretty shabby state. She hadn't realized gryphons could get shabby. Her motmots were always cleaning and preening themselves.

There were gryphons of all shapes and sizes, most of which she'd never heard of before. She wondered why they weren't with their prides. Then there were gryphons she knew didn't have a pride. A white-tailed kite gryphon was huddled up next to a peafowl gryphon for warmth. These had opinicus plumage, the results of liaisons between opinici and gryphons that had been born with paws instead of talons. They would have no home, pride *or* eyrie.

The greyfeather led them to a small makeshift building. The food there had been stolen from the butchery or bakery.

Stolen from the bakery's trash heap, more likely.

Still, Stripes knew how to be polite. She ate the food without commenting on where it had come from. Finding enough to feed a thousand gryphons wouldn't be an easy task.

"Where do you lot hail from?" the greyfeather asked. "Can't say I recognize the plumage. Are there more in your pride, or did the alabasters wipe them out?"

Before the motmots could answer, Stripes replied, "An island. We had opinici and gryphons living together."

"The bastards don't like that," the greyfeather said with a laugh. "Always figured they'd turn on Alwren one of these days. I'm sorry for what happened to you. We don't have much, but we've gathered all the lost gryphon prides here. We can keep you fed and housed if you want. Just don't go near the border. Out of sight, out of mind, but if they see you coming in here, they'll bring patrols in to 'thin our numbers.'"

Stripes shivered both at the opinicus's words and at the idea that there were patrols trying to wipe out gryphons.

She'd always known that the motmot pride had a raw deal with the Blackwing Alliance. Same with the glacier gryphons. They were treated as lesser, and their issues were never given priority. That was one case where both she and her brother were in agreement. They'd spent years working on gryphon rights.

But if the alternative was living as a nestless gryphon, stealing tarts out of the trash and waiting to be culled by opinici? Well, it was no wonder the glacier gryphons and motmots had joined the blackwings.

Still, it made her mad. She'd been ordered to die before

she explained who she was, but as she looked out at all the gryphons, a plan formed.

First, however, she needed a little more information. "It's nice of you to help take care of these gryphons. Why do you do that?"

The greyfeather laughed, a sound like crinkled paper. "Same as you and your lovers, I suppose. Fell for a gryphon, had children. All were gryphons. Things went to hell, they're dead, but I feel an obligation to keep doing what I can. The alabaster gryphons can sneak through the night, crows are good at that, too, but I take the beads they steal and buy medicine for them."

Stripes was starting to regret having told the motmots to act like spies and follow her lead. When the greyfeather referred to them as her harem, they all cuddled closer to her and started purring to add to the illusion.

"Not in front of the others." She tapped one of the motmots on her beak, and the gryphon looked offended.

"You can sleep in your own nest tonight," the motmot said.

Stripes sighed but turned back to the greyfeather. "You said the alabaster gryphons can move through the city at night? How do they do that?"

"After something in particular?" the greyfeather asked. "We give 'em specialized boots that hide the shape of their front legs. Make them look like fishers or like they work at the tannery. So long as no one checks too close, they can move around the city at will."

"And all of them came from the country, where they no longer feel safe?" Stripes asked. Once the greyfeather nodded, she added, "What if I told you that the border eyries are gone, and the country is safe again?"

He stared at her, noticing her harness for the first time. "That's an eyrie badge. An island village wouldn't have that."

"Answer the question," she pressed. "I assume you can't get everyone out because of the patrols, but what if I could cause a distraction. What if I could open the way out of here. Would you help me? Do you hate your king as much as I do?"

She'd attracted the attention of the alabaster gryphons nearby. They were listening to her words. "You asked who I am. I'm probably crazy telling you this, but I come from an eyrie across the continent, deep in the sea. The king's armies have gone to guard him near the Abyssal Naze where he follows a fool's dream of ascension and purity. He's left this city undefended.

"Reevesport is gone. We burned it to the ground. Smaller eyries along the way are also under our control. The might of the combined eastern eyries is near, ready to strike.

"I thought this city was too large to take. Now, I see that's wrong. You can leave now, if you want, and head back to the wilderness. We're about to cause enough chaos to let you all escape from this valley and see for yourselves how much of the kingdom we've liberated.

"But I know what it's like to be hated. I know what it's like to feel like a stranger in your own home. Don't step too close to me. My skin is poison."

There were a few rumblings there, talks of a Reevesbane. She wasn't wearing Rybalt's silly outfit, or they might have assumed she was him. But what really seemed to persuade them was her motmot bodyguards.

"If you don't want to stay to fight, that's fine. If you head east and can get across the desert, that's where we live. Tell them Stripes sent you. You're welcome on my island. Or, if you've had enough of opinici, there's a gryphon utopia south of the Crackling Sea. Eyries ruled by gryphons, opinici and gryphons living together on the shore. They'll take you all in. They call themselves the Ashen Weald, because when the opinici there tried to burn down their homes, they rose up and freed themselves, reclaiming their valley."

Her blackwing allies would not care for her sending a thousand gryphons to the Ashen Weald, but she felt indebted to them for finding out about Impir's plot to spread bloodbeak when they did. She also owed them for keeping Iony alive. He was like a second cousin to her, maybe third.

"Or you could stay. I think some of you are probably just as angry as I am. My army comes tomorrow night. But our victory would be secured much easier by having some alabaster gryphons placing saltpeter around the city for us, unseen. And I could use a more detailed map of the eyrie. I hear crows have a good memory for such things."

Whether it was her speech or the motmots going and telling their own tales, she slowly rallied the others. If she were trying to handle some sort of long campaign here, she'd never have spoken to a thousand strangers like that. But everyone here looked terrible. Even if some were willing to sell her out, the local Reeve's Guard would want proof, and the traitor's conscience might delay them. That was all she needed.

The alabaster gryphons planned to sneak out to get saltpeter tonight. Some of her motmots were showing them the way in small groups. But the most interesting intelligence came from the crows.

"We can show you the portmaster," they said.

It took her a moment to remember that the portmaster was the blue peafowl's reeve. "I'll stick out in the city proper."

A bit of cawing from the crows, then their leader spoke

again, shaking his bushy tail with anticipation. "We have a secret path. We can show you."

She checked to make sure she had a few red vials left. Her motmots wouldn't appreciate her taking this risk, but the portmaster's office was one of the buildings she needed to burn down.

"Okay," she said at last. "Lead the way."

THE CROWS' path through the city took Stripes into abandoned buildings, construction sites, empty crates, and even past a shipyard, moving from one empty hull to another. She did her best not to get her poison anywhere they might touch on the way back.

By the time she was done with the obstacle course, Stripes found herself atop a derelict rookery staring right into the large building where the portmaster lived when she was away from Reevesport.

Stripes watched the portmaster, the reeve. Clearly, the peafowl had begun to realize that something was wrong when her home shipments stopped arriving. But based on the snippets of words coming from the building, she had no idea Reevesport was rubble.

In fact, she was blaming the trade families. She assumed there was some sort of minor conflict that had escalated to sabotage.

Everything is set. We could take this city tomorrow if nothing goes wrong.

That was a big request from the universe, but Stripes had been fortunate so far. Sometimes, all of the pieces just fell into place.

She was about to thank the crows for their service and see if they were willing to plant some saltpeter here tomorrow when a new peacock came into view. A peacock whose face she recognized, whom she'd been tasked with killing—and failed. One from the Redwood Valley, not Reevesport.

Impir the Mad spoke to a smuggler, a black cockatiel with a stripe of green along his face and crest. The smuggler didn't seem happy to be here. What they were arguing about, she couldn't tell. But it provided her with a new target and a complication.

She let the crows lead her away, back to the Garden of the Forbearers, where the other gryphons were packing up to leave.

The greyfeather looked her over. "I'm not sure I would have invited you in if I'd known you were going to incite a rebellion."

She laughed. "I didn't know that's what I was doing. I just hate to see you all living like this. I need to head back and make sure the commander knows to let you pass tomorrow. Will you be leading them?"

The greyfeather shook his head. "No, you were right when you asked if I had anger in my heart. The Reeve's Guard murdered my daughter. The alabaster gryphons can place the charges, but you need someone with talons to light the fuses, I assume. I can do that."

"It's going to be okay," she assured him. She almost reached out to touch his shoulder but remembered her poison. "They have no army, and I assume the king took the royal guard with him. Victory is on our side."

The greyfeather shrugged. "Destroying an eyrie is easy. What comes after that is the hard part. Can you occupy the

Alabaster Eyrie when the Golden Sky comes home? Do you even have a way to return home yourself?"

She didn't respond. The blackwing commander's hope was that the kingdom would turn on itself. She didn't know if it would or not. She just wanted an excuse to go back to her island, and if this is what it took, she'd do it.

"Well," the greyfeather continued, "I hope you know what you're doing. You're playing with a lot of lives."

Do I know what I'm doing?

32

BARK BEETLES

Zeph and Cherine both took Kia's yolkbloom elixir. The copper hawk didn't feel any different. He sort of felt the same. Maybe a little taller?

"I don't think it's working," he said. "How do I know if it's working?"

Cherine stretched his wings and talons. "Go lick a starling. If they bite you, it didn't work."

Zeph rolled his eyes. He'd been practicing with a glass vial for hours, and his paws hurt. The original plan had Kia and Cherine unleashing the bark beetles upon the unsuspecting glyphs. Then they decided Zeph wasn't a good enough flyer to be bait and the starlings might catch him, so Kia had been placed in charge of that part, leaving Zeph to handle the bugs.

"Don't eat them," Kia teased. "The trip through the river was not kind to these beetles. We're going to need all we have."

She rolled up the map. Zeph had memorized it, and he could also sniff out the glyphs, so he wasn't too worried. With the cave gryphons' help, they'd found Nighteyes's corridor along the border of the Argent Heights and Abyssal Naze.

With the previous leader of the naze dead, it had taken some searching to find a pride leader who was part of the pact with the Emerald Jungle.

She was a small, elderly oilbird, but Slate and Chert had taken her around to add in a few new cave glyphs. If Kia's diagram was right, they'd now created a funnel of glyphs that would lead the starlings straight at the workshop.

"I… don't feel good about this," Zeph admitted. "I wish we could go and ask Nighteyes. I know what Erlock *said* she said, but… this feels wrong."

Kia and Cherine didn't respond. As they were normally talkative, he took that to mean they agreed with him.

"We can stop," Zeph pushed. "We don't need to do this. Maybe the cave gryphons are enough."

Kia looked up from her box of beetles. "What happens then? The Ashen Weald is depending on us. Rybalt and Iony are risking their lives to help us. And… what? The Nighthaunt escapes, the king gets his wish? No. *No.* If we wanted to turn back, the time to do that was before we left. Everyone is counting on us."

Zeph allowed her to put vials of beetles on his harness. He didn't know how to respond, but he still felt like this was wrong. Even if Nighteyes had come up with the plan inadvertently, that didn't mean the other starlings in her pride agreed with it. Opinici tended to act like a pride leader was a reeve, but that wasn't right.

In fact, between the combined poor judgement of Jun, Vosk, Strix, Merin, and Vitra, many of the gryphons were putting pressure on their pride leaders to change. None of the gryphons in the weald were particularly keen to follow a gryphon who made ultimatums. Not even if they liked their leader.

Cherine finished with his harness. "Okay, I'm ready. Don't worry, Zeph. If the yolkbloom worked, we're going to be doing the easy part. It's Kia who has to fly for her life."

Zeph gritted his tomia, but he didn't want to let down Kia or Cherine, so he accepted his beetles. They needed time to work, so the plan was to go out now and place them on the farthest glyphs, working towards the border. Then they'd place the last of the beetles on the glyphs along the edge of the Emerald Jungle, look around for some starlings, and report back to Kia.

Like all plans, it sounded simple to say, but there was a lot of room for things to go wrong. Once the starlings were swarming, the trio should be able to duck into the Abyssal Naze without being followed. But... well, there was no way to know for sure.

They were also depending on the Seraph King being too busy with his ascension to replace the glyphs himself. There was a lot going on, and Kia took him aside to talk to him.

"Zeph, I know you have reservations," she said. "I do, too. But no matter what, we *cannot* let the Seraph King or Nighthaunt escape. You know how many gryphons and opinici they've killed. We need to stop them."

"We're not assassins," Zeph countered. "We don't just go and kill opinici. We're not Rybalt."

"But we *are* reevesbanes," she pressed. "We did it once before, with Reeve Brevin. And as horrible as that was, as much as I never wanted to repeat it, we made the world a better place. We paved the way for the Ashen Weald to free the wingtorn."

He forced his hackles down. He hated being upset in front

of Kia. “We went up there to stop the fire. She attacked us. That’s... that’s different. And it was just us. We didn’t use the starlings for our own purposes. It’s not the same.”

“Zeph, I need you to promise me that you’ll go through with this. No matter what.” Kia’s sincerity was painful to see.

He looked into her eyes and saw the same doubts and pain he felt, and so he finally relented. “I promise.”

“You two lovebirds doing okay over there?” Cherine called. “My beetles are starting to chew through the stoppers. I think we need to get started.”

Zeph turned and left Kia behind, not looking back, and made his way into the borderlands between the Argent Heights and the Abyssal Naze, removing glyphs that had protected both lands for hundreds of years.

He tried to think of Xin, of Xavi and Pink Paw, of Hatzel, and even Younce. There were a lot of gryphons back home depending upon him. He wouldn’t let them down.

But using the starlings left a bad taste in his beak. A sticky, gooey taste he couldn’t spit out.

I’ve been spending too much time around the cave swiftlets.

33

NIGHTSKY

Wendl lit incense she'd specially formulated to match her scent, then disappeared into a cave on the border of the Nightsky Pride's territory. Most of the nearby gryphons were turning in for the evening, but if any starlings came close enough to smell it, that information would be passed along to the pridelord.

She'd discovered—by accident—that the pridelord's awareness was based on pride territory. So if she entered this cave from the Nightsky side, and her false scent showed her as being in their territory, the pridelord wouldn't know where exactly she was unless he came looking for her.

Her colleague came in from the other side, using his own incense to make it seem like he was in the territory of the Newmoon Pride. This would also work if they just stood by the territory markers and shouted back and forth, but she didn't want to be overheard.

"I need more of the salts," she said. "I'm running low."

Across from her sat a starling who looked nearly identical

to her, down to his ears, tail, and talons. That wasn't a coincidence. They'd both taken their blood from the same test subject. They even shared a set of four slightly larger white dots above their beaks.

"You're going through them quickly," he said. "I'll do what I can, but once we're out, we're out. Don't use it to reset the starlings just to delay their bloodbeak."

Wendl ignored him. He'd been an arrogant scholar, now he was an arrogant starling. He was useful because he was one of the only other scholars who had retained their talons when they transformed.

"I know," she retorted. "We'll have enough to fix them if we find a cure. I assume you've already set aside a vial for yourself in case we get a chance to leave, so how I spend *my* salts is no business of yours, is it?"

He bristled but didn't respond. He needed her as much as she needed him. These meetings were so rare because he'd been assigned to the temple itself, going through the relics in its depths. That gave him plenty of places to hide the salts Khalim had given her, but it meant he rarely had the freedom to see the jungle.

"I'll get it to you next time," he said. "Earlier, if I see one of our brothers or sisters."

She rolled her eyes. That was a strange way of looking at what the salts had done to them. "I need one more thing, and this may require some help to figure out."

"Ask away. Apparently, I live to fulfill your whims." He wasn't usually this grumpy, but there were strange rumors coming in. Just the barest whispers, and she didn't know how they were reaching the starlings, but something was brewing outside their borders.

"I need a list of every stormtail who has left the Winter

Jungle and taken a mate with another pride. Who their mate is, where they're staying together, all of it," she said.

Her request was an unusual one, and he responded the way she'd expected him to. "Stormtails? That's... odd. There aren't many. The pridelord has forbidden them from breeding outside their pride this year. Does he know why you want them? Don't bring his wrath down upon us, Wendl. He's not as dumb as most gryphons."

She didn't think most gryphons *were* dumb, which was why she'd managed to stay alive for this long. She was nothing if not careful. "I think he fears them for the same reason I want them. They're not... how do I say this? If the theories are correct, the fur patterns gryphons and opinici share came from somewhere. They all look the same. *Gryphonic,* as it were. But the stormtails are different. They're living here as starlings, but I think they're something new. That's why he doesn't want them breeding with the other prides. He worries they're going to break free of the hive."

Her colleague considered this. He was smart enough not to ask any more questions, not until he figured out why she wanted them on his own. The intrigue of universities and scholars was something they'd brought with them to the jungle. "It's a short list, but I can get it to you. I assume you have a way of... incapacitating them and erasing their memory?"

"You remember our old base camp?" she asked. "The pridelord put up a scent there that causes their memories to turn fuzzy. It's the perfect place for my purposes."

Her colleague left, promising salts and a map of the stormtails. He might figure out what she was up to. Maybe not. She crawled back out of the cave on the Nightsky side of the territory and put out the incense. She waited a little, letting her scent become established here in case the pride-lord was searching for her, then she headed to a small garden she kept near the northern border.

She picked a few of the forbidden herbs and tubers, hiding them in her pouch under more fragrant flowers, lest Nighteyes catch what she was up to.

In a sense, she was doing what she was doing to help free the nightsky. More of them suffered from bloodbeak than any other starling pride. And, after years of research and going over Mally's abandoned notes at the ruins of the camp, she'd finally figured out what was missing.

He'd claimed to have experimented upon all of the starling prides, claimed he'd come close to finding a cure. After the starlings, blackwings, and alabasters obliterated his old expedition base camp, he'd fled the jungle and never returned.

But Wendl had stayed, living as a starling. She'd taken the scraps of Mally's research she could find, then travelled throughout the starling prides, trying to fill in the missing gaps. There was only one partial success among his experiments, but no note of what pride that starling had come from.

It had taken her years, but Wendl thought she'd figured it out. By process of elimination, the only entry that showed promise *must* have come from one of the stormtails. Since then, she'd been ambushing them when they left their territory, stealing their blood, and using it on the nightsky chicks.

So far, there hadn't been any results. Mally's rotting notebooks didn't have names or even descriptions, but she was fairly certain that whatever stormtail gryphon had shown promise in the Nighthaunt's experiments had escaped alive. She wracked her memories of that day and her later searches, and she didn't remember any stormtails among the dead. She just needed to find the right one.

Then she could stop bloodbeak. Something which benefitted the Nightsky Pride.

I'm doing the right thing. I know it.

She sighed. Nighteyes wouldn't see it that way. The advantage of living among a group of gryphons who believed that no starling would harm another starling was that it made it very easy for her to lure the stormtails out on their own. And, despite the pridelord's insistence, stormtails were still leaving their pride and searching for mates.

When she reached the violet nesting grounds, she found them empty, which was unusual. Not even Nighteyes's stormtail was there, a gryphon who spent so much time with his mate that Wendl hadn't been able to get him alone to steal his blood.

Yet.

To the north, she heard some chittering of the friendly, curious variety and went to investigate. The Nightsky Pride was on the border, staring at several trees missing large swathes of bark. Nighteyes and her mate were in front of one in particular.

"It looks like the beetles are only eating the trees with glyphs," the stormtail said. "That's weird, right?"

Nighteyes shook her head. "No, the bark beetles really love the smell and taste of the paste we use. I mean, it's a little weird, but it happens."

Wendl approached cautiously. The Seraph King and silver reeve would never interfere with the border, but the blackwings might. While the violet starlings checked on the trees with glyphs, Wendl looked around at the other trees. None of them were showing signs of bark beetle infestation.

Nighteyes and her mate continued to speculate, but Wendl searched the ground and found what she was looking for—glass vials, an empty one between each tree.

This is deliberate.

But who had done it? She weighed her options. If she told the pridelord, he'd want to investigate everything happening along this border. If he did that, he might discover what Wendl was up to. For now, it seemed harmless enough. No attack had come, and she certainly didn't want anyone looking into the old expedition ruins.

She'd been dousing Nighteyes's food with just enough orange to give her a little free will, not enough to let her break free, but Wendl wanted to keep the levels high for when she needed Night later.

She turned back south to check on the pride leader. Wendl had gone a little beyond the glyph markers, but no one seemed to notice. She opened her beak to speak to Nighteyes, then closed it again. A flash of red, blue, and green flew overhead.

There was no starling pride that was red. And behind the interloper, a swarm of jadebeaks and some newmoon starlings followed.

The opinicus flew quickly, past the missing glyphs. The Nightsky Pride's altruism kicked in, and they joined the swarm.

Wendl swore.

Wendl had exactly one of her smoke bombs—really, explosive incense—left in her harness. Nighteyes was her friend as well as her pride leader, and Wendl didn't want her to die in the swarm. The starling opinicus lit the fuse as fast as her talons permitted and threw the scent bomb ahead of Nighteyes, catching both her and her mate in the explosion.

The other starlings flowed around the couple, but the scent in the bomb was designed to cut starlings off from the pride and calm them. Wendl waited for the smoke to clear out, something she'd had to learn from experience, and then grabbed the catatonic Nighteyes and dragged her back towards the nesting grounds.

As a mothfeather opinicus scholar, it would be natural to assume Wendl didn't have much strength, but she'd grown up on a farm. Even after she'd begun attending the university, she still had strength beyond what her small stature would have suggested. And as a starling, that strength had grown when she'd had to learn to hunt for herself.

So dragging Nighteyes back home was doable, but keeping her friend's paws from dragging was another matter. Wendl didn't think Nighteyes would begrudge her a little dirt.

To her right, the small nesting ground was full of gryphlets in a kind of trance. Their older siblings had been watching them, and while many had flown off to the swarm, a few were still young enough that the altruism had a mesmerizing effect on them instead of a homicidal one. One of the fledglings even had the markings of bloodbeak, born after Wendl had started treating the eggs here.

The scholar went back north, figuring she should save the stormtail, too, when a thought occurred to her. All around, swarms of dark and light green starlings were mindless, lost in their frenzy. None of them could really see Wendl, none of them would remember what happened here.

She dragged the stormtail's body behind some brush and pulled out her sharpest knife. It was a fish gutting knife taken off the corpse of a ranger in the bog, but it felt good to have tools again.

Life so rarely gives you exactly what you need, but today...

She pulled out the glass vials she'd found on the forest floor and filled them with the stormtail's blood. Then she stitched him up as best she could and dragged him back to the nests, laying him next to Nighteyes.

The swarm was still going, more starlings coming to investigate and 'catching' frenzy from the others. It was such a strange opportunity, Wendl decided to do a little more work.

She found the stunned fledgling with the worst bloodbeak symptoms, put the child on her back, using her wings to stabilize their body, and headed off to her workshop.

If the swarm lasted long enough, she could treat this fledgling with the blood and get back before anyone noticed. And if not, well, she would just claim she found her wandering around and brought her home again.

No rest for the wicked.

34

A COORDINATED ASSAULT

The sky over the Seraph King's capital city was gold, bringing new life to the buildings and stonework. It was beautiful in its own way. Not like an apple or a flower, but as a kind of testament to opinicus society.

Stripes took in the scenery because in a few minutes, she was about to blow it all up. She finished handing out flint and tinder to the crow gryphons, who swished their striped tails with anticipation. Despite their lack of talons, they were incredibly adept at using tools and navigating the less populated areas of the city.

Of course, the blackwing commander didn't want her and her new gryphon allies only blowing up targets that were out of the way. She'd given the greyfeather some long fuses for their other targets.

"The fuses being used by the..." She wasn't sure what to call the crow gryphons. She was so used to gryphons being in prides that it was unusual to talk to them as individuals. She didn't want to call them the *trash pride,* though that's really what they did: they lived in and stole trash.

She shook her head and started again. "The fuses on the saltpeter bombs the *city pride* are using don't last long, so as soon as the nighttime lanterns are lit, that's your cue. For our good greyfeather friend here, *your* fuses should last about an hour for the first one, then less time for each past that. By the time you light the last fuse, you'll have minutes to get away from the source of the explosion. And they should all go off at relatively the same time."

Only these gryphons and opinici were staying for the attack. The others had come here after the king's soldiers attempted to wipe them out, displacing them from their home territory. They were excited to return to the forests or plains. The crow gryphons, however, seemed to have arisen from the eyrie itself. It *was* their home.

The city pride were cagey with how they lived, but it seemed like they had nests and homes hidden within the walls. These nests were moved monthly, but they existed wherever the bright, shiny white opinici weren't looking.

At least, that was how Stripes understood it. They were a mystery even to their peers. The other gryphon refugees weren't allowed to follow the crows outside of the Garden of the Forbearers unless they had a city gryphon mate. It was an interesting situation, and it brought out the scholar in Stripes. She wanted to know more.

She'd given the crow gryphons a little more time to evacuate their homes and nests from the blast radius. She had no idea where they had been moved to, but she'd been assured they were safe.

She gave the word, sending the greyfeather and crows out into the world. No matter her reservations, in about an hour, the entire city would light up with fire, and the attack would begin. It was out of her talons now.

The motmots stood at her back, feeding her scarabs while she removed her red cave silk covering and put it into a spare pouch. Her companions hated wearing anything, were known for wanting to be naked all the time—who didn't, honestly—but she'd found she could trick them into wearing their battle harnesses if she filled them with gryphon snacks.

"You must keep up your poison," one told her, holding a scarab in her beak and trying to push it into Stripes's.

The pitohui was a little embarrassed, but she'd learned long ago that if a gryphon offered her food, it was best to just eat it. She'd forgotten to tell them they didn't need to pretend they were her lovers, that they didn't need to play along with the greyfeather's misconceptions, so sometimes when she accepted food from them, they'd purr and then wink at her.

Sigh.

She crunched down on the scarab. She was already oily, but she didn't think there'd be another time in her life when she needed more poison than now.

She made a final check of her map, one of several copies she'd made for the army with the help of the crow gryphons. While the army attacked the Reeve's Guard headquarters and the palace first to take care of any opinici with weapons, she had another task—marked with a skull and vibrant tail-feathers.

When she'd left the glacier pride's mountain months ago, she hadn't arrived back in time to stop Impir. This time, she was going to be ready. When the explosions went off, she'd strike.

A remaining crow led the way. They liked to touch things with their beaks, so now that her covering was packed up,

Stripes put the motmots between her and the city gryphon. They would wipe their beaks on her after they arrived at their target.

The sky darkened. The lamp lighters were out, planting small seeds of flame across the city.

And then Stripes's bombs erupted into fiery wildflowers, bathing the city in their vibrant orange glow. Parts of the palace collapsed. The arch into the city housing the Reeve's Guard fell down upon itself, and the skies to the south filled with the armies of the Blackwing Alliance.

"Now!" she shouted at the motmots, and the five of them flew for the portmaster's office.

THE STARLINGS CHASING Kia quickly closed the gap, one managing to slash away a few of her tailfeathers. To her right rose the mountains of the Argent Heights. To her left was a cascade of waterfalls disappearing into the Abyssal Naze.

And ahead, just a little too far ahead, was the lone workshop perched above the inky depths. She flew towards it, trying to get the starlings close enough to let their altruism latch onto the alabaster opinici, but she wasn't fast enough.

A starling took a bite out of her back leg, the sharp edges of its tomia allowing it to dig in.

She screamed and twisted mid-air, shaking it off. Pieces of her orange tabby flank, thankfully more fur than meat, came off in its beak.

New plan. Get out of here!

She dove towards the Abyssal Naze, crossing the cave gryphon glyphs. The starlings followed her until she was past the glyphs, then the altruism wore off and they became confused.

That's no good.

She landed to tend to her wound, hoping to get back up in the air, but some of the starlings had snapped out of their fervor and were turning back.

Just when hope seemed lost, a patrol of white opinici glided into view. The lead had black eyes and her markings were dripping. She stared right at Kia, missing the starlings until they began to chitter.

The darkstalker swore, fleeing back to the workshop, newly altruistic starlings in tow.

"That was close," Kia muttered. She stitched up her bite, covered it with some leaves that killed infection, and flew over the large pit beneath her. The starlings were fixated on the eastern side of the workshop now. A few alabaster patrols caught sight of her, but they let her go, worried more about starlings than a single parrot.

She dipped down by a waterfall, following it up to a cave entrance. She sniffed around, and Zeph had to chirp to get her attention.

"It's done," she said. "The starlings are attacking. Now's our chance to break into the workshop and kill the Nighthaunt."

Tiny black eyes appeared from a dozen hiding spots. They streamed out like an overturned anthill, swarming along the ground to the infamous workshop where their own kind had been experimented on for years.

35

ESCAPE FROM THE CRACKLING SEA

Storms crashed off the cliffs of the Crackling Sea Eyrie. The balconies were once again abandoned, even the dock workers had given up for the night. Only two blue heron shapes spoke in the shadows, staring out at the luminescent waters.

Bruen had missed his old home.

"They're starting to get suspicious," Llore said. "The flamingos opened one of the crates early and were snacking on its contents up in the library, and several scholars died."

He shook his head. "The dose shouldn't have been high enough to kill them. Not so quickly."

"An allergic reaction, then?" Llore seemed to consider this. "I wish I had my old journals. I used to have a chart showing which opinicus species were allergic to what. It figures a lack of preparation would bite us in the tailfeathers."

Bruen shrugged. "We're nothing if not prepared. Sometimes we just get unlucky. As long as we have enough foresight to stay alive, hey, that's all I ask."

He hid from the winds and rain long enough to fill out his report, toss it in the bag, and drop it off the cliffs and into the water below.

A few minutes later, a small, dark shape swam down and retrieved it. He couldn't be sure, but he thought it might've been Quess checking up on him. He left messages for her in the reports, but he had no way of knowing if the Ashen Weald was passing them along.

Llore was staring at him when he turned his gaze from the sea. "I'll be honest. I was surprised you two found some common ground at the Flower, and I'm even more surprised it stuck. When's the… fisherfolk mating ceremony?"

He laughed, but it was a little forced. "I don't think we're at that stage. We're just better together than separate. And don't knock the fisherfolk villages until you've been down there. They're hardworking, but there's also this purity of purpose on the coast."

"There's also sand fleas," Llore countered. "Rock crabs. Oh, and everyone I ever wronged in my previous life."

He hesitated, then did something he never would have done when Ellore was the Ranger Lord of the Crackling Sea or even his captain.

He gave her a hug.

She looked surprised, but she didn't toss him off the cliff, either. "What was that for?"

"We all lost our way, there at the end," he said. "But we've missed you. And inside the bog, you did right by us. There were quite a few rangers, red and blue, who spoke up for your pardon. Even two salty fisherfolk."

She considered him. "Did Quess?"

"She might've sat that one out, but can you blame her?" he asked. Before the starlings had made allies of enemies, before

Vitra had captured them, the rangers and fisherfolk had been at each others' throats.

"No, not at all," Ellore said. "I need to get back. Satra was cagey on giving me the details of her plan, but she said to be ready. Any day now, the supply lines will run dry, and the Ashen Weald will attack. We just need to avoid discovery until that happens."

He nodded. "I'm not worried. We've done enough harm in the world. I don't mind getting roughed up trying to do some good."

She hesitated, never the hugging type, but tapped the top of his head with a wing before disappearing down another wet ramp back into the eyrie.

Bruen stared out at the water a little longer, looking for shapes among the bright jellies of the sea. He didn't spot any, so he left.

When the day of the attack came, he'd have little to do. He'd already weakened the barriers and walls the pink reeve had put up to keep the wingtorn out. It wouldn't take much to break them down.

He'd still try to help where he could, but for the most part, he'd get to go home and relax once that happened.

It'll be good to curl up with Quess again.

He entered the stairwell, shaking off the rain, and made his way down to his quarters. He passed a few flamingos, but they paid him no mind. He felt invisible, which was bad for eyrie relations but good for espionage.

Daydreams of returning to the shore were going through his mind when he pushed the tanned goliath hide blocking the view to his nest and entered.

Inside, his things were ransacked. Everything he owned

was on the floor, broken, as though someone were searching for hidden trinkets or writing.

And if they'd come in earlier, before the drop, they might have found something.

That meant they were onto him specifically. He pulled out his fishing knife and scraped off the layer of his badge that marked him as a stabletalon, revealing a more polished version underneath that denoted him as a captain of the rangers and someone trusted by Jonas.

He needed to get out of here as soon as he could. But first, he had to warn the others. He'd been exceptionally careful, so if the pink reeve was onto him, they definitely knew about at least one other.

Ex-Ranger Lord Ellore wandered through the hallways, dripping water on her way. Some of it had seeped into her fur, and she shivered, but she didn't mind the cold and wet. She was back home, a task that had seemed impossible many times, and she was just happy to be here.

She also didn't mind the spying. That had always bothered her about her time in the swamp. Back then, it was the promise of getting to come home that kept her on the blackwing's leash. But she was already home. Now she spied because she wanted to see the other herons able to return here. And, perhaps, because during her time in the north, she'd stopped thinking about what she wanted and began to wonder what her daughter would have wanted.

The answer to that was clear. Mignet would have wanted her friends to be safe. And so Ellore had forced herself to make peace with the same gryphons she'd long blamed for

Mignet's death. She didn't start with Satra because she thought that'd be easiest. Ellore started with Satra because, deep down inside, she knew Mignet had cared most about Satra. For her part, while Satra was skeptical, she'd made small steps towards peace, including allowing Ellore to take her own team into the Crackling Sea Eyrie.

Zeph and Younce had been similarly uncertain, but they were each willing to sit and talk to Ellore once. They gave her stories about Mignet. They advocated on behalf of Satra. But when that one session had ended, neither had been willing to come back, though Ellore hoped that would change. Only Deracho had flat out refused to meet with her.

As she climbed the hallways back to her quarters, she thought of the other opinicus she wished she could speak with one more time, Lei. She didn't know where he lived. The last time they'd met, he claimed to be a fisherfolk salt trader, but she had no way of confirming that. Bruen wouldn't tell her about the fisherfolk. His trust for her was limited to him personally and the mission.

Bruen. How did I not ruin your life?

The hug was unexpected, especially from him. But if he could change, so could she. She shook off her feathers, nearing her small nest, then froze when she saw the colors of the chimes hanging in the hallway. She'd chosen this particular set of quarters because it was away from the others and populated with some of the seedier Reevesport merchants supplying the Seraph King with goods from up north.

The nice thing about seedy merchants was that they could be bribed. In this case, a hefty sum of beads if he'd keep watch on Ellore's nest and change the chimes in the hallway if someone had disturbed her things. A second sum when Ellore arrived and saw them.

She found it was best to have a merchant's financial well-being tied in with her own will to live. She took out a few beads and slid them behind a jellyfish carving for him to retrieve later, then she took a quick glance around the corner.

A dozen flamingos were sitting outside her nest. They wore the glass Crestfall badges of the pink Reeve's Guard.

Ellore turned back the way she'd come and made a break for it. Her quarters were on the southwest side of the eyrie. Most of their escape routes were in the northeast, but there was one near the center. It was a bit of a run, but if she got lucky, she might make it.

She stuck to the tunnels until she heard the sounds of Reeve's Guard patrols, then she took to the balconies. There was a light mist. That was enough to keep workers away, but it would make her stand out if someone was patrolling from the air. Did they know what she looked like, or had they just found some contraband while searching her nest?

She scratched off her stabletalon badge. There were still some loyalists who wore the ranger badge. If they were looking for a stabletalon, this might help her get away.

She reached the large, open center of the eyrie that looked out at the sea. She waited behind a pillar for the airborne patrols to pass. She was taking a great risk flying across one of the most populated sections of the city, but she couldn't think of any better options. She calmed herself, groomed a few feathers, and flew over the merchant area, trying to look like she belonged.

So far, so good.

She landed on the other side, walked calmly past a set of dozing guards, then made a dash for the closest secret passage out of here. Just off the intersection of three hallways was a small resting area that was too cramped for any guards to actually use it. Part of the reason it was cramped was that it contained a giant heron statue with a fish in its beak.

She'd nearly turned the fish to open the passage when she noticed that the dust had been disturbed. A pair of talons had already twisted it recently.

Bruen? she wondered. *If it was him, did he trigger the explosive to close it? Or would he have left it open for me, knowing I was stuck across the eyrie from most of the remaining passages?*

Her instincts told her to flee, but she didn't think she had time to find another way out. She twisted the fish, and one of the pillars gave way, revealing the hidden path. The tiny bits of saltpeter the Ashen Weald had installed were designed to quietly collapse the tunnels after they were shut without letting anyone know they'd been here. This one had been left open.

She hoped that meant Bruen had come this way, but the little light coming in from the hallway glistened off an orb of glass. The sphere floated towards her.

A flamingo stepped forwards, his pink glass eye sparkling in the light. "Ah, I see we located one of the missing spies. Clever things, these passages. Every time I think we've found them all, another springs up."

Flint and tinder clutched in separate talons, she backed up, but she could already hear a patrol approaching. There were only three behind her, but they were crouched down with nets. One was even using the jelly toxin on his sparkling glass talons.

Designed to shatter in the wound. How... sadistic.

The worst imitation of a coastal bird came from behind the patrols. They ignored it, but she knew what it meant.

She struck flame to the hidden fuse, and the tunnel

collapsed. To her disappointment, the pink-eyed flamingo's assistants pulled him back before he was buried alive.

The patrol in the hallway ran at her, but Bruen and four of her other rangers took them from above. A few quick scratches and they were tied up in their own nets and hidden just out of view.

"Seemed like you were in a bit of trouble there, boss," one of the herons said.

She laughed. "I'm glad you five are all fine. Were you looking for me or are all the other tunnels full?"

"Looking for you," Bruen confirmed. "But if they found this tunnel, we have to assume most of the others are compromised. Should we fly for it?"

Great blue herons were not the fastest flyers. They wouldn't make it across the sea, not when the Crackling Sea Eyrie housed a dozen argent hawks to run messages. But there was one secret passage that was probably still good.

"Head for the butchery," Ellore commanded. "I heard patrols and goliath birds in the back tunnels. All the meat in there should have kept it hidden from the birds' sense of smell. Let's fly for it. Speed over stealth. Everyone in, blow the fuse, and run."

The rangers who were putting away their metal talons pulled them back on.

"I like a good fight, but won't they dig us out?" Bruen asked.

Ellore shrugged. "I don't have a better idea. We'll just have to move fast once we're inside."

Ellore hung back once they were in the air. She and most of her rangers had simple badges, but Bruen had a captain badge, so it made sense that he'd stay in the front. She remained behind to make sure no one was chasing them.

They'd just reached the butchery balcony, slashing through the damp, non-stormcloth curtains, when the first airborne patrol spotted them and switched directions.

"We need to hurry," she told Bruen.

The problem with having a secret passage no one can find is that, if it's in a large shop, there's an even chance someone decides that's the perfect spot for storage and puts a bunch of crates of fish jerky in front of it.

They began moving the crates out in pairs, taking them to the balcony and the front door to stop the patrols. Only the butcher and a single customer were here, and Ellore tossed them both a few beads and told them to come back once the fighting was over. They were happy to oblige.

They'll probably tell the first guards they see, but we've already been spotted from the skies.

The shop itself had a back area for storage, a front area with a counter for orders, and then a large receiving area. The balcony and main entrance were now closed, the way to the secret passage was open, and they were just struggling to find the switch to open it. It was a lot easier to spot when this back room had been empty. They moved boxes and hoped for the best.

Ellore glanced at the receiving area and a thought occurred to her. These crates were too large for opinici to move them easily. That meant goliath birds needed a way in here. Goliaths couldn't fly, so the balcony was out. And the main entrance came through a small hallway that even she had to duck to get through.

She heard a pounding from the receiving area, and then what she'd taken to be a large, wooden wall decoration exploded, and a goliath bird wearing a metal, shovel-like helmet burst through with its handlers behind it.

She screamed at Bruen to run. Bruen screamed at her that he'd found it.

The heron statue twisted back, revealing a long passage that came out miles from the Crackling Sea Eyrie. There was only one problem. The goliath birds were already here. Even if they flipped the switch, there wasn't enough time to run miles through the passage before someone caught up with them.

Unlike the extra tunnels the Ashen Weald had added while they owned the eyrie, this one had been put in by the original butcher, who smuggled meat out to sell when rations were low. It was big enough for a goliath bird to pull a small wagon through it, and no opinicus was going to outrun a goliath bird.

"Go, run!" she shouted, pushing Bruen and the others inside. Then, without joining them, she lit the fuse, collapsing part of the tunnel. She pulled the statue back and knocked over some crates in front of it.

From her right, she heard an argent pulling aside the cases of jerky blocking the balcony. From the main corridor, two guards were shouting and pushing against the door, trying to dislodge another set of boxes.

And from the receiving area, a metal-clad goliath bird *mronked* loudly and charged her.

Ellore dove behind the stone counter, and the goliath bird's helmet destroyed half of it. It reared back, and Ellore did the only thing she knew to stop a goliath bird. She used her long, long beak to peck at its eyes.

The first hit missed, but she caught part of its eyelid, drawing blood. The bird squawked in fear and anger.

She went for the other eye, but her beak plinked against the metal helmet. Still, the noise startled the bird, and it backed up. She continued her attacks, knowing that if she let up, the goliath bird would kill her with one kick.

She'd forced it back to the receiving area when its opinicus handlers finally broke through the other ways. She chose a random section of the butchery that had a set of mismatched stones she hoped they'd think led to a passage, and ran that way, spreading her wings like she was going to defend it.

"Stay back! I'll never let you catch my friends!" she shouted, hoping she was convincing.

One of the tenders ran to the goliath bird, cleaning the blood around its eye and making sure it was unharmed. The others circled Ellore. She grabbed a pronged spear from a stack of them—apparently the butcher liked to fish now and then—and used it to deflect the loyalists' nets.

She held them at bay for the better part of fifteen minutes before the glass-eyed flamingo arrived.

"For crying out loud." He shook his head, the pink eye catching the light. He put a glove over his talons, spread the jelly toxin over a handful of flechettes and flung them at her.

Ellore covered her eyes, taking the spikes in her chest. The toxin worked its magic, and she collapsed.

36

WATER LIKE LIGHTNING

Ellore awoke in Jonas's old workshop, and her first thought was to check her wings. They were still there, though someone had stripped most of her feathers down.

Looks like I won't be flying for a while.

She started to stand, but she had a leather strap around her neck and more around her legs. Each was held by a nearby guard from a different eyrie of the Seraph King. The Argent Heights representative seemed less happy with her role than the others.

"Ah good, you're awake." The pink reeve sat on Jonas's old throne. "I assumed you'd have built up a resistance to your own toxins, but I suppose that's not the case."

Ellore shook her head a little, clearing out the cobwebs, then looked around. The pink-eyed opinicus who had caught her stood next to the pink reeve. Unlike when he was out in the hallways chasing her, he now wore the usual glass trinkets of Crestfall.

Though they paled in comparison to what the reeve

himself wore. The slightest breeze made him jingle. The brazier light caught on the teardrop crystals hanging from each set of necklaces on his abundant neck. He wore glass over his own talons, tinted pink.

Though something had changed, and she only noticed it by seeing the pink reeve up close. He wasn't the usual shade of pink. In fact, he was the same shade of pink that the taiga gryphons were, suggesting the flamingos had found a store of Biski's dye.

The other flamingos were similarly not *Crestfall pink.* Without access to the shrimp that granted them their colors, they were fading to whites and greys. It was a little sad and left her wondering if Zeph and Kia's poison had killed off more than just the salt-making organisms in the pools.

"Not going to plead for your life?" the reeve asked. "Not going to offer up intelligence on your blackwing masters?"

Ellore tried not to show her surprise. She didn't think there were any records of her real identity. Not even the prison at Whitebeak had known who she was. They'd just locked her up because of her Blackwing Eyrie badge. Yet these Crestfall opinici still assumed it was the blackwing reeve pulling the strings here. They were unaware of the Ashen Weald, waiting in the mountains and bog, ready to strike once the supply lines were cut.

She opened her beak, felt how dry it was, and decided there was nothing she could say that would be more misleading than what they already thought.

"Excellent. I enjoy expediency," the reeve said. "If the king's representatives have no objections, perhaps we can toss her over?"

The Reevesport peafowl, the Alabaster Eyrie white-tailed kite, and the duck opinicus voiced their assent. The argent hawk abstained, speaking neither in Ellore's favor or against her. Llore expected the pink reeve to be annoyed, but apparently this was the reply he'd expected.

"Perhaps Reeve Silver can send us someone who cares one way or another with the next shipment," he drolled, then waved a sparkling talon.

The guards lifted Ellore and walked her to the edge. She didn't particularly want to die, but there was a poetry to dying here. This was where she'd started down a path she'd been unable to stop. She had vivid memories of Jonas telling her to toss a baby gryphlet off the edge as a ploy to keep Satra in line. And now she, Ellore, would also get tossed over the edge.

What goes around, comes around.

There was no ceremony. They simply chucked her over, and she fell. Despite knowing her best bet was to die upon impact or aim for a rock, her survival instincts righted her as best they could with so few working feathers.

She fell like she was diving for fish. Into the darkness, which illuminated a bright blue-green ahead of her in response to the storm. She prayed the swarm's toxin rendered her unconscious immediately. There were rumors that if you were stung underwater, you remained paralyzed but awake, and that's not how she wanted to be when she drowned.

She crashed into the water, missing the stony spires, and went down a good fifteen feet.

Did the jellyfish leave? Am I safe?

Lightning crashed above, and the sea all around her lit up. Lanterns of living electricity surrounded her, drifting closer with the tide. She swam up, but she'd only just gotten her beak above the surface when she felt a sting on her back leg, and she lost consciousness.

Ellore was surprised to wake. The storm still raged overhead, more lightning than rain, but she was somehow floating on her back, her head propped above the water. She shook her back paw. It ached from the sting, but that just reinforced her belief she was still alive.

"Stay limp. Do not talk." The voice came from the water itself, yet it felt familiar to Ellore.

Perhaps death has just become an old friend.

When the next flash of light came, she opened her eye to see where the swarm was at. They were south of her now, near the eyrie, which led to the realization she was floating out to sea.

That was both good and bad. On the good side of the equation, that moved her away from this swarm of jellyfish and away from the sailfins, who preferred the coast. On the, well, *other* side of the equation, her feathers meant she wouldn't get to fly, and while the reeve's pet was long dead, there were still fish in the Crackling Sea large enough to take a bite out of an opinicus.

She must have twitched again because the same voice returned, "You're almost there. Remain calm."

No, not the same. A new voice, but also familiar.

Her brain reeled from being poisoned twice, but while it wasn't telling her who the voices were, it told her she was in danger. A sense of panic rose in her.

She pushed it down. Lying on the water, staring at the stormy skies. She'd dreamed of doing this as a chick. Her parents would never allow it, of course. There were the large turtles to worry about. The crackling jellies. The sea monsters. And, well, the chance of being struck by lightning.

There was a saying among the Redwood Valley opinici that *lightning never strikes the same place twice.*

It was, in fact, the stupidest thing she'd ever heard any opinicus say. Of *course* lightning struck the same place twice. Why did the reds think they were selling so many lightning rods at their metalworks? For exactly that reason!

Llore calmed herself. Crackling jelly turned the brain into, well, jelly for a bit. She hadn't been rendered unconscious in many years until today, but it wasn't something she'd ever forget.

She thought she heard the sound of choppy waves against a shore, and she wondered if she'd drifted all the way out to the old island fortress.

Not drifted. Pulled here.

Both voices returned.

"There are some jellies ahead. Do not be afraid," one said.

"You'll want to take a deep breath, though," the other continued, "because you're about to go underwater. We'll be fast, I promise."

They were already tugging her underwater, so she took in a breath as fast as she could. Beneath the waves, she saw dark shapes surrounding her, keeping the jellies at bay. A flash of something that resembled a shark came across her vision, making her wonder if this was the afterlife.

The shapes closed in on her and swam quickly, faster than she thought possible, in the direction of the island.

But they didn't bring her up to the shore. Instead, they went down, into an underwater cave, and then up again. Just when her lungs were at their limit, she breached the surface, finding herself in an old smuggling hideaway.

She righted herself and coughed, taking stock of her situation. There were several fires all around her, stacks of supplies, and... fisherfolk.

A *lot* of fisherfolk. The voices now connected to the visuals, and Ellore recognized the two standing in front of her.

Turresh the Shark took off her mask, revealing her jagged beak. "It has been a long time since the bog."

"A *very* long time," Quess emphasized. The petrel opinicus would forever have silver eyes in Ellore's memory, and it was strange seeing her healthy again.

They both brandished weapons. The gryphon's claws had been sharpened. Quess wore an old pair of Bruen's talons, though it seemed only to be out of habit. Quess made a show of putting away her weapons, and Tresh's claws returned to their sheathes.

"Bruen made it out okay," Quess said. "He sent us. Don't worry, you're not our prisoner, but we're going to be stuck here for a week or two. We need the jelly swarms to leave the entrance to move you out, and we need to find some heron feathers to get you imped up again."

Ellore stared at one of the fires. This was the third time she'd been certain she would die. She didn't mind being held in an old smuggling cave. Especially not one that seemed to have barrels of fresh water and food.

She started to move towards the food, then she remembered Bruen's kindness on the balcony that day. The words were difficult, but she still got them out.

"Thank you," she said to the petrels from the bog. Then she gave them a hug, wrapping her wings around both at the same time.

They returned it, though Quess whispered, "Must be the toxin," to Tresh after Ellore released them.

37

THE SILVER ASSASSIN

Rybalt sat atop a small mining town near the lumber mill and watched the Argent Heights garrison. When the darkstalker still lived, he never would have dared do this. But now that Tinkt had passed on, Rybalt felt a little freer to scout, and he'd spent the evening getting a feel for the enemy's movements.

Iony's grey plumage made him hard to spot against the mountains, and his owl microfeathers meant no one would hear him. Rybalt was waiting for him, looking for him even, and didn't see his friend until he was nearly right on top of the pitohui reeve.

"You're getting better at reconnaissance," Rybalt commented.

Iony laughed, short hoots in succession. "Or you're getting worse."

Rybalt grumbled, handing some rock candy to the gryphon. The nice elderly couple who watched the mine were tied up below, unharmed. In fact, they seemed delighted the pitohui and glacier gryphons had taken such a shining to their confections.

"Don't you dare kill them," one of Iony's pride had told Rybalt. *"Don't you dare kill those strange sugar-spinning wonders."*

Rybalt had been threatened by many gryphons and opinici in his time as an assassin, and he tended to respond poorly to threats. Having an easy way to make Iony happy felt worth letting it slide.

"You'd better hope I haven't lost my touch," Rybalt responded. "We have to go in tonight, and it's all riding on us. That garrison is housing a much larger army than we expected. If they get loose, our blackwing allies are dead."

Iony's head tilt was one Rybalt was familiar with.

"Yes, and Stripes," he amended. "I just trust my sister not to stay and die with the rest of the idiots. Her motmot body-guards have orders to evacuate her if things go horribly wrong. They're the best at what they do."

Iony huffed, a common response when someone praised the motmots over the glacier pride. "Well, let's get to it, then. Garrison's too busy for us to plant the explosives ahead of time. We're just going to have to time it as best we can if you get caught."

"I won't," Rybalt said. "When has anything ever gone wrong with me around?"

"Luminaire," Iony stated. "Whole island blew up."

Rybalt rubbed his beak against his oil glands, slicking his fur and feathers with poison. "The seraph in the bog was our true target, and we burned it to a crisp. That's a victory."

The glacier gryphon didn't correct him. Rybalt would be going in alone for this one. Iony would remain behind to handle the explosives. Precision was out of the question for a garrison this well-defended, so instead, they were going to have to trust the mountain itself to do the heavy lifting.

Teams of glacier gryphons, motmots, and pitohui all held saltpeter bombs courtesy of Bario's new flameworks. Pitohui would light the fuses, and the gryphons would drop them. So long as they were overhead with lit bombs before the Argent Heights figured out they were under attack, it should be an easy victory.

When a plan has a single key to making it all work, it's important to make that key as simple as possible.

Still, Rybalt felt off. Something was going on. Seeing Kia, the Redwood Valley opinicus, at Whitebeak had been suspicious. He didn't think his Ashen Weald allies would turn on him, but information was critical to what he did.

He and Iony had a rule never to be sentimental before starting a mission, but Rybalt broke it as subtly as he could.

"You recall how when the bee is sent out, it doesn't know it's going to die?" Rybalt asked. "Whatever happens here, be certain you are not that bee."

Iony didn't respond, allowing Rybalt to fly off into the night, approaching the eyrie beyond the garrison. With the darkstalker and the argent reeve dead, even if some of the garrison survived, there'd be no leadership. They'd probably mill around, not realizing they had it in their power to stop the Blackwing Alliance.

FOULTNER WAS HAVING A STRESSFUL EVENING. She'd sharpened her barnacle scraper to a point. Then it had broken, and she'd had to sharpen it again, giving her a kind of crooked blade. In addition, she had her fishing knife, and she'd allowed her talons to grow long, making her feel like a gryphon.

And also annoying Henders, who constantly asked why she was clicking when she walked. It was a valid question. Sneaking with clicking talons was hard. So she'd used bee's wax to tip them, allowing her to walk through the eyrie undetected.

Not that anyone was *trying* to detect her. She'd just decided that tonight was the night. She couldn't let the Argent Heights continue to funnel troops and supplies back to the sea. She couldn't risk them going after Satra and Blinky.

Silver needed to die.

Unfortunately, the entire world seemed to be conspiring to stop her. She kept running into friends who wanted to chat. Somehow, despite her surly attitude, everyone *liked* her. And they *loved* Henders. She'd chosen a time when she thought he'd be with Tilly the Goliath Bird, but instead, she ran into him in the hallway by the great hall, coming back with food for her.

"Hey Foult!" he chirped, setting down the little kegs of stew. "I thought we could eat in our rooms and sing songs again. I'm sorry I've been down at the ranch so much. Tilly's doing a lot better now, though."

Foultner tried to look calm, but she knew Henders could always see through her when it came to her mood and feelings.

Thankfully, as much as she hated herself for what she was about to do, he was incredibly trusting of words.

She pulled him into a closet. "Hends, it's time to go home. I need you to grab what you need, then leave the eyrie. Blinky is waiting for us, but you know how she is, she's probably going to wait for me to come out, too."

His eyes grew wide. "Blinky's here?"

"Yes," Foultner lied. "But you don't wait for Blinky or for me, do you hear? I need to do one small thing before I leave. You don't tell anyone where you're going. If they ask, say you're going to stay with Tilly at the ranch. Then you fly like the wind, Hends. You fly along the Jadebeak Mountains straight south until you hit the bog and find our friends."

He was a falcon, and she was a songbird. When things went wrong, he was always going to stand the greatest chance of making it home okay, but only so long as he left her behind.

"And you'll meet me down there?" he asked.

"Of course!" she lied again. "Do you think I want to stay here? Now, go on. Move quickly."

"Okay!" he said a little too loudly. He exited the closet, forgetting the stew on the ground as he left.

With all of her being, she wanted to tell Hends that she loved him. But his ability to sense emotional honesty might give the game away. So she just thought it and prayed he knew.

Once he'd disappeared, she grabbed the two stew kegs by their string and turned back to the alternating ramps leading up to the top of the eyrie. She attached the badge Silver had given Henders to be allowed access anywhere, and she climbed.

Foultner waited in the stairwell, trying to catch her breath. She wasn't winded from the ramps, she'd just never had to psych herself up to murder another opinicus before. She was a poacher. She killed tasty animals, and even then, her traps did the work for her. The closest she'd come to murder was killing infected starlings, and that didn't require the same mental fortitude.

Starlings had lost their minds and were attempting to eat her. Silver was trying to give Foultner a good life. Had even tried to save Foult's life back at the Clover Ranch. And she had no idea that Foultner was thinking of killing her.

The songbird put on her best calm face, then exited to the top story, prepared to confront the single guard.

"Hey!" Foult said. "I brought some dinner for Silver. I thought she may have forgotten to eat again, and Henders is down at the ranch. Thought it might be good just to... Oh, no one is here."

There was no guard. That wasn't entirely strange. The problem with having one guard for an entire floor was that everyone had to pee at some point.

Seems like a bit of a waste to have gotten this magical access badge and there's no one here to use it on.

Though... no guards meant that if she did kill Silver, she could, at least in theory, get away. She doubted she'd make it from the Argent Heights to the bog before *someone* caught up to her, but she might get lucky. Dying was no longer an inevitability.

She carried the stew to Silver's door and knocked lightly. No response came, but the door was ajar. She shrugged and pushed it open.

"Hey Silver, I just wanted to give you some food before we..." Foultner stopped, dropping the two small kegs on the floor.

Reeve Silver, ruler of the Argent Heights, lay on the floor twitching.

A million thoughts and emotions passed through Foultner's mind in an instant. She could do nothing. Someone, probably Rybalt Reevesbane, had done the hard work for her. She could stay here with Henders and continue on, never having done wrong.

Seeing Silver like that, seeing her on the floor twitching, brought up more emotions. It was the friendship she'd shared with Blinky, with Satra, with Orlea. She was seeing a friend in pain, a friend dying, and it was in her power to fix it.

For all Foultner's scheming, for all of her plotting, she now realized she was never cut out to be an assassin.

She yanked the leather strap holding the charm around her neck, and it snapped. She smashed the clay, revealing the vial of pitohui antitoxin inside, and she forced Silver's beak open and poured it down.

The argent reeve looked up, the light slowly returning to her eyes as her muscles regained control. She turned and coughed, and Foultner was worried Silver was going to spit up the medicine.

The argent hawk stared into the eyes of the songbird, seeing the smashed clay and the vial of antitoxin, and there was an understanding there that frightened Foultner.

Silver now knew Foultner wasn't just a rancher, that she was something more. What Silver did with that knowledge, Foultner had no idea. But that was for another day.

"Help me up," Silver coughed. "We have to warn the garrison!"

RYBALT SLIPPED OUT of the argent eyrie and into the darkness. All told, he'd hidden five bodies in storage, and he'd killed most of the cooking staff. Despite the eyrie's fancy front door with its guards and fortifications, nobody had thought to lock the kitchen entrance.

He slipped into the night, preparing to return to Iony and give him word to begin the explosives.

Unfortunately, he was halfway between the eyrie and the garrison when the clanging of giant bells sounded.

Rybalt swore, flying low to try to avoid detection. The garrison sprang to life, brazier flames illuminating the dark.

Against Rybalt's warning not to put himself into danger, Iony took to the sky, leading all their gryphons and opinici towards the garrison, but they weren't fast enough. Even where the saltpeter bombs exploded against the mountain, most of the enemy forces were already aloft.

Suddenly, the combined glacier pride, motmot pride, and pitohui forces looked small in comparison.

Rybalt changed course, trying to get to Iony. The glacier gryphon had been knocked out of the air, but he was a brawler on a mountain side and used the cover of the trees to force his opponents to the ground.

The Reevesbane watched his forces die to get the last of the saltpeter bombs dropped. He had a deep hatred for the Blackwing Eyrie that predated his imprisonment in its depths. But the motmots, the pitohui, the glacier gryphons, they represented the best of the alliance of eyries and prides. They didn't deserve to die like this.

He wracked his brain, trying to find where he'd gone wrong, but he couldn't see it. He'd been so careful.

The silver reeve is dead. That's all that matters. These forces won't realize the capital is under attack until it's too late. These deaths will not be for nothing.

A dozen half-armored alabaster opinici descended upon Iony's hiding place when Rybalt caught up to them. He fought like the spirits of everyone he'd killed were inside of him trying to get out, slashing and splashing his poison on everyone he could.

By the time he made it to Iony, the gryphon was in a bad state.

"Rybalt, get out of here," the glacier gryphon grumbled. A chunk of his left ear had been sliced off by a pair of metal talons. "The hidden cave... take the stargazer and *fly!* That's more important than me."

And it was. To the world, to their plan for a better tomorrow, to the betterment of the Blackwing Alliance itself.

But not to Rybalt.

He pulled off strips of leathers that had once bound him to the prison beneath the Blackwing Eyrie and used them to set Iony's leg and stop the bleeding where he could. "Come on, you giant oaf, we're headed into the caves."

"The others..." Iony began, but Rybalt cut him off.

"They know their way home. The plan was always to split up. They'll be okay. They're all going to be okay. And we're going to be okay, too."

Iony coughed, spitting blood out of his beak, but he let Rybalt lead him through the forest to the mining town, their mission forgotten.

38

RULER OF THE ARGENT HEIGHTS

Once, long ago, Silver had sat and watched as the previous argent reeve died at Rybalt's talons. She'd been the guard who watched this floor at the time, and she'd attempted to stop him. Only grabbing one of Rybalt's vials of antitoxin as the Reevesbane left her for dead had allowed her to survive.

Since then, she'd lived in terror of that night. It had fueled every decision she'd made to accept the Seraph King's offer, to safeguard her opinici. That single night had haunted her for so long she'd forgotten what it was like not to live in fear.

And then he'd appeared in her doorway. She hadn't screamed. She was wearing her comfortable, vibrant harness with all the pockets. She made a dash for her official harness, the one that always included the antitoxin, but didn't even come close to grabbing it before he'd slashed her chest and pushed her to the ground.

He'd spoken very little, holding her close as her muscles began to twitch, and her body lost control.

"I remember you." His voice was both smooth and scratchy from underuse. "In the end, you were unable to save two argent reeves."

He'd slipped away quickly, leaving her alone, and Silver was certain she was going to die here, a failure. As her vision blurred, the fear inside of her melted away, and she felt a kind of... contentment. She'd hated being part of the Seraph King's machinations. She hated causing harm to other eyries. She just didn't want the opinici in her care to suffer any more.

Then the face of a rancher appeared, holding a vial of antitoxin. How a rancher knew about the antidote, Silver had no idea. Maybe she'd been hiding and saw Silver reach for it in her harness.

As her mind cleared, she began putting things together. The trinket Foultner always wore lay smashed on the ground. Silver's two vials on her own harness were intact.

No rancher carried around protections against assassination. Not unless they either worked with assassins or feared them. But if Foultner was fighting the blackwings, why hadn't she let Silver know?

There was no time. Rybalt's attempt last time had been a precursor to an invasion. And with the reserves all sleeping in the garrison, the effect could be devastating.

She flung herself down the hallway, stumbling on legs working off the toxin's effects, keeping Foultner in tow—whatever she was, she had just saved Silver's life—and smashed through the entrance to the old reeve's lavish quarters.

The reeve shoved aside mirrors, glass, and silks, opening a set of doors that seemed to mark a bathing area or perhaps closet. Inside, however, was a thick rope hanging from the ceiling. One that they hadn't been able to use last time. One that sounded the bells to alert the eyrie.

Silver pulled as hard as she could and prayed the garrison still stood.

THE DEFENSE of the Argent Heights took no time at all. The attacking force was small, which was suspicious, and while one of Mally's abominations was discovered dead outside the confectionery, the army escaped the explosives.

Silver found Henders waiting anxiously for Foultner in the hills nearby and ordered him to take the goliath birds, affix their metal headgear, and get them excavating the few tunnels in the garrison that had collapsed. With a little luck, anyone who had survived the rockslide would have enough air.

The rest of the garrison she ordered to armor up and figure out their supplies.

"We've repelled the Blackwing Eyrie's attack," a confused captain told her. "We've already won."

That opinicus was an idiot, and she told him so.

"Check the dead," she hissed. "There are no red-winged blackbirds among them. This was a small force, meant to take us out so we couldn't stop the real attack. That means we need to leave *now*."

Without his darkstalker superior, the idiot captain had no choice but to obey. Even a backwater reeve like her outranked him.

She ordered her messengers brought together and immediately saw a problem she wished she'd identified the significance of days ago: the Reevesport and Whitebeak messengers were missing.

She reassigned two and began issuing orders, "You, head to the Crackling Sea Eyrie and tell the pink reeve to watch his defenses. We'll send more troops when we can, but the supply lines are down temporarily."

An argent hawk disappeared into the sky, and Silver turned to a pair of new ones. "I need you two to find out what happened to Whitebeak and Reevesport. Maybe they're gone, maybe they're in trouble. Let me know."

Those were all long shots, and she knew it. If an attack was coming, it would be somewhere much more important. The king's ascension should be at any moment now. But he had an army with him, the Golden Sky. An army that wasn't defending the capital.

She looked west, her eyes darting in the dying light, trying to see across an impossible distance. Finally, she made her decision.

"Captain, return to the Alabaster Eyrie with all haste. Bring the entire army with you."

"Reeve...?" he asked. "We have orders to assist the border eyries."

Idiot.

"The border eyries our enemies wanted to take are already taken. We've failed at protecting them." She slipped off her colorful harness when one of her hawks brought her official one and its metal trappings of station. "I'm going to fly to the king. If he needs help, I'll call for you. But he has an army, and your families don't. Tell the others that. They'll fly twice as fast."

She wanted to stay and make sure he didn't countermand

her orders, but hearing she was going to see the king had the intended effect on him.

"Reeve Silver," the commander of the Argent Heights said with a bow. "We're ready. Do you want us with you or with the... white opinici."

"Send our fastest to scout the farmlands, looking for signs of trouble," Silver ordered. "Everyone else, come with me. I can't imagine anyone would dare go after the king on the night of his ascension, but we must be certain."

She'd nearly taken off before she remembered one final matter. "Oh, and have Foultner thrown in the prison. Tell Henders she was hurt but she's okay, and they're treating her there, but don't let him inside."

The commander looked startled. "Is she in trouble?"

Is she? She saved my life.

"No. Tell her this is for her own safety, but don't let her leave," Silver said. "She may be... frightened or confused by her encounter with the Reevesbane."

With that, Silver flew west. If there was one single thing she was good for, it was flying fast, and she moved like a shooting star across the dark sky.

THE ARGENT REEVE arrived before dawn and could not believe what she was seeing. From the skies, it looked like a snake of green and purple flowed out of the Emerald Jungle and attempted to swallow the workshop whole. Most of the king's forces were holding the eastern walls, but it was a bloody battle. The starlings had no sense of self-preservation when they got like this.

On the western side, cave gryphons were taking advantage

of the chaos to break in. So far, the Golden Sky army was holding, but they wouldn't last forever. Something needed to be done about the starlings so more forces could be moved to handle the cave gryphons, and every opinicus who died here wouldn't be alive to defend the Alabaster Eyrie.

Allying with starlings. It sounds like a fantasy. How did the cave gryphons pull it off?

Her escort dove to assist their allies, but Silver remained in the skies, trying to figure out how this had happened. That's when she saw it. A team of cave gryphons climbed up the southern cliff face, running into a line of peafowl, who knocked them back. Most of the cave gryphons spread their wings and disappeared back into their burrows, but one took a moment to do so, putting him over the line of starlings.

The fluttering mass reached up and plucked him out of the air. He screamed as he died, and that's when Silver realized what was going on.

Once she knew what to look for, it was obvious. You couldn't fight alongside the starlings, and, in fact, none of the cave gryphons were. She saw a few hiding, but they always had a line of trees between them and their 'allies.' She watched until her suspicions were confirmed. There were new glyphs along the trees.

She came around the northern side of the workshop where the fighting was less fierce. A dozen little bridges along the cliffs allowed goliath bird caravans access to the main entrance, several of which had collapsed. Even as she watched, she saw a small team of Redwood Valley opinici light a fuse and destroy the main bridge inside, stranding a few goliath birds in the workshop entrance.

She let out a screech and dive-bombed the cave gryphons

crawling up this side of the workshop. One of the eyrie soldiers recognized her and let her inside without question.

Redwood Valley. Emerald Jungle. Abyssal Naze. Then the Blackwing Alliance struck at my eyrie. The scope of the assaults was alarming. She needed to see what was happening at the Alabaster Eyrie.

She moved past doctors and nurses. Many were Mally's cult-like worshippers: plumage pale, beaks and talons red. Not all of those wore medical badges. She passed by a large room. Inside was the first vat of purple salts, the stone around it dyed bright colors. She poked her head inside to see if the king was here, but another sight greeted her.

A spoonbill's head, elongated and unmoving, stuck out from beneath a sheet where Mally's assistants drained him of blood.

The blue reeve? He lives? That couldn't be right. She grabbed one of the assistants and demanded to know what was going on. "What is Mally doing to this reeve?!"

"The k-king ordered us to d-drain his blood," the assistant stammered. "He was too close to death when we put him in, too late to save him. Please, I must hurry. We need to take as much blood as we can before his body gives out."

She stared at the stained sheet, dumbfounded. She'd assumed Jonas had died in transit from his wounds. It hadn't occurred to her that they'd kept him alive—if this could be called life—just to test the salts on him.

She pushed down her emotions and carried on, deeper into the workshop. While the Golden Sky held the outer walls, the entire royal guard held the inner sanctum. She passed by door after door, challenged at every step, until she reached an ornate barrier that blocked the way into the final chamber, the vault where the salts had been sealed away from the cave gryphons when the workshop had been abandoned the first time.

"Let me in," she ordered the imperial woodpecker guarding it.

He shook his head. "The ascension is nearing completion. No one is allowed in or out."

"You know who I am?" She hated to play that card, but the title of *reeve* still held weight some places.

"Yes, Reeve Silver. That doesn't change things." His demeanor had softened a little. "How are things going outside?"

She didn't have time to spare, so she embellished. "The Blackwing Alliance razed both Whitebeak and Reevesport. They nearly assassinated me, and they *did* manage to kill the darkstalker leading the garrison. Meanwhile, the starlings are starting to overrun the outer defenses. They'll be in here at any moment. I can stop them, but *only if you let me through this door!*"

The woodpecker flinched. The other royal guards stared at him with pleading eyes, imploring him to let her through.

He turned and knocked on the bulky metal, the sound resounding through to the other side. *Tap-tap-tap, tap, tap-tap, tap.*

The door creaked open, revealing Hi-kun. "Ah, Silver. Come in. And here I thought managing the supply lines was too important for you to show up. I'm glad you changed your mind."

"I didn't, and you're about to be extremely glad that's the case." She pushed her way inside and the door shut after her. While she explained what was going on—a slightly more honest version than she told the guard outside—she looked around the workshop.

Off to one side, the vault was open, and most of the salts had been put into metal containers wrapped in netting. There were places for several opinici to grab on and fly the salts out of here.

Good thinking, considering the state of the goliath path. There were several empty vats, thick Crestfall glass glistening in the brazier light. These were where Mally had experimented on the cave gryphons who now clamored for his blood outside. At the far side of the room was a large, golden seal. All around its outer edge were alabaster opinici securing small explosives to it. It was beautiful, its six-wing design appropriate to what was going on here. It had also been designed as an escape hatch. It appeared the king would not be walking out the front door.

If he even survives. Jonas certainly didn't.

Rows of cabinets and low tables full of elixirs, salts, and chemicals filled the room. Beneath the seal was the only full vat of purple salts. As they swirled and bubbled, sometimes she caught sight of a wing pushed up against the glass.

"Is... is the king already in there?" she asked. On one of the tables, puddles of water emptied into drains, the remains of the ice around the seraph. The actual seraph's body was being catalogued, every drop of blood carefully preserved. The feathers had been saved. Even the pelt of this seraph, this sapient being, had been carefully removed.

The sick feeling in her stomach grew. She'd deliberately avoided going into Mally's Whitebeak workshop. Even in New Eyrie, she'd demanded he treat her outside, afraid to move into the darkness with him.

The Nighthaunt crawled atop the last vat. "Ah, my dearest Silver! It's good to see you. Bit busy at the moment. Could you go outside and do something about the noise, perchance?"

"That's what I'm trying to do." She explained what she'd seen with the glyphs and the starlings.

Hi-kun was a pompous bird, but where many of his subordinates had lived so long with victory after victory that they'd grown cocky, he still remembered what it had been like to lose. "What do you need?"

"I need ten of your best to protect me outside, and I need ten minutes with some of Mally's apprentices *right now.*" She didn't wait to see if he said yes or not. She grabbed a pale, red-beaked opinicus and shoved him into the cabinets. "I need your strongest but least fragrant insecticide, then I need the following items."

The assistant looked to the Nighthaunt, who shrugged and gave his blessing. "What do you want me to do with these ingredients?"

"Turn them into a paste." She was already massaging her back paws, trying to find the scent gland. "And hurry. We don't have much time."

39

BORDERLANDS

Reeve Silver's paws were numb when she exited the ascension room. On her way out, Hi-kun ordered six of the royal guard to follow her. They were used to unconventional combat after witnessing several assassination attempts, and they knew how to keep an opinicus safe.

For the other four, she had a royal decree that would let her pick whatever team she wanted. As tempting as it was to grab more woodpeckers, she'd seen a ragtag group fighting in the valley north of the workshop, and they looked like what she needed.

At the moment, they held off an attack from a small group of cave gryphons. A Reevesport opinicus in Reeve's Guard armor, a duckbill with no metal on her harness, and two alabaster opinici who didn't wear the Golden Sky's colors. They pushed the cave gryphons back to their hole, which looked new judging by the dirt around the opening.

Silver swept down with her handful of woodpeckers and

helped them out. Once the tunnel was secure, they tossed down some saltpeter to seal it.

"I need help stopping the starlings. You've been reassigned to me." She expected an argument, but they just nodded. She was about to head south when an argent hawk called for her from the moonlit sky.

"Reeve Silver! The Alabaster Eyrie is under assault by the Blackwings. We need to redirect the—" the messenger looked out at the swarm of starlings consuming the workshop like locusts. "Oh. I didn't realize. Are those starlings?"

One of Silver's new recruits, the peahen, wiped off her long talons. "I need to go. The portmaster is at the Alabaster Eyrie. She'll need me."

"I need you more," Silver said. "The king won't redirect the Golden Sky until after the ascension is complete, but I'll make this deal with you. If you help me shore up the glyph line, I'll order you north. If you get in trouble, you can blame that on me. But we need to hurry. Every minute we spend here is twenty more starlings reaching the workshop."

The peahen bristled, but she ultimately backed down. "So be it."

"I'm coming, too," the messenger said.

Silver shook her head. "No, with the bridges out, I want you to find the goliath caravans and any soldiers guarding them and redirect them north. Once you've finished that, guide the forces from the silver eyrie garrison to the Alabaster Eyrie."

When her messenger left, Silver filled the others in as they flew over the workshop. Several starlings fluttered up after them, but Silver had chosen her bodyguards well. Peafowl weren't known for their flight, but as long as they had the higher altitude, they could handle themselves against a mindless starling.

The best version of Silver's plan involved her flying right next to the workshop wall and sealing its side. The starlings had coated half the workshop with their bodies at this point, so that was no longer an option.

When she tried to fly down along the path, she discovered there were teams of cave gryphons lying in wait, guarding their own glyphs. There was no way to tell how many were hiding in the underbrush, so that plan was out.

The starlings, as much of a problem as they were, gave her a good idea of where the cave gryphons had put up glyphs. They also told her which of her own glyphs still worked. She flew over her own territory, poking around until she found a section without any cave gryphons. The flow of starlings here was too wide to stop them, so she continued south until she hit the border of the Emerald Jungle.

"There," the duckbill fighter said. "It's narrowest right where the jungle starts."

Not where I'd have preferred, but I think we can make it work.

Silver ordered the others to keep a close watch on her as she worked her way along the eastern side of the breach. She stopped at her last functioning glyph and looked out at the gap. It would take three glyphs to close it. "See the tall broadleaf? Cut me a path, then guard me until it takes effect. Stick close and the glyph should protect you, too."

Before she could act, the peahen flew up, then dove into the mass of starlings, swirling her long talons and chopping them up before they registered they were under attack. In the confusion, the duckbill charged forwards, clearing a path for Silver and the others. The woodpeckers stuck close, but the alabaster opinici stayed a little farther out.

When one of the white-tailed kites issued a challenge, the starlings swarmed him. Within moments, there was nothing left of the opinicus.

Silver didn't look back. She pushed onwards, reaching the tree. She grabbed a bag of the paste, stuck her talons into it, then pushed it against the bark, a little higher than the old glyph had been.

Several small beetles crawled out of holes in the tree, but she used her other foreleg to locate the insecticide. The two conflicting scents might cause an issue, but she had to risk it. She spread the poison around the glyph.

A bark beetle infestation along the border of the Emerald Jungle. This is going to be a disaster to try to fix. How could the cave gryphons be so irresponsible?

Her team closed ranks, huddling close to her, and the starlings began to flow around the tree. As the scent took hold and expanded, starlings stopped going east, only moving west through the open gap.

"Not so bad," the duckbill said. The remaining alabaster survivor shot her a death glare.

While there were several pressing reasons to move quickly, Silver stayed and waited until she was sure the poison would keep the beetles at bay. Maybe she could find a way to put the glyph on stone in the future. She'd need to experiment, see if that worked. Once the hungry beetles were twitching on the ground, she ordered her guards into the air.

The starlings stayed fairly low as they swarmed, so Silver's team was able to fly high enough to get over top without incident. Getting to the next tree was a little harder. She looked around for any broadleafs in the area, but her only options were spiketrunks.

"Do you want to go for the glyph in the center first?" the peahen asked.

Silver shook her head. "No, we'll save that for last, just to give the far glyph time to set. A few starlings are still going around it. Does one of you have a knife? Can you get the spikes off?"

"I'll do it," one of the royal guards said. "I can peck them off faster than you can peel 'em."

They attempted an encore of their last attempt, the peahen falling next to the tree, the duckbill charging in. This time, things didn't work as well.

Halfway through her charge, one of the dark-plumed starlings caught the duckbill's leg and pulled her down. Silver leapt over the opinicus, nearly losing her woodpecker guards. When they arrived, three tried to keep the starlings at bay while the fourth started removing spikes to create enough room for the glyph.

While the opinici were shy about the sharp points sticking out of the spiketrunk, the starlings were not. One landed on the tree and crawled down it, catching the pecking guard unaware and killing him. The duckbill had disappeared, and the peahen was having trouble against the dark-plumed starling pride.

Silver grabbed a bunch of the paste, then pushed her talons against the tree. The spikes went through her foreleg. They contained a mild anticoagulant toxin on their tips, and her blood dripped down onto her grey plumage as she waited for the glyph to take effect. The starlings backed off, avoiding the tree. Another woodpecker took advantage of the opening. He smashed his beak against the tree, listening to sounds, and then peeled away part of the bark to reveal beetles. He grabbed the poison out of Silver's harness and applied it to the crack in the tree.

"Can we take his body with us?" a woodpecker asked about their fallen comrade. "I don't want him to be eaten by the starlings."

The peahen stared out at the duckbill. "No, it's too risky. Prop him against the tree. We'll try to send someone back for him later. That's the best we can do."

The trickle of starlings going west around this glyph slowed, then stopped. There was just one more place left. To the south, the jungle was full of chittering. Their murmuration was like a river that cut through the sky from all directions.

"Just one more. Another bloody spiketrunk." Silver looked at one of the oldest examples of that tree species she had ever seen. Its spines were long and gnarled, twisting in weird directions.

A woodpecker stepped forwards. "I'll handle the spikes."

"No. That didn't work last time. I'll just deal with the pain." Silver looked at her talons. She sniffed, trying to detect if they had any of her unique scent on them. She'd used a different pair for each glyph, and she thought she might be out.

Guess we're going with my back feet this time.

She had three imperial woodpeckers, an alabaster opinicus, and a peafowl left. Without the duckbill to lead the way, they opted to drop in from above. A woodpecker and a white-tailed kite flew over the starling swarm to slow them down, then the peahen landed next to the tree.

Silver came after. Where her old glyph had been located was spongy and covered in beetles. The starlings were starting to focus on her again, and the peahen tossed one of the purple variety over Silver's head.

The reeve rolled onto her back, put one of her rear paws into the paste, and without looking, kicked as hard as she could.

Several spikes went into her foot. Her eyes teared up from the pain. The woodpecker and alabaster opinicus were pulled from the air and killed.

And then things stopped. A few starlings got through the gap. Then the flow ceased. The starlings on the jungle side snapped out of their frenzy and wandered south, a few pausing to look down at the dead opinici and wonder.

They didn't see Silver, like she was invisible. At least, most of them didn't. A single male opinicus, four larger dots forming an arc above his beak, watched her.

Silver had never heard of a starling *opinicus* before, and she stared him in the eye, trying to figure out what it meant. When he realized she was looking at him, he disappeared into the other starlings.

What was that about?

"We need to get back to the king," the last two imperial woodpeckers said. "Can you fly?"

Silver pulled her paw from the tree, eliciting a gasp of pain as the twisted spikes left her foot and more blood spilled out. "Go, I'll be okay."

"Here, let me patch you up." The peahen's black dye job must not have been recent because she didn't drip even when she was sweaty. She remained behind while the others left to give word to the king. Though no more starlings flooded out of the jungle, there were still over a hundred trapped in the small corridor with nowhere to go except to the workshop.

Silver's talons and paws all felt terrible. This wasn't the

worst she'd felt. That had come from being knocked out of the air in the bog defending Mally from Rybalt's ambush. But she wondered if she'd have full use of one of her talons in the future.

"Let's go find your reeve," she told her last companion.

"Are you sure?" The peahen seemed surprised. "Don't you want to stay and defend the king?"

Silver shook her head. "I can save a lot more lives in the north than down here. This battle is only half over. The real fight is at the Alabaster Eyrie, and the longer we can delay the blackwings, the better the city will fare."

The peahen helped Silver to her feet. Then grasped onto the reeve's harness and pulled her up until she managed to stay airborne on her own. Landing would be hell, but that would come in the future. For now, she had a lot of flying to do.

40

KINGSBANE

Zeph stalked the canopy. While they weren't redwoods, they still let him see the ground battle from above without attracting the attention of the patrols flying overhead.

Things weren't going well for the cave gryphons. Nor were they going well for the defenders, many of whom had been tossed down into the giant pit of the naze. Really, the battle was going poorly for everyone.

Such a loss of life. His heart ached, but he'd made a promise to Kia, and he owed a lot to his friends back home. He wouldn't fail them.

A pawful of starlings made it over the workshop and fell upon the guards at the western entrance. One of the soldiers, hearing the cry of the starlings, panicked and opened the door to retreat back inside.

"Now!" Zeph shouted at the cave gryphons.

Slate smashed through an opinicus, shoving him in the doorway to keep his friends from closing it. Several more cave gryphons came with him and grabbed the doors. The mass of black-eyed gryphons parted, allowing Silky and her pride through, and they bound the door open with their silk.

Zeph slipped past the guard and into the opinicus building. The scientists and guards retreated behind a set of makeshift barriers that clogged the corridor. Judging by the path they'd chosen to block, that's where the Seraph King waited.

"Wooden barriers, eh? Someone fetch the woodpeckers! They'll make short work of these," Slate shouted.

The oilbirds clicked, getting a feel for the area, then proceeded east. But Zeph wasn't so sure. He decided to try crawling around north.

Unlike the oilbirds, who had bad memories of this location, the silkmouths remained calm. They reinforced the way out with silk. They even chased several scientists into a closet and then webbed it closed, saving the opinici's lives.

When Zeph moved north, Silky followed behind him. There was a large room to the right, and the door was ajar, but he ignored it for now. He recognized the scent of Mally's apprentices, the iron tang in the air, and nearly caught up to them right as they left through the north exit. The soldiers behind them closed the door.

"Can we lock the soldiers out from this side?" Zeph asked.

Silky was already tapping her beak together to produce silk, so her response was sticky. "Sure can. That'll keep the soldiers holding this gate from getting back in to help the king."

While she worked her spidery magic, the copper hawk went back to the large, open door. Several supply rooms and other paths were being webbed closed by silkmouths, but none had reached this one yet. He pushed it open, letting his eyes adjust to the darkness. There was a single body on a slab, and the face looked both familiar and not familiar.

He pulled back the sheet, revealing a tentacle necklace. The metal talons sat on a nearby table.

The regalia of the Crackling Sea Eyrie. But I thought Jonas was dead?

He looked at the corpse. Its shape beneath the sheet generally resembled that of the bog mummy, and it even had a desiccated look about it. He stared into the cold, dead eyes and recognized them.

"Jonas." He whispered the word into the cold room. "How did you come to be here? How did you come to be like... that?"

The answer was simple. The ascension was real, at least in theory. Zeph didn't know if Mally's elixirs had killed Jonas or if Blinky's wounds had done him in. Either way, the opinicus who had set Zeph's home on fire, who had done so much harm, was finally gone. None of him was left in the world.

Or... is it? What are these vials?

The scientists had evacuated in a hurry when the oilbirds broke open the gates. Zeph rolled a partially filled vial in his paws, attempting to read the label. The opinicus language was similar in the Redwood Valley and Alabaster Eyrie, but the way they wrote their letters was a little different. The sorts of additions and subtractions to each character that were acceptable to opinici would have greatly changed the meaning of a pride glyph, and he struggled with the words.

"Zeph? Are you okay?" Kia called from the doorway. "What're you doing in here?"

He balanced on his back legs and carefully lifted the vial in his paws. "It's Jonas's body. He's... whatever the king wants to become."

"I see." She reached out and took the vial, reading the statistics, comparing it to the notebooks nearby. "Once he was a seraph, they took his blood. They'll be able to use it on chicks to create more like him. I guess they knew that, with so few salts, they'd need to concentrate on eggs."

Zeph covered Jonas's head. His usual curiosity had left him, and he didn't want to see what the blue reeve had looked like after the change.

Kia put the vial down. "I get it now. This is it. *This* is the king's plan. Jonas's blood, the king's blood: both will create more and more seraphs. Each new seraph becomes another source of blood, and when there's enough, they can treat all the eggs until there are no more opinici left."

Or gryphons if he's trying to round them all up.

"It's extinction." Kia looked around the room, then picked up a chemical labelled hemostabilizer and put some in the few forgotten vials before tucking them into her harness. "I'll see what I can do with this, but the Nighthaunt's assistants escaped with most of the blood."

Zeph turned from Jonas's body. He'd genuinely liked Jonas the first time they'd met. That didn't last past the initial conversation, but it always amazed him that someone who could speak such friendly words could be so cruel. "So his legacy lives on. We shouldn't tell Satra about this. There's no telling what she'd do to his... children."

"Not *his* children," she corrected. "Just... children treated with his blood. But I understand what you're saying. Should we take back the necklace and talons for Grenkin?"

The copper hawk shrugged. "They're just *things*. Grenkin didn't need them before. I think there're more important things to worry about now."

"I suppose." Her talons lingered, but she left them there.

They weren't designed for fighting, and Zeph didn't think the necklace would fit around Kia's short neck. It was designed for a heron, then modified for a spoonbill. "Zeph, do you think we made a mistake coming here?"

He never got a chance to answer. Chert burst into the room, shouting for the two of them.

"We've got a problem," the light-colored oilbird said. "We need an opinicus."

THE HALLWAY outside the Nighthaunt's, well, *haunt* was full of destroyed crates, dead bodies, and a lot of webbing. Silky's cooler head had prevailed, and all of the wounded opinici, and those who had surrendered, were wrapped up with promises they'd be released later.

The effect was as unsettling as it had been in the tunnels near Whitebeak. Zeph felt, once again, like he was walking through a spider's lair. He followed Kia across the chamber, catching up to Cherine and Slate. A giant, metal door stood before them. The imperial woodpecker guards had surrendered upon seeing their ivory-billed cousins, and some sort of tearful reunion was happening along the eastern web.

"We were told you hadn't survived," a red, black, and white opinicus said. "They told us you'd all died."

The white, black, and red gryphon served as his mirror image. "No, we were locked away after the presentation with orders we were to be put down, but the oilbirds saved us. We've been living in the caves ever since. I think we're the reason the darkstalkers were sent down there."

At the bottom of the silk wrapping, a black feathered tail stuck out from black fur. Outside of the silk, free of its bonds, dark red fur and a long, fuzzy tail twitched back and forth. Two woodpeckers, similar but not identical.

"This is all nice and friendly," Slate said, "but we need to know how to get through this door. It's solid metal. I don't even think saltpeter will blast through it."

Silky began building nests on the roof above the entryway. She built up a few pawholds, then used her spiked tail to stick in place. "Once it's open, we can try to hold it. A door this heavy is going to be tough. Looks like they treated it with something, too, so the silk isn't sticking."

"What's the deal with the woodpeckers?" Zeph asked Chert.

She was starting to cut one of them free now that they seemed friendly. "I guess they all started as Reeve's Guards, those past their prime or with terminal diseases. They were given to Mally. Half, he turned into ivory-billed woodpeckers, a bird that had no matching gryphon. The others, he turned into imperial woodpeckers, another bird that had no matching opinicus. The opinici were promoted. The gryphons we pulled out of a lampworks not far from here. They were scheduled to be burned."

Once the lead imperial woodpecker was free, he leapt at his ivory-billed friend. Zeph tensed into a crouch, preparing to pounce, but Chert put a paw on his face to hold him back.

"It's okay," she said. "Those two were lovers before the change. I think he's going to help us."

Ivory's long, red tail wrapped around the two of them. They sat like that for a few minutes until the sounds of bodies landing on the roof shook them out of it.

Finally, the royal guard spoke up. "I can probably get them to open it a little, but Hi-kun is in there with more guards. You're going to have to work fast."

Several alabaster opinici made muffled protests from their silk wrappings, but the other imperial woodpeckers remained silent. Whatever lies they'd been told, seeing their brothers- and sisters-in-arms alive and well had an effect on them.

Zeph leapt against the wall, then pushed off with a twist and dug his dewclaws into a patch of silk on the roof, startling Silky. He tested each paw, figuring out how well he could cling, and Silky modified his upside-down perch so he'd be ready to pounce.

Slate and the oilbirds moved to either side of the door, ready to strike. Cherine and Kia stood atop an overturned crate. The door was tall, several opinici tall, but that meant there should be a gap above whoever opened it, and Zeph wanted to be ready for that moment.

"Everyone good?" the imperial woodpecker said. Then he tapped on the door. *Tap-tap-tap, tap, tap-tap, tap.*

No response came. The door was thicker than the roof, and while the sounds of battle were loud from above, nothing could be heard from the other side.

"Do we hit it again?" Zeph asked.

Slate shook his head. "No, it'll open or it won't."

The royal guard stood in front of the door so he'd be seen first. The wait was unbearable, but a loud bang came, as though someone had removed a piece of metal blocking the way, and the door opened the smallest amount.

"Is Reeve Silver back?" Hi-kun asked. Then he saw past the royal guard. "Close it! Close the door!"

Slate slammed into Hi-kun, but the armored opinicus was unmovable, and the oilbird fell backwards. Zeph looked into the open space above both of them and leapt past, Silky breathing down his neck.

"Zeph!" Kia shouted, leaping from atop her perch after him, with Cherine hot on her tailfeathers.

The four of them tumbled inside before Hi-kun kicked Slate back and got the doors closed.

They were in the inner sanctum.

Their gryphon army was not.

ZEPH LOOKED AROUND THE ROOM, marveling at just how *tall* it all was. This was a chamber large enough to allow flight. Where other parts of the workshop had several levels, this room was like all four stories had been combined into one.

His instincts kicked in, and he shoved Kia and Cherine into the corner. The room was full of soldiers and scientists. He even recognized the slithering form of the Nighthaunt up on the pedestal that housed a swirling purple elixir.

"I'd have brought more cushions if I'd known we were expecting guests," Mally rasped. "Oh, dear me, you two look familiar. You were there the night the pools were poisoned."

Zeph and Kia shared a look before she spoke. "We stopped your experiments then, and we're going to stop them now. This is for Olan."

The Nighthaunt's black eyes were unreadable, but he tilted his head slightly, inviting her to go on.

"Experiment 429-7341," she repeated.

He nodded. "I remember. He'd had the egg treatment, but I still managed to activate the disease in him. Is he still alive? How far has the disease progressed?"

"Stay on task, Mally," Hi-kun said. A row of soldiers blocked the way to the swirling vat that housed the Seraph King.

The Nighthaunt didn't listen. "Scholar Cherine. Neider and Felicio sponsored you at the Redwood Valley University. Your thesis was on foodborne pathogens if I recall from our last meeting. It's good to see you again. I could use a new apprentice."

"Sure, just let me up there," Cherine said, but the guards closed ranks. "Well, it was worth a try."

"Hmm, *you* I don't recognize. But the silk around your mouth is familiar. I thought the portmaster had you all locked up in a textile mill making cloth for them," he said to Silky.

The silkmouth hissed stickily. "I'm here on behalf of the oilbirds. I've come for your eyes."

The vat churned. A grey beak stuck out and gasped for air. Two wings with talons gripped the sides, dripping purple salts down the glass. An additional set of wings stuck out, no taloned hands on them. The lanterns in here were bright, and Zeph spied the barest hint of iridescence in the feathers.

"It… worked," Cherine said. "It actually worked."

Kia shouted at the guards, but they stood firm.

While their attention was on her, Zeph went behind her back and whispered to Silky, "We don't have much time, and I don't think we're going to get more than one shot at this. Can you cause a distraction?"

She nodded. The silk in her mouth was a red color, and she only had eyes for one opinicus.

The guards were so busy blocking the way to the king that they weren't watching the Nighthaunt. When Kia approached, one of them slashed at her, just barely catching her chest, and pushed her back.

That was the moment Silky needed. The Nighthaunt moved to his workbench, and she shot forwards, latching onto his chest with her sticky beak.

Mally let out a screech that echoed through the cavernous space, and the opinici either covered their ear holes or rushed to his aid.

But not Zeph.

Zeph ran around the far side of the room, behind the empty vats, and flung himself up at the king. The glass containers stood four times the gryphon's height, and he had to beat his wings to get up to the edge. From the swirling dark purple, the king's head rose out again.

His beak had grown longer. His feathers sparkled in the light. Both his forelegs looked like taloned wings, and his real wings spread out behind them, longer than they had been before.

Hi-kun had already turned and ran to the king's aid. Zeph looked at the king, helpless as a fledgling, and hesitated.

I have to do this. I promised Kia I would. If I kill him, we can stop the war.

He pushed down his feelings and pounced. His beak found purchase on the king's neck, his claws sprang out and dug themselves into the king's chest.

Yet as the king rose out of the purple elixir, his wounds healed before Zeph's eyes.

41

TRIUMPH

Emin's mind had gone blank partway through the transformation. The Nighthaunt had used four times the dose he normally prescribed for this procedure, not knowing what would be needed for such drastic changes. The salts were at their most potent, and the king had felt like he was being boiled alive.

His old feathers had drifted loose, rising to the surface, where his assistants skimmed them off and saved them. For what purpose, Emin had no idea. For posterity, he supposed. They were the plain, dull feathers of an opinicus. He was becoming so much more.

The heat burned his skin, but the chemicals burned in a different way as they seeped into the gaps left by his feathers. A lesser opinicus might have screamed or asked for help, but not Emin. He'd lived enough lives. If burning to death was the price of transforming his entire race, so be it. He was ready.

When he'd finally arisen from the vat, clinging to the

sides several tries before sinking back in, he felt like he was seeing in color for the first time. His vision had expanded. His sense of smell had changed. He had fewer digits on his talons now, several having grown long to form the basis of his extra pair of wings. That took some getting used to. He couldn't wait to find out what it felt like to fly with two sets of wings.

When he surfaced for the last time, he looked into the face of a small, brown gryphon. As the creature's jagged beak caught his neck, as its claws pierced his chest, he wondered where his guards were.

The gryphon looked so sad as it thought it was killing him.

Don't fret, little gryphon. This isn't the first time I've felt the sting of an assassin's claws.

His body's strange internal systems, charged by the salts and blood, rushed to fix the damage. The beast's eyes grew wide as Emin reached out with winged talons and wrapped them around its neck.

He picked up the animal and looked at it with curiosity. Despite ordering their eradication, it had been a long time since he'd seen a foreign gryphon, let alone been in the same room with one. He'd listened to the ethics scholars talk about how gryphons were just like opinici, but now that he saw through the same eyes as the shipwrecked stranger's, and he knew he wasn't looking at an opinicus.

He was staring into the eyes of a capybara, of a little brown squirrel. This vermin wasn't his equal. To think that the fisherfolk bred with these animals.

Disgusting.

Holding the beast with one pair of sharp talons, marveling at how the wing on that leg felt, he looked down at his other limbs, using his back wings to prop himself up on the vat. His talons were long, sharp. They were different, but not worse. He wiggled his toes and felt a new set of talons down there, too, and dug them into the glass to steady himself.

He held up his free foreleg and raked his claws against the beast that had dared bite him. The creature struggled, but he tightened his grip. Only when it stopped moving did he toss it aside and climb out of the vat.

His hind legs no longer had paw pads. The long feathers there weren't wings like his forelegs but probably served some purpose in flight. He flapped his back wings a few times, feeling how much lift they provided. His body felt lighter but also stronger.

He looked down at his assistants. Had they always been so small? They were in awe, as they should be.

"My adornments." His voice had deepened. No, that wasn't right. It had more resonance now. It was close enough to his old voice that his attendants jumped to obey. Several used towels to get the elixir off him, then preened his new feathers into flightworthiness. Others fetched his crown and armor, but not the fake light armor he'd worn as an old opinicus. This was a new set, forged of real metal, designed around the replica skeleton of the seraph that hung in his throne room.

The attendants made a few modifications, but everything fit. He smiled, testing out the muscles around his beak. It was hard at the tip like an opinicus beak, but there was a little more give at the top. He resisted an urge to stick a talon inside and see if he had tomia. That exploration could wait until later.

"Where is the one who made my ascension possible?" he asked.

"Here, my King." The Nighthaunt limped over to him. There was a sticky red substance on his chest, and at first, the king mistook it for blood.

He waved the scholar over. "Do you require the salts? Are you wounded?"

"No, I will wait until a cure is found," Mally said. "We have no time. The Abyssal Naze and Emerald Jungle siege our workshop from outside. But the Blackwing Eyrie swoops down to take the Alabaster while we wait here."

The king looked up at the seal, rigged with explosives. Some parrot-like opinicus next to an eagle rushed over to help an unconscious gryphon on the floor, but he paid them no mind. He had a kingdom to save.

"Blow the seal. Order the Golden Sky to fall back." When Emin had gone into the vat, it had been just after sundown. Now, as the seal fell away to reveal the sky, the heavens were lightening. Morning would soon be here.

Despite the Nighthaunt's warning that the starling hordes had come upon them, his army was still intact, and the starlings lay dead. Even the cave gryphons had been beaten back into their holes.

He laughed, a sound more musical than his old rasp. He'd done it. He'd actually *done it.* He'd become a seraph. He stretched his wings, fore and back, and leapt into the air.

"What do we do with the prisoners?" Hi-kun asked, struggling to keep up with the king's flight. He looked smaller than he had a day ago.

"What need have I of prisoners? Release them, for all I care. We must leave. My subjects must be told of my ascension." The king flew north ahead of his army. They hurried to keep up. He flew as easily as he breathed, ascending higher and higher. The thin air of such altitudes no longer bothered him. He felt like he could fly up to the stars and pluck them down.

I am a god.

42

COPPER HAWK

While Cherine attended to Silky's unconscious form, Kia ran across the stone workshop to the small, brown body of a copper hawk in a pool of blood. Tears fell down her face as she cradled his lifeless form.

And then she felt his heartbeat.

"Cherine, help me get him into the vat!" she screamed across the empty room that had just housed a small army. "We can still save him!"

Cherine hesitated, and she had never felt more frustrated at him in her entire life, not even when they'd broken up.

"He's too far gone," the golden eagle said. "And that vat has already been used. It's full of seraph blood. If you put him in there, even if it works, he's not going to come out again as Zeph."

She grabbed Zeph's harness, no longer worried about causing him more harm and pulled him onto the pedestal. "Opinicus. Gryphon. Seraph. He'll be *alive,* Cherine. That's what matters!"

She didn't have time for Cherine's ethical considerations. When Zeph had doubts, she'd been the one to push him here. He'd promised *her* that he'd kill the Seraph King, and it had nearly cost him his life.

Nearly.

Cherine finally flew atop the vat and helped her get Zeph over the edge. The glass container was much larger than the small copper hawk. When they lowered him in, he sank, his head dropping below the surface.

Kia swore and dove in after him, catching her wound on the side and gashing it open again. The Nighthaunt had left a fire going under the vat, and the liquid inside boiled. It burned against her side, but she managed to get Zeph's head above the surface again.

She put her face in front of his beak and could just feel his breath.

"Kia, you have to get out!" Cherine's pleading never stopped.

She ignored him. If she had to stay in here to save Zeph, she'd do it. She held him close, his head on her shoulder, and watched as his feathers floated to the surface. She used her wings to steady herself but soon saw her own feathers mixing with his, a sea of brown and red and green.

"Get more wood for the fire," she ordered Cherine. "We need to maintain the heat it was at while the king was in here."

His eyes pleaded with her, but he obeyed without offering up more objections. The Golden Sky disappeared into the pre-dawn morning, and some of the Silkmouth Pride came through the hole to find Silky. One of them landed on the edge of the vat and reached down for Kia, but Kia yelled at her to leave them alone.

Kia shouted at Slate when the oilbirds brought him to reason with her. By then, her voice had started to change. She no longer recognized it.

Cherine came over, trying to say something to Kia, but she had trouble hearing. Something was changing on the side of her head, but she couldn't catch her reflection in the thick glass of the vat. He pointed up at the hole where the seal had been. Silkmouths were now building a web around it to hide the vat from view.

She nodded to show she understood. Her whole body felt like it was on fire. Part of the ceiling collapsed for reasons she couldn't tell from her current position, and the vat rocked back and forth, waves covering both her and Zeph for a moment.

Now her eyes burned, too. She grew weaker. Hope faded.

And then he coughed. Zeph coughed and opened his eyes.

His bright blue eyes.

43

STRIPES

The Alabaster Eyrie burned. The massive arch housing the Reeve's Guard had been the first to fall. By the time the survivors pulled themselves from the rubble, the Blackwing Alliance's forces were upon them.

More explosions wracked the city, destroying guard outposts and collapsing the entrance to the palace. The blackwings flooded in, attempting to root out any resistance before it built. And yet, even on fire, the city refused to die; its citizens refused to surrender.

Sailors at the docks took up weapons. The portmaster, the wayward leader of Reevesport, led a counteroffensive, trying to hold the docks against the blackwings as ships fled to sea. Bells sounded across the city, rallying the common folk to defend their homes against certain death.

Everyone who could hold a weapon, everyone who feared for their families, took to the night sky and fought for their lives. The battle raged on, and the alabaster opinici screamed in indignation that anyone *dared* attack their eyrie.

The blackwings' strategy depended on the city surrendering, but it refused, and the blackwings gave them no quarter. Stripes couldn't bear to watch. There was so much death on both sides. This was a battle that could only be won if the Alabaster Eyrie suffered terrible losses, and she didn't know how to reconcile herself with that fact. Instead, she concentrated on only one thing.

Impir.

The mad peafowl had looked into her pitohui plumage and fled before she could strike. He'd led Stripes and her motmots on a chase through the port authority, across the docks, and into a half-constructed dreadnaught. He'd gone underwater and come up in a raftworks, but her motmots had tracked him down.

He'd fled through apartments full of opinici, trusting them to attack Stripes and her bodyguards and buy him time. She'd done her best not to kill anyone just defending their family, but she left a trail of twitching bodies in her wake.

She pushed aside those thoughts. For an old peacock, Impir was fleet of foot. He ducked through an office, went through a prison—releasing the scariest prisoners when Stripes arrived—and took shelter in an abandoned Reeve's Guard building.

Or so she thought. When she came in, she saw that several guards were hiding here. Too cowardly to fight the Blackwing Alliance's army outside, but not too cowardly to try to kill her.

The long beaks of her motmots made short work of the alabasters, but the gryphons were breathing heavily. Stripes's injuries were superficial, but their wounds would need to be tended to soon.

Is this a fool's errand? Am I getting us killed when we should be running for our lives?

The motmots twitched their long, feathered tails the way they did when hunting prey. She was doing this because she hated Impir for cursing their children. But they were doing this because they were hunters.

When she hesitated, the gryphons pushed her onwards. She entered a warehouse and couldn't see where Impir had gone. The motmots sniffed the air, one sneezing blood, and ran to an underground passage she never would have spotted.

The path led into the palace itself, and the sight of it took her breath away. The ground was a golden carpet over white marble. Stone statues lined the hallways. Lanterns burned brightly, smelling faintly of cooked poultry.

A motmot approached one, putting its nares almost against the lamp itself, then hissed. "Made from gryphons."

"Made from what?" Stripes asked without answer. Already, they rushed off down the corridor, into the throne room. Thankfully, if there'd been Reeve's Guard posted here, they'd gone to find a way out. Several glass vats had been dragged into the center of the room. What purpose they served, she had no idea. Firewood was stacked nearby. Several smaller cauldrons lined the room.

A white-tailed kite turned the corner and looked at Stripes, dropping the cauldron he had balanced on his wings. He reached for his harness for some weapon, but a motmot ran back to defend her. The gryphon wiped her beak on the pitohui's oily feathers, and the alabaster opinicus reconsidered and fled.

Stripes let out a breath she'd been holding out of concern for the stranger's well-being. The lead gryphon let out a cry, and they ran to a large vent on the far side of the room that had been knocked loose. They crawled through the center of the palace, passing by rooms. The warm and cool air created a kind of airflow throughout the building. Above her, another metal grate was tossed aside.

"Hurry!" she ordered the motmot in the lead. "Don't let him get away!"

By the time she exited, standing atop the stone opinicus's head, Impir had just taken flight. The motmots were on his tail, literally and figuratively, pulling him down and pinning him atop the statue's beak.

Stripes limped to catch up. She was ready for this day to be over. She pulled out a pair of manacles like the sort that were used to imprison her brother, attaching one of them to her foreleg. She reached out for Impir, but the motmots hissed at her.

"We are not taking this one alive," one said.

"It is not just *your* children who were harmed," a second continued. "Glacier gryphons, motmot gryphons were also treated."

The third stared Stripes in the eyes, their beaks touching. "Iony ordered you to kill him. You must do so now to restore your honor."

Still, she hesitated. The fourth gryphon took Stripes's talons and pressed them against her orange and black plumage, getting them nice and oily.

Impir held his talons over his face and beak. The motmots pulled back his forelegs so he was staring at Stripes, keeping his neck down so he couldn't strike out like the cobra he was.

She took a deep breath, then pushed her talons against his chest. Like Mally's other agents, Impir had a tolerance for her poison, and it took a moment for the twitching to begin. Stripes thought of all the gryphlets and chicks who would die. The motmots were right. There was no time to take him back. Knowing Impir, he'd just escape again. These were her orders. Despite her protests, she was a soldier now.

Yet she couldn't meet his gaze while she did it. She could feel his soft feathers, his heartbeat, his warmth. She could feel where one strap of his harness was starting to wear away, where another had been patched.

She opened her eyes, but only to look down from the giant statue at the city below, hoping to find some kind of distraction. Her blackwing allies were exhausted. There were a few pockets of resistance, but for the most part, the doctors and their assistants were tending to the wounded. The port burned, though most of the ships had survived by fleeing into the deep water. The portmaster, the reeve of Reevesport, sat in a cage next to the blackwing commander. The strange green and black smuggler she'd seen arguing with Impir had disappeared in the fighting.

Did we win?

When she'd started chasing Impir, it had been dark. Now, the sky was bright, the morning sun shining. She looked up at it, blinded for a moment, and thought she saw a shape in the sky.

It can't be. Her first thought was of the seraph from the glacier mountain, defrosted and alive. Then she saw the golden armor and the spiked crown.

The king's ascension wasn't a lie or a myth.

Soon, the heavens above the Alabaster Eyrie filled with an unending number of white opinici. The Golden Sky had come home to roost.

She looked down at Impir and saw he had something in his beak. Before she could grab it, he bit down, and red juice squirted everywhere. She wiped some off her face and recognized the texture and smell of the antitoxin.

The mad peafowl lashed out, knocking back the motmots who were holding him. Stripes didn't pause to think, she just reached out, grabbed his leg, and attached the other side of her manacle to him.

They plummeted off the statue, flapping their wings together to stay aloft, creating their own seraphic form. They struggled, pulling against the chains and pushing off each other.

"Release me!" Impir hissed. "If I die, I will pull you down with me."

He was right. Of course he was right. Still, Stripes slashed, managing to catch his neck. She wrapped herself around him, pulling her wings in and grabbing onto his to keep him from flapping. It was a long way from the top of the palace to the ground. She closed her eyes partway down, opening them again when it was taking too long, and she saw the roof of a building rising up to meet her.

She twisted, putting Impir on the bottom, and prayed this was a warehouse of nesting material. If the king's insane prayers could be answered, why shouldn't hers? As they crashed through a glass skylight, she was surprised to see water rushing up to meet her.

44

MOTMOTS

The motmots dove after Stripes, knowing they were in a lot of trouble if they returned without her. The four gryphons fell, tails like streamers, slowing only to slip through the broken skylight.

Despite the outer appearance, this wasn't a warehouse. It was a waterworks. Some of the aqueduct system was still aboveground, as it was in the Pitohui Eyrie, but large sections were hidden under the earth. The motmots searched, curiosity etched in their ears, and landed on various stone platforms guiding water in different directions.

"Rybalt will not be happy," one said. "She is definitely dead."

"Tsk!" another scolded.

The third examined the various waterways and the directions they went. "This one has damage. She must have hit here."

"Perhaps she *is* dead, then," the fourth said. "Unless the peacock hit first."

The first dipped her toes into the water. "This is shallow, but if she is still bound to the peacock, she will drown when they arrive at deeper water."

Time was of the essence, so the motmots split up. One gryphon leapt into the gutter damaged in Stripes's fall. Another flew overhead. The third noticed some trash that had been stuck to the walls in the shape of a glyph and went to see if there were city gryphons here. And the fourth, an avid reader, saw an emergency sign for waterworks employees and went to see if anyone lived here who could explain how all of this worked.

SHORTCLAW, the fourth gryphon, ran through the hallways of the waterworks. It all smelled kind of strange, both wet and chemically. And the obvious sewage once she got away from the main area.

She could also taste fear in the air, and she followed that scent until she reached a barricaded door. She excavated it, pulling pieces of wood away as she heard screams and worry inside. She paid them no mind. She was a skilled hunter, and it was natural for opinici to fear her.

Once the crates of strange bottles were moved, she faced the toughest dilemma of her entire life: a door. She tried to get her beak around it, but she couldn't get traction. She bit harder, digging her jagged tomia in, but the metal resisted her best efforts.

She placed a forepaw on it, but it was a strange, round shape. She tried adding more paws to the equation, getting three on it while balancing on the fourth and stabbing her beak into the ceiling for support before deciding that was the wrong approach. Instead, she looked around for a tool she could use. There were all sorts of strange opinical devices, but their purposes eluded her. Instead, she saw what she really needed, a universal tool, a multitasker that solved all problems: a strip of leather.

She wrapped the leather around the door handle, giving it traction, and pulled it tight. Holding the leather strap in her beak, she went *under* the doorknob, twisting it a little in one direction. She scurried under, keeping the leather taut, then she leapt off a crate to go *over*, twisting it again. She continued this until the door popped open.

Easy!

She left the leather strip wrapped around the doorknob in case other gryphons needed to get in here and stared at twenty frightened opinici.

"Who are you?" one in a harness with a blue drop on his badge asked.

"A friend fell in the water. I need help finding her," Shortclaw said. "You, come with me. The rest may stay. I am not here to hurt you."

They were startled, but perhaps it was Shortclaw's polite demeanor or incredible attractiveness that won them over because the waterworks employee agreed to follow her.

"Come, back to main room," she said. "This is where she fell. Where will she end up?"

The waterworks employee looked at a map on the wall. It had many different routes in different colors, and he traced one that went into the depths. "Looks like she'll end up down here, where the water gets treated."

"Is it deep?" she asked.

He nodded, and she started to fly off.

"Wait!" he shouted, perhaps overcome by her demeanor

and beauty a second time. "There's a shortcut. Come, I'll show you the way."

She followed him until they reached a door. "These can be tricky. I left my multitool back at the other one. Let me go get it."

But the opinicus was crafty. He was able to take his strange talons and wrap them around the metal sphere and turn it.

This will be much faster, she thought. Opinici were terrible with strips of leather, but they made do despite their shortcomings.

SPLITTAIL, the third gryphon, followed the trash glyphs until she found a bunch of crates propped up against the wall. She nuzzled at each, finding which ones were hollow and moving those out of the way to reveal a hole.

She made friendly chirping noises as she went. Gryphons who hid their nests were often nervous, and she wanted these to know she was a friend. Also, concealed nests often meant gryphlets, and some gryphon prides were very defensive about their young.

"Hello," she chirped. "I met your friends at the garden. It is me, a motmot. I could use your help."

The motmot pride often introduced themselves as *a motmot* because names brought with them a level of responsibility. If someone knew Splittail's name, they could ask a favor of her or talk about her to other gryphons. That was a lot of power to grant someone else, so most of her pride, when around other gryphons or opinici, preferred the simpler *a motmot.*

She followed the aroma of trash, but when it turned left, she thought she detected the scent of gryphon to the right. *This must be a way to keep from being tracked. The city pride is very clever.*

She continued, and the path diverged again in an open room. It went in all directions. But when she spread her wings to flutter up to the ceiling, she found another trash glyph, and the scent was stronger here.

This is a fun scavenger hunt. Back home, the motmots were often given scent or sound hunts, where they had to track something that resisted being tracked by sight. The prize at the end was often a colorful bird or a piece of fruit. Splittail was a fan of eating pretty things, and she won these games as often as she lost.

She continued her climb, chirping greetings as she went, until she stumbled upon a barrier of trash that had been sewn together.

City gryphons must be good with their beaks.

She knocked, repeating her greeting, and a muffled sound came from the other side.

"What do you want?" a crow's face asked.

Splittail repeated her introduction, explaining that she was a motmot and needed help finding her lost charge. When that didn't work, she spoke in the language that all city-dwelling gryphons understood. She rifled through her harness for an empty glass vial and some food.

The door opened, revealing a small room packed full of stolen opinicus bedding and fifty gryphons, most of whom were adorable, ring-tailed crow gryphlets.

"This is a big pride," Splittail said. "Are there several city prides?"

There was some discussion on this matter, and she realized she should have first asked about the whereabouts of Stripes. "Wait, wait. I need to find a friend. She fell down the sky-window in the big building and washed away. Where could she have gone?"

One of the trash gryphons had a striped pattern, and Splittail mentally called him *Not Stripes* to avoid confusion. "It depends. They all come out in one of a dozen places. Do you want us to show you where they are?"

He led Splittail over to a wall. Bits of different maps showing lines and corridors and tunnels had been spliced together to create a new map of the underworld beneath the Alabaster Eyrie. It was stuck to the wall.

"Blue marks the exits," he explained. "Green is places she could end up, but they have grates over them so you can't get in or out there without some planning."

Splittail considered. "Do the skulls mean danger?"

"Oh, no." Not Stripes laughed. "They're good places to find dead things to eat. The Alabaster Eyrie emblem means danger of all sorts, not just opinical. That one there is actually where part of the old aqueduct system has collapsed, and alligators have begun coming in from the retaining pools."

The motmot considered her options. There were too many places to check, but if Stripes ended up at one of the safer places, presumably she would be just fine. Whereas if she ended up at one of the dangerous places, she might need help.

"Okay, split up and check the dangerous places first." Splittail recognized a few familiar faces from the gardens, but most were new. "Stripes is an opinicus, but she's poisonous, so do not touch her. Her stripes are different from yours. I have a little song to help you remember. *Stripes has stripes on butt, not tail.* We will meet in the big room with the broken glass to find my pridemates. Good?"

The trash gryphons nodded but remained seated. Splittail realized she wouldn't help, either, if she wasn't given food. She emptied out the pockets of her harness.

Thankfully, Stripes always put a lot of treats in there. In this case, those same treats may have saved her life, something Splittail would remind her of if it came up again in the future.

"You, Not Stripes," she said to the confused one by the map. "Take me to the alligators first."

The gryphon started to give his name, but she shushed him by softly closing his beak with her paws.

"Too much responsibility," she explained. "Just show me the alligators, and we'll find you more treats."

He purred and led her into the old aqueduct system. There were spiders up here and little squeaky birds that liked the cold. There were also weird things swimming in the water, which she knew opinici hated. Not her, though. She stabbed a water scorpion on her way.

She'd given away her own treats, so she'd need to make do with whatever she could find.

I wonder how alligator tastes.

Brighteyes leapt down into the water and was whisked away, hopefully in the same direction Stripes had gone. She let out a loud cry of happiness, which Sharpbeak hushed from overhead.

"There are opinici in the city now! It's not safe," Sharpbeak scolded.

The appropriately named motmot rolled her bright eyes. “Just try to keep up!”

Several of the ducts of fast-moving water smelled of sewage, so Brighteyes was happy that Stripes had fallen into a relatively clean water area. This smelled more like... saltwater runoff from the raftworks, sometimes mixed with fresh water. It wound around a platform, heading deeper into the earth, and Bright saw her first problem.

The tunnel split in two. It seemed like it was made to handle a lower water level, so when this area got too wet, the other path was designed to divide the water. She looked back and forth, trying to locate evidence of opinici in either direction. All she could see was that something metal had hit right on the divide.

That could be the chains between the manacles. Hmm.

Right was her favorite direction, so she shouted overhead for Sharpbeak to go left. The flying gryphon changed direction, and Brighteyes leaned to the right.

The tunnel soon went underground, confirming she’d made the correct choice. Sharpbeak hated to get wet. She would save a friend’s life, sure, but not if it meant that she’d have to go *inside* the water to do it. That was a hassle.

Stripes was lucky that Brighteyes was here, too. She let out another whoop of excitement as she descended into the darkness. Fast water rides were even *more* adventurous in the dark. She’d have to bring Splittail down here later. Did all eyries have secret water slides beneath them? Brighteyes couldn’t imagine the Pitohui Eyrie doing this.

I should run for pride leader. I could promise water slides.

Strangely, as she went deeper, she saw lit braziers. She’d register a light in the distance, and as she’d approach it, she’d get a glimpse of city pride sneaking through the sewers holding goodies. She tried to shout hellos to them, but the water was moving too fast.

As she went deeper, the lighting changed from city gryphons with braziers to a kind of glowing substance on the walls. She couldn't tell what it was, but she could make out black eyes in the light. They blinked at her as she floated by, and she tried to blink back.

"You have a very pretty beak!" she shouted to one, and the gryphon hopped in after her. She latched onto the brown and grey gryphon, the cute stranger's long whiskers tickling her beak.

"Is this safe? I didn't know you could just ride these like this!" The stranger was purring, which Brighteyes took as a good sign.

The tunnel curved again, sending them into a spin. "I don't know! I'm looking for a friend in trouble."

"Exciting! Have you found anyone for mating season?" the tunnel gryphon asked.

"I think I just did!" The motmot slow-blinked at her new friend, and the tunnel gryphon blinked back.

Brighteyes didn't know why Stripes had such a hard time finding someone for mating season. It was easy. Stripes always overcomplicated things.

They passed through another lit section, and the walls were full of strange, silky nests with little swift-like gryphons staring down at them.

"Hello, swiflets!" the tunnel gryphon shouted. They chirped back happily. At least, it sounded happy. Brighteyes also thought she heard one of them say, "Brace yourself," which could just be a greeting they often said to each other.

Stripes was certainly someone who could use a *brace yourself* greeting every morning. Alas, it was a warning and not a salutation, as a bright light and metal bars were quickly approaching.

Brighteyes did what she could to decelerate. The tunnel gryphon joined in, and back-to-back, they pushed against the sides of the slide. They managed to slow themselves down just enough that they didn't break anything when they hit the metal grate.

The same couldn't be said for the body of Impir, which had smashed against the bars.

"Is this your friend?" the tunnel gryphon asked. He held a paw over his black eyes to block the light.

"No, this one is prey." The motmot chewed through the mad peafowl's harness. It would have to do as proof. She'd rather bring the whole body back, but Stripes had complained the first time the motmots dropped a dead assassin in her bed.

And the second time.

And the twelfth.

Stripes was excitable and not good at finding a mate, but she was Brighteyes's friend, and the motmot hoped the pitohui was still alive. Sharpbeak should be finding that out any moment now.

Bright's new mate let out a screech, the noise building as it filled the chambers, then pointed at the ceiling. "There's a way up here, then I can get you back. Where did you come from, by the way? Do you live here? Are you with the ringtails up top?"

Brighteyes pulled herself out of the tunnel and into the dry passage, then worked on preening her feathers and fur. "I'll tell you on the walk. My friends are up in the big room with the glass. Do you know it?"

The tunnel gryphon shrugged. "The swiftlets will know. We'll ask them on our way."

Sharpbeak listened to Brighteyes's warning and veered left, staying just above the duct as it went off in a new direction. She shouted a warning to her friend not to get into any trouble, but Bright had already vanished down the other tunnel.

Sharp sighed. Her pridemates were not the best at search and rescue. They had all been taught to seek out attacks on the reeve's sister and foil them. There had only been one evolution to their training. Over time, they'd come to realize they also needed to defend other opinici against Stripes's forgetful poisonings.

The duct continued for a long while, eventually feeding into a large cistern. Based on the smell, this was some sort of water purification system like they used on Pitohui Island, just on a much grander scale.

And underground.

Sharpbeak searched the cistern, not seeing Stripes under the water. She had to make two rounds before she noticed a body under one of the other pipes draining in here. She perched on the side, not wanting to get wet, and checked to see if it was Stripes.

The pitohui floated on the water, beak only partially submerged. Sharpbeak pulled her friend out, putting her face down, and Stripes began coughing up water.

"That is a good sign," the motmot attempted to reassure her. "I am not a medicine gryphon, but you probably just had too much water inside of you."

While Stripes caught her breath, Sharpbeak searched the

room. Her companion didn't look to be in any shape for flying or climbing, so they'd need to walk back. There were a few hanging walkways, and they all converged along a stone wall, disappearing into darkness.

Generally speaking, motmots didn't care for ominous, dark caves. They preferred sunlight, fruit, and puddles of water to splash in. But there didn't seem to be any other alternatives.

Sharpbeak fetched Stripes. It took a little effort to get her over to the hanging walkway, but once she was there, it was easy to keep her on the path.

"What happened to Impir?" Stripes asked.

The motmot didn't know and said so. "Save your strength. You are weak still. We must hurry. The white opinici's army is searching for us."

It wasn't a good sign that the pitohui didn't remember that. Unless they could get back to the blackwing army, Sharpbeak wouldn't be able to find a doctor for Stripes. And there was no telling what would happen to the gryphon refugees who remained in the garden if the king found out they'd aided the blackwings.

Worries for tomorrow. The sun still shines today.

The stone was slick, and she had to help Stripes back onto her feet a few times, talons being inadequate in situations like this. Sharpbeak went to the right first, but that path led deeper into the waterworks and away from where they'd come in. The incline the other way was harder on Stripes but seemed to go in the correct direction, though it was completely devoid of lamps.

"Where are we going?" Stripes asked.

"Up," Sharpbeak replied. "Away from the inverns."

The pitohui shook her head. "What are inverns?"

"Dark empty space inside the earth. No light. Strange bugs. Do opinici not have this word?" the motmot asked. When Stripes just shook her head, Sharpbeak continued, "It is a good word. You should use it. Then you will sound smart. Maybe find a mate."

The light was long gone, and Sharpbeak found herself crawling forwards as though she could run into a wall at any moment.

"Do I not sound smart?" Stripes asked, but there was a strange noise coming from off in the distance, and Sharpbeak hushed her, putting a paw on her beak.

The noise repeated. High-pitched, almost a squeak. There was no place to hide, and no way to see what was coming. In searching for a hiding place, Sharpbeak came across several splits in the passage, making her wonder how many offshoots she'd missed already.

No hiding, then. Next option, fighting.

She positioned herself in front of Stripes, turning to wipe her beak on the pitohui's oily feathers, only to find them ruffled and clean from the water, the toxins washed into the aqueducts.

With a sigh, Sharpbeak spread her wings to hide Stripes, then stuck her beak out like a spear. She was prepared for a fight when she heard a familiar sound: Brighteyes's sneezing.

45

STRIPES, AGAIN

The last thing Stripes remembered was falling from a great height and landing in water. After that, everything was a blur, though she recalled a sudden jolt of pain in one of her foretalons and a desperate struggle to keep her beak above water.

Rybalt often told her pain was the body's way of showing joy it was still alive. Stripes now knew her brother was a liar. Pain was the body's way of punishing the mind for doing stupid things, and she ached down to her bones.

"What's going on?" she asked the motmot protecting her, but she was hushed. She couldn't see what was going on, but she felt like a chick being protected by her mother when the motmot spread her wings.

A sneeze came, and the motmot with Stripes turned to reassure her. Though they still couldn't see anything, a moment later she felt another of the motmots nuzzle her with a greeting of "brace yourself." And... another, squeaky gryphon.

"Will guide us," the new motmot explained between social grooming. "Is good with darkness and caves."

"An inverns gryphon?" Stripes ventured.

The motmots chirped back and forth a few times, then the new one said, "She hit her head and now she's smart? If that works, why aren't *you* smarter?"

The old motmot hissed, but it was the playful kind of hiss, not the one where they were actually about to fight. The inverns gryphon led them towards a passage with glowing fungus and checked Stripes's wounds, sometimes rubbing something on them.

"You're lucky," the *not*-mot gryphon said. "You fell into pretty clean water. If you'd landed somewhere else, you'd be riddled with infection by now."

Stripes remained still so she didn't bump into anyone in the darkness. "Are you a medicine gryphon?"

"Apprentice," he chirped. "It's really exciting to meet more gryphon prides. We lost our cave when they made the aqueducts, so we've been living down here ever since the alligators broke it open."

The motmots let out squawks of alarm. "Alligators?"

"Don't worry, I can usually hear them," the apprentice medicine gryphon said. "Are you headed back to the surface? You're welcome to come live with me."

"We need to find our friends," Stripes explained. As the medicine gryphon finished rubbing ointment on her wounds, something occurred to her. "Wait! Careful, my skin is poison!"

The ointment stopped, and one of the motmots interposed herself between Stripes and the inverns gryphon. "It's okay. The poison washed off into the drinking water."

How is that okay? Stripes wondered, but she was glad she hadn't hurt the new gryphon.

"If you feel a dizzy or a tingle, let me know," the new motmot told her friend. "I took Impir's harness, it has anti-toxin in it."

"He's... dead, then?" Stripes asked. It seemed impossible that she'd actually succeeded at her task. "The mad peafowl is finally dead."

A motmot groomed her face like she was an anxious gryphlet. "Current was too strong to bring his body back, so brought back harness. We should keep moving. Nighthaunt could come looking for him, and he can see down here."

The inverns gryphon served as their guide, using some sort of echolocation to pull them closer and closer to the surface. Just as the darkness turned from black to grey, he reported a problem. "Someone has put a kind of metal barrier over the exit."

Both of her motmots ran up and began pecking at the metal bars, searching for a way through. While they weren't successful, they managed to attract the attention of a third motmot on the other side who had her own guest.

"Stop being so loud!" the new motmot said before turning to an opinicus with a waterworks harness. "You can open, yes?"

The employee looked exhausted. He also did not look happy to see Stripes, whose ruffled appearance and leather binding with chains hanging down from one leg moved her one step closer to looking like her brother. "Yeah, sure. But your feathered friend here promised not to hurt any of us hiding down here. I need you to make the same promise, Reevesbane."

I'm not a Reevesbane. Just a... scholarbane? No, just a murderer, plain and simple.

"We're just trying to get out of here alive," Stripes explained. "We won't hurt you."

Whether her word was enough or whether he was just afraid of the gryphon standing next to him, he worked the mechanism on the other side and the bars lifted, letting them back into the light. Then he disappeared into another hallway, presumably to resume hiding with the others he'd spoken of.

The new motmot interrogated the other two with chirps, but Stripes was busy inspecting the roof of the waterworks. Broken glass, some with blood on it, was scattered across the floor. She looked down at herself for the first time since stepping into the light and saw surprisingly few cuts.

Impir must have taken the worst of it. I guess I should be grateful.

Overhead, she saw the Golden Sky army searching for her blackwing allies. "We need to go. When they see this is broken, they'll come searching here for any survivors. They'll probably think we came down here to poison their water supply."

"Which you did," the first motmot pointed out. "Though only the cistern that purifies the water. So everyone should be safe."

Stripes counted the motmots and realized one was missing. "Hey, where'd your fourth go?"

More chirping, then the motmot who pulled her out of the water said, "She went through one of the upper paths. Can you climb? We'll take you there."

Stripes looked down at her wings. They didn't seem to be broken, but they were drooping, and she didn't think she had energy to do more than stumble. With a little help, which mostly involved the motmots locating leather straps and

Stripes tying them to her harness to be lifted up, the pitohui reached the upper chamber. She was weak on her feet and collapsed in front of a bunch of empty boxes.

She was ready to take a nap until the crates shook, and one exploded in front of her, revealing the face of an alligator. She leapt back, falling again on her wobbly legs, but then she saw the alligator's eyes were closed.

A few moments later, the entire alligator squeezed through the hole, pushed from behind by a city gryphon and Stripes's final motmot bodyguard, who chirped a greeting to her three pridemates.

"You found her! Good, good," the final motmot said. "I brought food to eat."

More chirping, then the third chimed in, "Food is good, but we need a place to hide Stripes."

The second motmot suggested they go back into the inverns with the black-eyed, long-whiskered gryphon. "Good pride! Friendly. Small. But dark. Also, this my new mate."

The darkness gryphon purred.

"See? Not so hard to find mate, is it?" the second gryphon bragged.

The third gryphon put a wing around the crow gryphon next to her. "I find mate, too."

The city gryphon shook his head. "No thank you, I don't take mates."

The third gryphon retracted that wing, and then put her other wing around Stripes, but Stripes very gently removed it.

"Thank you, but we all get into enough trouble as is." The pitohui poked once at the alligator, but its hide was too tough to eat even raw. "I don't suppose there's a place to cook it?"

There wasn't, but after some negotiations for half the

meat on the alligator, the city gryphons agreed to take in the five refugees.

"Should we search for the blackwings?" fourth motmot asked. There was shouting coming from the waterworks, but they managed to get the crates back in place to hide the path to the city gryphons' nests.

The plan had been to leave before the Alabaster Eyrie's army returned. If they were here now, it didn't seem to Stripes like things were going well outside. "No, it's better to wait for everything to die down. We'll make a run for it later."

Did you make it home okay, Rybalt? Is Iony with you?

Stripes shook her head. There'd be time to think of that later. For now, she needed to recover.

The four motmots closed in, leaning against her to help keep her upright and on the path. She almost told them how much she appreciated their aid, but every time she dozed off, one of them pecked her haunch to wake her, and she remembered why they were as much of a pain as they were a help.

46

VICTORY

The air currents were strong this high, and the king spread all four wings and hovered in the air, staring down at his beautiful city. Smoke rose from every quarter, but the palace still stood, minus part of a stone wing. The docks were gone, but he could rebuild those. His gardens were untouched. And, against all odds, the blackwings hadn't killed the portmaster. Hi-kun found her locked up in a cage, battered but alive.

The king opened his beak and heard the cry of a seraph, his own cry, for the first time. It was beautiful but powerful. It was the sound of a species that needed to communicate across long distances in the sky.

It was a good voice.

The bodies of red-winged blackbirds filled the rooftops. His adversary, the Blackwing Eyrie reeve, had acted in desperation. He'd nearly burned down the Alabaster Eyrie, sure, but what did any of this matter next to unlocking the secrets of their ancestors?

The king landed among his prisoners. Hi-kun was assisting the portmaster. She was in poor shape, but Emin had plans for her. Several of his strongest opinici had taken turns in teams, flying the recovered workshop salts here. They hadn't arrived in time for the battle, but they now descended upon the palace, where several armored goliath birds pulled away the rubble.

The blackwing prisoners balked at the sight of the king. He stared down at them the way an opinicus might look down to a gryphon. They were the past. He was the future.

The Nighthaunt arrived late. His body was nearing death, but he'd refused the blessing, saying he needed to find his cure first.

So be it. He would do better to live briefly as we were meant to be, but he's earned the right to make that choice himself.

Emin's main concern was that the Nighthaunt would die before they began converting next generation's eggs into seraphs. They had the blue reeve's blood. With the last of the salts, the Seraph King would create a new generation of seraphs, and then *their* blood would change the eggs of the next generation.

And then we return home to see what awaits us there.

"Gather my reeves and commanders," he ordered Hi-kun. "Bring them to the throne room."

The Seraph King sat curled around his throne while he gave his speech, his four main wings spread for effect. He offered up medals and praise for everyone who had helped save the Alabaster Eyrie. In honor of those who had lost their lives at

Whitebeak and Reevesport, he promised to retake those cities.

The room contained his most loyal advisors, his bravest warriors, his craftiest scholars. Everyone here already knew what he was going to ask of them. There were only three who would not receive his blessing in one way or another.

Mally waited for the cure to his disease. Instead of ascension, Emin had made certain that every scholar in the kingdom was working on the problem. Funds and opinici had also been moved around to aid with his *less conventional* methods to the south. His final darkstalker had also declined, though her hesitancy was drawn out. She had no children, no eggs, and she didn't wish to sully the public's view of seraphs with her black eyes and inky markings.

Also missing was the reeve of the Argent Heights. Under normal circumstances, the king would have taken this as a grave insult. She'd lived along the borderlands for far too long, and she had a level of autonomy that allowed her to offer haven to opinici whose views would have gotten them killed in the capital.

Yet she'd proven herself one of his most valuable assets. Only through her quick thinking had the starlings been stopped, the workshop saved. And, in turn, her messengers had helped rally the forces to come to the aid of the Alabaster Eyrie. That was not enough for him to save any of the frozen seraph's blood for her, but it was enough that he forgave her absence.

With a feathered talon, the Seraph King used flint to light fires beneath each of the vats. Hi-kun would go first, as would the Alabaster University headmaster. Then Emin's reeves would become seraphs. For their commanders and the other heroes, there wasn't enough purple salts to go around.

Instead, those with eggs of the appropriate age would see them treated with the blue reeve's blood.

They would become the first. And from them, their blood would be taken until all new eggs in the kingdom would hatch as seraphs.

Hi-kun took off his armor, handing it to the assistant on his left, then stepped into the boiling vat. His face was steel, unreadable, as his feathers melted away. The Seraph King nodded to an assistant waiting in the wings. The commander of Whitebeak was partial to the specific metal used in his regalia, so Emin had ordered the royal metalworks to reforge it into something that would better fit Hi-kun's new form.

The reeve of Reevesport stepped into her vat. She let out a small gasp at the heat, despite already being on a large dose of painkillers. There was no fear in her eyes. The wounds the blackwings had given her would have left her unable to fly more than short distances, would have left her in pain for the rest of her life. With the last of the salts, Emin granted her the skies again.

The other reeves—ospreys from the south, a mallard from Duckbill—looked like they'd been gathered up for execution. Little did they know what awaited them. They may resist now, but once they felt the joy Emin did, they'd come around.

Last came the eggs. A hundred seeds, a hundred baby seraphs. And from them, more and more.

Emin retired back to his throne, wrapping his long, feathered tail around it. He looked up at the replica bones of the stranger, hanging from the ceiling, and smiled.

EPILOGUE

THE OTHER MOUNTAIN

Every day for two weeks, a fantail arrived at Satra's hideaway along the northern edge of the kjarr. Every day, they reported that the supply lines had dried up, that the time to strike was now.

The Kjarr waited because she was cautious. No word had come back from the teams she'd sent into enemy territory. Even the Emerald Jungle had gone silent. The small cave over the Jadebeak River had been cleared out and was collecting dust.

What did it mean?

Today was different. Satra didn't wait alone this time. The aneda forest north of the goliath bird pass housed an army composed of taiga gryphons, Strix owls, and other weald prides. The island fortress housed an army of fisherfolk in partially submerged caves. Both the bog and kjarr prides filled the wetlands around her, ready to strike. They wore armor made at Orlea's metalworks. They were surrounded by fantails clutching bombs made from saltpeter taken from

Felicio's old mines and the flameworks, which was finally up and running. Even the sand gryphons had sent an army after Satra promised they could loot what they wanted from the Crackling Sea Eyrie.

All they waited on was the final word.

A small dark spot in the sky dove down far from here, hiding in the cypress to see if she was followed. Twenty minutes later, Erlock Chartail crawled out of the underbrush.

"What news?" Satra asked. The gryphons around her tensed, ready to fight.

Erlock shook her head. "The Argent Heights are active again. A new caravan is en route with supplies for the pink reeve."

"Any sign of our... cave explorer friends?" the Kjarr asked.

"Nothing." Erlock's ears were straight back. "I received word from Hoppy that the guest caves haven't seen any activity, either."

What happened? Satra wondered. *Did I send you to your deaths?*

"So be it," she said at last. "Order the retreat."

A medicine gryphon next to her with a green spiral pattern around her missing eye stepped forwards. "So that's it? The war is over?"

Black Mask, the quills on his armor making him look like an entirely different species, pulled her back. "No, the war continues, but the battlefield and tactics have changed."

Satra put her paw on the outspoken bog witch. "Thistle, is it? The king has taken over half the continent at this point. That's impressive, but let's see how he feels about us by the time winter is over. It's one thing to conquer the world. Let's see if he can hold it."

Erlock gave the orders, and she and Satra waited while

small groups disappeared back into the kjarr. When everyone was gone, the fantail asked, “What are your orders?”

Satra stared out across the grasslands at the cliffside eyrie. It took an act of will to retract her claws and look away. “Tell Ninox and Blinky we’ll do things their way.”

Pip returned to the family ranch from Blacktalon, bringing with him a crate full of metal beads hidden under a large number of sugar beets. The king’s army had begun taxing the local farmers, but Pip had just enough sway with the commander that he was able to requisition back some of the funds for his own use, which he distributed to the same opinici it had been taken from, starting with his own family. While they didn’t know who he was, they were starting to like him.

Which was good, because it looked like he might be stuck here a while.

He finished unloading the beets, then handed the wagon over to some of his mate’s family, who would distribute the funds to whoever needed them most. Technically, because he’d told the commander he was using the money to bribe the locals for information, it shouldn’t be a problem if they were caught. That didn’t do much to ease his anxiety. The last thing he wanted was to cause harm to the blackwings here.

He rinsed off outside, getting relatively dry, then returned to his private wing of the ranch. He wandered out onto the balcony to preen in the sun.

“Any word?” Vilessa asked. His mate had gone through several phases of anger, and while they still slept in separate rooms, they’d gone back to confiding in each other like they’d used to. They didn't want the others to gossip, and neither of them wanted to raise the ire of their family members by disrespecting *Khalim's* memory, so separate rooms made sense.

He finished his face, letting her adjust the black markings around his eyes so he looked less like the Eyes of the Seraph King. "Yes, though none of it is good. The king survived an assassination attempt of some sort. The blackwing army was defeated, and the few blackwings who make it across the desert got picked up by the king's patrols near Blacktalon. Short term, there's no new forces coming. Instead, there's some sort of religious movement that's caught on around the capital. I don't think the lull will last, though. It's only a matter of time before they move on the Blackwing Eyrie."

"What news of, er, your friends?" Vilessa looked around to make sure no one was close enough to hear them before whispering, "Iony and Rybalt."

"Both missing, but they're as hardy as palmetto bugs, so I'm not worried." That was a lie. Pip *was* worried. He already stood a good chance of getting caught by the alabaster opinici, but he was depending on Poisonbird and Longears to save him if the blackwings got to him first.

Vilessa pointed across a field, where Lei and Lemmy were coming out of the woods with a small herd of capybaras following them. "It's nice that those two are doing well. Lemmy's had a hard time since you left. Then, suddenly, his dad comes back from the dead and brings a new sibling with him."

"I'm not sure sibling is the right choice of words," Pip countered. Even at this distance, Lemmy's parents could see he and Lei sneaking the occasional cuddle. They might need to adjust the rooming situation. In retrospect, putting those two in adjacent nests might have been a mistake. "My wagon is back at the fort, but I'll see if I can steal away some red fern for Lei."

Vilessa, medicine opinicus, took a moment to make the connection. "That's right, I'd forgotten. We might get grand-chicks yet. Not sure I'm quite ready for that day to come."

Pip finished with his feathers and slipped his harness back on. He was still wet on the back of his head, and Vilessa *tsked* at him and preened those feathers dry.

He cleared his throat. "I've been thinking. We're between two armies here, and the one that's likely to win isn't the one that's going to provide you safety. And even if the blackwings somehow succeed, Lei and I will need to leave for our own safety. What if… what if you and Lemmy come with us back to the south?"

"I don't think that's a good idea." Her tone was neutral, but her posture had stiffened. "We're farmers, Pip. Is there enough farmland in the weald to support us? I have a hard time imagining the kjarr and bog have much of it. Are any of those fisherfolk islands of yours large enough for farming?"

He knew it was a long shot, but he'd hoped she'd reconsider. "A few. They're not big, and you can't stay on those islands during the stormy season. But there are a talonful of farms."

"Enough for all your family and mine? Or were you going to leave your siblings and cousins behind?" she asked.

"No, you're right. I just hate thinking we're going to leave soon." He looked at Vilessa, something he tried not to do when out in the open lest it betray something about him. "I guess I'm not ready to go, and that time is coming. I can't imagine how Lemmy and Lei will react when we tell them."

"You can't change the seasons. You can't change the tide.

Enjoy what you have, then wait and see what tomorrow brings." She reached down and took his talons.

He squeezed back, but he was watching their young charges. "Will you do me a favor? I know it's a lot to ask, and you don't owe me anything, but... if something happens to me, will you look after Lei?"

She squeezed his talons again, and they watched as Lemmy and Lei were so caught up in each other that the capybaras made their escape and reached the tree line before the two young opinici noticed.

FOULTNER SAT in a prison cell in the middle of a mountain she had attempted to infiltrate several times without success during her stay at the Argent Heights. Now that she was finally here, she just wanted to leave.

This section was a prison inside a prison. She'd passed by dozens of cells on her way being led back here. Officially, this was for her protection. Of course, weeks had passed now, and she was still 'in need of protection.'

Her only connection with the outside world was one-way. Henders had been told that Foultner was sick and under quarantine. At least, that's what Foultner *thought* they'd told Henders. All she knew was that every few days, a new get well card arrived with his artwork and signature on it.

"I don't suppose I can send one back to him?" she asked.

The guard grunted. "Can't trust you won't include a coded message in it."

"How long do I need to stay here?" she pushed.

He shrugged. "Until the reeve says you can go."

"Can you ask her now?" Foultner tired of this game.

The guard looked up from his book. "She's still out."

"Where?" Foultner began, but the guard just reiterated.

"Out."

The poacher sighed, looking around at this inner prison. Two ducks played a game. They had a large cell to themselves, and it even had a bit of privacy. She'd tried asking if one of them was the Duckbill Murder Hen, but they'd glared at her. Several ospreys were lodged with a couple of gryphons and a peafowl.

"Why am I by myself? How do I get a friend?" she asked. "No, wait, let me guess. *Ask Silver.*"

The guard just grunted. They'd performed this routine so many times, Foultner could play both parts. It wasn't that they were mistreating her. She had food and things to read. Mostly boring personality books or ranching reports, but occasionally, pamphlets would come from the Alabaster Eyrie.

Thus, word of the attacks on Reevesport, Whitebeak, the Seraph King, and the Alabaster Eyrie reached her. She tried to read between the lines, but none of it made sense.

Starling attacks on the rise? Did that mean there was a new outbreak?

Cave gryphons stealing babies to sacrifice in weird chthonic rituals? How did that mesh with the friendly ones who visited Crestfall?

The Ashen Weald and the Blackwing Eyrie working together? Insane. Satra would never stoop so low. Foultner had full faith in her.

None of that told her what had *really* gone on, however. What's more, after the initial downpour of information, the news had gone silent. There was word of an ascent, something about a seraph, but none of it made sense to her. She was too far from the capital here. The messages must have gotten garbled through repetition.

Foultner growled and slammed her food bowl against the bars, earning her some insults from the duck opinici next to her. The guard, for his part, didn't even look up from what he was reading.

She was about to pick up a book and fling it at him when the sound of a key in the metal door to the inner prison sent all of the incarcerated into a tizzy. Everyone here knew when the door was supposed to open, only for meals, when the guards would switch.

This was not mealtime.

Several argent hawks filed in, and Foultner worried that they were here to escort her to her own execution. That fear didn't alleviate when the reeve herself stepped in, peppered with a dozen new scars and limping something fierce.

"As you were," she ordered her soldiers. She took the cell key from the guard and unlocked it, sitting down next to Foultner. One of her escorts came in holding two kegs of stew, warmed but not burned, setting them down in front of Foultner and Silver.

The reeve began eating. Foultner shrugged and joined in. The food in here wasn't terrible, but it was cold and bland. She missed the taste of salt and heat.

Once she finished, Silver spoke. "You're not a rancher."

"I am not." Foultner didn't see any point in denying it.

"I'd ask who you are, but as a spy, you'd lie to me." Silver handed her keg back to one of the guards. The cell door was still open. "So I went searching on my own. It's not easy to keep an inquiry away from the king's new spymaster, but I believe I succeeded, and I'm fairly certain I know who you are."

Foultner didn't respond, though her curiosity was piqued.

Silver unfolded a scroll. "To the Redwood Valley Eyrie, you were a criminal. You joined up with the Ashen Weald when you were promised wealth beyond imagining."

"Food," Foultner corrected. "I was promised I could hunt wherever the Ashen Weald held territory. Reeves have a tendency to look at hunters and tell them where they can and cannot hunt."

"I see." Silver continued. "For which you infiltrated one outpost, then helped overthrow the Crackling Sea Eyrie and a fishing village called New Eyrie. It looks like a lot of opinici died because of your actions. What makes an opinicus turn on her own kind?"

Foultner shrugged. "My *kind* have never been *kind* to me. What's more, your report is leaving out a crucial detail. There were hundreds of wingtorn slaves held in the depths of the Crackling Sea Eyrie. Not to mention the ones whose paws had been mutilated who were tied up in New Eyrie. So if you want to know why I hold no loyalty to opinici, you should ask yourself the same. Why do you hold *any* loyalty to the sorts of reeves who would do things like that? I'm not anti-opinicus. It's just that I know the difference between right and wrong and a lot of my *kind* have forgotten that. Hence why you're alive."

"Thank you for that," Silver said. "The antitoxin, that is. Not the lecture. How did you come into possession of it?"

"When Rybalt attacked the Ashen Weald, some of the blackwings were carrying it. I took it off their bodies," Foultner half-truthed.

Silver unrolled more of her scroll. "It seems you later served as a spy at the goliath bird ranch, but this time I was your target. What did you learn?"

There was no mention of Henders, which worried Foultner. Did they think he was a spy, too? "I learned you weren't nearly as loyal to the Seraph King as your compatriots. That sometimes, you didn't do terrible things *like locking up the opinicus who saved you in the darkest prison you can find.* That's what I discovered."

Though some of the soldiers drew weapons, Silver waved them off with a bandage-wrapped talon. "Did you stay behind at the Clover Ranch so we'd invite you here?"

"No," Foultner admitted. "That was an accident. Thank you for saving us. Though it turned out the other prisoners were all rescued at the lumber mill, so it's more of a *thanks for trying.*"

"So you saving me, that was us being even?" the reeve asked.

"I wouldn't say that," the poacher countered. "You've got me locked up. If you'd let me go free, then it'd be different. Plus, we rescued you first, after Rybalt nearly killed you. So we're one ahead, *and* we didn't lock you up when we found you in the bog."

Don't say we, don't bring Henders into this, the voice inside Foultner's head kept repeating. *Don't get him into trouble. Please let him be safe.*

The soldiers behind Silver looked at each other. Apparently, they weren't aware Foultner had saved the reeve once before.

"I suppose that's correct." The reeve handed the scroll to another of her soldiers, and he took it over to one of the braziers and tossed it in. "It's not easy figuring out what to do with a spy who appears to be doing more good for your side than the enemy's. Had you let me die, you would not have later found yourself here to save me from Rybalt. And without the warning bells going off in time, the garrison would have been buried under a landslide. Without me alive, the Seraph King would have died at the claws of the Emerald Jungle and Abyssal Naze. In fact, reports say that there were Ashen Weald gryphons and opinici there, too. They made it into the ascension room. They match descriptions of operatives Kia, Zeph, and Cherine from the destruction of Crestfall."

"They're not really Ashen Weald," Foultner corrected. "They're more... independent contractors."

Silver didn't comment on that. "The garrison's army met with the king's army and routed your Blackwing Eyrie allies, who were attempting to burn down the Alabaster Eyrie. The Ashen Weald, the Abyssal Naze, the Emerald Jungle, and the Blackwing Alliance all moving as one. And they may have pulled it off, had you not given me the antitoxin. Everything hinged upon a single act of kindness."

A feeling of dread made Foultner's stomach feel heavy. "That can't be true. The Ashen Weald would never treat with the Blackwing Alliance."

The entire world was counting on just me, and I screwed it up. If I had just done nothing, they would have succeeded. Yet Foultner didn't feel any better about the alternative, a world in which she'd killed the Silver Reeve.

"Fine, I'm a hero for your cause." Foultner stood. "So why am I still in this cage?"

Silver beckoned around the room. "This is where I put traitors to the Seraph King."

Something about the gesture stuck with Foultner, and she looked around the room again, seeing it with new eyes. Everyone in this room *was* a traitor to the Seraph King, and what was more, all of them were his subjects. There were no red-winged blackbirds here, no glacier gryphons, no Ashen

Weald. In Foultner's case, she'd even been wearing an Argent Heights badge when she was arrested.

"These are all... what? Dissidents?" she asked.

Silver stood up and walked over to the neighboring enclosure. Several of the other *prisoners* stepped out of their cages, none of which were actually locked, and greeted her. "Dissident is a rather mild word. These two duckbills are assassins and counter-propaganda specialists. The peacock ran one of the largest smuggling rings the kingdom has ever seen, stealing money directly from the king's coffers. Several others liberated gryphons from the king's prisons, handing them over to the Abyssal Naze to take to safety. This is a room full of opinici—and a few gryphons, I see you, Sven—whom the king hates above all others and believes were executed."

Foultner stood and attempted to open her own cage door, which Silver had closed when she left, but it was still locked. "What are you getting at?"

Silver returned, though she didn't enter until Foultner was seated again. "Your mistake was in thinking an opinicus like the king could be killed, that it would even solve your problems if he could be. Do you know what would've happened if Zeph Reevesbane had killed the king? Every eyrie in the kingdom would rally together. They'd have hunted the Ashen Weald to the ends of Belamuria to get revenge. The king's strange, seraphic faith would have lived on. He'd have become a god to the opinici here.

"No, if you want to take down a monarchy, you have to work from inside the system. You need to bring every eyrie here to your side and let *them* overthrow the king from within. That's how you stop a monarch surrounded by zealots."

However Foultner had expected this conversation to go, it was now wildly off script.

"You've already proven that you're willing to work with a devil." Silver tapped the necklace she wore around her neck, *Henders's necklace.* It was a reminder of Rybalt Reevesbane. "Would you be willing to work with... a different sort of devil?"

Foultner considered her options. "Just what are you proposing?"

Silver raised a talon, and the guard unlocked the gate. She handed over Henders's necklace, and the soldiers brought in a new harness for Foultner, but not a rancher's harness. No, it was an Argent Heights harness of a military design.

The argent reeve tossed over a shining captain badge. "Insurrection, Captain Foultner. I'm proposing you help me start a rebellion the likes of which the continent has never seen. And I want you to get the Ashen Weald to help me do it."

K. VALE NAGLE

PRIDE LORD

GRYPHON INSURRECTION: BOOK EIGHT

OILBIRDS AND CAVE SWIFTLETS

AUTHOR'S NOTE

Let's just get this out of the way quickly: there are some really weird cave-dwelling swifts and swiftlets out there in the world. I'm sure, much like me, you come into each new GryphIns book expecting that you've already had a taste of the weird birds the world has to offer. And then, like me, you find yourself surprised once again.

I thought I knew swifts. When I go for early morning walks past the dam, the fields are full of swifts dancing about like sentient boomerangs intent on catching any bugs stirred up by my passing. They seemed like normal, friendly birds. They did not seem like silk-spinning spiked spider-birds.

You can see cave swifts building their sticky, gooey silk nests in many documentaries, but I kept seeing references to their tail spikes without any images to back it up. I finally had to reach out to ornithologist Oriana Pokorny, whom you may remember for her information on the infamous godbird woodpeckers, who was able to pass along images of the tail spikes. I could have stopped at silky webbing (did I mention it sells for more per ounce than silver?), but I needed to know what bird tail spikes looked like.

And Oriana delivered. The center of the feather forms the spike that extends out from the 'end' of the feather, and they use their tail spikes to dig into the cave walls while they build their nests.

While the cave swifts were a new addition, this book was really focused on the cave gryphons. As it turns out, oilbirds are some of Maria Puenchir's favorite birds, and oilbird gryphons are her all-time favorite gryphon. In addition to providing an interior art piece for this novel, Maria also helped me with the echolocation sections. While the cave gryphons had their own, specialized echolocation with a fantasy flair to it, Xin was using something closer to how humans learn to echolocate. Her advice was invaluable, and any mistakes in the text are entirely mine.

And because I know I'll get emails asking about this, the feline halves of the woodpecker opinici and gryphons are jaguarundis and bay cats, two felines with impressively long tails!

Of course, cave gryphons weren't the only fancy new addition. After years of mummified or frozen glimpses, we finally get a good look at living seraphs, courtesy of Brenda Lyons' interior art. Brenda has known what they looked like for some time, having had to hint at them in the art for *Starling* and *Crackling Sea*. I was really nervous about how they'd look in the flesh, so to speak, but Brenda showed me the sketches, and Emin was already perfect.

The seraphs (or *opinithings*, if you prefer) are a little

pterosaur in the forelegs, a bit microraptor in the hind legs, and a healthy portion of Eastern-style dragon in the long body. As I've said before, what I love most about gryphons is that so many different, unconnected cultures came up with their own. Making bird-cat hybrids is something humans do; it's part of who we are as a species. What's more, we don't just create gryphons, we're inspired by the gryphons of other cultures. Egypt and Greece are a good example of that, trading back and forth hawks, eagles, lions, kitty paws, bird talons, cat ears, and bird tails. Even North America's influence is visible in how common bald eagle gryphons are in fantasy art today.

Where am I going with this? Well, I was writing from a hotel last year, and I didn't have the map nearby, and I couldn't remember if King's Reach or Alwren was farther north. Searching for Belamuria brought up a long description of "Belamurian gryphons" along with a character someone made set in the Gryphon Insurrection world, a fisherfolk.

Then, as I was going through and finalizing the author's note for *Opinicus* and getting signed copies of *Crackling Sea* ready to mail off, someone asked if I'd seen the Gryphon Insurrection original character (OC) on Reddit.

I had not. I was only barely aware that one person had made a character. Now there were two. Maybe even more! Complete with art.

I've always been pretty clear about my goals for writing this series. Catastrophic APS nearly killed me twice, and I wanted to be sure my spouse had books to read to help him grieve if it killed me the third time. Our love of gryphons is what brought us together as middle school friends, then best friends, then a married couple. So when I hear other authors talking about how they know when they've 'made it' as an author, I never stopped to think about what that meant for me.

Really, finishing the series before a clot killed me was how I viewed success.

Yet here I am. I live in a privileged place now where signing onto social media or typing "Belamuria" into a search engine brings up fan art, where fans love the world so much they've created their own (very stylish) characters.

It's humbling, and I just want to say: thank you. Everyone who has made GryphIns fanfiction, fan art, original characters, or just enjoyed the series and talked about it—thank you all.

Opinicus is behind us now, and it's time to head deep into the Emerald Jungle for *Pridelord*. I'll see you in the author's note for the next book. Until then, be well and stay awesome.

-Vale

ABOUT THE AUTHOR

K. Vale Nagle is alarmingly hard to kill.

After surviving several pulmonary embolisms and multiple organ failure, Vale kicked their writing into high gear and saw their first short story and novel publications. When they're not writing creature fantasy or fighting for their life, they enjoy reading, archery, and exploring the Rocky Mountains with a tabby cat by their side.

They can be found online at kvalenagle.com, via their newsletter, or on Patreon.

- patreon.com/kvalenagle
- facebook.com/kvalenagle
- twitter.com/kvalenagle
- bookbub.com/authors/k-vale-nagle
- amazon.com/K-Vale-Nagle/e/B07ND33BHW

ALSO BY K. VALE NAGLE

THE GRYPHON INSURRECTION

Eyrie

Ashen Weald

Starling

Reevesbane

The Ruins of Crestfall

The Crackling Sea

Opinicus

Pridelord

SHORT STORY COLLECTIONS

Blue Eyes and Other Tales

ANTHOLOGIES

Tales of Feathers and Flames

www.ingramcontent.com/pod-product-compliance
Lightning Source LLC
Chambersburg PA
CBHW020604310726
48979CB00008B/1337/J
* 9 7 8 1 6 4 3 9 2 0 4 7 4 *